Black Silver

INDIGORIVER
PUBLISHING

Black Silver

WAYNE ABRAHAMSON

Indigo River Publishing

ACKNOWLEDGMENTS

While this novel is a work of fiction, it would not have been possible without the help from friends along the way. I would like to thank Siska Williams and Kendra Kennedy (both excellent writers in their own right) for reviewing my rough draft and encouraging me to continue with the project. I also want to thank Keenan Finkelstein, a former US Navy submariner, for letting me bounce a couple of ideas off him. Lastly, I would like to thank Indigo River Publishing for allowing me to fulfill my dream of becoming a writer and for providing excellent editors, namely Dianna Graveman and Regina Cornell, to help bring this project to fruition.

Please enjoy Black Silver, and stay tuned for future works of adventure and intrigue.

CONTENTS

Prologue

....

SOUTH CHINA SEA, 1965

Darwin Pinky exhaled through his mouthpiece and turned to watch the column of bubbles race to the surface seventy feet above. The scuba diver turned his attention back to the corroded steel beneath him. He floated above a ragged gash that exposed the interior of the tubelike seaplane hangar bolted to the main deck of the submarine. None of the sun's rays entered the gash. An inky blackness teased him.

Pinky, an English building contractor from Hong Kong with a penchant for the easy life, turned his head from the void and looked down at the forward section of the submarine's hull. Plate-sized holes, resembling blossoming petals of sharp steel, pitted the seaplane hangar, deck, and hull. Evidence of cannon fire and at least one bomb blast was obvious, but the submarine and the muddy plain it rested on showed no other sign of human disturbance. Not so much as a Coke bottle stuck out of the bottom mud. There was no marine growth on the submarine, not a single barnacle. He didn't see any fish. He and his companions were two weeks into their spring cruising vacation, and this dive was the first one during which they had not seen any fish or marine growth.

The absence of marine life seemed strange, but Pinky dismissed the oddity as he looked for his dive partner. He looked aft, toward the stern of the vessel. A column of rising air bubbles marked Geoff Dalrymple's location. He had just floated over the stern. Like Pinky's, Dalrymple's midsection resembled the bulbous curvature of the submarine's outer hull. Pinky pulled his dive knife out of the sheath strapped to his calf and hammered the blade's thick metal handle against the submarine's hull three times. The sound of the sharp, metallic clicks reached his partner's ear. Dalrymple swam toward Pinky, and when the two men were together, Pinky gestured with his hands for his partner to remain outside and shine his light into the gash.

Pinky pulled himself past the incisors of the monstrous grin, and as he entered the hangar, an awareness seemed to speak to him. It was as if the bubbles from his regulator were warning him in a foreign language to leave the wreck alone. The hangar's interior was now visible, along with a pile of broken wooden crates, pieces of rope, and thermos-like metal containers that lay huddled under a thin layer of sediment. The crates had probably been stacked and secured at one time, but because of the bomb blast, the list to port, and corroding salt water, they had broken from their lashings and settled against the opposite curved bulkhead.

Pinky glanced at his air gauge and noticed that he was down to 50 bar, or about 725 psi. The two men had simply been out for a sport dive that morning and had not been expecting to find an intact submarine. Now, in his excitement, Pinky had lost track of time while exploring a wreck that appeared to have been undisturbed since it sank, probably sometime during WWII. Pinky knew that he had to surface soon, while he still had air in his tank, but images of treasure raced through his mind. He took a brief second to remember his training about out-of-air emergency ascents, deciding he could perform the emergency maneuver if needed, before letting his thoughts return to images of gold bars and diamonds. His eyes darted about, looking for a canister that might be easy to pull from the pile.

Both Pinky and Dalrymple had been engineers in the British Army. They had been stationed together in India during the war, but after the war, they resigned their commissions to take advantage of lucrative construction contracts to rebuild cities like Singapore and Hong Kong. It was during their time in the service that they had heard tales of wealth pillaged from all over Asia and the Pacific Islands by the Japanese, who placed it on board ships and submarines for transport back to Japan. The thought that now the two men may have stumbled upon some of that lost treasure made Pinky feel euphoric.

He selected one canister and tugged at its base until it broke free. As he pulled, a cloud of silt ballooned from the pile, blotting out all available light. Pinky held on to the canister with one hand while pushing himself out of the hangar with the other. The fingers of his left hand began to itch, so he rubbed them together after transferring the canister to his right hand. He promised himself that he would wear gloves next time.

Once outside the hangar, Pinky gazed up at the wavering outline of his yacht, and both men slowly ascended toward the silhouette. They rose no faster than their bubbles. As soon as they reached the surface, they spat out their regulators and swam to the aluminum dive ladder. Pinky looked up and saw the tall wooden mast swaying ever so slightly, brushing against the sun behind it.

"Evelyn!" Pinky shouted as he grabbed a rung. A woman's face suddenly peered over the handrail. Her head and an enormous hat blocked the sun.

"Yes, dear?" his wife answered.

"Here, take this."

Evelyn kneeled in the open dive gate and grabbed the canister; then she walked aft to rejoin Jane, Dalrymple's wife, who sat in a folding wooden deck chair at a small table mounted to the deck just beyond the cockpit. Pinky and Dalrymple removed their fins before flinging them up over the handrail, onto the deck. They labored up the ladder, one at a time. Once on deck, they bent forward, taking a minute to catch their breath, before unbuckling their straps and loudly dumping their scuba tanks on the deck. Minutes later, after recovering from their exertions, they sat gulping gin and tonics with their wives, the canister standing like a large centerpiece on the table between them.

"By Jove, Pinky," Dalrymple said after taking a long pull of his drink, "I do believe we found the jackpot. What do you think is in all of those canisters?"

Pinky, lost in thought, took a few seconds to answer. "I suggest we don't get too excited just yet. If there is treasure in these things, I'll wager there's a whole line of people who would want their property back. The Japanese looted gold and other precious items from many countries throughout the war."

The men's wives, clothed almost identically in khaki shorts and white flowing button-up tops, lounged in their chairs. While Evelyn had been writing in her journal, Jane had been reading an article in the April edition of Playboy. Now Evelyn reached for her drink, which sat beside the canister on the tabletop. "What's the name of this dreadful island?"

Pinky looked up from his drink, at their surroundings. They were anchored in a long bay that ran from east to west. Other than the top of an exposed rocky volcanic wall that rimmed the western shore of the island about four miles distant, all he could see was a dense tropical forest that bordered the bay.

"I think it's called Terumbu Island," he said, "but we'll have to be sure of the name and find out who owns this island if we're going to think about salvage."

Evelyn returned to her journal. Jane was still intent on the article. The men looked at the canister, inspecting its dents. They noticed a thin black liquid running down the tin side of it, one drop at a time, each drop vaporizing before it reached the table. Out of curiosity, Dalrymple touched a drop with his bare finger.

Suddenly, Evelyn began to gasp.

"Evelyn, what's wrong?" asked Pinky.

"I don't know!" Evelyn snapped as her journal fell from her hands. "I am sorry. I didn't—"

Evelyn's eyes clamped shut, and her body snapped, forcing her to sit straight. She wrapped her arms around her midsection and bowled out of the chair, landing heavily on the deck before vomiting and writhing sporadically. Jane followed with spasms of her own, dropping the magazine and falling to the deck next to Evelyn.

Pinky lurched to assist his wife but collapsed instead. Dalrymple did the same. As Pinky struggled on the deck, his bowels and bladder emptied. It was the last sensation he felt below his waist. Pinky tried to reach for Evelyn again, but found that his arms had lost their mobility too. He lay helpless, watching his wife's upper torso and head convulse like a dying animal until, finally, her once-lovely face transformed into a mask of torture.

Although they were not dead, the four immobile bodies could do nothing but lie on the deck as the tropical sun burned their retinas. Pinky knew they were dying, and the seconds seemed to drag forever. Spittle ran slowly from the corner of his mouth as he waited for death, and his failing brain told him that whatever had prevented that wreck from flourishing as a living reef was taking their lives away too.

1

....

SUBIC BAY, PHILIPPINES
EARLY JULY, PRESENT TIME

Joseph Havok slouched in a broad-backed rattan chair, quaffing a draft beer. A ceiling fan mounted to an overhead beam hewn from tropical hardwood slowly rotated. However, the fan offered little respite from the tropical morning air. A rain shower had passed through earlier, leaving the sky a cloudless, dark blue, but the air heavy and damp. Over Havok's left shoulder, a 1970s soft-rock tune streamed from a speaker mounted high on the rear wall of his bar. As he lifted the glass to his lips, a drop of condensate fell from the glass and stung the warm skin of his chest between the open V-neck of his white polo shirt. Lowering the glass, Havok savored the yeasty taste while wiping froth from his thick mustache with the back of his hand. A large yellow envelope lay on the glass-covered table in front of him. A bonded courier had just delivered the envelope, but Havok was in no hurry to open it. Instead, he simply looked at the envelope, anticipating its contents.

"Stone, it looks like we have another offer from SPAN Expeditions," he said loudly, not looking up from the envelope.

"Where to?" asked a male voice off to his left. Havok's longtime friend and business partner, Pete Stone, stood five feet, ten inches tall and weighed in around 175 pounds. He had steel-gray hair cut military-style short, as was Havok's, and his eyes were grayish blue. Stone had a habit of talking and laughing out of the right corner of his mouth.

"Does it matter?" asked Havok.

"I know Costa Rica isn't an option ever since you got us caught. Anyway, I'm getting tired of jumping from one tropical paradise to another. How about a job in the Baltic? Or Japan? It's been a while since we've had some quality time in Japan."

Havok clamped his eyes shut. Damn, will he ever forget about Costa Rica? After a deep sigh, he answered, "Let me look at the offer in a minute."

"All right. I'm going into the shop to help Junior for a few minutes."

Havok looked over the wooden handrail that lined the rear deck of his bar and across the shimmering bay, toward a row of lofty, verdant hills that formed the northern boundary of the bay. Immediately in front of him, a wooden dock extended from the deck and pointed north as if it were a compass needle. A fifty-foot wooden boat, moored to the right side of the dock, tugged gently at its mooring lines as the dissipating wake from an unseen boat disturbed its slumber. Even though he had owned the boat for a number of years, he never failed to appreciate its beauty: its hull consisted of rich reddish-brown mahogany planks; the upperworks built from teak. Brightly polished brass and chrome fittings enhanced the natural beauty of the varnished wood. On the transom, hand-painted bright green letters, resembling sections of bamboo, identified the boat. Its name was Outfit.

On the left side of the dock sat a low-winged, two-seat WWII Kingfisher seaplane. Aside from the central float, which was located under the plane's fuselage, two smaller floats extended down from the wings' tips. Two planked walkways protruded perpendicular to the dock, one in front of the starboard wing and one behind it. Mooring lines from the central float secured the plane to brass cleats on the dock. The upper halves of the plane's fuselage and floats were painted sky blue; the bottom halves painted cloud white. Following WWII tradition, a vivid image adorned the stubby front-engine cowling on the starboard side. The woman in the mural had flowing black hair and bright red lips. She wore a black bikini and rode sidesaddle on a broom. She held on to the broomstick with one hand while holding a bottle of beer high in the other. A trail of flames followed the broomstick. The name Esmeralda was painted under the icon.

Havok used Esmeralda mostly for taking his and Stone's customers up for joyrides and flying lessons. Esmeralda would have looked as if she had come straight off a 1941 production line if it weren't for the tail numbers indicating current American registry. After surveying his gilded cage, Havok's eyes returned to the envelope.

SPAN stood for Special Projects Archaeology Network, and the company conducted archaeological, architectural, and historical research. The last time he and Stone had worked for SPAN was about a year ago, when they were assigned to act as backup for German Navy divers working in conjunction with the History Channel. The purpose of that joint effort had been to investigate an IX-class long-haul U-boat that lay in two hundred feet of water off the coast of Sumatra and to document that investigation. The History Channel production team was following up on rumors that this submarine had carried Hitler to a secret hideout in May 1945 but had been sunk by British aircraft in transit. Havok knew that the program was a farce made to satiate conspiracy junkies who reveled in such innuendo and that he and Stone were simply props on the project. However, two weeks of paid diving and living on a German Navy salvage tug, drinking good German beer at the end of every day, and taking a week off in Bali was reward enough. But, at least for Havok, the real reward was not the pay or the revelry in Bali. The real reward was the opportunity to dive on an authentic U-boat. History and adventure meant more to him than money. It was his fix for a severe addiction. He craved adventure just as a heroin addict hungers for his deadly poison.

Havok finally leaned over to open the envelope. He pulled out several typed documents and an old leather-bound book. A piece of stationery poked out from the pages of the book. He opened the book and saw that the author had written a note to President Chester A. Arthur on the inside cover. It was dated 1883. Havok turned the title page and read the brief note on the stationery. The cursive writing read, I hope you don't already have one. Love, M.

Havok smiled while he held the book, feeling the embossed lettering on the binder with his fingertips. How many times have I read this book? he thought. He placed the first-edition copy of Treasure Island on top of the empty envelope and turned to the documents.

The first document laid out the plans of an expedition. SPAN was aiming to find and excavate a lost pirate fleet located off Panama's Caribbean coast. As Havok scanned copies of old charts, survivor accounts, manifests, and contemporary drawings of what the ships supposedly looked like, he realized that this job would be extremely simple. Any well-trained underwater archaeologist with some competent students or shovel bums could easily map and excavate this site. Simplicity didn't attract Havok, but he needed some relief from his stifling routine. A working vacation in the Caribbean would do nicely.

With a satisfied sigh, Havok grabbed his beer as he pushed his six-foot frame up from the chair. He stretched as he walked around the wooden deck, idly surveying his surroundings. Centered on the deck, a brass spiral staircase led to the sundeck above, where his customers, who occupied the guest rooms on the second story of the building, could sun themselves in beach chairs. Over the waist-high wooden railing of the lower deck, and beyond an eight-foot wide alleyway, was another building and patio similar in appearance to the one bordering Havok's bar. Both cinder-block buildings, owned by Havok and Stone, were only two of a number of resort hotels that lined the stretch of Baloy Beach. The building in which Havok currently stood was a guest resort hotel and restaurant, with the first floor being the bar, known as P.J.'s to locals. The other building served as a dive shop, artifact conservation lab, and residence. The first floor of that building housed the dive shop and the lab, while the second floor was comprised of two studio apartments: one for Havok and one for Stone.

On the deck of the opposite building was a waist-high square steel table at which Stone had just sat down. Sitting in a swivel office chair, its stuffing poking out of cracked leather, Stone held a length of rope in his hands, and a cigarette dangled from the corner of his mouth. On the table were his lighter, cigarettes, and cell phone.

Havok stepped up to the deck railing and spoke across the alleyway: "The job's off the Caribbean coast of Panama, and we're looking for Captain Morgan's lost pirate fleet. We'll be flying into New Orleans to pick up a boat and then crewing it to Pensacola, the Keys, and Panama."

Looking up from his work, Stone pulled the cigarette from his mouth and tapped the lit end against the rim of a five-gallon trash bucket on the floor next to him. "Well, it isn't Japan, but I know a good gentlemen's club in each of those places."

"I'll take that as a yes," Havok answered.

"Good, and did my Alabama chrome make it over there?" Stone asked as he popped his cigarette back into his mouth.

Havok's eye darted around the deck. He spied a roll of duct tape sitting in the dirt of a potted palm tree. "Here," he said, grabbing the roll and flinging it across the alley.

Stone reached to catch the roll of tape, then put it on the unpainted steel table and returned to splicing a loop into one end of the rope. "I'm making a new mooring line for Esmeralda, and I'll preflight her in the morning. You've got three scheduled flights."

"Thanks," Havok said. "I'm going for a swim. You got everything under control for our charter tonight?"

Stone waved a dismissive hand.

Havok was happy to let Stone take care of the blue-collar side of the business. He went back to the envelope, replaced its contents, and laid it upside down on the table beside his now-empty beer glass. He peeled off his polo shirt, used it to wipe sweat from his face, and dropped it on his chair; and wearing only a pair of green board shorts, he stepped off the deck and onto the dock. He walked past his boat and his airplane, to the end of the dock.

Havok dove into the water and enjoyed the relief it offered from the humidity. Using a variety of strokes and kicks, he quickly reached a sandbar about two hundred yards out. He waded up to exposed, packed sand and knocked out twenty push-ups. Afterward, he dove in the water and was back at the beach within eleven minutes of having dived off the dock. Slightly out of breath, he sat in his chair at the table and heard the screen door that led into the inside bar and restaurant open. He turned to see one of his employees step through the open door to bring out his lunch, a T-shirt, and a towel.

"How was the swim?" The employee wore sneakers with white ankle socks, a pair of dark blue shorts hemmed to reveal a good amount of thigh, and a white blouse. The blouse was loose fitting and short sleeved and had her name, Apple, embroidered over the left pocket. The company name was embroidered over the right pocket in yellow: Peso Pete and Olongapo Joe's Eco-Adventure Tours.

Apple dropped the towel into Havok's lap, draped the T-shirt over his chair, and placed a tray on his table. On the tray, next to the covered plate, was a bottle of San Miguel beer and a glass of water with some ice cubes and a lemon wedge.

"I need to work on my swim time," Havok replied as he finished toweling himself off. He put on his new shirt and looked at the plate heaped with steamed white rice topped with adobo, chunks of pork and potatoes stewed in a mixture of soy sauce, vinegar, and black pepper. To the side of the rice and adobo were pickled banana peppers, each about the size of his index finger. He realized suddenly how hungry he was.

"Thank you," he said as he picked up a fork. "Now, get my clothes ready for tonight."

"Yes, sir!" she replied with a smile, and turned to leave.

Apple was only one of Havok's many employees, but all his employees were from one extended family with one patriarch. This system worked out well, as the patriarch could be trusted to run the business while Havok and Stone were not around.

Havok dove into his food while watching her walk away. Small and pretty, with straight shoulder-length black hair, Apple never failed to be attentive to all of his needs.

It took him only a few minutes to finish his lunch. As he munched on the last banana pepper, the screen door behind him opened again and a couple came out. The man was wearing an obnoxiously loud Hawaiian shirt and beige shorts and had a beer in one hand and his cell phone in the other. The shirt was an overwhelmingly brilliant lime-green color, covered with images of colorful tropical birds. The woman behind him was petite and had green eyes and short red hair. Her skin was creamy and smooth, and it appeared she wore few cosmetics. She held a gin and tonic in one hand and a phone in the other as well.

The man looked over at Havok and spoke: "You must be Joe, the owner."

"Yes, I am. And you are?"

"My name is Steve Johnson. This is my wife. Mind if we sit down?"

"Please do." Havok noticed that the man did not introduce his wife by name.

"Thank you," Johnson said, plopping into a rattan chair with a sigh. His wife sat next to him. "We just checked in, and I have to say, your website doesn't lie. You have some toys, inside and outside," he said, inspecting his surroundings and subconsciously brushing his thin, trimmed mustache with his index finger.

"Well, thank you." Havok slowly sipped a glass of water as he watched Johnson appraise the boat and airplane. He watched the woman out of the corner of his eye. She looked at Havok discretely.

Johnson turned his attention to the patio deck and then to the deck above him. "This entire patio seems to be made from mahogany. Must have cost you a fortune."

"Not really," Havok replied, looking at the thick planks that made up the deck and the eight-inch-square stanchions and ceiling beams supporting the deck above. "Over the last few years, my partner and I have had the occasion to salvage tropical-hardwood logs from shipwrecks. One reason the Spanish wanted the Philippines as a colony was that it was right between the Spice Islands to the south, or modern-day Indonesia with its spices, and China to the north with its silks and porcelains. The Spanish needed wood to build their ships, and the Philippines provided that wood."

"I know what you're talking about," Johnson added after taking a pull from his beer bottle and straightening his shoulders. "We're from northern Minnesota, and the salvaging of old-growth logs from the bottoms of lakes and rivers has been quite a gold rush up there. Some of those logs go for as much as twenty thousand dollars."

"Same here," Havok said, "but an old-growth teak log would go for a lot more than twenty thousand dollars."

Johnson, his shoulders sagging slightly, turned his eyes from Havok and looked at his beer while Havok continued.

"Instead of floating log jams of harvested logs down rivers or across lakes, the Spanish would send men into forests on nearby islands to chop them down and process them just enough to get them craned aboard the decks of their ships. And sometimes these ships sank because of storms or running aground. Salvaging tropical-hardwood logs may not be as sexy as brining Spanish doubloons, but these logs will stand up to any typhoon, Teredo worm, or termite, and are sorely wanted by musical-instrument makers and millionaires."

"What about that lovely staircase? Is that solid brass?" the woman asked. "By the way, my name is June." She held out her hand and leaned forward, revealing her freckled bosom.

Havok shook her hand and guessed she was in her late thirties. He tilted his head toward a low-lying wooded island at the entrance of Subic Bay. "We took the staircase off an old steamboat. The Spanish sank it in the pass just south of Grande Island, trying to blockade the bay so the Americans couldn't enter when Dewey came down in 1898 to fight the Spanish fleet in Manila."

"It is in remarkable condition," June said.

"My business partner is pretty good at restoring and fixing just about anything. He's the one that finished processing our recovered teak and mahogany and put this deck together." Havok turned to look across the alleyway. "That's him over there."

Stone looked up and waved.

June waved back, and her husband finished his beer just as Apple came out with a tray of refills.

Johnson perked his shoulders up again as he handed his empty bottle to Apple. "One reason we're here is to see that boat of yours. We're on our way to Hong Kong for a business symposium, and I saw your advertisement. If I am not mistaken, that's a fifty-foot custom-built raised-deck express-cruiser-style 1930 Stephens gentleman's motor yacht. Plumb bow and transom stern. Now that was a classic era of construction: everything square, the bow, stern, and upperworks all at right angles to the keel, and constructed completely out of mahogany and teak.

But . . . it seems a bit different. Perhaps more robust than the ones I've seen back home."

"It's a 1926," Havok answered. "And yes, it is a bit more robust than when it was originally built. We've had the occasion to be in places where we shouldn't have been, and it has deflected more than one bullet."

"I grew up on Lake Superior, and we have boat shows all the time. I always wanted a Stephens, but I've always been too damned busy with business." Johnson sighed and dipped his chin slightly before straightening his back. "How did you come by it?"

"I salvaged it from a cove on Mindoro," Havok said, turning to look at the boat himself. "It has quite a varied history. The boat company built it especially for a Canadian millionaire for his personal use, so although it's built of tropical hardwood, it's light in construction, for economic reasons. And it had rather basic diesel engines. But the millionaire soon realized that the American Prohibition Act could add quite a bit to his bank account, so he had it modified slightly to include beefier engines for speed and leased it out to a rumrunner called The Swede. Both The Swede and the boat proved to be quite successful. At least up until 1931, when the Coast Guard finally captured it."

"You're kiddin'!" Johnson exclaimed. "That's The Swede's boat? The Red Duck?"

"You've heard of him?" Havok asked as he sipped his beer.

"Nobody grows up along Lake Superior without hearing about The Swede, perhaps one of the most successful rumrunners in Prohibition history," Johnson explained, pointing his bottle at the boat. "I can't believe I've read about his exploits for so many years only to find myself sitting ten yards away from his boat, the infamous Red Duck."

"Well," Havok continued, "now it's my dive boat. Are you scheduled to dive with us?"

"No. I got certified years ago but haven't dived since," answered Johnson, a hint of shame in his voice.

Havok noticed that June furrowed her brow, and he guessed the closest Johnson had ever gotten to a scuba tank was page 159 of an adventure novel.

"You said that boat can deflect bullets. How so?" Johnson asked.

"The Coast Guard, after capturing the boat in 1931, commissioned it for their own use. What better way to capture other rumrunners than to use a boat used by rumrunners? Anyway, after Prohibition was repealed in 1933, the Coast Guard had no need for it. But the Navy figured out that it would be of use to them, so they commissioned it and had it shipped to the Philippines. They had planned to use it as an early version of a PT boat, or high-speed gunboat, throughout the islands. However, when the Japanese invaded the Philippines in 1941, the Navy didn't have time to use it. Instead, they stashed it in a cove on Mindoro Island, where it was forgotten. Over the years, the jungle claimed it and typhoons beat it up. We had to take it apart and bring it back up here to Subic in sections.

"Stone stripped it down to its keel and tried to save and reuse as much of the original wood as possible while rebuilding it, but even though the entire boat was built of mahogany and teak, it was still lightly built. Again, for economy and speed. Since we had access to tropical hardwood ourselves, we replaced what needed to be replaced with the same wood that we used for this patio deck. As we put the boat back together, though, we realized we were rebuilding something that would be quite substantial and needed special engines, as any basic diesel engine would not do. Stone managed to find two 1918 Liberty L-12 aircraft engines with extra parts."

Johnson chimed in: "Twelve-cylinder aircraft engines with three hundred horsepower and a high speed-to-weight ratio."

"Four hundred horsepower actually," Havok said. "But with larger, more robust engines, we had to continue to strengthen the boat's internal framing structure, which we covered with hull planking almost twice the thickness of the original planking."

Johnson sighed. "So what you've Frankensteined together is a classic 1920s gentleman's motor yacht on steroids?"

"That's right," Havok said, "and it has served us well over the years and has deflected quite a bit of small-arms fire when needed."

The table fell quiet as everybody tended to their drinks. Meanwhile, Johnson seemed to drift off to another world. He took on an expression that Havok's parents had accused him of having after reading a novel. It looked as if Johnson had suddenly been transported to a world a hundred years away. Havok could almost imagine the daydream taking over Johnson's mind.

There he was, standing with legs spread wide while firmly holding the helm of the Red Duck as it powered its way across the black water of Lake Superior in the dead of night. Armed only with a crumpled captain's hat perched jauntily on his head, a holstered M1911 .45-caliber pistol on his hip, and his guile, he was transporting over a hundred cases of Canadian Club to waiting trucks near Thunder Bay.

Suddenly the night disappeared as a spotlight targeted Big Johnson and his boat. Knowing that capture by the Coast Guard was out of the question, Big Johnson once again defied the law and the impossible. With one hand remaining on the wooden helm, Big Johnson pulled his pistol out of its holster and pointed it at the blinding glare. He fired four rounds at the spotlight, which was over two hundred yards away. Exploding in a shower of sparks, the light was suddenly extinguished, leaving the Red Duck in total darkness. Big Johnson returned his thoughts to his mission and the thirsty customers who would soon be imbibing the fruits of his adventurous exploits and cheering his name.

"What about a flight lesson?" June asked Havok, disturbing the quiet of the table. "Can you give me a ride?"

"Anytime you want. Just let me know when." Havok kept his eyes on her while he asked Johnson, "Do you want to go up for a flight?"

"No, thank you," he said. "After having flown halfway across North America and all the way across the Pacific, the last place I need to be is in another airplane just yet. We're going to be here for only two days. We're flying to Hong Kong for a symposium."

"You mentioned that before," Havok stated. "What's up in Hong Kong?"

"I'm in manufacturing," Johnson explained, a bit of pride in his voice. "Setting up a business venture between my company and China's leading appliance manufacturers. By this time next year, I think I can have five plants up and running back in Minnesota."

"Appliances," Havok said slowly. "Huh."

Johnson fell silent as he turned his attention to the airplane.

"We recovered it from Taal Lake, just east of Manila, a few years back," Havok said, seeing Johnson inspecting the plane. "It's a type of seaplane that battleships and cruisers launched from catapults. The pilot sat in the front seat, while a spotter sat in the rear seat. After we salvaged the plane, Stone restored it and installed an extra gas tank for long-distance flying. He also installed a gauge console, a steering yoke, and rudder pedals in the rear cockpit so I can give flying lessons."

Johnson thought pensively for a moment and then asked, "Is it legal to salvage this stuff?"

"It's the Philippines," Havok replied. "Everything is legal as long as you have pesos."

"It must be wonderful being a successful treasure hunter," June said.

Havok shrugged his shoulders slightly. "Treasure hunting is a dirty word. I like to refer to myself and Stone as artifact-recovery-and-relocation specialists."

Johnson looked as if he'd had a sudden realization. "I thought flying and diving weren't a good mix."

"Well, you're not supposed to fly for a while after diving. You have to allow the body to off-gas," Havok explained, adding, "I try to follow the rules most of the time."

The table fell quiet for a few moments as Johnson, lost in thought, continued to look at both the boat and the plane.

Havok silently finished his beer while surveying Johnson. The man looked like one of those washed-up actors who had been a heartthrob in his heyday but was now simply a heart attack waiting to happen. In that moment, Johnson could have been David Hasselhoff, Erik Estrada, or Val Kilmer dreaming of earlier days, or even The Swede himself.

After a couple of minutes, Havok broke the silence. "Just let me or my staff know if you need anything. How are your rooms? I hope you sleep well and enjoy your stay."

While her husband was still lost in thought, June spoke up: "I am sure we will, but if we . . . need anything, where do you sleep?"

Havok hooked his thumb over his shoulder and across the alley. "Second floor. Bedroom's on the south side."

Havok took a final sip of water and then grabbed the beach towel, the envelope, and his beer. "It was nice to meet you two, but Stone and I have guests coming in for a night dive. I have to help him get the boat and the dive gear ready."

"Before you leave," Johnson said, bringing himself back to the present, "let me give you my card. I own a restaurant supply company in Minnesota, and I think we can work out a deal when you're ready to spring for an upgrade." He reached into his shirt pocket. "It helps to carry a few of these around." He pulled out a wad of cards.

June looked down at the table and put her hand to her forehead.

Havok accepted the business card. "Thanks."

Once inside, he stepped past the door to the kitchen and into P.J.'s, stopping long enough to throw the card into a trash can just behind the bar. Upgrade my ass, he thought.

Inside the cool barroom, rotating ceiling fans offered comfort for the several customers sitting at the long wooden bar or at a few of the dozen tables on the barroom floor. Havok saw Apple's mother, Catalina, sitting on a tall stool behind the end of the bar. One of Catalina's wrinkled hands was busy making tally marks in a notebook. She was counting the number of drinks served so far that day. The inside bar was Catalina's domain, and she took excellent care of this part of the business.

Havok put his empty beer bottle on the polished tropical-hardwood bar and walked toward the front wall, where an open window allowed sunlight to enter. Next to the street-facing window stood four uniformed Chinese sailors ogling the contents of a wall-mounted display case. The men spoke in Chinese and pointed to shiny gold doubloons lying on black velvet inside the case.

Indeed, space that was not taken up by the long bar or the dozen tables was occupied by shelves and display cases filled with curios of the sea: an old Spanish conquistador helmet, a Japanese samurai sword, various types of ordnance that Stone had rendered inert, brass fittings salvaged off historic wrecks, even a collection of rum bottles. Each rusted, dented, or coral-encrusted artifact represented a slice of Havok's past, as if its purpose were to record his life.

Havok nodded to the sailors as he passed them on his way to the front porch. From there he watched Filipinos race by in the unique multicolored jeepneys that roared down National Route 1 until a mostly red jeepney, which was dragging a trail of dust behind it, came to a screeching halt in front of the bar. The spring-mounted chrome horses on the sun-faded hood still jostled for position as their driver, Manny Magsaysay, bounced out from behind the steering wheel and up three cement steps to the porch. Dressed in hiking boots, khaki shorts, and a green bush shirt with Peso Pete and Olongapo Joe's logo, Manny weighed just over one hundred pounds. At seventy-five, Manny still had a full head of thick, short hair. He ruled his clan with an iron fist, making sure everybody in his family pulled their load. Havok and Stone relied on the patriarch, and Manny was extremely loyal to his two employers. In return, his employers offered everybody in Manny's family well-paying jobs.

Manny leaned against the concrete railing of the veranda and pulled a pack of Champion cigarettes from his shirt pocket. He popped one into his mouth and lit it as he watched two of his sons, and Apple's brothers, get out of the back of the jeepney.

"Did you get everything?" Havok asked.

"Sure did, boss," Manny answered. "I'll go back to the Marvista Hotel to get our night divers as soon as we are off-loaded."

Cases of beer and soda were stacked in the back of the jeepney. The two young men started lugging them into the bar.

"Looks like you got it under control, Manny," Havok said as he treaded down the steps to walk next door.

Havok climbed the stairs at the back of the dive shop and entered his apartment. He stripped and entered the small bathroom. After a leisurely shower, he toweled himself dry and walked naked to his bed. Sunlight shone through the open windows on either side of the bed, warming the sheets and the clothing that Apple had set out for him to wear: briefs, khaki shorts, leather flip-flops, and a green company shirt. Next to his clothing was Apple's favorite pair of pajamas: pink shorts and a pink tank top, both with white bunnies. Havok quickly ran a comb through his short brown hair and long reddish-brown mustache before leaving the room.

A few minutes later, he was standing on the back deck of the dive shop, pulling his dive gear from a drying rack and placing it into his dive bag. As he pulled on the zipper, closing the gear bag, he heard muffled voices coming from inside the shop. He looked through a window and saw customers for the night dive charter. They were Japanese and all wore the typical tourist uniform: new, name-brand tropical attire. Junior, one of Manny's other sons and the company's divemaster, was assisting the group with checking out their dive gear. Although Havok could speak and read a sufficient amount of Japanese and was a certified scuba instructor himself, he chose to delegate as much as possible so his employees could max out on tips. Not only had Junior attained scuba instructor certification, he had learned Japanese along the way, and was certainly well rewarded for it with extra income.

Once all the Japanese divers filled their gear bags, Junior led them out to the Outfit, where both he and Manny, who was already on the boat, stowed their gear bags on top of the raised roof of the engine room. The engine-room structure took up the center-aft portion of the deck. It was three feet high and ringed with circular brass portholes on the sides. The raised structure vibrated slightly from the idling engines inside. Scuba tank holders lined both sides of the boat. Once Manny and Junior had secured the gear for sea, Manny went into the pilothouse and nodded through the windowpanes to both Havok, who was on the bow, and Junior, who was on the stern, indicating that he was ready for them to bring in the mooring lines.

Apple had staked Havok out for herself, and her mother, Manny's wife, controlled the bar, but the Outfit was Manny's domain. When not attending to other duties, he spent every second taking care of the old vessel. He doted on the boat. The only downside for Manny was that Stone still took care of the engines. Manny would fume at the greasy fingerprints Stone managed to leave now and then throughout the boat. Havok suspected that Stone left the marks on purpose just to mess with Manny.

After Manny guided the boat away from the dock, Junior opened an old fifties-era metal Coca-Cola cooler and passed around sodas, bottled water, and small bags of pretzels. Junior, like his father, was small in stature but muscular. He wore his jet-black hair short like his father. After passing out the Cokes and snacks, Junior began his mandatory dive brief as everybody settled down for the trip out to the site.

This was not the Japanese divers' first dive with Havok. The day before, he and Junior had taken them out to Grande Island for a leisure shore dive and then for a more intensive dive. The object of the intensive dive had been the sunken USS New York, a 1890s-era battle cruiser. Tonight the divers had signed up for a dive to explore a Japanese WWII destroyer. Junior finished his briefing and was about to order the divers to suit up when one of them interrupted him.

"Excuse me, please," said the Japanese diver, who appeared to be about forty. "This is nice boat, but why do you have those holes? They look like bullet holes." The man pointed to a line of thumbnail-sized holes that scarred the length of the starboard side of the engine-room structure, which was part of the original construction.

Junior looked down at the holes. An application of clear varnish sealed them. "Yes, they are. Mr. Havok and Mr. Stone had a run-in with some pirates a couple of years ago down Mindanao way." He paused and looked at his audience. "Yes, we still have to be careful."

The Japanese diver turned to his companions and spoke to them in Japanese. They all looked at the bullet holes and remarked quietly to each other as they started to assemble their gear.

Havok, meanwhile, went below to the forward cabin, changed into his swim trunks, and slipped on a pair of faded dive booties. Afterward, he went up to the bow. This was the best part of the trip for him. He sat on the deck, leaned against the front of the pilothouse, and gazed into the purple-orange sunset that separated the blue sky from the South China Sea. The throbbing hull massaged him. The air rushed at his face, tugging at the flowing ends of his mustache. He raised his hand to push the ends of his facial hair down, and as he did, his thumb ran across the scar on the left corner of his mouth. He smiled inwardly at the thought of the scar, which was a result of the time he and Stone had been in the custody of the Unidad de Intervención Policial, Costa Rica's militarily trained, and best-trained, police force. It was only after his contact at SPAN made some quick moves, transferring a substantial amount of money into certain foreign bank accounts, that the police had seen fit to release him and Stone.

Havok turned his attention to other scars on his body, rubbing one on his right forearm and touching one on his left leg. The scars were to him like the lines parents draw on a kitchen doorframe to record the height and events in the lives of their children. Like the relics at his bar, each scar on Havok's body marked an adventure in his life. He felt proud of them, except for the scar on his lip. Although he never cared much what people thought of him, refusing to be enslaved by other people's opinions, he did feel self-conscious about that particular scar; hence, the audacious mustache. The mass of reddish facial hair clashed with his short brown military-style haircut, which accentuated strong Nordic facial features.

Havok stretched and relaxed. He felt the dying rays of the sun on his shoulders. He looked at the mountains to the north. The sun had set to the west, behind Grande Island, and the last of the rays escaped the hold of the setting sun, illuminating a line of clouds that surrounded the lofty mountain peaks. Beneath the awe-inspiring sky, steep mountain slopes covered with green tropical forests stretched all the way to narrow strips of beach, which were strewn with rocks that had tumbled down from the heights above.

It was seven thirty p.m. when the Outfit approached the wreck site. Havok stood and moved to the bow. Manny, using three lines of sight—the northeast corner of Grande Island, a tall coconut tree on low-lying Chiquita Island, and the end of the old ammunition pier—and using two throttles, positioned the boat over the wreck. He raised his hand, and Havok reached down to the six-foot chain shackled to the stock of the boat's anchor. He grabbed the chemical light stick clipped to one of the links on the chain by a metal shower-curtain clip and bent it with both hands until it snapped and started to give off a rich blue aurora. He released the pelican hook that held the fifty-pound anchor in place and stepped back. The anchor splashed into the black water below, the six-foot length of chain and anchor rope racing noisily after it.

As soon as the line slackened, indicating that the anchor had hit bottom, Havok snatched the line up. He waved his left hand in the air, signaling for Manny to reverse the engines. The Outfit idled backward, dragging the anchor until it bit into the bottom of the bay. Manny continued to reverse the boat while Havok played out another hundred feet of anchor line. He cinched the line around the cleat and raised a fist. Manny moved the throttles to their neutral position. On either side of the boat, about twenty yards away, were two pre-positioned white Styrofoam buoys, one tied to the stern of the wreck and the other to the bow.

Junior gathered his charges under the darkening sky while Manny flipped switches on the boat's helm console, turning on the deck lights. Havok looked around as he walked aft. He saw a couple of narrow outrigger boats anchoring twenty to thirty yards off.

Havok put on a rash guard before slipping his arms through the straps of his buoyancy compensator. Standing up with the load on his back, he met Junior by the portside dive gate. He and Junior divided the group into two teams, with Havok taking three divers to the bow marker and Junior taking the other three to the stern marker. This methodology allowed each dive leader to keep control of his group while decreasing the risk of confusion from crowded diving conditions and the stirring up of the bottom sediment that came with it. Each diver stood hunched over to support the weight of the scuba tank and weight belt, and each had a glowing chemical light stick tied to his mask strap. Under the shadow of darkness, they looked like Navy SEALs getting ready to jump out of a C-130.

"Is your shotgun ready?" Havok asked Manny while surveying the narrow-hulled outriggers bobbing in the darkness around them. A weak bow light marked the location of each one.

"Don't worry," replied Manny, holding up a Remington 870 twelve-gauge pump-action shotgun.

The divers' eyes widened at the sight of the shotgun, and they all looked back at the bullet holes on the engine-room structure.

"Pirates!" Havok emphasized with a mischievous grin.

He stepped up to the open gate that gapped the bulwark, pushed a button on a strobe light, which was tied to the handrail by a ten-foot piece of rope, and watched the light flash several times before he dropped it into the water. The beacon would serve as a reference point for the divers. He then turned to his group of divers and ordered, "Iki massho."

The divers obediently fell in line behind their leaders. Havok placed his right hand over his mask and regulator, put his left hand over the gauge console looped under the waistband of his buoyancy compensator, and then stepped out into open space. On the other side of the boat, Junior followed the same routine with his team.

Manny's responsibility was to remain topside in case of emergencies, to assist divers, and to keep an eye on the boats that bobbed in the darkness. The boats in this bay were owned and operated by simple fishermen, but given the opportunity, the fishermen would paddle silently over to unattended boats to take everything that was not bolted down. Manny lit a cigarette and made one complete round of the main deck, stopping for a brief moment under each deck light. The two boats had pointed their bows toward the Outfit, but after seeing Manny, they pulled up anchor and left the area.

Neither Havok nor Manny worried about these harmless pests, most of whom probably already recognized the vessel as Havok's; they were simply anglers looking for an extra peso. Real pirates would not have stopped because of a single guard. Fierce Asian cutthroats would board their victims' boats and do as they wished. Piracy still existed in many parts of the world, including Southeast Asia, where pirates found safe operating bases among the islands that made up the Philippines, Indonesia, and Malaysia. Operating from secret lagoons, villages, and towns, the latter two of which openly supported the trade, the pirates could pillage with impunity.

After about thirty-five minutes, the first of the Outfit's divers surfaced near the blinking strobe light Havok had dropped into the water earlier, and Manny assisted each diver up the short ladder until all were safely on board. It took another thirty minutes for the divers, including Havok and Junior, to gear down and stow everything away for the trip back. As the divers stood on the fantail, toweling themselves dry, Manny motored the boat toward the anchor while Havok, on the bow, brought in the slack of the anchor line. Once the anchor line tended straight up and down, Havok threw up a fist, cinched the line around the cleat, dove headfirst into the water, and pulled himself down the anchor line to the other end, which was sixty-five feet below. Reaching the anchor chain, he grabbed at the fuzzy blue light in front of him, snapped the clip, and, with the plastic light in his hand, returned to the surface. The watching tourists applauded and spoke quietly among themselves as Havok held up the faint blue light.

Manny began steering the Outfit home while Junior passed around drinks. Havok remained in the background with a beer, listening to the excited babble. The divers talked and gestured, bragging to each other about what they had seen and who had used the least amount of air. Havok forgot about his customers and turned to look at the eerie shadows in the valleys of the Zambales Mountains. He watched as the clouds became luminescent under the full moon. He never failed to appreciate the natural beauty of the Philippines.

Arriving back at the shop, the tourists returned their dive gear and migrated to P.J.'s for drinks and food, and to talk about their adventure that night. Havok went to his bedroom for a shower and a change of clothing. He decided to see how things were going at the bar, so he walked across the alley and onto the deck at the rear of P.J.'s. He opened the screen door and walked into the beginning of his own adventure, not knowing that a chance encounter that evening would drag him into a life-and-death struggle with others thousands of miles away.

2

HONOLULU, MAY

Two months earlier, the bow of the research vessel Kona Wave sliced through the dull green waters of the channel leading out of Honolulu Harbor. The ship pointed west, into the Pacific Ocean, as the black hands on the Aloha Tower clock behind her struck noon, marking both the time and the ship's departure.

On the enclosed bridge of the Kona Wave, the ship's captain, John Morgan, stood by his helmsman, Fetu, and together they piloted the 180-foot motor vessel past the red and green buoys that led them safely out to sea. Briefly taking his eyes off the channel, Morgan looked through the window in front of him at the thirty college-aged students on the bow. He saw that although Professor Pilar Bonne-Bouche stood near the mixture of graduate and undergraduate science students, she held herself a few feet apart from them. Pilar, the chief scientist, or "chief sci," for this field school, was a trim and fit young woman with short coalblack hair. Both Morgan and Fetu had known Pilar since she was an undergraduate student at Honolulu State College. Pilar was the result of a marriage between a French geologist and a young Filipino woman who died when Pilar was a baby. Pilar had studied under her father, Professor Jacques Bonne-Bouche, who had been head of the Environmental

Sciences Department. She was full of curiosity and wanted nothing more than to work in the field with her father.

Morgan turned his attention to the doorway that led to the starboard wing of the bridge. Over the top of the waist-high bulwark and about forty yards distant, a line of people stood along the narrow strip of brownish-white sand that defined the shore of the east end of Sand Island. The students on the bow were waving goodbye to family members who had come to see them off. Morgan spied familiar faces in the crowd, and he turned to look at his helmsman.

"Oy, Fetu, I see Emere in the crowd. Want me to take the 'elm so you can wave bye?" Morgan's deep voice retained the vague hint of a cockney accent left over from his days as a London youth.

"No t'anks, Cap'n," replied the large Polynesian seaman, keeping his huge brown eyes on the channel markers ahead and his large brown hands on the spokes of the helm. "Said goodbye 'nough times last night."

Morgan accepted the curt reply and continued to wave back to the people in the crowd, including Emere, a Polynesian woman who matched the girth and weight of Morgan's helmsman.

Emere returned Morgan's wave with a ham-sized hand, mouthing something.

"Emere says she loves you," Morgan translated.

The helmsman gave him a simple nod of acknowledgment.

Universally respected along every waterfront from Honolulu to Bombay for his seamanship, Captain John Morgan presented a tough physical appearance, which was also well respected. Built like a steel marlinspike and just as resilient as one, he stood five feet, eight inches and hovered around 170 pounds. His torso was thick and powerful, and his legs were lithe but muscular. His flaming-red hair was wire-brush stiff and closely cropped on the sides. A dense but neatly trimmed red mustache with sharp ends extended beyond the corners of his mouth and arched up toward his temples. Beneath the mustache and determined lips, a beard grew down his jawline, ending in a bushy yet well-groomed point that accented Morgan's already-protruding chin. His ruddy and worn complexion spoke of a lifetime spent at sea. His scarred, callused hands indicated that he was not the type of captain who lounged about while others did the work. While his physicality presented a hard and stern person, his startling green eyes and their large black pupils gave off a mischievous glow and evinced an adventurous soul.

Anybody who looked at his lined face, merry green eyes, and beaming smile could tell that he was glad to be at sea again. He had left school at sixteen to fulfill his dream of becoming a world-traveling merchant seaman. Now approaching sixty years old, he was just as excited about this departure as those that had already come and gone, including those that had occurred during the last ten years, which he had spent as master of the Kona Wave. Wearing a pair of sun-faded blue jeans and a worn but freshly laundered Dickies khaki work shirt, Morgan looked out the windows of the pilothouse, searching the channel with experienced eyes. His scrutiny landed once again on the group of students near the ship's bow. This group was the reason for their westward journey.

On the high-profile bow of the Kona Wave, the HSU students leaned over the wood-capped bulwark. An occasional streak of running rust marred the white-painted bulwark. A good number of the students waved to relatives in the crowd. Other students watched the rushing water slide past the white bow as the ship carried them toward the islands of the western Pacific. All the students, though, eagerly chatted about the adventure that lay ahead. The publicized reason for their expedition was to conduct environmental impact studies in the wake of international mining conglomerates.

However, one rascally student, Stephan, had introduced himself to Morgan the day before and had immediately followed his introduction with asking if Morgan had any experience with the Pacific Vortex, the Pacific's version of the Bermuda Triangle. The area in question covered a large portion of the South China Sea, with points stretching from the west coast of the Philippines to Vietnam and north to Taiwan. That imaginative student, holding a torn paperback, now stood at the end of the line, right beside his professor, Professor Pilar Bonne-Bouche.

"How's Pilar doing, Cap'n?" asked Fetu.

"You know her," Morgan answered without taking his eyes off the bow. "Right as rain anytime she's in the field."

"I know, but I think sumptin's in her head," Fetu offered as he adjusted the helm slightly.

"I agree. The itinerary for this expedition's a bit busy," Morgan responded, "but she knows what she's doing."

After graduating with a PhD from HSU, Pilar had become part of the university's faculty, working in her father's department. Morgan and Fetu had watched the father-daughter pair for years, shuttling them around the islands of the Pacific and Indian Oceans as they conducted research for the university and other schools, institutions, and government agencies. Morgan envied their relationship. It was a type of family relationship not often seen these days.

Unfortunately, that relationship had ended two years before, when Jacques Bonne-Bouche was killed in an accident while on a research trip to the American mainland. Since then, Pilar had become distant and introverted, cold and empty like the Arctic landscape. At one time, her black almond-shaped eyes had glowed with wonderment and curiosity. Now they seemed to be looking at something beyond the distant horizon. Pilar knew that she had changed, and she knew people noticed it. She told everybody that her only reason for staying on at the university was to carry on her father's work. However, Morgan and others guessed she had her own reasons for remaining—a secret agenda that only she could fathom. While she kept herself remote from most people, she occasionally sought fatherly support, along with a comforting hug now and then, from Morgan.

On the bow, Stephan turned to Pilar, who still stood about four feet away. "Are you looking forward to the field school, Dr. Pilar?" he asked.

Pilar turned left and looked up at the gangly, redheaded student who towered over her five-foot, two-inch frame.

"Yes, Stephan, I am. However, I believe it would be wise to replace that drivel"—Pilar paused to point out the paperback in Stephan's hand—"with my report on soil degradation in eastern Russia. I spent half of last year there waist deep in swamp water, and I would hate to think my time was wasted. That book is alien fantasy. Soil denitrification rates are scientific facts."

Stephan, who was trying to grow a beard but had more pimples than hairs, looked down at the book in his hands. It was about how aliens were responsible for the large statues of Easter Island and the perfectly engineered roads and temples in Peru and Mesoamerica.

"OK, Miss Pilar," Stephan conceded. "I can take a hint, but you ought to look into some of this stuff. You never know where there might be a connection. Life is full of surprises."

"I'll think about it," Pilar replied, turning away from the student. She looked up at the bridge and saw Morgan's head and torso framed by the wood of one of the large bridge windows. She waved to him and walked aft to the port breezeway and down three steps. Turning right, she grasped a brass doorknob, pushed open the wooden door, and entered the dimly lit passageway that led to her stateroom.

Later that night, with the ship safely out to sea, all aboard were sound asleep except for a few souls. Fetu, along with one of the students, stood near the console that ran along the front of the darkened bridge interior. His eyes alternated from the dimly illuminated instruments on the console to the sea outside, watching for other craft that might cross their path. Behind him, the helm moved ever so slightly, as if an invisible helmsman were handling the wheel, though the movement was actually the result of the automatic pilot and computer keeping the vessel on course. Outside the bridge, Morgan reclined fitfully in a swivel-mounted chair on the port bridge wing. He was holding a steaming mug of black coffee laced with a shot of whiskey. The Pacific blackness rushed at his face. He relished the smell of fresh, clean salt air. Behind him, he could hear the muffled roar of the ship's diesel engines as their rhythmic noise escaped from the smokestack. Deep inside the hull, Cheng, the ship's engineer, made his rounds. Wiping up a drop of oil there, checking a gauge here, he was making sure all was in working order before he went to his stateroom and bed. The alarm panel in his room would summon him if necessary.

In her small two-person stateroom, Professor Bonne-Bouche reclined in her lower bunk. She was showering after a brisk workout in the ship's gym: two miles on the treadmill, a set of sit-ups, and several reps on the bench, where she confidently pressed 135 pounds of iron.

Though weighing twenty pounds less than the weight she lifted, she had no problems bench-pressing it. Now, wearing white panties and a dark blue men's V-neck T-shirt, Pilar rested on top of freshly laundered sheets that smelled of fabric softener, and leaned against two pillows, which were damp from droplets that had escaped her hair. The inclined position flattered her visible cleavage. Under the light of a bunk lamp mounted to the bulkhead beside her, she read the topic of the lecture she would be giving the next day: "Sedimentary Denitrification Rates across the South China Sea's Oxygen-Minimum Zone." While she held the pages, the muscles in her arms spasmed, causing her reading material to quiver slightly.

After finishing the last page, Pilar twisted her torso to place the reading on a small metal desk. Re-centering herself on the bunk, she thought for a moment before twisting again to grab something from under the pillows. She didn't immediately find what she was looking for, and she paused again, listening for the quiet snoring of her roommate. The graduate research assistant who slept in the bunk above her sounded fast asleep, so Pilar continued her search. Her hand found what she was looking for, something that was hard and about twelve inches long.

Pilar retrieved a black cloth-covered rectangular case and placed it on her lap. She pulled at the zipper and opened the small flat satchel, about the size of a book. Four 9 mm magazines were nestled inside, each in its own little pocket and each fully loaded. Facing the magazines was a 9 mm semiautomatic pistol. Pilar pulled the Sig Sauer P226, a favorite among elite military special operatives, from its cloth holster. The cool, subdued metal felt good in her hands, but she knew, deep down, that her ability to use the weapon for one intended target was simply an unattainable dream. She noticed that the muscles in her arms had stopped their spasms. With the deftness of trained hands, she quickly and quietly pulled the pistol's slide back, giving her weapon its own workout. She brought it up at the ready, aligning both front and rear sights on some unseen target in front of her. Stephan, her student, was right: life was full of surprises.

3

THE HAGUE, EARLY MAY

WHILE THE **K**ONA **W**AVE STEAMED OUT OF **H**ONOLULU **H**ARBOR, A SMALL BALDING MAN, TAKING A MIDMORNING BREAK FROM MANAGING HIS CELL-PHONE STORE, ROUNDED THE CORNER OF AN ANCIENT-LOOKING BUILD-ING AND WALKED DOWN A NARROW STREET. He saw a taxi, its engine running and meter clicking up quite a fare, parked along the curb in front of the doorway of his destination. The taxi driver was playing a card game on his cell phone. The balding man pushed the door of the building open and entered. There were only two customers: one bland-looking man wearing a wrinkled black suit and another man who wore a dark blue tailor-made suit. Both customers sat in straight-backed wooden chairs at one of the tables in the center of the room. The bland-looking man slumped dejectedly, while the other sat poised and erect. The seated men sipped liquor from glass tumblers. The man sitting straight up was reading a newspaper. Above them, the thick wooden ceiling beams were stained almost black from hundreds of years of swirling tobacco smoke. The sable stains helped darken the room.

The balding cellphone-store owner walked past the men to his regular stool against the back wall. He moved the stool away from the pock-marked plaster wall and then wiped away plaster chips from the seat before sitting down. The young man behind the bar was already drafting a blonde lager. After accepting the beer and taking a sip, the balding man spoke in Flemish: "Who's His Royal Highness?"

"I don't know, Stojan," the young man answered. "They ordered in English, but I think they're Russian. They've never been in here before."

Stojan glanced at the man reading the newspaper and then thought about the taxi. Taxis rarely drive down this street much less wait outside. He guessed that the man in the expensive blue suit had the taxi on standby, which meant its meter was still running. Stojan then looked at his own reflection in the mirror behind the bar. Sweat glued thinning hair to his rounded skull. His suit was worn.

"Hope he never comes back," Stojan said. "Wouldn't want Bartel to raise prices. Once that bastard sees money, he always wants more of it."

From there, Stojan and the bartender began to discuss the previous night's football match.

The two men at the center table remained silent for a few more minutes, until the rich man's companion finally spoke.

"Nicholai, why do you go on these tirades? Now look at us. We are hiding from the shit press and drinking shit vodka in a shit bar." He looked into the liquor in the glass as if it could tell the future. "All we have to look forward to is a recall back to Moscow, and I'm not looking forward to meeting the boss."

Nicholai remained intent on the newspaper throughout his companion's opining. He wore a strikingly dark blue suit with a contrasting brilliant-white silk shirt and soft-blue silk tie. The fit of his attire accentuated his solid 190-pound frame. Its color accentuated his looks. His neatly combed wavy black hair, strong nose, and prominent chin revealed his confidence. His physical and aristocratic appearance spoke of a person who could be sitting at the head of a corporate board meeting, directing workers in the gardens of a European estate, or leading men into battle.

Nicholai held a tumbler while his sapphire-blue eyes moved to read the text of a newspaper article.

MAY 29—The steps outside the Peace Palace became a scene of violence this morning after a group of human rights activists gathered to protest the presence of Deputy Commissar Nicholai Anisimova as part of a visiting Russian delegation. The delegation is in The Hague to discuss an aid package with the leaders of the European Union, which they say will finance an environmental recovery program in Siberia.

Waiting protesters jeered and taunted specifically Mr. Anisimova, an ultranationalist and dedicated white supremacist, as he and other delegates emerged from their limousines. One protester jumped from the crowd to throw a bucket of pig's blood at Mr. Anisimova. Mr. Anisimova managed to dodge the blood and punched the protester once before the security detail rescued the delegation and ushered them into the palace.

Mr. Anisimova is a cofounder and member of the Yedinaya Rossiya Party, or United Russia, which advocates for the restoration of Russia's old imperial borders, the reannexation of Alaska, and the rebuilding of Russia's military capabilities. Mr. Anisimova is a former Soviet military intelligence officer with a specialty in Asian languages and an Olympic medalist in the martial arts, and is at the end of a long lineage of the Anisimova family, which dates back to at least the sixteenth century.

Security personnel removed Anisimova from today's scene, while the remainder of the delegation met with European Union officials throughout the afternoon.

"Idiots," Anisimova muttered as his eyes moved up to the headline article and to photos of the American president and Putin. The article compared the two leaders and their international policies.

"Look at that self-centered, arrogant fool," Anisimova stated, speaking to the photo of the president. "I could play that buffoon like a puppy."

Anisimova's eyes crooked to the photo on the right. Putin, on the other hand, was used to dealing with the unforgiving facts of life and making life-and-death decisions. As Anisimova studied the photos of the two leaders, his fingers tapped a slow Morse code on the table. It was as if the fingers were telegraphing his thoughts. While the American would be an easy target, Putin, the boss, would be much more of an adversary.

Anisimova knew he would have to be careful with his plans. He put aside his thoughts about the two world leaders to read a side article about another Russian, Dr. Alik Dubrinsky, an award-winning chemist who had been at the Peace Palace conference to discuss chemicals leaching into groundwater systems.

That doddering old fool has no idea what he's mixed up in, Anisimova thought, even though it was he who had asked Dubrinksy to become part of his future plans. He should be home playing koldunchiki with his grandchildren.

Anisimova brought his glass to his lips and downed the liquor in one swallow. He thumped the glass on the table.

Grabbing a liquor bottle, the young bartender approached the Russians to refill their glasses before returning to his post behind the bar. Anisimova downed the fresh drink and then reached into his pocket to pull out folded money from which he peeled a one-hundred-euro note. After slapping the currency down, Anisimova stood and straightened the front of his suit and pulled at his cuffs. He stepped through the door to his waiting taxi as his companion finished his drink and followed behind him. Upon exiting, a devious smile of anticipation finally broke Anisimova's stoic face.

After the pair opened their respective doors and sat on the taxi's back seat, the driver spoke without turning: "Where to?"

Anisimova quickly replied, "Airport."

As the driver put the transmission into first gear, Anisimova thought about his next move. He smiled.

4

SUBIC BAY, PHILIPPINES
EARLY JULY

HAVOK OPENED THE SCREEN DOOR AND ENTERED THROUGH THE REAR DOOR OF HIS BAR. He looked into the large room and out through the front windows. A number of customers were quietly talking and enjoying themselves either inside the bar or out on the veranda. An original 1963 jukebox sat in the corner. A Johnny Cash song, "I Walk the Line," intermingled with the patrons' voices. Catalina was behind the bar, loading up a tray of drinks for Apple to deliver. Havok peered through the open kitchen door. Stone, wearing a pair of faded jeans, flip-flops, and a yellow T-shirt, stood at the kitchen counter about five feet away from Havok. He was making a sandwich.

"How was the dive?" Stone asked, keeping his attention on the food in front of him.

"It went OK," Havok answered flatly. He looked at a brass nautical chronometer mounted above the veranda door. The black hands pointed to just after ten p.m.

Stone accepted Havok's answer as he remained focused on his sandwich. On the steel countertop was a tray with a round loaf of pumpernickel bread, a plate heaped with thick slices of ham and Carr Valley

Wisconsin cheddar cheese, a jar of spicy brown mustard, and a jar of German gherkins.

"Not much of a Dagwood," Havok commented. "It almost looks like a normal ham-and-cheese sandwich."

"Ran out of olive loaf and limburger cheese last night."

"Thank God," Havok remarked. "Hey, do not concern yourself with my gastronomic issues."

Havok smiled slightly as he stepped into the kitchen, opened the refrigerator, and removed two San Miguels. He grabbed the bottle opener, which hung from the refrigerator door handle by a piece of kite string, and opened the beers, placing one on the steel counter in front of Stone. Havok turned his back to Stone and leaned his shoulder against the doorframe, looking out into the bar. "How did it go here?"

"Quiet," Stone answered. "The couple you met this afternoon is out front, and apparently Mr. Johnson saved your life during the war."

"Cool. I'll have to go and find out how he saved my ass."

Leaving Stone to his sandwich, Havok walked into the barroom, nodding his head, first to Catalina and Apple and then to some regulars sitting at the bar. He made his way out to the veranda, where there were ten customers sitting in small groups. The concrete deck of the veranda was painted blood red and reflected a dull, gloomy light. Diesel exhaust from worn jeepney engines mingled with the muggy night air, but the pulsating breeze from the slowly rotating ceiling fans helped to evaporate some of the sweat that was forming along his hairline. Vendors shouted, trying to overcome their competition and the music from several nearby bars, as they hawked hand-carried wares. The throaty roar of truck engines and the piercing screech of jeepney horns tried their best to drown out the sounds of large insects frying on the electric bug zappers that fringed Havok's bar.

A group of four customers sat at one table, five at another table, and one man sat by himself. The Johnsons were part of the five-member party. The lone man, wearing a pair of jeans and a Hawaiian shirt, seemed to be waiting for somebody. Havok sat down with the group of four, chatting with them for a few minutes while eavesdropping on Johnson's exploits around the world. Havok noticed that Johnson's face was flush. Probably from a day's worth of drinking, Havok guessed. In addition, Johnson was so into his tale that he failed to see Havok sit only a few feet off to his left.

"I recall bein' down to six hundred fathoms just off the coast of Michigan," Johnson slurred. "And we're trying to salvage an airplane that crashed back in the fifties. It was sitting a ledge and could've gone over the side at any minute. Havok was on the other side hookin' his cable, but all of a sudden, the plane lurched to starboard. I knew if I didn't get over there quick, Havok was dead."

Johnson paused to sip his beer. June sat next to her husband, and Havok noticed her downcast look, narrow eyes, and tight lips. Her embarrassment was evident.

"But the problem was that my surface-supplied air hose wasn't long enough," Johnson continued as he pulled the bottle away from his lips. "So I ripped my face mask off and swam over the top of the plane to Havok, and just in time. He was trapped under the wing, so I placed my feet into the mud and lifted up the wing just enough for him to slip out from underneath."

After taking another sip of beer, Johnson finished his tale of rescue. "I signaled him to go up. Then I swam back over the top of the plane, put my mask back on, and finished the salvage job." Johnson sighed pensively as he leaned his chair back slightly. "Yes, sir. I'd say I've saved his life at least two or three times."

It was not the first time Havok had heard such outlandish tales from people, and he chuckled inwardly. Six hundred fathoms is 3,600 feet underwater, and no human outside a submersible can work at that depth. It's amazing what people can come up with in their own heads, he thought. Even believe their own lies.

June finally looked up and saw Havok. She straightened, and her eyes widened. With a slight nod toward the dive shop next door and a poke of her tongue out of her mouth, she gave Havok the "get me the hell out of here and take me to your bedroom and screw the hell out of me" signal.

Havok winked at her.

She smiled.

The other three people at Johnson's table, a middle-aged American couple and a young adult who might have been the couple's son, were drinking sodas. The trio appeared to be swallowing every piece of crap Johnson was spewing.

Havok shifted his eyes to the lone man. He looked to be about seventy and approximately six feet tall. He was also balding, sported a rotund gut, and had a bulbous drinker's nose with tiny capillaries that road-mapped the blotched and porous skin. His arms, though, still possessed the thick, knotty muscles of a working man. Havok noticed that the man's beer was almost empty. He waved two fingers in the direction of the bar's front window. Apple, who was inside the bar, saw Havok's request. Havok chuckled to himself as Johnson started on another outlandish story of derring-do involving Havok. Something about chasing pirate treasure off the Florida Keys. Havok stood and walked over to the lone customer. Johnson was still too into himself to have noticed Havok.

"I'm Joe Havok, the owner. Buy you a beer?" Havok asked the old man.

The man looked up. "You sure can, mate," he accepted with an easy-going grin. "I'm John Wheatley." He spoke with an Australian accent.

Apple swung by, placed two beers in front of the men, and then moved off to Johnson's table. Both Havok and Wheatley took a heavy pull from their bottles. Wheatley pulled a white handkerchief from his shirt pocket to wipe his forehead and then looked up at a bug zapper in the corner as it sizzled another insect.

"And I thought they grew 'em big in Queensland," he remarked.

"Is that where you're from?" Havok asked. "Queensland? Australia?"

"No, I'm from Alice Springs, but I visited Queensland a couple of times. We're up here on a short holiday. My son-in-law, Jack English, is part owner of a hotel at the other end of Baloy Beach. He invited Mum and myself up for a visit. We've been here a week but are leaving tomorrow around noon."

Havok recalled meeting Jack English some time ago, as most of the resort owners either helped each other out on occasion or just had drinks together. "Where's your wife now?"

"She's shopping," Wheatley said. "I told her when she gets done, I'll be right here."

"What do you do back in Australia?" Havok asked, raising his beer bottle to his lips.

"I'm retired. Used to run a sheep station, but now all I do is listen to my wife complain about me being underfoot." Now it was Wheatley's turn to ask a question. "Why 'P.J.'s'?"

"Short for Peso Pete and Olongapo Joe's. Named after me and my business partner, Pete Stone."

"Sounds catchy. How did you end up with this place?"

Havok looked down at the glass on the table, appreciating a time long past. "At the start of the Second World War, millions of Philippine silver pesos were about to be captured by the Japanese. So, to keep the silver from falling into the hands of the Japanese, the Philippine government, with the help of the US Navy, smuggled as much of the silver out as they could with submarines and used boats to dump a bunch more in various places around Manila Bay, figuring the latter portion could be recovered after the war."

He paused to sip his beer and noticed that Wheatley's mood had changed over the course of the short account. The old man had lost that merry-old-grandfather face and had taken on the expression of a man searching a distant past.

Havok continued: "I've always been a reader, especially when it comes to lost ships and treasure, and after coming across some first-hand accounts, I just thought I would give it a shot. Did my research and talked Stone into coming here with me. We rented a boat and gear, and found a cache of silver pesos. After paying off a long line of government officials, we put the rest in a bank in Manila and settled up with business elsewhere before opening this place."

Havok finished his story and noticed that Wheatley was sitting ramrod straight in his chair.

"You know how amazing this is?" Wheatley's voice trembled with shocked disbelief.

"How's that?" Havok asked.

"My old man was in the Navy during the War. He saw an American submarine crew dumping pesos, boxes of them!"

"Where? When?" Havok drilled in quick succession.

"Is he telling you that old muck?" asked a strong feminine voice.

Both heads turned toward the voice.

"Hello, Mum," Wheatly said. "Mr. Havok, this is my wife, Alice."

Havok stood to meet Mrs. Wheatley. She was about five feet, six inches tall. She had a trim, sturdy frame and steel-gray eyes. Her silver-blue hair was drawn back into a bun, which gave her a stern but somewhat benevolent appearance.

"Please sit down, Mrs. Wheatley," invited Havok just as Apple walked up to the table. "Would you like a drink?"

"Why, yes, thank you. A double Maker's Mark," she said, taking a seat and placing her shopping bag on the concrete floor. She poked her slouching husband. "Straighten up, please."

"What do you mean, 'muck'?" Havok asked.

"It's OK," Wheatley said, straightening up in his chair. "She always kids me about that story. She says if it were true, my old man or I would have got it a long time ago. Everybody else thought he was just blotto."

"Why didn't you go back and get it?" Havok asked. He ignored the doubt that was creeping into his mind.

"You know, I really don't know why. Money? Family? The fact that my old man had a rough time after being captured by the Japanese?" he reflected. "I guess I just got too busy with my sheep station in the middle of the Australian outback and didn't have a clue where to start even if I wanted to."

"Go ahead and finish," Havok said. "It sounds like great 'muck' to me."

Apple returned with the drinks and placed them on the table, which gave Havok a moment to think. Two people who know where treasure was dumped, and they didn't get it.

"Well, my father was a sixteen-year-old ordinary seaman in the Australian Navy. In April 1942 he was on destroyer duty. They were trying to get back to New Guinea when two Japanese airplanes attacked. The planes shot the bloody hell out of the crew and ship with bombs and cannon and machine-gun fire. Dad said the ship's crew tried to evade, but the bombs damaged the steering gear and they abandoned the ship, but the Japanese kept shooting as the survivors tried to make it to rafts floating in the water. Fortunately, it was almost dark and the planes were shooting blind. When the Japs gave up and left them alone, there were only seven survivors and one damaged raft. When morning came, they could see an island way off to the northwest. Dad said that it was part of the Spratly Islands."

Havok immediately pictured that group of islands in his mind. The Spratly Islands were a widely scattered and largely uninhabited group of islands east of the Philippine archipelago.

"He said the way the wind was blowing, they would get close to the island around sunset." Wheatley paused to sip his beer. "Finally, the wind brought them to a beach on the island's southeastern shore."

"Sounds like a pretty wicked tale of survival," Havok commented.

"Yes, it was," Wheatley said. "Fortunately, none of the survivors were badly hurt in the attack. All were well enough to walk. He said they walked north along the beach until they came to the edge of a mangrove swamp. They were looking for fresh water and a native village. Dad said they followed the edge of the mangrove until they came across a path that looked like it led through the swamp. As they walked that short path, they heard splashes, and once they got through the mangrove, they saw a surfaced submarine on a long, narrow bay. The sub was about two hundred yards offshore and the sun had just set, but Dad said they all could see well enough. Several men were on the foredeck of the submarine, and three men were up in the conning tower. The men on the foredeck were dumping wooden crates over the side and talking quietly to each other. Dad and his mates listened until they heard English, at which point they ran across the beach like a pack of dingoes, yelling at the sub. One of the men in the conning tower gave an order to the men on the foredeck, and they dropped what they were doing and climbed into a rubber raft tied alongside the submarine. Two men paddled while a third man, armed with a Thompson submachine gun, stood in the bow. The sub and crew turned out to be Yanks. Dad said he and his mates identified themselves and explained their predicament. The men in the raft paddled back to the sub. About five minutes later, it came back and picked them up." Wheatley paused to wipe his forehead.

"Dad and his mates entered the sub through the aft hatch and were led forward. When they stepped through the control room, Dad glanced at the chart table. The Yanks had a chart out, and on it was the island that they were just picked up from."

With calculating anticipation, Havok asked, "Did he tell you the name of the island?"

"He said it was named Terumbu," Wheatley answered quickly. "The Yank captain joined them in the mess. He said Bataan had fallen a few days earlier, and only Corregidor was holding out. He had been ordered to smuggle out vital personnel and equipment and make his way to Australia. Before the captain left the mess, one of my father's mates asked him what they were dumping over the side. The captain said his submarine was dangerously overloaded and he stopped at Terumbu to dump excess gear. The captain said that for the remainder of the journey, the Australians needed to remain mostly in the mess. They could leave to use the privy or go up on deck in pairs while the sub was surfaced. Dad said the sub got underway, and for the remainder of the night and well into the next day, he and his mates slept in the crowded mess. The next night, the Yank submarine surfaced to charge the batteries. My father and a quartermaster from his ship were the last pair to go up. They sat on deck, just forward of the conning tower and by the main hatch, ready to jump in just in case they were attacked again.

"The quartermaster was wondering why the Yank captain had stopped at Terumbu if he was escaping to Australia. The island was at least a hundred miles out of his way. The quartermaster said that if they wanted to dump the stuff for recovery later on, there were plenty of uninhabited islands all along the shortest route to Australia. The quartermaster figured out what he thought were the captain's motives—the captain had said that the Japs had set up a blockade between all the narrow island passages in their effort to trap escaping ships, and he was avoiding the noose. The quartermaster also said, if the cargo was dumped closer to the Philippines, it might be discovered. He even joked with my dad about gold ingots being in those crates instead of radio equipment."

Havok sipped his beer with rapt attention, but he could tell Wheatley had started to tire. Alice gulped her whiskey and watched her husband as if she could tell when it was time to go back to their room.

"My dad then said a Jap airplane suddenly attacked from the east. It turned on its spotlight and dropped two bombs. Both landed square on the deck behind the conning tower, and the explosions rocked the sub so hard they knocked Dad and the quartermaster into the air. They landed in the water forty feet from the sub. The sub went down so fast that only two Yank lookouts remained on the surface. The four survivors spent the rest of the night just trying to stay afloat. They were picked up by a Jap destroyer the next morning." Wheatley stopped talking to sip his beer.

Havok noticed the other customers, including the Johnsons, had left.

Wheatley continued the recounting: "They spent two days on the ship while being taken to a POW camp in Singapore, and while onboard, one of the Yank lookouts told my father something fantastic. The night before the Yank submarine had left Corregidor, while the crew was loading stores and those crates of vital equipment, the lookout was working in a guard shack on the pier when he overheard the captain and somebody else talking outside. It turns out that those crates were full of thousands of silver pesos. The Yank lookout told my father that if he helped him stay alive, he could have half of the silver after the war."

As Wheatley described his father's adventure, Havok could feel his own heartbeat quicken word by word. The force of the blood pressure pounded thunderously against his eardrums.

"Dad said that he and the other prisoners were dropped off at Singapore, where they were assigned to a small work party made up of captured Allied soldiers who were forced to work in the city itself. A few days later, one of the Japanese guards, called Old Bad Eye by the prisoners, beheaded the Yank lookout for some reason. I think the lookout tried to bribe the Jap with his knowledge about the silver. Later on, my father's mate, the quartermaster, was also executed. Old Bad Eye tried to have my father killed on some charge, but the guard was transferred out before he could lop my dad's head off. Dad survived the war and was freed in Indochina."

"Do you think that the lookout told your father's mate, the quartermaster, about the silver pesos? And what about the other American lookout? Do you think the lookout who knew about the silver tried to bribe him as well?"

"Oh, yes, I'm sure of it," Wheatley answered, wiping his forehead with his handkerchief before yawning widely. Alice finished her whiskey.

"Did the second lookout get beheaded like the other two?"

"I couldn't tell you. He might have been. It seemed Old Bad Eye wanted to kill the four of them especially."

"What about your mates in Australia? Do you think any of them took your father seriously?"

"Not those sots," said Wheatley. He pushed his empty beer bottle from his hand and stared through the glass tabletop. "Even if they did, I doubt it if any of them could muster up enough courage to step ten paces away from O'Leary's."

Wheatley went quiet, and Alice stood. She gathered her bag and nudged her husband. Silently and unsteadily, he pushed himself to his feet.

"The drinks are on me," Havok said as he helped Mr. Wheatley steady himself.

"Why, thank you," Alice replied. "We're leaving at noon tomorrow. Why don't you come down and see us before we leave? Did Mr. Wheatley tell you where we're staying?"

"Yes, he did," answered Havok. "And I would love to see you off."

After Havok helped Alice Wheatley load her husband into a passing jeepney, he returned to the veranda to think. His finger traced the rim of his beer bottle while he was lost in thought. Some of the world's most valuable archaeological sites, artifacts, and historic wrecks have been found by chance encounters or passing words. He recalled hearing such stories, including the story of a Ming vase worth over $3 million bought at a garage sale for two dollars. Hell, even the Dead Sea Scrolls were only found because of a donkey hoof going through the ceiling of a small cave. As a diver, he'd had his encounters with drunks at docks and in bars from Spain to Panama to the Indian Ocean, and all the drunks seemed to know where Spanish gold, hordes of WWII plunder, or pirate treasure was buried. Nine times out of ten, it was bullshit, but Havok knew that all it took was that tenth encounter. A plan started to formulate in his brain as the minutes slipped by.

As Havok pondered the possibilities, a movement disturbed him. Bringing his attention to the veranda, he saw that Mrs. Johnson had returned without her husband. She stood inside the bar, framed by the large front window, watching Havok. Apple stood in the doorway next to the window, playing a videogame on her phone and waiting.

5

....

SIBERIA, EARLY JULY

"**HERE COMES KISS-ASS,**" SAID THE SOLDIER SITTING IN THE DRIVER'S SEAT OF A **BRDM-2** AMPHIBIOUS ARMORED SCOUT VEHICLE. The soldier removed his brown beret to wipe his forehead with a damp handkerchief as he looked out the open window in front of him. Both the hinged Plexiglas windshield and the protective covering plate were propped up, allowing sunlight and air to enter the enclosed patrol vehicle. He replaced his beret and pulled a cigarette from the pack, which sat on the middle console between him and his passenger.

The soldier sitting in the passenger seat smoked a cigarette and looked out the small square window in front of him at another slope-sided, four-wheeled BRDM-2 coming down the narrow dirt road that sliced through the primeval woodland. The two soldiers saw a man, his head and torso exposed, standing in the low-profile 25 mm gun turret that was centered on top of the vehicle. The passenger soldier let out a puff of smoke with disdain while waving a gnat away from his face. "My God, I get so tired of seeing Petroske riding around like he's a conquering general entering Rome, riding a golden chariot."

"No shit," the driver responded. "I'm tired of him screeching on about his special secret mission, petting that pistol of his, and strutting around like a peacock. I hope he goes on that op soon. It's bad enough we have to spend our time guarding bunkers, but having him around all the time makes it even worse."

This particular bunker, buried under the damp black earth, was composed of five-foot-thick concrete inlaid with iron rebar. Over the concrete, the dense taiga, a vast evergreen forest, grew prolifically, disguising the mound from any distance. This reinforced bunker, like others scattered throughout eastern Siberia, had been used for Soviet civil-defense storage during the Cold War, but since then, an economically troubled Russian government with a splintered army and more important worries closer to home had forgotten them. Now the bunkers were being used again; this time, by a group of Russians with vastly different designs than the original Soviet owners.

This particular shelter contained a dozen long-range Soviet SS-19 and SS-24 missiles. Still entombed in their original shipping containers, the missiles were capable of delivering deadly nuclear, biological, or chemical warheads; however, the deadly material needed for the warheads had long been removed and destroyed—a result of previous disarmament talks between ex-Soviet and Western powers.

Within minutes, the second BRDM-2 stopped in front of the first and its two soldiers. The soldiers remained in the vehicle and watched Petroske grab the edge of the turret and use his arms to push himself up and out. Throwing his legs over the side, Petroske slid down the sloped metal of the vehicle, landing on the grass-covered ground. Despite his height, he was not an impressive-looking man. He was thinly built, his shoulders pinched, and he looked as if he were missing a section of his abdomen. His mid torso seemed to rest on his hips. As a result, he walked with a jerking stride. The two soldiers looked at the man's face. His eyes were mere slits, his nose was large and hooked, his face was long, and his chin was almost nonexistent.

Petroske, like the two soldiers, wore the standard Russian field uniform: a short brown-green camouflage jacket, which was tight around the waist, and identically patterned trousers with cargo pockets. All three of them wore a patch on the upper-left sleeve of their sweat-stained jackets. The patch was round with the outline of a white bear centered on it.

Above the bear was the Russian flag, and under the bear was the name of the unit: the First Russian Militia. The only item that set Petroske apart from the other two soldiers was a shoulder holster securing a SR-1 Gryza semiautomatic pistol under his left arm.

Petroske stepped toward the vehicle while pulling at the hem of his jacket and stroking his leather-bound pistol. "Is everything secure here?" he asked the men through the open windows.

"Da," the driver replied flatly.

Petroske jerked his head ever so slightly. Annoyance for the lack of respect was evident on his face, but the two soldiers didn't care.

In an effort to gain some sort of respect from the two men, Petroske straightened his shoulders before speaking. "Good. I am finally turning my duties over and will be leaving for my secret mission today. Deputy Commissar Anisimova has personally asked for my assistance." He looked down and flicked an unseen gnat from his sleeve.

Since leaving the army and joining what was, at first, a small group of disenchanted ethnic Russians, Petroske had steadily risen in rank. Though he was never able to gain the confidence or respect of their military leader, Colonel Yeshenko, he was able to ingratiate himself into Deputy Commissar Anisimova's confidence. Anisimova had given him the responsibility of guarding the militia's supply reserves. Petroske and his security section were constantly on patrol, covering hundreds of kilometers of what would soon become a pure Russia. The bunkers spread throughout this part of Russian Siberia were filled with weapons and material for new Russia, and beneath the soil lay the natural resources that would sustain the nation for years to come.

"I received a secret communiqué from Anisimova," Petroske now said. "My orders are to make my way to Singapore covertly. From there, an airplane will take me to an undisclosed island location. I will be his aide."

"I understand Sonny is down there as well," the driver said. "Tell Sonny we wish him success on his mission."

The two men in the vehicle had served under Colonel Yeshenko recently and had quickly learned to respect the man. Yeshenko, called Sonny by just about everybody who served with him or under him, was a soldier's soldier. He had been part of the Russian airborne forces for years before becoming a member of Directorate A of the Federal Security Service Special Purpose Center, an elite standalone subunit of Russia's Special Forces. The members were dedicated counterterrorism specialists. Sonny was a decorated combat veteran and professional down to his bone marrow, but like other Russians, he was able to read the tea leaves when it came to the future of ethnic Russians and their nation.

"I will," Petroske stated with irritation. As he turned around, he wondered why his men never said anything like that to him. Hell, they don't even bother to salute me.

The two soldiers watched as Petroske climbed back into his vehicle.

"One hell of a security officer," the driver commented. "He can't even keep his own secrets to himself."

The passenger responded by flicking his cigarette butt out the front window toward Petroske's vehicle. "I hope he accidentally shoots himself with that pistol of his. It's bound to happen as much as he plays with it."

He and the driver fell silent as they watched Petroske's vehicle reverse and turn back in the direction it just came from. Petroske stood in the turret.

6

....

SUBIC BAY, PHILIPPINES
EARLY JULY

THE NEXT MORNING BEGAN TOO EARLY FOR HAVOK. The clucking of chickens roaming below the windows on both sides of his headboard woke him from an all-too-brief sleep. Moments later, sharp blades stabbed into his eyes as Apple turned on the lights. She was wearing her pink pajamas. Reluctantly, he rolled to his left, uncovered a sleeping body, and cracked his hand sharply against the firm white buttocks, startling the woman from a deep sleep.

Apple approached the stand next to her employer's bed. She plunked down a steaming mug of black coffee without glancing at the woman.

"Here's your coffee," Apple said as she leaned over to kiss Havok on the cheek. "Go for a run, and I'll get your breakfast." She went into the bathroom.

Havok rolled over and reached for the gray cotton shorts on the floor. He picked them up, swinging his legs into them as he stood. "We gotta get you back to your room before your husband wakes up." He spoke with his back to the woman.

June Johnson, half asleep, stared at the ceiling.

"Don't worry about him," she said as she stretched lazily on the bed. "When he goes on benders like last night's, he's out for a while, especially since you two had a dick-measuring contest yesterday and he lost. Did you enjoy what you did to him?"

"Sort of," Havok answered slowly. "I got you as first prize, right?"

"Now you're just being a jerk," June said. "But did you have to do a victory dance on his corpse?"

"How'd I do that?"

"I'm lying in your bed wearing nothing but your old, smelly shirt."

"I didn't invite you up here. You could have stayed faithful to your husband."

"You didn't say it in words," June said with a regretful sigh. "Marrying money isn't all it's cracked up to be."

"Sorry to hear that," Havok said nonchalantly. He picked up the mug and sat on the edge of the bed, enjoying the breeze from the ceiling fan and the soothing warmth of the coffee.

June gave herself one more lazy stretch and sighed heavily. She looked at his back and ran a finger down his spine. "I hope you don't think I do this sort of thing all the time."

"Just some of the time?" Havok asked.

June did not answer right away. After a few seconds, she asked, "Can I call you a douchebag?"

"You're gonna have to take a number," Havok responded, looking at the black liquid in the cup. He felt June roll out of the bed behind him.

Wearing Havok's polo shirt from the day before, June walked sleepily around the end of the bed to Havok, tousling his hair with one hand while taking the cup of coffee from him with the other. She looked at him with downcast eyes. "My husband and I have a silent understanding," she said as she strolled about the room. "And when he's capable, he has his occasional indiscretion as well."

June fell silent and continued to survey the spartan furnishings and sip the coffee. She stepped toward the side of the room where the kitchenette and bathroom took up one wall. She heard Apple changing in the bathroom two feet away. Two wooden floor-to-ceiling bookshelves covered another wall. A Victorian rolltop desk with a framed map of the world above it took up five feet of space between the shelves. Holding the cup with both hands, she tilted her head to read the titles of the books.

"You seem to have an interest in all kinds of subjects," she observed. "History, language, literature, science, archaeology, dive manuals."

"It came with the job," Havok answered groggily.

While stepping around the wooden chair in front of the desk, June commented, "An uncluttered desk with a simple laptop and bargain-basement printer. You don't possess much."

"Sometimes having less means having more."

June tilted her head again and read the spines of some of the leather-bound books on the bookshelf to the right of the desk. "I used to love to read, especially the classics like you have here. I also liked novels about female detectives on the hunt for international criminals, but I haven't picked up a book in years."

"Why'd you stop?" Havok asked, holding his face in his hands and rubbing his eyes with his fingertips.

Still dwelling on the titles, she answered, "I guess I've been married too long to a man who worries more about business than about having a little adventure. I became jealous about having to live a life through fictional characters." She paused to run her finger down the spine of one of the books. "I see that you live in the past: Dafoe, Poe, Melville, Stevenson, Verne, London, Dumas, H. G. Wells, Rice Burroughs, Fleming, Hemingway, Clancy."

She stopped reading as her eyes fell on a row of books on the bottom shelf. She turned to Havok and threw him a glare. "Really? Cussler?"

"Sorry."

With a sudden strike of inspiration, she blurted, "Why don't you write a novel? I know you have enough life experiences to fill a whole room with books, and with you as the main character." She placed the coffee cup back into Havok's hands before reaching down to grab the bottom of her shirt, pulling it over her head, and balling it up in her hands. Standing naked, she brought the shirt to her nose and closed her eyes. "I can be one of your characters," she purred, her eyes still closed.

"A sexually frustrated homemaker whom you rescue from a boring marriage and ravage anytime you wish."

"I couldn't tell you the difference between a split infinitive and a sentence fragment. Besides, the protagonists in most novels are supposed to be some sort of good-looking and chivalrous knight in shining armor who, at no time, sleeps with another man's wife, always puts the toilet seat back down, cooks the perfect eggs, and never burns the toast." Havok shrugged his shoulders. "I have a habit of burning toast."

With the shirt still against her nose, June opened her eyes. "Somehow, I think that you make it a habit of burning your toast."

Havok raised his coffee cup in salute.

"Well, if I can't read a book written by you, then can I have this old shirt?"

Havok raised his coffee in affirmation again.

After another sniff, she walked back around the end of the bed to the opposite nightstand to place the shirt on her handbag. "Are we still on for a flight lesson?" she asked, slipping on the dress she had worn the night before.

Havok affirmed by raising his coffee cup.

Apple came out of the bathroom, now wearing a bar T-shirt, cutoffs, and a pair of sandals. She walked to the door. June did the same, but only after giving Havok a kiss on the top of his head.

Havok nursed another cup of coffee for five minutes before finally deciding to go for a short run. He walked to the closet, opposite the bookshelves and desk, which ran the full length of the wall. He slid his clean but faded running clothes and shoes from a hook at one end of the closet and put them on, then left his room.

Under the awning in front of the shop, he stretched while remembering the conversation with Wheatley. With the anticipation of an adventure in the offering, he started into a slow trot, thinking about fuel, time, distance, and supplies while absentmindedly waving back at acquaintances who waved to him. Havok ran with a slow, steady gait and turned around after one mile. He relished the mild exertion.

When he got back to his apartment, he slammed down a bottle of water and took a shower, barely toweling himself dry before getting dressed, leaving wet skin to stain his light-colored shirt. He sat at his desk and removed the napkin that covered a fork, a bowl of sliced fruit, and a few chunks of sharp cheddar cheese on a separate plate. His breakfast and juice both sat next to his laptop, and he slowly ate while searching the internet for information on the Spratly Islands, specifically Terumbu.

According to the internet, the islands consisted of a wide-ranging collection of reefs, cays, and a few larger islands, including Terumbu Island centered in the South China Sea between the Philippines and Vietnam. Havok also knew, from keeping updated with international news, that the islands themselves were not significant in terms of providing natural resources, but the waters around these islands were rich fishing grounds and possessed a wealth of mineral and petroleum deposits. These resources had led China, Vietnam, Taiwan, the Philippines, Brunei, and Malaysia to establish military installations on some of the larger islands and to argue over boundaries. However, China, over the last few decades, had increasingly pushed for dominion over the entire region, claiming the South China Sea as its own sovereign territory. One couldn't open an internet article or lift a newspaper without seeing photos of artificial islands, complete with airstrips, under construction by the Chinese. The South China Sea was also the major maritime shipping nexus between the Pacific Ocean and the countries that bordered it and the Indian Ocean and the countries that bordered it. Control of the South China Sea meant control of a major portion of the world's international maritime shipping.

Havok poked through various sites and found several images of Terumbu on Google Earth. He could see that the island was round in shape, about five miles in diameter, and completely covered with a tropical forest except for a rocky ridge that ran from north to south along the western edge of the island. On the eastern side of the island were two bays. There was a long, narrow bay in the southeastern corner. Havok assumed that was where Wheatley's father claimed to have seen Americans dumping the silver. There was a smaller, rounder bay farther to the north. Both bays ran east–west. The image was several weeks old but still useful.

Havok spent another hour reviewing more files and websites that referred to Terumbu Island. He printed out what he thought would be valuable, including an old US Navy report regarding the construction of a small base and a concrete wharf for the Philippine Navy back in the 1970s. The file also contained a detailed map on which two rows of single-story barracks ran from east to west, parallel to each other. A two-story headquarters building with a large front porch stood at one end of the barracks, while a single-story mess hall stood at the other end. Havok, judging by the number of rooms, estimated that the encampment was built to house about three dozen men. There was also some sort of single-story storage building off to the side.

The Americans had constructed everything out of cinder blocks and mortar, which gave permanency, but the Philippines had abandoned the encampment after only two years. The island had been unoccupied since. Havok looked back at the image of the island and could see that the tropical forest now covered everything, with no sign of the buildings that the map outlined. However, he could see what remained of the wharf. What was once a fine concrete pier where small ships and patrol boats could tie up was now two jagged chunks of concrete piling and slabs pointing out into the larger of the two bays.

Havok looked at the clock on his laptop. It was ten a.m., time to take his customers up for flight lessons. He grouped the papers together into a file folder and grabbed both the folder and his cell phone before walking downstairs and across the alleyway to P.J.'s. He saw that Apple had a glass of water and a coaster waiting for him on the table he had sat at the day before. He placed both the coaster and the water on the folder, along with his cell phone, before walking out onto his dock and to the side of his seaplane. Esmeralda bobbed ever so gently in the wake left by a passing banca boat. Her canopy was slid back, and he could see Stone sitting in the front cockpit. The back of Stone's head bobbed with the rhythm of the seaplane. His steel-gray hair was dark with sweat.

"Ready to go?" Havok asked.

Stone popped his head up. "Gas tanks are full, did the run-up and radio check, and your flight bag is on board."

"Great," Havok replied.

"Oh, by the way," Stone added, "Catalina said the Johnsons checked out early, so you're down one lesson."

Havok thought for a minute about their sudden change of plan. Maybe Mr. Johnson had a sudden attack of jealousy.

Voices from the patio interrupted Havok's thoughts. He turned and saw the same six divers from last night enter the patio with glasses of juice or water in their hands. Apple seated them at one table and gave them all menus. The women accepted the menus but turned to look at Havok.

"Looks like we're going to get busy," Havok said. "Be back in a few minutes."

He went to sit with the group to go over the flight plans, starting with briefing them on what to expect, and allowed them to pick who would go first, second, and third. Minutes later, Stone was strapping the first passenger into the rear observer's seat while fitting her with a set of headphones. He slid the rear canopy forward as Havok grabbed a handhold high on the fuselage, pulled himself up, and stepped onto the wing, then slid into the pilot's seat. He donned his headset and then fired up the original Pratt & Whitney radial engine. After letting the engine warm up and seeing that all the gauges read normal, he gave Stone a thumbs-up. Stone untied the mooring lines and pushed the plane out of the dock socket. Havok taxied away from the dock with his canopy still slid back.

Havok took his passenger for a thirty-minute flight over Subic Bay, and after a series of demonstration air maneuvers, gave her the controls, talking her through the flight, but taking the controls back when it came time to land. He repeated the process for the two remaining women passengers, and by noon, the last passenger had climbed out of the plane. On the dock, the three women huddled around Havok for pictures, which Stone took with their cell phones.

After the tourists left, Stone met Manny at the dive shop so they could run errands together. Havok returned to his folder of papers that he had left on the table and sifted through them idly while sipping a beer. As he did, a plan was coming to fruition. He also tried to estimate how much silver might still be sitting on the bottom of that bay. He reached for his phone to place a call to a friend and realized it was almost one p.m. He had missed seeing the Wheatleys off.

Well, he thought, I can always get their address from the owners of their hotel. I'm sure they wouldn't mind a last-minute visit accompanied with a cashier's check.

Havok punched in his friend's number and left a message on his voice mail. He also called Stone's cell phone and left a message.

An hour later, Havok was still sitting in his chair, mulling over the silver cache, his plan to retrieve it, and one small discrepancy that he noticed during his research. The discrepancy offered an air of mystery, and it excited him.

Returning to his room, Havok got back on his laptop and scrounged the internet for additional information. Finally, the sun had inched its way toward the western horizon, casting long shadows through the windows by his bed. He estimated travel times, distances, stops, fuel, and water requirements. A paramountcy of foreseen variables pieced together like a jigsaw puzzle. The unforeseen variables made only a brief pit stop in Havok's mind. If he could not control something, he did not worry about it. The often-unpredictable tropical storms did not concern him, nor did the fact that somebody may have already recovered the silver.

Havok was interested, however, in the minor discrepancies that had grabbed his attention earlier. An old US Geological Survey map identified the island as Bass Island, not as Terumbu. Some English sailor or explorer probably inspired the name Bass long ago. Additionally, an obscure college text identified the island as Karipot. Havok inwardly laughed at the name, which loosely translated to "cheapskate" in Tagalog, or "someone who refuses to give up his wealth." But the island's international name, as printed on modern nautical charts, was Terumbu. Havok's subsequent research did not reveal any recent occupation or interest by any of the countries who claimed the Spratly Islands, but his biggest concerns were naval patrols and pirate ships from disputing countries. At convenient times, the naval patrols and pirates were the same, and the last thing Havok wanted was to have any recovered goods confiscated by some opportunistic naval commander turned pirate. He thought about the bullet holes in the engine-room housing on board the Outfit.

Havok stopped riffling through the files on the laptop and his papers. He stared at the pages in front of him as if they could tell him something that wasn't written on the pages. His mind kept going back to the word karipot. Sitting back in his chair, Havok realized that although he had quite a bit of textual information, firsthand information was also crucial. He considered two options for obtaining firsthand information. One of the options would mean he'd have to fly down to the island himself for reconnaissance. The other would merely mean he'd have to meet with his friend.

Twenty minutes later, Havok walked up the staircase that led to the door of the Matacumbe Key Resort Hotel, which was about a half mile down the road from P.J.'s. This hotel was a three-story concrete structure. It was painted white, trimmed with dark red accents, and had a wide front porch. While the theme at P.J.'s represented Havok and Stone's lifestyle, the theme here represented its owner's lifestyle: it had a carefree vibe and a Key West atmosphere.

As Havok crossed the porch to enter the building, he saw his friend Scott Kilgore. Kilgore sat with a Caucasian customer at the square island bar in the center of the large room. Havok, now standing in the doorway, touched the arm of a passing server. The female server wore white capris pants and a red short-sleeved blouse with a Caribbean island print.

"Hi, Mercedes," Havok said. "Can you get me a Duval Crawl and tell Scott I need to talk to him?"

"No problem, Joe," she said, turning toward the bar.

Havok went back to the porch to select a newspaper from a pile stacked on a small table just outside the front door. Grabbing an empty table in the corner farthest from the other customers, he scanned the front page of the World Tribune while listening to Caribbean music coming from a speaker mounted somewhere above him.

He also thought about June Johnson but didn't know why. After all, she isn't the first married woman I've slept with.

He forgot about June and put the paper down when he heard Kilgore's voice.

"Hello, Joe," Kilgore said. His teeth flashed in a broad smile that went perfectly with his blond hair, sparkling blue eyes, and beachboy looks. Although he was in his forties, Kilgore's tanned and velvety-smooth skin made him look ten years younger, masking his years as a decorated Navy SEAL and combat veteran. Havok and Kilgore had first met at the Naval Special Warfare Center in Coronado, California. Kilgore was with SEAL Team 5. He was a good operator and an even better friend. After twenty years of service, he had retired from the military and relocated to Subic, opening two businesses—his bar and a marine-repair facility—as a front for what he was really doing. In reality, he was a field agent for the CIA.

Now, Kilgore held two Duvall Crawls, which were quart-sized Mason jars, each containing ice cubes, a wedge of lemon, and high-octane lemonade. "Come to spy on the competition?"

Havok feigned revulsion. "Spy on an old dump like this?"

Even though the two men pretended to compete like two old dogs trying to own the same backyard, their friendship was real enough. Havok replaced his look of horror with a genuine smile. "No. I wanted to talk to you about something else."

"Thought so," Kilgore said as he placed the drinks on the table and sat down.

Havok grabbed a jar and took a pull while reclining in his chair. "Have you heard of any action about the Spratlys, specifically a rock called Bass, Karipot, or Terumbu Island?"

"What kind of action?" Kilgore asked. "The Chinese view the entire South China Sea as their own private lake and, as a resource-rich waterway, claim it as such. They've been occupying a number of islands and creating artificial ones as airbases. Ever since the Hong Kong Accords last November, China has bullied the leaders of all the countries surrounding the South China Sea into uninviting any US presence, which is why I've been looking out my office window at a Yantai-class guided-missile frigate."

"Well, at least their crew is helping me stay in business," Havok replied.

"Although Chinese sailors have been enjoying this place as well, it would make me feel better if it were American sailors spreading the wealth. Anyway, nothing has crossed my desk lately about that specific island, but if you want, I can make some calls."

"That's fine," Havok said, accepting the offer.

"Is there something special going on there?"

"I'm gonna fly Esmeralda down there for a recon, then go back with the Outfit for a few days. Ran into an Aussie last night, and he gave me a hot tip about some World War II silver."

"Off on another treasure-seeking adventure," Kilgore joked.

"Ain't nothing wrong with getting outta town for a couple of days and getting some air under my ass," Havok responded in kind.

"Just let me know if you need anything else," Kilgore said. As he placed his drink on the table, he looked past Havok, at the steps behind him. "Oh my god!"

Havok turned as Stone bounded up the steps. His partner was wearing banana-yellow shorts and a bright blue aloha shirt covered with pink flamingos and islands of the Keys. Behind Stone, the sun had set and Grande Island was backed by a rich orange-blue, cloudless sky. Stone stepped up to the table. He pulled a pack of cigarettes, a lighter, his phone, and his wallet from the pockets of his shorts. After placing the items on the table, he sat down.

"Would our meeting have anything to do with the Aussie from last night?" Stone asked.

"I didn't get a chance to tell you earlier," Havok replied. "But he told me about a cache of silver. Figured we could take a few days off and take the Outfit to check it out. Are you in?"

"You know I don't let you take that boat anywhere without me," Stone answered. "You might burn out the engines."

"Good," Havok responded. "And I also need you to preflight Esmeralda for me."

"No problem with Esmeralda," Stone replied, "just as long as this little distraction won't screw up our trip to the Gulf."

"All I know is if you're dressed like that when we get to New Orleans, I don't know you," Havok said, looking down his nose. "Do you and Johnson shop at the same thrift store?"

"Remind me to remind you that you're still a douchebag," Stone said, pulling a cigarette out of the pack on the table.

Havok downed the last of his drink and stood. "I've gotta get some sleep. It'll be a long day tomorrow." He placed the empty jar on the table as Mercedes returned. She smiled as Stone looked at her.

"Hi, Mercedes. I'll have a full serving of Louisiana Viagra, a double order of spermicide, and a big-ass beer."

He winked at her as she giggled and twirled away.

7

TERUMBU ISLAND, EARLY JULY

PILAR GLANCED THROUGH THE OPEN DOOR INTO THE PILOTHOUSE. She looked at the brass chronometer mounted on the wood paneling of the interior wall. The black hands of the instrument showed it was just after nine a.m. She stood out on the port bridge wing, monitoring the dive operations while holding a metal clipboard in her right hand. A pencil was perched behind her right ear. Most of her students were divided into pairs and were collecting sediment cores from the bottom of the bay using five-foot sections of aluminum piping. It was her responsibility to monitor the divers and their dive times. Pilar watched as bubbles broke the surface of the smooth cerulean water in intervals.

Stephan, wearing only a pair of swim trunks and sunglasses, sat on a white fiberglass life-jacket locker on the main deck in front of the bridge. The pimply faced student diver held a hardcover field book in his hands. His dive gear was staged next to him, and he was ready to put it on and jump in if there was an emergency.

Stephan looked up at Pilar. "Hey, Professor, what's the name of this island again?"

"Terumbu," she replied.

"Thanks." The student looked back down and wrote in his field book.

Meanwhile, Pilar decided to pop into the pilothouse to get her water bottle, which she had left sitting on the helm. Captain Morgan, who was bent over the chart table, shifted his eyes from a chart to the small island in the middle of the bay, then back to the chart.

"Still confused about that island?" Pilar asked.

Morgan straightened and turned to look at her. "I don't get it. We're obviously looking at an island about one hundred fifty feet long and half as high, smack in the middle of the bay. It even has a bit of black smoke coming out of the top, but the island isn't on my charts."

He dropped a pencil on the table and looked past Pilar to the southern shore about two hundred yards away, before speaking again. Far away from the divers, two students zipped around in a gray inflatable Zodiac, collecting water samples from the bay. A few more students flitted in and out of the mangrove swamp that surrounded the small white beach on the shore. The students' clothing flashed against the dense green foliage as they collected leaf samples. "How's it going out there?"

"We're doing great for our first morning here," Pilar replied. "I suggest we remain anchored in this bay until tomorrow morning. We can go to the bay north of us tomorrow and perhaps anchor off the western shore the day after that."

The Kona Wave had arrived at six a.m. that morning, and this was their first full day of fieldwork on the island. Pilar and Morgan had agreed to spend three unscheduled days at Terumbu, which would be their final stop of the two-month field school.

Morgan turned back to Pilar. "I have no problem with how you've run this expedition, but every place we've stopped at so far had some sort of government or law-enforcement presence nearby. This island's a little farther away from the safety net."

Pilar sensed his concern. "I know this stop wasn't part of the itinerary we submitted to HSU, nor did we mention it in the plans that we submitted to the Philippine government, but it isn't too far off our intended track from Mindanao to Manila. Don't worry. Three days here, a stop in Manila for fuel, and we'll be on our way to Guam, then home. Besides, the students are having a blast, and they're learning good fieldwork."

"Do you think something's here?" Morgan asked.

"Too soon to tell, but we can start analyzing our soil and water samples on the way back to Hawaii. Besides, I don't think that fisherman back in Mindanao would lie to me. If he says the water around this island is poisoned, then we should believe him. He lost family members in that gold mine cave-in outside of Davao City, and the same corporation and its CEO, Kang, who owned that mine, conducted manganese mining throughout these islands. There is no reason to think that CMPC isn't responsible for anything happening here."

Shouts came from outside the pilothouse.

"What the hell?" Pilar blurted, turning back to the door. Morgan followed her onto the bridge wing. The students ashore lined the beach, pointing to something back at the ship, just under the bridge wing.

"Professor! Captain!" yelled voices from below.

Pilar looked over the wood-capped rail and down at the two divers in the water thirty-five feet beneath them. Two female students, about ten feet from the side of the ship, held their hands high, clasping black discs about the size of half-dollar coins. The students were so excited that they had forgotten to inflate their buoyancy compensators. Their legs and fins kicked frantically under the surface of the clear water as the students attempted to keep themselves afloat.

"What's going on?" Morgan asked.

A diver yelled, shaking her fists, "Look what we've found. Coins! And there's piles down there."

Pilar and Morgan looked at each other. "Coins?" they said in unison.

"What'll we do now?" Pilar asked Morgan as she looked down at the students below her.

"I'll wager that any further work scheduled for today just went into the loo," Morgan answered. "Call everybody in until we can sort this mess out."

Pilar pulled her phone from her back shorts pocket to call the two students in the Zodiac. Afterward, the students in the boat went to collect the students on the beach to bring them back to the ship. Meanwhile, the two students who had found the coins re-submerged to move the floating safety flag's anchor to mark the spot where the coins lay. Then they swam to the other dive teams to signal them to surface. While all of that was going on, both Stephan and Pilar left their stations and met at the dive platform located on the ship's transom to help each diver out of the water. By pairs, students surfaced and swam to the dive platform, including the two students who had found the coins. They didn't even have time to get out of the water and remove their gear before they were flocked by their fellow students, who wanted to see the coins. Because of such insistence, the two divers each pulled a handful of loose black discs from the pockets of their buoyancy compensators.

Both Pilar and Morgan realized that this accidental find created a fun diversion from mundane specimen collecting, but they also knew that any sort of serious fieldwork was impossible now. Pilar removed her outer clothing, stripping down to her one-piece swimsuit, and donned her personal dive gear, which was staged on the ship's main deck at the stern. Leaving Morgan in charge of the topside operations, Pilar and Stephan dove to look at what the students had found.

Within an hour, after returning from her dive, Morgan and Pilar had discussed the situation and made the decision to organize a recovery process to gather up the coins. Stephan and Pilar, as well as three dive teams, went back down with five-gallon buckets to scoop up the coins by hand. The remaining students and the crewmen, including Fetu, mustered on the portside of the ship, right above the spot where the coins were piled on the bottom of the bay. When the buckets were full of coins, the divers would tug on the ropes that were tied to the bucket handles. After the students and crew members on deck felt the tugs, they hoisted the buckets to the deck. Then the topside students and crewmen poured the coins into other rope-less buckets, which were then carried aft to the fantail. The students on the fantail hosed the coins with a freshwater hose, counted them, and then placed them in buckets filled with a 50-50 mixture of salt water and fresh water. Morgan inspected several of the coins, concluding that they were Filipino silver pesos.

By sunset, the divers had scoured the bottom of the bay, but they could find no more coins. All that remained was a gouged seascape and pieces of rotten crates that once held the coins. The ship's deck lights were turned on, and Pilar and Morgan stood back to watch the students wash and count the coins. Pilar and Morgan also listened to their jokes and the lively conversations about their newfound treasure.

"How do you think the coins got here?" wondered Pilar. "And do you think it was a wise decision to recover them? We didn't get ahead of ourselves, did we?"

"The first question is easy to answer," Morgan replied. "No coins appear to have been minted after 1941, and the boxes they came in were piled up like they were dumped. The American navy obviously chucked the crates of coins to hide them during the Japanese invasion of the Philippines in 1941. The second question is a bit harder to answer. No, we didn't have a salvage permit, and there is a bit of controversy about who owns what in these islands. That said, we did mark the spot with GPS, and the coins did not appear to be associated with any sort of wreck or structure, so we're not destroying any sort of provenance. Lastly, we are counting them and taking the best care possible to prevent any damage."

"I agree that recovering the coins was the right move," Pilar said, looking at the excited faces of her students and Morgan's crew. "But who gets to keep them once we inform the American government? Them or the Philippine government?"

"I'll have to check the laws on the books," Morgan answered, "but for right now, I suggest we document everything we did so we can't be accused of hiding some of the coins. After we're out of these waters, we can contact HSU, and they can figure out what to do next. After all, we're not scheduled to be here, on this island."

Morgan wrapped his arm around the young professor, giving her a fatherly hug. Pilar responded by wrapping her arm around his waist and giving him a squeeze.

After a moment, Morgan let go of Pilar and announced loudly in his best pirate accent, "All right, you scurvy dogs! Best we strike our booty below! I'll break out the grog!"

A hearty roar from the students, along with three cheers for Blackbeard's ghost, answered Morgan's demands. What better way to top off the summer than to discover a secret cache of World War II treasure? So, in keeping with the holiday-like spirit, Morgan broke what little stores of wine and beer were on board and allowed everybody a beer or a glass of wine while they worked. He kept his scotch to himself.

Finally, close to midnight, the students finished filling all the available five-gallon buckets with the coins. Once each bucket was full of coins, it was topped off with a freshwater-saltwater mixture before the lid sealed the contents. Then the students formed a bucket brigade to move the heavy buckets to the forward bosun's locker. Morgan locked the compartment's only door and placed the key into the pocket of his jeans.

Once the coins were securely locked away, the students continued their party-like mood into the ship's wardroom to finish their drinks. Captain Morgan had told his crew to go to sleep or to find other duties, as he felt this was a night for the students to enjoy their find. Morgan himself found solace on the bridge wing with a glass of scotch. Pilar found her own solace on the fantail near the dive platform, which hadn't yet been raised. Her hands clasped a bottle of Heineken as she leaned over the bulwark to watch the dark water lap the side of the ship and listened to the revelry in the wardroom behind her. Even with what had happened that day, she felt empty. The evidence they had collected would not be enough to file charges against the CEO of CMPC. Even the finding of the silver was only a brief distraction. While Pilar was picturing the 9 mm under her pillow, she heard a soft thump coming up from below her. She looked up and down the side of the ship but could see nothing but black water.

Probably just a log or coconut floating up against the ship, she thought.

But as she raised the bottle of Heineken to her lips, she looked at the dark stains at the edges of her fingertips, a result of the black silver oxide rubbing off the coins and onto her fingers as she had processed the silver coins that appeared to have been lying on the bottom of the bay since 1941. Captain Morgan called them treasure-hunter hands, and he said that, no matter how much you scrubbed, you would never lose that stain of black silver.

Suddenly, she detected movement out of the corner of her eye. An apparition, holding a sack of some sort, emerged from the darkness.

Before she could scream, Pilar felt the presence of a person behind her. An arm reached around and across her throat.

8

....

SUBIC BAY, PHILIPPINES
MID-JULY

A COUNTRY-WESTERN SONG BLARED FROM HAVOK'S CELL PHONE NEXT TO HIS HEAD. Startled, he reached over to the nightstand to turn it off before lapsing back to sleep.

Five minutes later, Apple, wearing one of Havok's old Magellan fishing shirts, entered the room. She turned the lights on, placed a tray of food on the rolltop desk, hit the brew button on the coffee pot in the kitchenette, and then went to the closet to get Havok's clothes ready, making enough noise to wake him and send him stumbling into the bathroom.

Thirty minutes later and just as they had done a thousand times previously, the couple sat quietly at the desk, enjoying a simple but filling breakfast of hot coffee, chilled pineapple juice, Filipino bread rolls, and canned liver spread while lost in their own thoughts.

As he chewed, Havok watched Apple. She was half naked, wearing only a simple shirt and a pair of white panties. Her demands had always been simple as she saw him off to another adventure. All she ever wanted was for him to return, whether the adventure was two days, two weeks, or two months long, or even two oceans away, with no questions asked. It did not matter. Havok then thought of his flight and the silver he had been told about.

Why do I always have to take something simple and make it so complicated? he asked himself, before looking around at his simple but comforting studio apartment. All he had to do was simply climb under those sheets with a woman who adored him and sleep in past dawn. With a silent sigh, he returned his thoughts to his flight.

"It's only five," Havok told Apple after breakfast as he stepped into a pair of faded jeans. "Why don't you get some more sleep?"

"OK," she answered from the other side of the bed, which she had started to straighten. The shirt that Apple wore engulfed her. It looked more like a nightgown on her. She had rolled the long sleeves up to her elbows, and the shirttails reached her knees. The front was unbuttoned, revealing the white panties, a flat stomach, and cleavage. Her small but shapely breasts moved with her breaths. She crawled into Havok's bed, watching him as she had done a thousand times before. Although she always felt lonely when he left on his trips, she knew she could not contain him. Doing so would destroy what time they had together. Apple had to force herself not to love him. She told herself it was better to have something for a time than nothing for an eternity.

Havok finished dressing in his normal flying clothes: a cotton bush shirt, a pair of faded jeans, hiking boots, a leather belt with a multipurpose knife, and a worn leather flying jacket. He stuffed a thermos of coffee into an old army rucksack full of extra clothes and emergency supplies, and double-checked the contents of the pack before closing the top flap.

"See you in a couple of days," Havok said, bending over to kiss Apple on the lips. He left the room without looking around, though he wanted to.

As he walked down the dock toward Esmeralda, he looked up at the black early-morning sky. It was clear with sparkling stars, promising good flight weather. He also saw a hint of gray in the eastern horizon, and he could hear the putt-putt of worn-out two-cycle engines as fishermen got an early start. He heard a noise and saw a dark figure next to the starboard wing.

"How ya doin', Pete?" he asked.

Stone was moving the wing flap with one hand while holding his other hand over his stomach. "I don't think I'll be ordering any of Kilgore's oysters anytime soon."

"Are you sure it wasn't the double serving of his nuclear horseradish?" Havok grinned. "You know that stuff will clear anybody's pipes."

Stone burped. "Stop gloating."

Havok grinned. "I filed my flight plan and left a copy on my desk. I have my stop times listed and will check in with you at each stop. You know what to do if you don't hear from me."

"Yeah, notify everybody on the planet that the world's greatest adventurer is missing. That'll get 'em running."

"Good," Havok said as he threw his bag into the rear cockpit. He slid the canopy forward and then climbed into the pilot's seat in the forward cockpit. After checking in with the Subic Bay Airport tower and test running the engine and the airplane's magnetos and other equipment, Havok waved to his partner, who untied the mooring lines and stashed them in a small line hatch inside the starboard wing. Stone gave the wing a push away from the dock and waved goodbye. The pilot looked back at Stone, who suddenly placed both his hands over his stomach.

Havok taxied his airplane away from the dock at idle speed, turning the aircraft toward the mouth of Subic Bay. Dawn had broken, and the water ahead was smooth and gray with no visible flotsam that might damage the main float on takeoff. Havok slowly pushed the throttle in and pulled back slightly on the yoke. Once achieving rotate speed, he pulled farther back on the yoke and waited for the airplane to break free of the water. When he felt the plane lurch free, he instinctively applied more backpressure on the yoke and pushed hard on the right rudder pedal to overcome the engine's spinning torque. Maintaining her climbing speed, Esmeralda effortlessly grabbed at the thick, humid tropical air and pulled its pilot skyward.

Leveling off at a thousand feet with a southwest heading, Havok maintained the required traffic-pattern altitude until the air traffic controller cleared him of terminal airspace. Havok acknowledged the transmission, thanked the controller for his assistance, and switched the radio to the open VFR frequency. He tapped the screen of his iPod, clipped to the dash, and tuned it to his music playlist. With Meatloaf blasting into the cockpit, Havok pushed the throttle all the way forward and maneuvered into a steep climb. The engine clawed its way upward toward the brightening sky above. He steadied out at seven thousand feet, settling in for the first leg of a long jaunt to Terumbu Island.

***

It took thirty minutes to get to his first stop, Puerto Galera on Mindoro Island. This stop was a brief but curious one. He took advantage of every stop he made: double-checking the weather, topping off the fuel tanks, and getting some refreshments. He had used the services here before and spent a few minutes with Mr. Mendoza, the man in charge of the small marina where he docked his plane. It was not even seven a.m. yet, but both men were sweating in the early-morning humidity as they stood on the dock.

"Anything going on south of here that I have to worry about?"

Mendoza was a small man who wore casual but immaculate clothing. His complexion was smooth and the color of doeskin, which was accentuated by gold-rimmed glasses. "An American ship named the Kona Wave has disappeared, and the American embassy is asking everybody to watch out for it and report if it is spotted. It's a research vessel from Hawaii State University. One of those students was in contact with his family over the internet. The student told his family they had found something on a deserted island. It ended with a strange message. The family told the university that all contact had been lost for over a day now. The university tried to contact the ship by radio and internet. No luck."

"Any explanation as to what happened?"

"No," answered Mendoza, but he paused and looked around to make sure he was not overheard. They were the only ones on the dock. "I think it was the Pacific Vortex," he stated firmly, with a nod.

Havok maintained his expression, as he knew not to scoff. He did not believe in the Pacific Vortex, but many of these islanders did. Most of them were staunch Catholics; however, they could never shake deeply rooted native superstitions. Mendoza believed in evil spirits as deeply as he did the Virgin Mary. Havok attributed any disappearances to bad seamanship, fire, storms, pirates, or even ISIS—to hell with supernatural forces.

"What makes you say that?"

"The family said the last part of their son's message was, 'They have us.'"

"Well, describe the ship to me. If I see anything, I'll let the authorities know."

***

After flying over or around a number of rain squalls, and a brief stop at Taytay, a sleepy seaside town on the northern end of Palawan Island, Havok took off and set his compass toward the expanse of the South China Sea.

It was just past noon when he sighted Terumbu several miles ahead and eight thousand feet below. He decided to first fly full circle around the island by following the shoreline. He had made good time on the smooth and quiet flight, and the only thing that had come over his radio was a call from a Philippine Navy ship, asking him to keep an eye out for the Kona Wave. He acknowledged their request, and although he sighted a few small freighters and fishing boats, the vessels did not match the description of the missing ship.

Havok began his descent toward Terumbu by easing back on the throttle, allowing the aircraft to drop five hundred feet a minute. The plane glided smoothly toward the island, and he welcomed the sight of the green-covered island on the rich blue sea. As he neared the island, its features began to conform to the printed-out image on the clipboard on his lap. He leveled off at one thousand feet, and as he approached the northeast corner, he eased the plane to port so he could follow the coast toward the southern part of the island. The entire eastern shore crept out of the sea at a shallow incline. The green waters were marked by underwater shadows, indicating broad expanses of reef flats. This half of the island was level, but toward the western side, the island's canopy rose slightly before giving way to a ridge running north–south. Reaching a height of about seventy-five feet, it looked like a purplish-white scar on green skin.

As a matter of habit, Havok took a few seconds to scan his gauges. He noticed nothing out of the ordinary and went back to viewing the island below. He reached the southern end of the island and turned to starboard, following the shore to the western side, where the slope from the top of the ridge to the shore was steep. He followed the shoreline north, coming around full circle to the island's northeast corner. There, a dark gouge cut through the shadowy green reef flat. Havok pulled back on the throttle, allowing the plane to drop, almost kissing the calm sea. He banked around and came back for another pass. A dark hole was visible amid the rocks and jungle. He knew the cut in the reef came from a freshwater stream that flowed away from the cove. The fresh water changed the salinity and temperature of the ocean, driving away coral-building organisms. The draft of the Outfit was less than three feet, so the channel should be deep enough for the boat. He saw no sign of human presence—present or past.

He thought about landing the plane for a better look but decided not to. There were rocks and coral heads all along this part of the shore, which would damage the seaplane's main float. However, he was able to see that the little cove would be just big enough to hide the Outfit if needed, so he powered up the aircraft and climbed back up to three hundred feet. He flew south again along the coast until he came to the smaller of the two mapped bays. He increased the engine's rpm slightly to maintain his altitude while he banked into a constant-altitude turn.

Angled sharply at sixty degrees so he could see over the wing, he spiraled over the still water and searched for any sign of human presence. The only thing he sighted out of the ordinary was a small point of land that poked into the shallow water from the southern shore. This did not match the image on the clipboard.

Havok thought about the oddity but dismissed it, blaming it on the jungle's prolific growth. He marked it on his image and came out of his turn, pulling back on the throttle and reducing the rpm to keep the nose of his plane from riding up as he leveled out. With level wings at three hundred feet, he crossed the stretch of land that separated the bays and reached the one where the submarine had supposedly dumped its load of silver. Once there, he went back into a steep turning configuration and inspected the bay below. The crossed shadow of his airplane on the bay's surface followed him. He spotted the small beach from where Wheatley's father was rescued, and he spotted another beach at the western end of the bay that stood in bright contrast against the dark jungle. Carving the beach in half was the black ribbon of a meandering stream escaping the jungle's hold.

In the middle of the bay was an island. It was about two hundred feet long and eighty feet wide, and about fifty feet in height at its center. Completely covered in vegetation, the island seemed to pop straight up out of the water, as there was no beach. Havok looked at the image on the clipboard in his lap as he circled over the island in the middle of the bay, but his attention was suddenly drawn away from the clipboard and to his right rudder pedal. While in his turn, he felt a slight jerk on the foot pedal. It was as if something had pushed against the rudder on the tail of the airplane. He released pressure on the right rudder pedal and pushed down on the left rudder pedal for a second before pushing back down on the right pedal. The airplane responded as he did.

A bird or something might have struck the rudder, Havok told himself. His thoughts returned to the island in the middle of the bay. Once again, the island possessed another piece of land not indicated on the image. He was noting the oddity on the image when the hairs on the back of his neck snapped to attention.

Click-click-click-click.

The noise and vibration from the piston-fired engine almost masked the rapid series of clicks that came up from the undercarriage. Havok checked his gauges. Everything was within parameters. Next, he tested his controls again, finding the plane as responsive as ever. Havok pondered the noises for a few seconds but convinced himself that he had just flown into a swarm of large insects. He went back to finishing his survey of the island. While landing was an option, he decided not to, as there was no need for it. Twenty minutes later, satisfied with the information he had collected, Havok looked at his gauges one more time and saw that the oil temperature had risen slightly but was well within limits. He made his final turn away from the island and began his 250-mile flight back to Quezon, a seaport on the island of Palawan.

After tuning into the weather channel on his radio, Havok decided to fly at eight thousand feet because the reported wind direction at that altitude would give him a good tailwind for his return to Quezon. He began his climb to that altitude while adjusting his GPS waypoints. Reaching altitude, the contented pilot, immersed in the sounds of Fleetwood Mac, flew eastward.

***

Thirty minutes into his flight, Havok pulled his attention away from the airspace around him and glanced at the gauge panel. The oil temperature had risen ten degrees since the last time he had inspected the gauges, fifteen minutes ago. Flying straight and level, the plane should have had sufficient airflow to keep its engine's temperature down. He quickly examined all of his other instruments, especially the oil-pressure gauge. The needle held steady.

Havok looked at his chart. He had less than fifty miles to fly before he would pass over the Tizard Banks. One hundred fifty miles beyond the Tizard Banks was Quezon. Between those two points was nothing except deep, lonely ocean, scarred by a few pieces of exposed reefs and barren islands. At the plane's current speed, Havok estimated he would cover the distance to Quezon in a little over an hour. He noted the sparse landmarks between his current position and Quezon as emergency landing areas where he could anchor out or tie up if needed. He hoped that the rise in oil temperature was due to slightly fouled oil cooler.

Playing the prudent pilot, Havok kept looking out the cockpit, and in a few minutes, the Tizard Banks appeared. But they disappeared as a grayish volcanic haze began to fog the air at his altitude. The automatic weather report said that a volcanic haze or fog layer hung over Quezon from eight thousand feet down to about a one-thousand-foot ceiling. Though not an impossible landing, the haze just added to the problem.

He tried several times to raise the Philippine naval vessel that he had spoken with earlier, but received no reply.

The next hour was the longest for Havok, as all he could do was get as close to Quezon as possible before the engine seized. Throughout that tense hour, he continued to send out calls for assistance, but to no avail. As he got closer to Quezon, he started to radio the airfield, but with the same result. Havok took a chance and glanced at his oil gauge, hoping his inattention had made the temperature decrease. Instead, the oil temperature was on a slow but steady rise toward the red arc.

Damn it!

Havok again attempted to contact the Quezon airfield with no answer. What a time to step outside for a cigarette, he thought.

Finally, after five calls, a disinterested voice answered: "This is Quezon. Are you asking for clearance to land?"

"This is aircraft November Charlie Foxtrot November Hotel Bravo," Havok said. "I am en route to your location. I am experiencing some engine trouble and am asking you to stand by on this frequency in case I need assistance."

The voice in his earphones seemed a bit more interested now. "We'll be standing by."

Havok gave up staring at the oil-temperature gauge, which was now in the red arc. Instead, he stared out of the cockpit, hoping the haze would disappear, but the closer he got to where Quezon was supposed to be, the thicker the haze became. He was not worried about getting lost, because the GPS was leading him straight to the airfield. He was thinking about the mountains around Quezon and other flying aircraft. He didn't feel like completing a power-out landing while trying to dodge unseen mountains or aircraft. He also feared Stone's wrath if the airplane were damaged.

Havok took a chance and glanced at the oil gauges again. The temperature gauge pegged out at maximum temperature, and the needle of the pressure gauge started to waver. Now he knew what the problem was: he was losing oil somewhere and was helpless to stop it.

Well, it's either stay at this altitude so I have air under my ass if I need it or get below one thousand feet and risk not having altitude in case the engine seizes.

After a moment of thought, he made up his mind: Screw it!

He pulled back on the throttle and pushed the yoke forward, but just slightly. Flying down at an angle, he lost altitude but was ready to pull up at any minute. After a three-minute descent, the fog disappeared and beneath him, as far as he could see on either side of the airplane's nose, running north–south, stretched the mottled brown-and-green coastline of Palawan Island. Directly in front of him was the municipality of Quezon, with its crescent-shaped bay. The maritime city occupied a band of land sandwiched between high, rugged mountains and a light-brown beach. He saw the working port of the city: a number of buildings and warehouses, with two wharves poking into the water. Alongside the wharves were a few small, rust-stained interisland ferries and freighters. On the water of the bay, various watercraft transited back and forth, leaving behind feathery white wakes in the dull blue water. He turned his head and looked alongside the starboard nose. Through the spinning propeller blades he spied the narrow airstrip, which ran parallel to the mountains. While he didn't intend to touch down on the strip itself, he felt the shoreline next to it was a safe area; it was free of boat traffic and had a repair shop nearby. He pulled back on the throttle further to reduce the engine's rpm and pushed the yoke slightly forward to lose altitude.

As he reached five hundred feet, he zeroed in on the water near the northern end of the airfield and switched off the engine before the wavering oil-pressure needle had a chance to drop to zero. The die was cast. Now, a strange silence replaced the smooth drone of the reciprocating engine. Without oil pressure, the high-performance engine would seize in seconds, so a power-out landing was his only option.

"Quezon Tower, this is aircraft November Charlie Foxtrot November Hotel Bravo."

The same voice responded, "We have you in sight and see that your propeller stopped."

"Affirmative," said Havok. "Engine's shut down, and will be landing north of the strip."

With the shoreline of the airfield as his target, he reached down for the lever controlling the flaps and put them at ten degrees. He felt the plane slow even more, allowing it to drop to two hundred feet. The nose rode up slightly. He let the plane react, and after another minute, when he saw all was clear in front of him, he put the flaps at twenty degrees and pulled back on the yoke, flaring the plane. He guided the plane in that configuration until he was twenty feet above the water, then pulled back sharply on the yoke, and Esmeralda roughly dumped herself on the bay. The plane bounced back into the air, but Havok kept pulling the yoke back, maintaining the plane's attitude. Esmeralda touched down a second time, and this time she stayed.

The seaplane plowed through the murky water for about one hundred yards before the center float grounded in the sand of an open beach near the airstrip. Havok slammed back the rounded canopy, unbuckled his safety harness, and stood up. Grasping the frame of the fuselage, he lifted his legs up, throwing them outside the plane. As he slid down the fuselage, he saw a yellow truck racing down the beach toward him. He let go of the plane's side and dropped into water about a foot deep. He stepped out of the surf onto the beach, and by the time the truck reached the plane, Havok was leaning against the warm metal.

"You all right, sir?" the driver asked, leaning out of the window to inspect the airplane.

"I'm fine, but I think I'm going to need a mechanic. Is someone available?"

"My cousin is a mechanic. I'll get him."

"That'll be fine."

As the truck roared away, Havok turned his attention back to his airplane. The engine crackled loudly as it cooled and contracted, and he could smell the stench of burnt oil under the late-afternoon sun. He listened to the cries of the engine and inspected it while he waited for the truck to return along with the mechanic. He got on his knees and looked up at the undercarriage, which was covered with black oil. The stream that had exited the cooler had stopped dripping because there was no more oil left. Turning his attention away from the film of oil staining the underside of the fuselage, Havok sighted the source of his nearly disastrous problem.

9

....

**PALAWAN ISLAND, PHILIPPINES
MID-JULY**

Ten minutes after the forced landing, the same yellow Toyota from before raced down the side of the runway toward Havok, who was sitting in the sand, taking advantage of the shade offered by a nearby palm. The truck stopped at the edge of the beach, its tires crunching noisily on loose gravel. A new man opened the passenger door, stepped out, and joined Havok next to the seaplane. The man wore clean but faded jeans, a T-shirt, flip-flops, and an Ohio State ball cap. The truck driver remained in the driver's seat, smoking a cigarette and watching them.

"I'm Victorino Balabac. My cousin say you needed help."

"Yeah, my name is Joe, and I hope you can help me."

They stepped up to the nose of the airplane and squatted down to look up at the underside of the engine cowling and fuselage. Havok looked quickly at Victorino, who pulled a rag from his back pocket. Yellowish stumps that used to be teeth lined the man's gapped mouth. The pungent odor of tobacco emanated from him, which overpowered the searing stench of burnt oil.

"I don't know where you been at," stated Balabac, "but I tink you were not welcome."

They stared at the seventeen neat round holes, about the size of .30-caliber bullets, that decorated the bottom of his plane from the engine cowling to the tail. Havok also spotted three more holes at the trailing edge of the rudder. They were at least .50 caliber in size, closer to 20 or 25 mm.

Thinking about what had happened to him and the plane, he decided to lie a bit until he could figure out what was going on. "I don't know, but maybe I got a bit too close to a Vietnamese ship or something."

The man grunted while he wiped burnt oil from the underside of the engine cowling. He poked his index finger into some of the holes. Havok saw the truck driver flick his cigarette butt out of the window, into the sand.

The man stood and looked into the open engine cowling. "It looks like one bullet cracked the oil line," Victorino said without looking at Havok.

Havok stood and looked into the engine cowling as well. A bullet had grazed an oil line before lodging in one of the radial engine mounts. The nick was small enough that only tiny drips of the hot, thin oil could flow out, causing him to run out of oil only upon his approach to Quezon. Havok squatted back down and looked at the other bullet holes. They all went into parts of the fuselage that were not vital.

Havok and Victorino finished their inspection, and they agreed on repairs and a guard for the night. Havok gave Victorino his cellphone number while retrieving his pack from the rear cockpit. He threw his pack into the bed of the pickup and climbed into the passenger seat. On the way to the airfield tower, Havok and the driver passed a beat-up GMC truck headed in the plane's direction. The truck was strawberry red with "Balabac Towing and Vulcanizing" painted in white letters on the door. Havok called Stone.

"Hi, Pete," said Havok after Stone answered. "I'm staying in Quezon overnight."

"What did you do to Esmeralda now?" Stone said accusingly.

"Nothing, she's fine," lied Havok.

"Bullshit. You're lying. You did something to Esmeralda, and there's no way you're going to hide it when you get back."

"Honestly, I'm not lying," lied Havok again. "And how do you know I'm lying?"

"Anytime you call to tell me you're staying overnight somewhere, you always start out by telling me you found a new shipwreck or met a girl. Since you failed to mention either one, all I can assume is you did something to Esmeralda. I swear, if there is anything wrong with her, you're going to be in big trouble when you get back!"

"Well, just don't worry about it. Christ, you act like we're married," Havok retorted. "I'll see you tomorrow."

Havok ended the call then and wondered how he was going to explain the bullet holes. He also thought about the holes in the rudder: a large-caliber, and probably crew-served, mounted machine gun or cannon had made the holes. It also appeared as if the gun crew had failed to lead their target properly. Any gun crew should have had no problem shooting a relatively slow-moving surface target, such as another patrol boat or ship. Conversely, targeting a faster-moving and flying aircraft required a bit more training in learning how to lead a target. Havok had just learned something new about the island. He and Victorino had agreed on replacing the oil line and looking for other mechanical damage, but the mechanic could do nothing about the bullet holes in just a few hours.

Havok sat back and looked out the window. Thankfully, the driver was more interested in having another cigarette and driving than having a conversation. By the time the driver finished his cigarette, the truck stopped next to a one-story concrete building beside a forty-foot metal tower with a glass-enclosed room on top. Although the building appeared to be in decent condition, with clean white walls and bright green trim around the door- and window frames, the orange-and-white-checkered tower seemed to be on the brink of collapsing. Large areas of severe corrosion ate away at the steel trusses. Havok saw a man in the top of the control tower looking down at him, and an aged and decrepit Mazda sedan supported an equally aged and decrepit taxi driver, who leaned against its dented fender, taking advantage of the shade offered by the tower.

"How much do I owe you?" Havok asked as he reached into his pocket.

The man waited to answer until Havok pulled out a roll of Filipino pesos. "Five hundred."

Havok peeled off two five-hundred-peso bills and held one out of the window, showing it to the man in the tower. "Make sure he gets one of these."

The driver nodded as he smiled at the money.

Havok opened the door and stepped out. He grabbed his bag from the bed of the truck and walked over to the taxi. He saw the taxi driver straighten up a bit and smile at him. An opportunity to overcharge a fare, Havok thought. He didn't mind, though; it was part of life here in the Philippines, and he really did need a shower and a beer, so he was in no mood to haggle. Havok opened the right rear door of the taxi and sat down. The driver jumped into the driver's seat and turned the key in the ignition. After several seconds of sputtering misfires, the engine caught. In unpracticed English, the driver began the conversation as they drove away from the airfield.

"Where you going?" he asked.

"A hotel, a nice one," Havok answered.

"OK, I take you to my brother-in-law's hotel. It is a nice one."

"Fine."

"Sir, my nephew at the airport said you were shot at."

While staring out the dusty side window, Havok repeated the vague lie.

"I guess you lucky man. Hey, maybe I wait for you at the hotel. I can be your driver while you are here. I know where you can meet some nice girls. They are clean, I promise," the taxi driver offered.

Havok turned his head and looked at the reflection in the rearview mirror. He saw the pleading smile on the old man's face. His wrinkled skin was tanned nut brown, and his puppy-dog grin revealed widely gapped teeth.

"No, thanks," Havok said. "I just want a meal, a shower, and some sleep. I'll be leaving tomorrow when my plane is ready."

"I will wait for you, then, in the morning. My name is Tabon."

Havok nodded his head in acknowledgment as his thoughts moved on to the bullet holes. He was intrigued, not by the .30-caliber holes, which was a common caliber, but by the larger ones. There were three of them, all near the tail. The rounds that had made the holes near the tail were at least .50 caliber in size. Somebody was toting around a rather large-caliber machine gun, and the average fisherman in these parts did not arm himself that heavily.

He was tired, so he decided to set aside his thoughts for now and look out the side window. The coughing taxi puffed its way down a narrow road and through a crowded collection of thatch huts and wooden and cinder-block homes, leaving behind a trail of dense blue exhaust that mixed with the smoke of roadside cooking fires. The heat from the late-afternoon sun seemed to be magnified by the dirty windows of the taxi. Though tired, Havok felt the stiffness in his legs. It had been a grueling day of flying over a thousand miles, and he needed a long walk to stretch his cramped legs.

To Havok's relief, the taxi, its engine complaining, jerked to a squeaky stop in front of a four-story building that stood at the end of a wide boulevard. The brilliant-white paint of the building matched the other buildings that lined the town's broad main street, which was packed with traffic and pedestrians crossing the road.

"Here's five hundred pesos. Be here at eight a.m.," Havok said.

Tabon turned in his seat to collect the fare. "Eight o'clock a.m. Yes, sir."

Havok stepped out of the taxi with his bag and entered the lobby, welcoming the shelter from the dying sun of the late afternoon. He walked up to an immense wooden desk and the smiling man standing behind it. The man was obviously Filipino, but Havok could see traces of Spanish ancestry in his sharp facial features and smooth coffee-colored skin.

"Good evening, sir. I am Mr. Coron, the owner. May I get you a room?"

"Yes. For one night, please."

"Good," he said as he tapped at a keyboard while looking at a computer monitor next to it. "That will be six hundred pesos."

Havoc placed his bag on the floor, pulled his roll of bills from his pocket, and peeled off two five-hundred peso notes. "I'm going for a walk before I go to my room," he said, placing the two bills and his bag on the desk.

The man accepted the money and pushed a key, a blank registration card, and a pen toward him. Havok had just begun to fill out a blank registration card already on the desk when he felt someone walk up behind him.

"We'll take care of your bag," Mr. Coron said.

Havok turned to see a young man waiting. He finished filling out the card, gave the bellhop some pesos, took off his flying jacket and placed it on top of the bag, grabbed his key off the desk, and left the lobby.

After leaving the hotel, he rolled his sleeves up to his elbows and strolled down the boulevard. The sounds of people selling their wares from street-side shops and carts and the eardrum-bursting sounds of jeepney engines racing to nowhere filled the early-evening air. As he walked, stretching his mind as well as his legs, numerous street vendors held up items for sale and barkers invited him to their cousin's bar or restaurant, grabbing at his attention. After about thirty minutes of walking, Havok had had his fill and escaped his entourage by ducking into a small restaurant. The crowd followed him to the doorstep, but they could not enter, so they disbanded.

"Hello," greeted a teenage female server standing near the door. "Do want to seat?"

"Yes," Havok said, pointing to a table next to the front window.

She ushered him to the seat, but as soon as he sat down, two die-hard street vendors pulled up to the sidewalk outside the window and held up seashells and woodcarvings for his inspection.

"San Miguel and a menu," Havok said, looking around the room. Framed photos and posters of Filipino movie stars and several out-of-date calendars decorated the pale-green walls. The large room held ten tables, half of which were occupied by men drinking rum or beer. The teenage girl walked up to a woman who stood behind the restaurant's bar, passed on Havok's order, and stepped outside to shoo away the vultures perched outside the window. The woman behind the bar adjusted the restaurant's radio for better reception before approaching Havok's table. She carried a bottle of beer, a menu, and a set of utensils wrapped in a napkin.

"Hello, sir. I am Belinda," she said as she finished setting the table. "What do you want?"

Havok gave the menu a quick look-over. "I'll just take the fried fish."

Belinda acknowledged the order with a nod before leaving for the kitchen.

Havok brought the bottle to his lips and took a long pull. The cool lager soothed his parched throat, reminding him how thirsty he really was. Havok knew he was better off with water but did not relish catching a stomach bug and spending ground time on the toilet. Even bottled water was questionable. Only half finished with the beer, he held up his index finger toward Belinda, who was back behind the bar, wiping out some glasses. She smiled, acknowledging his order.

While waiting for his second beer, Havok looked outside the window at the northern half of Quezon Bay and the normal maritime traffic, which one would expect to see in any Asian port. However, one vessel did stand out.

Located about four hundred yards from the seawall was a splendid yacht riding at anchor. Its gleaming white hull and multilevel superstructure contrasted with the rust-stained hulls of the fishing boats and freighters that were also at anchor or tied up to the wharves. He looked for a name on the large boat, but the vessel swung with the tide. The stern was pointed westward, toward the setting sun, so only the starboard side was visible, and only at a severe angle. Havok didn't remember seeing this vessel when he flew in.

"Mind if we sit down?"

Havok turned toward the voice that had disturbed his solitude. It belonged to an Asian man who looked to be about fifty years old and five foot eight. He was dressed in a white silk dress shirt and tan slacks, both neatly pressed. In his carefully manicured hands he held an expensive Canon EOS 1X camera. Havok looked up at the man's smiling face. His perfectly straight teeth flashed brilliantly, and the skin on his face, smooth and flawless, glowed almost pink as if he had just stepped from a steaming bath. His straight, thick black hair was neatly combed and closely cropped on the sides.

Next to him stood a young Asian woman who was perhaps twenty-five years old. She wore a two-piece halter-top-and-short-pants outfit, revealing an exquisite body under the cerise cloth. Instead of a camera, she wore a matching Louis Vuitton leather purse, its thin strap looped over her left shoulder. She and the man both wore gold-and-diamond jewelry, but not in a gaudy way; instead, the gold and gems seemed to accentuate their freshly scrubbed skin, as if the precious items were a natural extension of their bodies. They both appeared to be Chinese.

Although irritated by the intrusion, Havok did not show his ire.

"You want more beer?" the man asked, even though Belinda had just placed another bottle on Havok's table.

"No, thank you. I'm set."

The man pulled a folded beige handkerchief from his shirt pocket and wiped the seat of a wicker chair before sitting down next to Havok. His companion pulled out her own chair and sat across from Havok. Once seated, he held up three fingers to Belinda, who stood behind the bar again.

"My name is Kang, Rong Kang. This is Xian," the man said as he offered an open hand toward the young woman.

"My name is Havok. Is there something I can do for you?" He took a glance out the window. There, standing along the seawall on the other side of the street, was a stout Asian man. He wore loose tropical attire and acted as if he was on his cell phone. It took a split second to remember, but the man standing outside the restaurant reminded Havok of an assassin in a James Bond movie.

The woman looked at Havok as if examining him. He felt like a lab subject.

"We were just walking down the street," Kang said, "stretching our legs, getting a bit of shopping in, and we saw you through the window. I thought it would be nice to have a cool drink and some conversation. Are you American? Canadian?"

The man's English was just as impeccable as his dress, but somehow that polite smile and demeanor and most specifically the perfect English seemed to be qualities that were alien to Kang.

"I have a reason for being here. What about you?" Havok asked.

"I am on what you would call a working holiday. I am traveling this part of the world, looking after some of my business interests while getting a little sun at the same time. What about you? Are you American? You did not answer my question."

Havok was tired and answered curtly. "From Subic Bay. Down here on business." He turned and pointed his beer bottle out the front window. "I'm guessing that's your large piece of real estate parked out there on the bay? And I'm also guessing that's your muscle out there. His name isn't Oddjob, is it?"

"Yes," answered Kang without looking out the window. "That is my sovereign part of China. And the man you refer to is Chiba, my bodyguard and handyman. I also understand the reference to Oddjob, the muscle-bound Oriental assassin in the James Bond movie Goldfinger, but without the frock coat and the top hat with hidden razor blades in the brim."

"Is that where you're from? China?" Havok asked. "And I'm assuming Chiba does a bit more than remodel kitchens."

"Yes and yes, but I consider myself a man of the world and have several degrees from prestigious universities in China, the United States, Canada, and Europe. But enough about me. What type of business are you in?"

"Scuba diving charters for tourists." Havok sat back in his chair and yawned. He looked at Xian before turning back to Kang. "I'm just scouting locations."

"Diving must be a good business. It looks like it has treated you well," said Kang as he appraised Havok. "You have a woman here?"

"I just rolled into town."

"Good," he said triumphantly. "I am sure I can make some suitable arrangements."

"No, thank you," Havok declined. "I've got to get some sleep. I'm tired, and I have a long day ahead of me tomorrow."

"I understand. It can be hard being a pilot. Where are you staying?"

"A hotel up the street."

Kang shook his head and stated, "You must stay with me on my yacht."

He paused and stared into Kang's eyes, trying to read what was on his mind. Kang stared back steadily, allowing nothing to be read.

Just then, Belinda placed Havok's plate of fish, along with a scoop of steamed white rice, on the cloth-covered table. Havok fell silent while poking at his fish with a fork to see if it was done. He hoped Kang would get the hint. Both Kang and Xian just sat there, patiently watching, as Havok grabbed a bottle of malt vinegar and sprinkled some on the fish. Christ, why won't this guy take a hint? Havok thought.

"No, thank you," Havok answered tersely. "My hotel room is just fine, and I've already paid for it." He felt like an animal tied to a stake, about to be set upon by buzzards from two different directions.

Kang did not seem to notice Havok's brusque voice, but he didn't push any further. Instead, he excused himself to the bathroom, leaving behind his companion, who had yet to utter a single sound. When the man was out of sight, Xian looked straight into Havok's mind with her dark, almond-shaped eyes that were refined by the silky, flawless skin of her face. She was beautiful in every sense of the word.

After a few seconds of staring at each other, she distracted Havok by sitting back in her chair and widely lifting one leg over the other. Her loose shorts remained open long enough to reveal a pair of tanned, supple thighs and peach-colored panties. Looking back at his food, he suddenly realized why this guy was so stuck on him. He probably wanted Havok to be part of a porno movie. He knew that many producers went to Asian countries, like Thailand or the Philippines, to make movies. In these poverty-stricken countries, it was legal and cheaper.

"Want another drink?" Kang asked as he returned unnoticed from the bathroom.

"No thanks. I'm hungry, and I need some sleep bad." Havok tore off a huge chunk of fish with his fork and swallowed it as if to drive his point home.

"Well, I am sorry for any intrusion," Kang said apologetically. "We will leave you to your meal."

Xian stood and nodded goodbye, and the couple silently departed the restaurant.

After they left, Havok finished his meal and remained there for one more beer, thinking. When he was finished, he held up his finger for the check. He pulled his roll of cash from his pocket and laid two one-hundred-peso notes on the check. Saying goodbye, he walked out of the restaurant into the humid night air and started up the lighted street, but he paused when he heard a boat engine. Walking over to the sea-wall, Havok saw a boat approach the starboard side of Kang's yacht. He watched Kang and Xian step up a short ladder into a doorway on the main deck. Back in the restaurant Kang had said something that bothered Havok, but he could not think of what it was.

The vessel had swung a little farther to the north, and he could now see the full starboard side. It was indeed an expensive-looking ship: the white-painted hull didn't have a single smudge or rust stain, white deck lights illuminated the two-story upperworks, and large windows on the second level revealed a luxurious interior with expensive furnishings and electronics. Havok could now see the name of the ship painted in black letters under the bow: Tu Er Shen.

As Havok walked back to his hotel, he kept trying to recall what Kang had said, but a phone call from Victorino interrupted his thoughts. His plane was ready. He thanked Victorino and said that he would be at the plane at eight thirty the next morning.

He arrived back at the hotel and told the attendant he wanted a wake-up call at six thirty a.m. As Havok stepped away from the desk and walked up the one flight of stairs to his room, he kept trying to recall the night's conversation with Kang.

10

PALAWAN ISLAND, PHILIPPINES
MID-JULY

AT FIRST HE THOUGHT HE WAS DREAMING, BUT THE KNOCKING WAS IN-
CESSANT. Finally Havok realized that someone was at the door. With a
groan, he rolled his stiff frame off the bed and struggled across the dark
room toward the door. He looked at his wristwatch. It was only ten thirty
p.m. He had been asleep for an hour. He grabbed the knob and yanked
the door open.

"This had better be good!"

Wearing only cotton shorts, Havok faced Xian. For a few seconds,
they just stood there looking at each other. While Xian studied Havok,
he noticed she wore the same clothes and jewelry from this afternoon.

He broke the silence: "Listen, I don't know what kind of kicks you
and Kang are into, but I don't need it."

"Please, do not misunderstand." Her voice was invitingly subtle and
apologetic but strong and confident, which caught Havok off guard.

"OK, what can I do for you?"

"That is much better. For starters, you can let me in."

He quietly sighed, and stepped aside. With a strong, purposeful
stride, she entered the room and casually flung her purse on the ruffled

bed as if it were her room and her bed. She stood in the center of the room, and the light from the hallway accentuated the jewelry she wore. After appraising the room, she sat in the only chair and crossed one leg over the other in the dark shadows of the room. The hallway light illuminated her crotch, but Havok did not see panties.

"Are you a fan of Sharon Stone movies?" he asked, still standing next to the open door.

Xian smiled as she leaned back in the chair. "Basic Instinct: a classic murder mystery in which the main suspect uses her physical sexuality to distract the police during questioning and to trick one police officer into being her dupe."

"Is that what you're doing to me?" Havok asked.

"Before I came up," Xian said, ignoring his question, "I took the liberty of ordering tea."

"That still doesn't tell me what you need or want."

Before she could answer, Havok heard somebody approach the doorway. He turned to see a young man holding a brown wooden tray with a sky-blue ceramic teapot and matching cups on it. He accepted the tray, thanked him, and pushed the door shut with his foot. He put the tray on the small table next to Xian and poured two cups, handing one to her. With his own teacup, Havok sat on the bed, reclining against the headboard.

"Again, what do you want?" he asked.

After taking a sip from the cup, she replied to his directness. "After visiting with you this evening, I found you very intriguing. I wanted to find out what kind of man you are."

"That's all?"

"That is all. There are no strings attached."

"I guess I can live with that."

"So, how is the diving business these days? Do you like your career?"

"It fills my rice bowl." Havok answered her questions simply, but he could sense she wanted more than his résumé. "So what about Kang? Does he know you're here?"

"I am what you would call a trophy wife or arm candy. He prefers his pretty boys. He employs me for show, and if he is having a tough time negotiating with a client or somebody, I go in to help secure the deal."

"So you're his whore."

Xian took another sip of tea dismissively. "I view myself as a valuable business asset."

"Are you here to help persuade me then?" Havok asked. "What do I have to offer Kang?"

"Don't worry. I'm off the clock. I take care of his special needs, and he allows me to take care of my rather particular needs."

"I've got a feeling when it comes to sex you're never off the clock," Havok said. "And what are your particular needs?" Did these two have something to do with the bullet holes in his airplane, or was she just honestly horny? Or both?

"That is not your concern right now, but I would gladly share them with you later. I just want to talk with you for now. Do you have family in Subic Bay?"

"No family. I'm just a loner with a dive shop, a small-time businessman in a small town."

Havok took another sip of his tea and put the cup on the nightstand next to his cell phone. He'd had enough and stated his ultimatum. After all, he had to get to sleep somehow.

"I'm really tired, so do me a favor and either get in this bed or close the door behind you on your way out."

Xian placed her cup on the nightstand, stood up, and began to unbutton the front of her pink halter top. She opened the top, allowing it to fall off her shoulders, revealing shapely, tanned breasts. Letting the clothing fall to the floor, she turned around and placed her hands on her shorts, pushing them off her gyrating hips and exposing firm buttocks. She bent at the waist, still facing away from Havok, and pushed her shorts all the way to the floor. After her leg kicked them away, she stepped across the short distance.

***

After a fitful sleep, Havok woke to the warmth of the morning sun shining on him through the window and to the sound of the phone ringing next to his head. He picked up the receiver.

"Hello," he said before pausing, "Thanks. Please send up some coffee."

After hanging up he stretched and turned his head toward Xian as she dressed herself next to the bed. "Were you a gymnast in a previous life?"

Xian chuckled quietly. "I'll take that as a compliment."

The pair fell back into silence, staring at each other while she finished dressing. Havok saw that Xian had that same look from yesterday: sultry, alluring, yet strong and confident. It was as if she always knew what she was doing and was always one step ahead of everybody. She had the same determined look as Sharon Stone's character in Basic Instinct. Havok tried not to show it, but he wondered if he'd just become the Michael Douglas character in the movie, a veteran cop seduced and tricked into becoming a puppet for a serial killer. He knew that he would see her and Kang again, but under what circumstances?

Xian approached the bed to give Havok a quick peck on the forehead before leaving the room. She never looked back.

Havok got out of bed and cleaned up while waiting for his coffee. He opened his bag to look for a new shirt. He stopped. For some reason, something seemed different in the bag. He poked around the contents: clothing, a few bottles of water, a first-aid kit, an envelope with more cash, a multipurpose knife, and a few other miscellaneous items. Nothing appeared to be missing, but it looked as if someone had gone through the bag. He looked at the door, thinking about Xian. Did he expect anything else?

After a lukewarm shower and a cup of bitter instant coffee, Havok walked into the hotel lobby, where he saw the taxi driver from the day before waiting by the front desk.

"Good morning, sir. Ready to go to your airplane?"

Fifteen minutes later, the taxi rolled up to Esmeralda, which was waiting patiently in the surf with the bow of its main float resting on the beach. A man, whom Havok assumed was the night watchman, sat on the float and smoked a cigarette. Havok strolled toward the sand, leaving the taxi gasping in its own noxious fumes. Just before he reached the plane, he heard a vehicle drive up behind him. It was the tow truck from yesterday. Victorino parked the truck several feet away and jumped out.

"Finished?" Havok asked.

"Yes, sir," Victorino answered. "We repaired the oil line and checked out the rest of the engine. Want to test run her?" He handed Havok a clear plastic bag with four bullet slugs in it. "It is all I could find. The rest went straight through."

Havok accepted the bag and examined the slugs. They were .30-caliber slugs with no identifying marks. However, he could tell, based on the length of the rounds, that they were not pistol rounds or rifle cartridges; they had been fired from a submachine gun or assault rifle of some sort. An image of an AK-47 popped into mind. He placed the rounds into his backpack, stepped onto the main float, and then clamored up the side of the fuselage. After throwing his bag into the rear cockpit, he climbed into the pilot's cockpit.

The preflight checks were completed, and after Havok fired up the engine, Victorino and the night watchman gave the plane a push off the beach so Havok could give it a test flight. He turned the seaplane toward the mouth of the bay and, when he reached rotation speed, pulled back on the yoke. The plane clawed its way toward the thick blue sky. For ten minutes, he pressed the engine hard, going into stalls and steep climbs. He tortured the aircraft with agonizing cruelty, trying to find its breaking point. The plane absorbed the punishment with no hint of weakness, and the gauges all read normal. He landed the plane back on the water and nosed up to the beach, where he and Victorino gave the engine one last look. Satisfied with the test flight, Havok paid Victorino and climbed back into the airplane for his flight back to Subic Bay.

Once again in the air, he decided to fly over Kang's yacht. In less than a minute, he approached the vessel at about five hundred feet. It was the most luxurious yacht he had ever seen. Polished brass and chrome fittings reflected the morning sun. Dark-stained wood railings outlined the classic gleaming white hull and the superstructure, which was topped with a pilothouse, an exhaust stack painted a light blue, and a helicopter landing pad. Various antennae poked into the sky above the pilothouse and exhaust stack. The wide array of antennae and electronic dishes indicated worldwide communication capabilities. Under the pilothouse and helo pad, taking up the entire mid level of the superstructure, was a large room enclosed almost completely by tinted glass.

The yacht was definitely capable of sustained ocean transits and looked stable enough to handle even the roughest seas. At first, the ship appeared deserted, but Havok spotted movement as a few men in white uniforms came out the open wings of the pilothouse. He also saw the muscle-bound bodyguard from last night. Chiba wore gym clothes that looked like they were soaked in sweat. The men watched as Havok performed a long, lazy circle above them. After Havok had seen what he needed to see, he banked the airplane toward the South China Sea for his first leg of the flight back to Subic Bay.

As he left Quezon and turned north, Havok casually thought about the bullet holes that punctured the fuselage. After tossing the idea around in his head, he decided to let the holes remain. They would make a good conversation piece, just like the bullet holes in the Outfit. He also tried to remember something Kang had said last night, but he couldn't nail it down.

It was now midafternoon, and after a stop for lunch on Mindoro, Havok was on his last leg of the flight. He had been in the air for ten minutes when it suddenly hit him. Last night Kang had said, "Being a pilot is hard work." How did he know Havok was a pilot? That hadn't come up in the conversation. Nor had Havok been wearing anything that identified him as a pilot. Havok now thought deeply about Kang and his motives. Kang could have easily questioned the locals back in Quezon. Also, he had only landed at Quezon two hours before meeting Kang, and he didn't remember seeing Kang's yacht anchored in the harbor before he landed. There were thousands of people living in that port city, so for Kang to know exactly whom to talk to in such a short time was no coincidence. Perhaps Kang already knew something about him before he arrived in Quezon.

Kang was more than just an innocent corporate executive.

Havok landed back at Subic Bay just before four p.m. Impatiently, he taxied up to his dock, where Manny was waiting. Once the plane was in position, Manny reached out, pulled mooring lines from the compartment in the main float, then secured the plane to the brass cleats bolted to the dock. Havok pulled the throttle back, bringing the engine's rpm to idle. He twisted the fuel-mixture knob, leaning out the fuel mixture until the engine shuddered to a complete stop. With Kang on his mind, he anxiously pushed the canopy back.

"Hi, Joe. How was your flight?" said Manny.

"Interesting. What are you doing for dinner?"

***

By seven p.m. Manny and Havok were sitting with Kilgore at a table off to a corner in Kilgore's bar. A Jimmy Buffett song played from speakers in the ceiling. They were drinking margaritas on the rocks while the pilot told his friends everything that had happened in the last two days. After two rounds, Kilgore had two pages of notes jotted down on a pad of yellow legal paper.

Stone walked up to the table and pulled out the last empty chair. "Sounds like you had one hell of a flight."

Havok could see that his friend didn't seem that upset about the bullet holes, and was relieved, as he did not want to listen to Stone's rant. "Checked out Esmeralda?" he asked.

"Yes, I did, and you were in the doghouse for a while. But on the way over here, I had a change of heart," replied Stone.

"What changed?" Havok asked.

"Well, you know how chicks dig scars, so I thought we could tell our customers that we got them in a running battle with Malayan pirates off the coast of Bora Bora or something. Just like we did with the Outfit."

"What's this 'we' crap?" Havok said. "Exactly how many times have you been shot at this week?"

"Yeah, well, if it wasn't for my abilities to keep you in the air and us in business, you wouldn't have the opportunity to get shot at."

Mercedes came to the table and smiled at Stone, who winked at her.

"I'll have an order of Montezuma's Revenge," Stone said. "And keep the margaritas coming."

Mercedes noted the order and walked away while Stone watched her.

Meanwhile, Havok completed his tale of the flight, including a discussion about the disappearance of the Kona Wave and a possible connection. The four of them shared various ideas, along with more margaritas and the cheese-stuffed jalapeño and habanero peppers.

After two hours of conversing and drinking, Kilgore stood. "I'll contact my brethren in Manila and Vietnam for any intelligence on Terumbu. And I'll get the lowdown on Kang and his associates as well," he said.

Manny stood and stretched his arms. "I'll guess it's time to get the Outfit ready to go." He followed Kilgore out of the bar.

Havok and Stone reclined in their chairs, sipping drinks, listening to Kenny Chesney, and mulling over the events of the last two days. Havok looked over to the bar and saw Apple walk in. She sat at the bar and chatted with Mercedes. The two of them were good friends, and Apple often came here after her shift to make sure Havok got home safely.

Lulled by the sights and sounds of the slow night, Havok spoke in a voice that matched the dawdling evening atmosphere: "What do you think, Pete?"

"How much scratch did you say was out there?"

"According to what Wheatley said, I figure it to be at least one hundred thousand."

"And you didn't see anybody down on Terumbu?"

"Nope, didn't see squat."

"You know that means whoever is down there didn't want to be seen."

"Yep."

"And you know they're packing some powerful heat."

"Uh-huh."

"It's my guess they even tried to kill you."

"No shit."

"This isn't some small operation. They probably got the backing of a government who's not too keen on sharing their secrets."

"Could be."

"You know we aren't politicians or soldiers."

"Yeah."

"I bet next time you see Boris and Natasha, they won't be so congenial."

"Suppose not."

"Do you think they're out there digging up the silver?"

"Could be."

"Or do you think they're out there for another reason?"

"Sounds possible."

"They could be waiting for us, you know. Seems like they got a pretty slick communications setup."

"Seems so."

"Do you think I'll be able to talk you out of this?"

Stone received no answer because Havok was lost in thought. Stone turned to see the two women from the bar walk toward them.

11

TERUMBU ISLAND, MID-JULY

"HAVE YOU HAD ENOUGH, SERGEANT OHMSKY?" asked Anisimova, facing his opponent amid a circle of hardened soldiers.

The circle of men occupied what was once a military parade ground bordered by two rows of single-story cinder-block barracks. The motel-like buildings had been built years ago by American Seabees but were now covered with peeling paint and green moss. In the open windows and doors, camouflage rain ponchos and ragged blankets replaced long-gone wooden blinds and doors. At one end was the two-story headquarters building with a large front porch. At the other was the mess hall. The spreading jungle canopy covered all the buildings.

They, like Anisimova, wore BEKAS trousers with a jungle tiger-striped pattern, black leather boots, and short-sleeved jerseys with horizontal blue-and-white stripes. None wore the matching blouses because of the previous physical training. They had hung the blouses from the branches of nearby trees. After the soldiers completed their morning training, Colonel Yeshenko, who also acted as referee, allowed Anisimova to continue the exertions by sparring with members of the militia, an activity that also provided some entertainment.

"Nyet," Ohmsky responded in Russian while standing opposite Anisimova. "You may have a black belt, but a good jab followed by an uppercut will do just fine."

Ohmsky wiped blood from his mouth with the back of his hand before lowering himself slightly into a defensive stance. He now stood level with Anisimova.

This morning, just as on most other mornings, he served as Anisimova's sparring partner. Ohmsky was the most senior noncommissioned officer and the biggest of any in the group. Towering over everybody else, Ohmsky outclassed the men in size and fighting experience, and the other enlisted men feared and respected that in him.

On the other hand, the morning bouts kept Anisimova mentally and physically sharp and fit; but most importantly, the fights provided him with a sense of domination and power. He conquered other men by beating them to the ground. It was almost orgasmic for him.

When the group first arrived on the island less than two weeks ago, others had volunteered to spar with Anisimova, including Chiba when he was available to do so, but the other Russians quickly learned to bow out and avoid needless injuries. Only one man, other than Ohmsky and Chiba, still volunteered to spar with Anisimova, but only occasionally: Yeshenko's young aide, Lieutenant Varonov, who even managed to win a couple of bouts. Varonov was in his late twenties and had blond hair and a full round face, a slightly broad nose, and blue-green eyes—a face that could have graced any military recruiting poster. This morning, though, he stood next to Yeshenko. Both of them held mugs of steaming tea. As Varonov sipped his tea and watched the bout, something distracted him, something in the jungle behind Anisimova. He looked into the foliage and, for a split second, thought he saw a face. Varonov closed his eyes quickly, and when he reopened them, the face was gone. He remembered hearing some of the men commenting about this island being haunted, as they, too, sensed they were being watched. Petroske, standing next to Varonov in full uniform, failed to see the face as he was adjusting the pistol holster on his hip.

Now, Anisimova moved around the opening, looking for an opportunity. It came when Ohmsky took his eyes off Anisimova. Ohmsky saw the same face Varonov had. During the millisecond of Ohmsky's distraction, Anisimova leaped off the ground to a height of five feet. His leg lashed out, and the extended blur collided with Ohmsky's skull, knocking the sergeant to the ground. Ohmsky quickly recovered, though, and was back on his feet before Anisimova could launch another kick. As Ohmsky straightened, he threw the handful of rocky sand he had grabbed while on the ground. Anisimova turned his head, avoiding the dirt, and kicked at Ohmsky's chest, knocking the man to the ground. But, with a recovery that surprised even Anisimova, Ohmsky jumped to his feet, lashing out with his right fist. The closed hand caught Anisimova on the right cheek.

Anisimova ignored the blow. He knelt down and swiftly brought his fist up into his opponent's crotch, and as Ohmsky doubled over, Anisimova stood, ramming his knee into his opponent's face. The sergeant's head snapped back and he landed heavily on his buttocks before rolling over, a result that ended the morning exercise.

"Good fight this morning, Ohmsky," Anisimova said, turning toward the old headquarters building. He occupied the large room on the first floor, but its furnishings were simple: a folding cot under a window with a threadbare blanket draped over the opening and, against the opposite wall, a length of pipe suspended from the ceiling by wire. Numerous coat hangers and uniforms hung from the pipe. A wooden stand with a washbasin stood next to the row of clothing, along with a mirror and towel slung from hooks in the wall. In the center of the room was a round wooden table with several camp chairs around it. Centered on the table was an unlit camp lantern, a carafe of red wine, and a glass.

"Good moves, sir," praised Petroske as he pushed aside the thin blanket draped over the doorway. He stepped inside, letting the blanket fall back into place behind him.

"Thank you, Petroske," Anisimova said. He inspected himself in the mirror and patted his chin with the towel. "What do you have for me this morning?"

"I visited our little flotilla out on the bay and have good news. The captain of Kang's yacht said that the Kona Wave is now registered in the Chinese Merchant Marine under a new name. In addition, the captain of our salvage ship said that his crew finished modifications to the Kona Wave, now listed as the Shanghai Mariner, and that no one should be able to recognize the ship. They are also almost finished with the special storage room for the nerve gas aboard our salvage ship. We should be ready to have the surviving students transfer the sarin from the shore laboratory to the Stalinetz in the next few days. The salvage captain said that the cargo removal from the Japanese submarine is continuing, but it is still a slow process because of the amount of gold bars. The salvage ship's bilges are nearly full, which is why the surprise visit from the American ship was so fortuitous. The salvage ship captain said we may have to ask Kang to store and transport some of the bullion for us either on his yacht or on the Shanghai Mariner, or both."

"What of the crew from the Kona Wave—I mean, the Shanghai Mariner?"

"They are still handcuffed and held in the engine room of the Shanghai Mariner. They have refused to cooperate in any fashion. Their captain, Morgan, has quite a bit of control over them. He's a rather difficult man, but the group may prove useful in the future."

The recovery of the sarin and bullion from the Japanese submarine had been going well until the Kona Wave entered the bay and anchored along the southern shore. At first, the Russians and Kang were quite alarmed, as they had no idea why the ship had suddenly appeared, but Anisimova, Yeshenko, and Kang agreed to wait and monitor the Kona Wave's activities. As that day neared an end, they realized that the people on the ship were conducting only environmental experiments. The problem, though, was that Anisimova and the others had no idea how long the ship would remain in the bay. Also, those aboard the ship might want to explore Terumbu further, including the false island anchored above a Japanese submarine full of gold bars and a cargo of nerve gas.

As the sun was setting, Kang proposed an idea that was acceptable to all. He proposed to capture the ship and use the student divers to recover the sarin, to reconfigure and rename the ship, and to use the ship to help transport the gold if necessary. That would leave the Russian divers free to recover the bullion and would free up space aboard their own salvage ship, the Stalinetz, to transport as much bullion as possible. It was a risky decision, as it might call attention to the island and their activities. However, the availability of extra divers and an extra ship was nothing to disregard. It was worth the risk.

That night Anisimova, Yeshenko, Varonov, Ohmsky, and ten other men paddled out in rubber boats to board the research vessel. Anisimova was the first to climb over the bulwark, and in doing so, was the first to encounter somebody from the ship, who turned out to be the ship's chief science officer, Pilar Bonne-Bouche. Throwing a cloth sack over her head, he subdued her while the other commandos filed past and burst into the wardroom. The students were no problem for the Russians, as they had no idea what was happening. Once the students were subdued, the Russians spread throughout the ship and subdued the crewmen who were either sleeping or standing watch in the engine room. Captain Morgan was the last to be captured, and it took four Russians to do that.

"How many students do we have left?" Anisimova asked, bringing his thoughts back to the present.

"We had to bury another one this morning. He's buried with the others. These students are going to have to be more careful while re-packaging the sarin if they want to survive." Petroske paused. "That was a good idea, taking the professor to the seaplane camp. Without leader-ship, these students are mere cattle."

"Speaking of the professor . . ." Anisimova turned from the mirror and reached for something under his pillow. "After we took control of the ship, I took the professor to her stateroom for further interrogation. In the process, she tried to shoot me." He tossed a flat-black case over to Petroske. "I know how fond you are of sidearms, so I thought you might like this piece."

Petroske caught the case midair and opened it.

Anisimova saw the glowing beam on Petroske's face as he opened his gift. What better way to keep the loyalty of a dog than to toss him a bone now and then? he thought.

"What about our pilot friend? Has Kang found out anything about him?" Anisimova asked.

Petroske closed the pistol case. "Kang said he has, but is looking for further information. He will let us know when he finds out more."

"Good. That research ship was obviously a chance encounter, but the plane that visited us the other day has me concerned. Now go ahead and make sure the men are on patrol and that our guests are taken care of. Also, have my breakfast brought to me."

"Yes, sir," replied Petroske as he saluted the other man.

Anisimova watched him leave. It was true that security was being maintained and everything was under control, but it was not true that it was Petroske's doing, as the man liked to think. Anisimova knew that Petroske thought too much of himself, and he had no problem reinforcing the other man's self-importance, which was why Anisimova had had him brought down from Siberia. Anisimova also knew that the men of the company only listened to Lieutenant Varonov, and that Varonov listened only to "Sonny" Yeshenko. Indeed, both he and Petroske were outside the military hierarchy, but Anisimova did hold a special place in this operation.

Anisimova finished patting his chin and smirked as he thought about Petroske, who was useless as a soldier but one hell of a dupe. Anisimova could count on Petroske to be his lapdog and do his bidding. He also liked having Petroske around as a fly on the wall. All Anisimova needed to do was to keep him in uniform, let him parade around while rubbing his pistol, and compliment him now and then. Turning from the mirror, Anisimova removed a fresh shirt from one of the hangers while remembering the event that had now brought him to this island.

A few years ago, Anisimova had spent a week at a resort outside Da Nang. The resort had once been a French plantation and had been re-occupied by the Japanese during WWII and used as a local headquarters. While relaxing by the pool one afternoon, a friend of Anisimova's had shown him a box of Japanese radio messages. The friend, who owned the resort, said his workers discovered the box in a hidden wall safe while they had been renovating one of the large bedrooms. He knew about Anisimova's linguistic abilities and asked if he wanted to leaf through the messages before he threw them away.

Anisimova had idly thumbed through the box of yellowed forms that afternoon until he was about halfway through and then suddenly sat up straight. He quickly finished going through the box, pulled two forms from the pile, and returned the rest to his friend, saying the box contained only supply invoices and requests. His friend accepted the report and threw the wooden crate away.

The first sheet Anisimova kept was a form that had been sent from the Japanese naval headquarters in Manila in the fall of 1944 to the Japanese military headquarters in Indochina. It simply stated that a submarine from the Imperial Japanese Navy, with two valuable cargoes, was attempting to escape the Philippines to make its way to Indochina. The second message was a report from the submarine commander, who, because of the importance of his cargo, had to report his daily position to the headquarters in Indochina. That way, the Japanese navy could backtrack the submarine's route and estimate an approximant position in case it was lost. One day in late October, the commander of the submarine reported he had surfaced in a bay on Terumbu Island in order to recharge his batteries and to vent the submarine. He also reported that the American air force presence was making his journey difficult. The headquarters in Indochina never received any other messages from that submarine.

The two messages intrigued Anisimova. A bit of curiosity, then reasonable deduction followed this intrigue along with historical research of the American fleet and air-combat actions in the fall of 1944. Finally, he asked a favor from another friend in the Russian Space Agency. This friend, with discretion, had been able to redirect a satellite monitoring maritime traffic in the western Pacific for a few precious seconds and use the satellite's subsurface-imaging capability to capture one important scan.

Once dressed, Anisimova poured himself a glass of wine and sat in the folding chair, waiting for his breakfast and thinking. His thoughts came around to Dr. Alik Dubrinsky and Chiba, Kang's bodyguard.

Poor Alik. Why did you have to change your mind about being here? You could have remained in Moscow, playing chess in the park and durak in your favorite bar and taking your grandchildren to the cinema.

Anisimova brought the wine glass to his lips and said aloud, "Instead you killed yourself."

12

THE DAY AFTER HAVOK'S RETURN FROM QUEZON PROVED TO BE QUITE BUSY, AS HAVOK, MANNY, AND STONE FELL INTO FAMILIAR ROLES. Havok went through the navigational gear and deck lighting on the Outfit, making sure all was in good working order. He also laid out a route on a nautical chart of the Philippines and the South China Sea, and plotted overnight stops, both on the chart and on his GPS. Lastly, he inspected the armory hidden in a compartment under the deck inside the pilothouse. There was enough room between two floor joists to hold an M14 rifle with a wooden stock, an H&K assault weapon, a shotgun, three pistols, extra magazines, and several boxes of ammunition. He pulled the weapons out one at a time, wiped them down with oiled rags, and cycled their bolts and slides. After taking note of the amount of ammunition, he decided to quadruple the amount. He looked into the angled doorway that led down from the pilothouse into the forward cabin. Manny was tightening a sheet on one of the two-tiered bunks.

"You need anything, Manny? I'm going up to my room for more ammunition."

"No, thanks. I've got a list of food and will get Junior to help me after I'm done here. Oh, by the way," Manny said, straightening, "do you know what this is?" He reached into his shirt pocket and threw a square object toward Havok, who caught it. It was about the size of a cigarette pack and made from black plastic. It had no identifying marks or features, but Havok knew what it was.

"Where did you find this thing?" Havok hefted the black box in the palm of his hand.

"It was under the linen in the drawer under this bunk." Manny pointed to the bunk at his feet.

"It's OK," Havok said, "but just let me know if you find any more."

He turned around and stepped into the small salon behind the pilot-house. At the aft end of the room, past a sofa, was the angled hatchway that led to the engine room. He saw Stone between the two one-hundred-year-old aircraft engines, wiping down a valve cover with a rag.

"Need anything?" Havok asked.

"We're topped off on fuel along with two five-gallon cans of gas for the outboards and the Homelite generator. They're secured on the stern along with four scuba tanks. Engines and the air compressor are also good to go," Stone replied. "I'll get our dive bags in a bit. Anything else you think we need?"

Havok pondered the question before answering, "Bring extra dive or duffel bags for the silver, and some climbing gear won't hurt."

"Why the climbing gear?" Stone asked as he threw the rag onto a toolbox mounted to the forward bulkhead of the engine room.

Havok really had no answer. "Don't know." He paused. "Have you noticed anything out of the ordinary down here?"

"No. Why?"

Havok answered by tossing the black item to Stone.

Stone caught it and inspected it for a few seconds. "Now what kind of shit did you get us into?" he asked, looking up at Havok. "Where'd you find this?"

"Manny found it under some linen up forward."

Stone tossed the item back to Havok. "Nobody plants a GPS locating device without a reason. What are you gonna do with it?"

"I'll figure it out," Havok said, "but in the meantime keep your eyes open."

Stone nodded, and saluted with his index finger.

Havok searched the rest of the boat for any additional hidden GPS locators. Once he was satisfied there weren't any more, he walked off the boat, toward his apartment. As he did, he looked at the stern of his boat. Along the starboard side were four aluminum scuba tanks secured to the wooden railing. Opposite the boat, along the portside railing, were the two five-gallon gas cans along with the two small outboard engines. The engines were used for the original wooden dingy that came with the 1926 motor yacht and a six-foot inflatable boat, both of which were now turned upside and lashed to the roof of the pilothouse.

When he entered his apartment, he saw that Apple was in his closet, taking some extra clothing off their hangers and folding them before placing the clothing in a laundry basket.

"How many days will you be gone again?" she asked.

"About two weeks. Just going down to the Visayas for some diving." Havok reached up to retrieve a wooden crate from the shelf above the hangers. He pulled the crate down and placed it on the bed behind him, noticing the look of concern on Apple's face.

He opened the crate's lid. It was full of cardboard boxes of 9 mm bullets, 7.62-caliber rifle rounds, and 12-gauge shotgun shells. He mentally counted the contents without looking at Apple, who had stopped pulling clothes from the hangers.

***

A day later, Apple, Mercedes, and Catalina stood on the dock as the sun broke free from the eastern horizon. Their concern was apparent on their faces.

Havok was in the pilothouse listening to the radio for a weather update when he looked out the windowpane and saw Kilgore walking down the dock, holding a white business-sized envelope. Kilgore stopped adjacent to the open door on the port side of the pilothouse and stepped onto the boat, entering the pilothouse.

"I got something for you," he said. He reached to place the envelope in Havok's hand.

Although never an outwardly serious man, Kilgore's voice did display a sense of concern this morning. "I've made some calls, and your friend Kang is not to be trifled with. He owns CMPC, the Chinese Minerals Mining and Petroleum Corporation, a multinational exploration and development corporation with home offices in Saigon, Beijing, and Victoria, Canada. It has multiple ongoing operations around the world, with current projects in the South China Sea, the gold region of British Columbia, and the Weddell Sea off Antarctica. And not only is he the head of a mining conglomeration, he also has close ties with a branch of the Chinese army known as Section Five. That's the computer-hacking arm where they conduct both industrial and military espionage. Make sure you go over my info, and if you have to get hold of me, watch what you say over the phone or on the internet. In fact, go ahead and pull your batteries and kill your cell phones and your laptop just so his sources don't ping onto your location."

Kilgore drew a breath. "I've reached out to my brothers and sisters for help. According to satellite imagery, those two changes in the island's profile occurred a couple of days before your flight over the island. Something is going on there, and I asked for further assistance but was told to stay out of it. The chain of command is testing the waters with their big toes, what with talks between Beijing and Washington coming up and all, but I'm not willing to give up just yet. I can call in favors, so let the good guys handle this one. You know you don't have to do this."

Havok looked at the envelope for another second while thinking about something June Johnson had said. He sighed. "I guess it's time to burn some more toast."

"I have no idea what that means, but it's your funeral," Kilgore replied with a sigh. "Also, watch out for that bodyguard of his, Chiba. Apparently, he is quite the man-crusher."

"Caution noted," Havok replied. "We'll keep in touch. By the way, do you think you can find a slow boat to China?"

Kilgore looked at Havok quizzically, but then he saw the GPS locator in Havok's hand. He reached out and took the device. He thought for a minute and then smiled. "I suspect that Kang had comms with the captain of the Chinese Yantai-class guided-missile frigate and that a crewman snuck this onto your boat sometime last night. I also suspect that the frigate is due to depart this very morning for a few days in Cebu. They'll be loading stores this morning for their three-day transit, which should give you time to get most of the way to Terumbu before they get suspicious. However, after Cebu, the frigate is scheduled to go to New Guinea. You know, to show the flag. If someone is monitoring the GPS locator, that'll tell Kang, or whoever, that they've been found out, since New Guinea is east and south of the Philippines, not due west. This should prove interesting."

Havok smiled. "How are you gonna return the gift?"

"Leave that to me," Kilgore replied. "Just make sure you get back in one piece."

Havok stepped back into the pilothouse and fired up the engines.

Two minutes later, as Havok steered the boat away from the dock, Kilgore gave his friends a salute. Standing next to him, Catalina, Mercedes, and Apple held one another's hands. Kilgore and the three women watched the boat until it disappeared behind Grande Island. The women were not privy to what had transpired recently, but they knew this was not a normal trip. They feared the worst.

****

Three days later, Havok looped a mooring line around a concrete piling, one of many supporting a concrete quay that extended out from Taytay's main street. The structure, occupied by a few other watercraft tied up on both sides, sported scars from years of enduring rough seas and typhoons, and the pounding of boats and ships against the pilings. The trip that had brought the men through the islands and to this town should have taken three days, but after the run-in with Kang back at Quezon, Havok decided to stick with the story he had told Kang just in case somebody was watching or listening. They followed a meandering course southward, navigating past dozens of islands, stopping and diving at various locations, and dodging spats of bad weather. Wherever the crew of the Outfit went, they planted the idea that they were just what

Havok had told Kang they were: a small-time dive outfit looking for places to take their customers.

Just past five p.m. Havok stepped onto the quay and turned to look past the four coastal freighters anchored in the bay, toward the band of burning yellow rays of the setting sun that separated the orange-blue sky from the sparkling azure horizon. Here, in Taytay, they were going to take on fuel and water and speak to a few locals about dive locations along the coast. Then, after one last fling ashore, they would disappear into the South China Sea.

Stone, holding a piece of folded paper in his hand, joined Havok on the concrete quay.

"Manny's going to make arrangements for fuel, and he gave me the shopping list." He looked down at the paper and grumbled, "What is it with Spam and beans with this guy, anyhow?" In defiance, he added, "Well, I'm gettin' pickles!"

Havok chuckled. "Come on."

Both men, wearing faded swim trunks, T-shirts, and flip-flops, walked toward Taytay's main street, passing several Filipino seamen who were working on their own boats. As they reached the foot of the pier and stepped around a pile of broken concrete and rebar, they saw a group of young boys waiting for them. Two of the older boys held beer bottles.

"Want beer?" one of the boys asked.

Stone reached into his pocket and pulled out pesos. "We'll have the beers, and how would you all like to make some money?"

Dark brown eyes widened, and the boys broke into anticipating grins.

"We're going shopping and want you to carry the stuff back. If everything gets back to our boat, the man on board will pay each of you. Clear?"

They all nodded excitedly and fell in behind the two Americans, who proceeded toward the row of sari-sari stores that vended general merchandise.

By six p.m. the Americans had purchased everything on Manny's list and Stone had found a jar of American pickles. A troop of young boys, each holding a full plastic shopping bag and a Coke, happily filed back to the pier.

Four hours later, the two Americans relaxed as they drank at a beer garden not far from the pier. Three local women had joined them, which drew a few stares from some of the other customers.

Absently listening to the babble of other customers and pop music, Havok looked out onto the black bay. White anchor lights high in the masts of freighters and the dim shadows of their superstructures dotted the black sky above the ships.

"I don't know about you, Stone," Havok said, yawning, "but I'm beat. I'm gonna hit the sack."

The woman who sat next to Havok squealed with triumphant glee, having mistaken Havok's words and yawns. Her immense smile was short-lived. Havok stood, laid down pesos for the drinks, and waved goodbye to the disappointed woman.

"Come on," pleaded Stone. "Stay for just one more. Can't you see your friend wants you to stay?" His face was flushed from the beer and the two women vying for his attention and money.

"Sorry," Havok said, "but we're underway at first light, and I don't want to have to come lookin' for you."

"Don't worry," Stone said, leering into the cleavage of a girl to his right.

Havok left his friend and started down the road that led back to their boat. Though tired, he was enjoying the night and the cool sea breeze. He subconsciously sniffed the salt air, relishing its freshness. As he reached the foot of the quay, lost in thought, he was quickly jerked back to reality by the sound of footsteps racing up behind him. He whipped around, lowered his body into a defensive stance, and raised his clenched fists. Someone loomed in front of him. Havok straightened, lowered his fists, and let out a sigh of relief. It was the woman from the bar.

The pair stood facing each other, looking into each other's eyes. He thought about sending her home with a swift pat on the rear but surrendered. He reached out for her hand, but suddenly a black shadow enveloped the woman and snatched her off her feet, ripping her from Havok's hand. Havok moved to help but was stopped by a crushing blow on the back of his head. The impact exploded through his brain, reaching his forehead like the shock waves of an atomic blast. In between the nauseating spasms that rippled through his skull, he heard the horrified screams of the woman and saw the specter toss her off the pier. Havok started to fall to his knees, but a set of enormous arms clamped in a vise-like grip around his chest from behind, trapping his arms.

The iron jaws closed upon themselves, painfully squeezing the life out of Havok. He could feel his rib cage near the point of implosion. While one man held Havok in a death grip, he saw the shadow of the man who had thrown the woman off the pier pull something from his waistline, shaking it. It looked like some sort of black bag. The shadowy man stepped up to Havok's side, out of reach of his legs. The pain in Havok's chest was becoming unbearable. He had begun to surrender to unconsciousness when suddenly the vise released its grip, and both he and the man who had been crushing him bowled forward. The human vise forcefully expelled breath that smelled of beets and sardines, sickening Havok as the two men slammed into the ground. Havok felt the great weight on his back roll off, and he quickly rolled the opposite way while sucking in an enormous gulp of air.

Havok jumped to his feet and turned to face the man who had held him in a death grip, while the shadow with the sack was attacked by another figure. With all his might, Havok kicked his attacker in the crotch. The man bowled over and threw up on Havok's bare leg. It was then that Havok saw his attacker's face. He was a large white man. The two other men fought silently, although it was not much of a struggle. The shorter of the two was sinking blows into the abdomen of the taller victim, who held his arms close to his midsection to ward off the blows. Havok looked down at his own victim, who was rising to his feet. He grabbed a piece of broken concrete with rebar sticking out of it, and before his crouching assailant could stand, he slammed the cement chunk into the side of the man's skull. Blood splattered on Havok's hand and arm. Still, the attacker would not give up. He swore in what sounded like Russian and regained his footing. Havok struck the unfortunate man in the temple, and this time the rebar punctured the skull. Without uttering a sound, the man fell, dead. Dismissing his victim, Havok ran to the side of the quay to look for the woman.

"You all right?" Stone asked as he stepped up to Havok.

Havok looked back over his shoulder at his friend's sparring partner. Stone's opponent lay on the ground, unmoving and curled in a fetal position. The man groaned quietly.

"Just ducky," Stone answered, "but I don't think this exercise program they got going here is gonna catch on."

Havok returned his attention to the woman. All he saw were a few footprints in the mud. If she could get up and run away, then she must be fine, he surmised. "What made you come looking for me?"

"After you left the beer joint, another woman came in. It was then I decided this place isn't all too healthy for us."

"Well, I don't feel like being questioned by the local cops, so you can tell me later. Let's get out of here."

They ran down the quay, the empty slap of their flip-flops chasing them.

By midnight, the Outfit stood well out to sea. At first, Havok pushed his vessel hard, but he eventually slowed down. They were surrounded by a dark vastness, but he could see the occasional weak lights of far-off boats heading to their own destinations. He decided to match their speed so the Outfit wouldn't stand out on somebody else's radar screen. Havok stood at the helm, staring through the window into the blackness of the South China Sea. In front of the helm, the small luminescent marine compass glowed, bathing his neck and lower face in its green light. Behind him, Stone sat and monitored the Furuno radar screen mounted above the chart table. Although there were several blips scattered across the monitor, none seemed to be following them.

"So how did you know I needed help?" Havok asked, breaking the silence. "And what about the woman who followed me?"

"The woman who followed you was just an innocent bystander," replied Stone. "Nobody your attackers had any interest in hurting. They just wanted to get her out of the way."

"So again, how do you know all this?" Havok asked.

"After you left the bar, another woman walked in, and she, like all the others, wanted a piece of old Pete."

"Your pesos is more like it."

Stone ignored the sarcasm. "The latecomer had an edge on the competition, and she used it to get one hundred percent stock in Stone, Inc."

"What was the hot stock tip?"

"She told me that some people stopped at her father's store earlier this morning looking for us," answered Stone. "Before we arrived."

"Boris and Natasha?" Havok interjected.

"Nope. This time our visitors were two men who said they wanted to dive with us, which seemed too fishy."

"Well, I don't think they will be too keen to dive with us now," Havok stated.

As an afterthought, Havok remembered that his victim had sworn in Russian. "Why would Russians be looking for us?" he asked.

"I asked myself the same thing, but since I didn't know, I figured your butt was just a tad more precious than my sex life. I followed after you and found you having your threesome without me, and since you didn't see fit to invite me to your party, I decided to crash it."

"I'm glad you did," Havok said.

"After I put my man down, I searched him for ID. All I found was a roll of rubles."

"Why would anybody in their right mind carry around a roll of currency that ain't worth toilet paper?" asked Havok.

"I don't know," said Stone. "Two huge white guys with no ID but carrying a roll of Russian rubles, looking for us in this one-horse town."

Havok stared through the glass in front of him into the darkness of the South China Sea before speaking. "First, the fact that they were carrying only Russian currency tells me one thing. Second, the fact that they didn't jump Manny and take over the Outfit to wait for us tells me something else."

Stone lit a cigarette. "They just pulled into town, and they're not that bright."

The intrepid adventurers fell back into silence as Stone put the cigarette in his mouth and moved back to the sofa behind the pilothouse, leaving Havok to stare toward an unseen horizon.

****

The following afternoon, the men dropped anchor on the leeward side of Ituba Island, gratefully accepting its meager shelter. The sunburnt, windswept cay, shaped like a horseshoe, barely broke the ocean's surface and was topped with a few scraggly palm trees. It was the last piece of land that managed to cling tenaciously to the southern end of the Tizard Banks. Their ultimate goal was a little less than eighty miles beyond this cay.

The three-member crew put the few hours of daylight left to good use. With the radar set at its widest range, Manny watched the screen and mumbled to himself, while Havok and Stone transformed the beautiful boat into an ugly duckling. The partners covered the deck fittings with wide strips of landscape cloth to break up their outline and used duct tape to hold the cloth in place. After the upperworks had been camouflaged, Stone jumped into their six-foot Zodiac and Havok climbed into a wooden dingy, and they set out to paint diagonal black, green, and gray stripes along the hull. An hour before sunset, the two men stood on the fantail in their shorts and paint-splattered sneakers, sweating profusely and surveying their handiwork.

"I don't think Manny will ever forgive us," Stone said, wiping his hand with a rag. "He doesn't look too happy."

"He's gonna have to," Havok replied.

After a water break, Havok and Stone positioned one roll of camouflaged netting on the bow and one on the stern. Once the craft was inside the cove on Terumbu, they would stretch the two nets over the entire boat. After securing the rolls of netting, Havok turned and looked across the early-evening sky. He saw the steel-gray curtain of a distant rain squall. Throughout the day, the easterly winds had gradually increased, causing the seas to become choppy. He hoped the weather would continue to deteriorate as the rain and rough seas would minimize or even hide their signature on radar as they motored toward Terumbu. The only thing left to do now was to ready their weapons, and get a hot meal into their stomachs.

Havok walked aft along the port side and stopped at the open door leading into the pilothouse. Manny was still watching the radar and tapping his cigarette hard against an ashtray. Havok saw the annoyance on his face.

"Manny," he said, "how about going ashore and finding some rocks to sink our empty paint cans? Also, see if you can scrounge up dinner. Maybe some crab?"

"OK." Manny flicked his butt over the rail. "But don't think that I've forgiven you." He turned and stepped down the ladder to the forward cabin.

Havok saw Stone sitting at the table on the fantail under a wood-paneled canopy, drinking a beer. He joined him, and in a few minutes they saw Manny with a dive mask, flippers, a net bag, and a spear gun, climbing over the handrail into the dingy. Manny used two short wooden oars to propel himself to the exposed coral rocks. The two men drank cold beer as Manny landed the boat and secured the painter around the base of a coral head. He stepped out of the dingy and carefully picked his way across the craggy surface. After a few minutes, he stopped and began to wave his arms wildly.

Havok and Stone sat straight up and looked at each other. Without a word, they ran for the Zodiac. Havok pulled the cord to start the five-horsepower outboard engine, and they quickly covered the short distance, driving the boat up onto the rocks, its fiberglass hull scraping harshly against the sharp coral. The two men jumped out of the boat and covered the few feet between themselves and Manny, who was looking into a shallow tide pool.

Bobbing gently in the clear water was the normal detritus of modern-day life: plastic shopping bags, foam flip-flops, and empty water bottles. But the pool also snared something else: a severed human head. The voracious crabs that still hid nearby, waiting for the humans to leave so they could finish their meal, had emptied its eye sockets and destroyed its ears and lips. Strands of thin gray hair and a wispy beard moved lazily with the subtle wave action as if it was a live sea anemone. The living men stared down at the open mouth where the lips used to be. Grotesque, exposed teeth greeted their gaze. A baby crab remained inside the mouth, patiently waiting for the humans to leave so it could start back on the man's tongue.

Havok spoke while watching the head bump against the coral: "Well, not much to go on, but it looks like he was Caucasian and in his fifties. Maybe sixties." He paused and looked up at Manny. "I think it will be fish for dinner tonight."

An hour later, after they had secured the boats, bottom side up, on the roof of the pilothouse, the men sat under the wood-paneled canopy, which extended aft from the combined pilothouse and lounge. They reclined in camp chairs around the table, quietly eating their dinner off paper plates: grilled bonito fillets seasoned with garlic salt and crispy golden-brown potato wedges and onions fried in oil. They washed the food down with glasses of ice-cold San Miguel beer. Each man ate in silence, lost in his own thoughts.

Havok took a break from his thoughts and looked over to his right, witnessing the final rays of light as they disappeared beyond the western horizon and dark, billowing clouds. He was pleased, as rain squalls could help mask their approach to Terumbu Island. The Outfit was now shrouded by the tropical darkness. There were only two sources of light. The first was the stainless-steel grill mounted on a handrail overhanging the stern. The embers in the grill glowed a dark red, and sparks blossomed when juices dripped from the fillets onto the hot coals. The other source of light came from a small battery-powered lantern that hung from a brass hook above the table where they sat, and swung with the motion of the boat. The Outfit tugged at its anchorage like an errant puppy who was disdainful of the leash that secured him to a kitchen table leg. It sought to be let go. A building wind further encouraged the irascible boat to be loose from her leash, and the wind was a signal to her owners that it was, indeed, time to release her from her tether.

Havok looked down at the deck at his feet and thought back to June Johnson again and her comment about his habit of always burning his toast. Speaking quietly to the boat, he said, "It's fine girl; we're going."

"Well, I guess it's time," Stone said sullenly.

The men stood, one by one, and threw their plates into a wastebasket. Havok went to the pilothouse. Manny collected the glasses and the wastebasket, and Stone flipped the grill over, dumping the briquettes and remaining fish into the sea. Once the Outfit was ready, Stone pulled in its anchor and Havok fired up the engines, pointing the boat toward a dark western sky.

13

SOUTH CHINA SEA, LATE JULY

THE BLACKNESS IN FRONT OF HAVOK SEEMED TO BE AN INFINITE VOID, AND HE COULD SEE NOTHING EXCEPT FOR FAT RAINDROPS ASSAULTING THE WINDOWPANES OF THE PILOTHOUSE. He'd been standing at the helm for several hours now, and his legs were numb from his wide bracing as the seas surged past the Outfit from astern. He did not notice the ache in his legs, though. Instead, he stared at the white lubber line under the hand-sized dome of the floating compass face. His hands maintained a 210-degree course, while his mind pondered the human head many miles behind him. Who had it belonged to, and how had it ended up on such a desolate lump of land?

The men had examined the lonely stub of Ituba Island but had found no other sign of human presence: no footprints, shelters, or dead campfires. Before they departed the island, they inspected the gruesome flotsam the island had snared and discovered a single bullet hole at the base of the head. Somebody had executed the man.

By three a.m. the narrow white lubber line had become a stinging blur. In what seemed like slow motion, Havok reached over and rapped his knuckles on the raised wooden hatch of the cabin below. Within a minute, Manny opened the hatch and stuck his head out.

"Take the helm," Havok said, yawning. "We're still a ways out. The seas are coming in from the port quarter, and I've embedded us in a line of rain squalls, so stay with them as long as you can maintain a direct heading to Terumbu."

"Got it."

They swapped places, and as Manny wrapped his hands firmly around the spokes of the old-fashioned wheel, Stone popped his head up from below. He stretched and yawned while he scratched his short gray hair. "What's going on?"

"Manny has the wheel and GPS has us on track," Havok said, still looking out the window. "We're still twenty-five miles out. Why don't you get some more sleep?"

"I'm good." Stone stumbled his way toward the chart table for his cigarettes. "I'll wake you when we get close enough."

Havok faltered down the steps to his bunk. Manny was getting used to adjusting the course to match the surging seas coming from astern.

***

It seemed only a minute had passed since Havok's head hit the pillow when somebody roughly shook his shoulder. He opened his eyes. Manny's face leaned over him in the darkness. The pounding of the engines and the surging sea had ceased. Raindrops still hit the wooden deck above the cabin, but their pace had slackened.

"What's wrong?"

"Nothing, we're here."

"No way," Havok mumbled. He brought his dive watch close to his face, and his gritty eyes focused on the luminous crystal. The hands indicated that he had been asleep for over two hours. "I'm up," he grumbled as he stretched his arms above his head. After a minute of stretching, Havok threw his legs out of the bunk and sat up. After another minute of rubbing his eyes, he headed toward the staircase leading out of the cabin.

A pitch-blackness enveloped Havok as he stepped onto the deck in front of the pilothouse. The landmass ahead was a shade even darker than pitch black, like the ebony of a shadow in the night. The rain squalls that had escorted them to the island continued to move on, passing over and beyond the island. He turned around and saw Manny in the pilothouse. The weak light from the compass and other gauges highlighted his outline. Manny was wearing the night-vision goggles he had borrowed from Kilgore.

Havok, no stranger to using NVGs, could imagine what Manny was seeing through the device. Havok turned to look at the ebony island, which took on a fuzzy green outline, and at the subdued surf, which was light green, and the break in the surf, which revealed the channel through the reef. Havok saw Manny in the pilothouse grasping the twin control levers with his right hand, pushing them with his thumb and pinkie, one forward and one in reverse. This directed the boat to twist to port and coast a short distance southward. When the break in the surf line was abeam of the boat, Manny reversed the positions of the throttle levers, turning the boat until the bow pointed into the narrow channel.

Havok turned to the island again and thought back to the day he had flown over and around this island. He remembered the broad reef flat along the eastern shore and the channel that cut through it. He could almost see the hidden cove at the other end of the channel.

After glancing at the LED readout of the fathometer above the chart table and then the details on the chart itself, Stone announced to Manny, "Looks like we're just off the channel entrance."

Havok stepped aft and entered the door to the pilothouse.

Stone looked at him and said, "We're right where we need to be."

"Good," replied Havok. "Now let's get into our swim gear. I would hate for a coral head to scratch the bottom of your precious boat."

Stone replied with an unintelligible mumble and followed Havok out the door.

Manny stayed at the helm while his employers went aft to get ready for their next task. Although the chart indicated that the channel was deep and wide enough for the Outfit's three-foot draft, Havok had to assume there might be scattered coral heads not indicated on the chart. The depth finder's transducer, mounted on the stern, would give no warning of them until it was too late. They would have to guide the boat past any obstructions.

Leaning against the handrail up on the bow, they each wore swim trunks and basic snorkel gear and carried a dive light. Duct tape covered the lenses of their lights, leaving one square inch uncovered. Havok waved to Manny before he and Stone rolled backward off the bulwark and fell into the black of the sea. The sudden temperature change from the warm, tropical night air to the cool water chilled Havok. He ignored the discomfort and turned on his dive light. Several feet to his side, the slim blade of Stone's light stabbed into the depths. Havok's eyes followed the light stiletto, but the only thing he could see, other than Stone's faint light, was an endless green space. He could hear the haunting throbs of the diesels behind him.

Havok rolled over in the water and kicked ahead until he could see the silhouette of the pilothouse above the bow. Stone had done the same, and when Havok was sure Manny could see the beams from their hooded lights, he rolled back over and kicked ahead on the surface.

The sloped, gravel-strewn bottom of the channel began to appear about fifteen feet under Havok. To his left, the channel wall rose out of the void. Although their lights were covered, the beams were still visible. Havok was not sure if the people on this island had patrols out and could have heard the diesel engines or had already zeroed in on this spot as a likely landing point for Havok to park his boat. After quite a bit of internal dialogue, he decided that whoever was on this island hadn't taken the time to post a guard on this spot—at least not yet, as that Chinese frigate was probably still in Cebu in the central Philippines. But there was also that run-in with the two Russians. Had the survivor had the time to contact others for help or to alert those on this island? Maybe or maybe not, but in any case, they were now on this island.

Still kicking into the channel, Havok swam over a coral head. Its rounded top crested ten feet beneath his fins, leaving plenty of room for his boat to pass over it. Soon, his light culled out a second coral head. It was about eight feet under the surface, which still allowed plenty of room for his boat to pass over. Suddenly, he felt it: the sudden movement of water against the side of his head. Havok shot his light over to his left just in time to see the angular tail of a shark disappear into the blackness.

Hope the sharks around here are well fed, he thought.

The bottom began to level out at about five feet, as Havok entered the cove. Thankfully, the bottom was clear of any obstructions and sharks. He rolled over and could see the ghostly shadow of his boat glide toward him. He moved a bit farther to his left as the muffled sound of the engines reached a deeper pitch. The boat slid past him into the small pocket of the cove. The sound waves, having no place to go, reverberated off the sides and the bottom of the narrow confines and thundered painfully against Havok's eardrums. The pain exploded as Manny put both engines in reverse and increased the engine's rpm to stop the boat. The propellers churned up the bottom of the cove, cutting out any visibility. Not wanting to lose a leg in the propellers, Havok remained where he was until he heard the engines go silent, and then swam to the plastic rungs of the rope ladder that hung from the portside dive gate. While waiting for Stone, he listened to the jungle and could hear the running of water somewhere in front of the boat. He could also see the rocky edge of the cove about three feet away. The boat fit nice and snug in its little refuge. Stone, who was still on the other side of the boat, free-dove down, squeezed under the keel, and surfaced next to Havok.

"Manny," Havok whispered loudly.

Manny's head loomed out of the darkness above the men. The bulky night-vision goggles were still strapped to his face.

"What do you see?" Havok asked.

"Looks like we found a perfect hideaway," Manny answered. "There's a rocky wall on both sides and in front of us about as tall as the boat. They're covered with jungle vines and roots that we can tie mooring lines to, and there is a waterfall in front of us."

Havok now recognized the sound of the falling water. "Drop the mooring lines."

Manny walked around the deck, dropping two bowlines and two stern lines into the water. Havok and Stone found the ropes and tied them to the nearby tree roots that snaked down the crevices in the rocky wall. They left enough slack in the lines to account for tidal changes.

Havok's stiff biceps bunched as he pulled himself up the narrow rope ladder. When he reached the deck, he stripped off his snorkel gear and, wearing only swim trunks, went forward to help Manny with the camouflage bow net, stretching it from the bow to the top of the pilothouse. When the net was in place, Havok helped Stone with the other net, while Manny removed his goggles and went into the salon behind the pilothouse for dry clothes, towels, and hot coffee. Havok and Stone stretched the stern net from the transom up to the pilothouse, leaving a gap between the two nets so they could get on and off the boat. Dawn was still an hour away, and the air was humid and motionless. Both of them sweated heavily, and the drying salt water on their skin, combined with thick sweat, created a sticky coating on their skin.

Havok accepted the towel and mug of hot coffee that Manny offered him. The rough cloth seemed to smear the coating of dried seawater and sweat. The bittersweet black coffee, though, washed the salt water from his mouth.

Stone was doing the same, and Havok saw a smirk develop on Stone's face.

"What's so funny?" Havok asked.

"I'm just remembering that time in the Keys," he replied as he threw his towel on the table behind him. "You know—when SPAN Expeditions gave us a boat and hired us to sneak onto Marathon and steal that stash of marijuana from Big Mike's gang."

"Yeah," replied Havok. "That stash of marijuana they stole from an international artifact smuggler with no idea that there was a golden Mayan idol hidden under the reefer. So what?"

"Nothing," mused Stone. "But those damned dentally challenged Keybillies sure were pissed as they tried to shoot up the boat during our getaway. I just hope that whoever's on this island are bad shots, just like those Keybillies."

"Somehow," Havok replied, "I don't think we're going to run into a bunch of Keybillies with Halloween candy corn for teeth, shooting at us with worn-out shotguns and secondhand AR-15s."

They both fell silent and finished dressing.

Havok peeked through the netting at the entrance of the cove and could see the black sky starting to turn a lighter shade.

"What about some sleep?" Stone asked. "Even just a few minutes?"

"One of us will have to stand guard," Havok answered.

"I'll stand watch," Manny volunteered as he joined the two to collect the towels and coffee cups.

"Keep your shotgun handy," Havok ordered.

An hour later, just after sunrise, Manny woke his employers and had a breakfast of canned guava juice, cold sardines in mustard sauce, and day-old rice waiting for them. Havok appreciated his friend's thoughtfulness, as the smell of frying meat would have traveled far and advertised their arrival. The group sat on the fantail, under the cover of the netting and the lush tropical canopy overhead, eating their simple fare off paper plates.

Havok looked out the round, tunnel-like entrance at a dark blue sky and the sun sparkling off the ruffled turquoise sea. A tiny fraction of the early-morning sea breeze was able to sneak in, providing comfort. The boat moved slowly up and down in synchronicity with the gentle seas. The sound of water falling over rocks in front of them serenaded the tranquil morning. While Havok bathed in nature's serenity, he wondered what kind of human ugliness awaited them that day. He also saw the rope that Manny had stretched from the roof of the pilothouse, over the four feet of space between the side of the boat to the trunk of a tree on top of the embankment, and just a few feet into the jungle.

After the meal, Havok and Stone prepared for the day's expedition. They had worn their camouflage clothing to bed, and now they pulled two olive-drab backpacks from under the padded bench seats in the salon. Havok also pulled out an overstuffed army rucksack. While the two men slept, Manny had removed all of their weapons from the compartment under the pilothouse deck and made sure the weapons were loaded, as well as their cartridge belts.

When breakfast had settled, they each drank a quart of water.

Havok turned to Stone, who was checking his MP5 assault weapon. "Ready?"

"We ain't gonna get back to Subic standing here," Stone answered while looping the strap of the weapon over his head.

Havok pulled a folded map from the left cargo pocket of his trousers. He opened it up and pointed to a red X that marked the southern shore of the large bay. "This is where we're going," he told Manny. "We should be back well before sunset. While we're gone, set up an observation post up on the bank. Never know who might come snooping around."

"Already done," Manny said. "I found a spot about ten yards into the jungle. Put my gear there before I woke you."

"Good," Havok said, slipping the straps of the day pack over his shoulder. "Now help me with the emergency pack."

After both bags were in place on Havok's back, he slung his M14 over his head and jammed his Beretta into his beltline and walked up to the taut line Manny had assembled. Before he grabbed the rope, Havok looked ahead of the boat, at the eight-foot waterfall cascading over the rocky edge. Havok felt the dried salt water and sweat on his skin. Well, a bath's going to have to wait. He hoisted himself up, swinging his legs over the rope, and pulled himself headfirst toward the bank. Once above ground, he dropped from the line, removed his rifle from around his neck and shoulder, and moved deeper into the jungle. Stone followed, and joined Havok in the jungle. They kept guard while Manny slithered across the rope bridge. Once Manny was on the ground, he silently moved off to his observation post hidden in a patch of ferns. Havok and Stone started their hike without a word spoken.

They hiked for thirty minutes, heading south and getting close to the island's largest bay. They had already passed the smaller bay, where they had stopped to rest, observe, and share a canteen of water. Sweat now soaked their fatigues. Although the walk was comparatively easy, humidity made the hike arduous. The interwoven canopy above kept the hot sun from reaching the forest floor, which limited undergrowth, but it also trapped moisture-laden air. Now, as they walked in silence, they searched for a cache site for the emergency pack.

Havok spotted a fallen tree surrounded by broad-leaved ferns. "How does this look?"

Stone looked around before answering. "We can use that big tree back there as a landmark." He pointed at a large banyan they had just passed. He also sniffed the air. "We can use that smell too. Is that a dead pig?"

"Not likely. I didn't see any game trails or droppings," answered Havok as he loosened the straps of the emergency pack and slid it off his shoulders. "I doubt there are any large animals on this island. I'll clear a spot for the pack. Keep guard."

Havok stepped into the ferns to look for a spot under the fallen tree.

Well, something died here, Havok thought, seeing a pile of leaves about seven feet long. The smell was proof of that. He squatted and poked the barrel of his rifle into the long pile of leaves. Suddenly, a sortie of enormous purple-black flies came to life within the pile. Having been disturbed from their meal and egg laying, they swarmed, darting over Havok's head as he ducked. Their sudden departure threw aside all but a few leaves and exposed a ghastly sight.

14

TERUMBU ISLAND, LATE JULY

ALTHOUGH THE CARCASS HAD LONG SINCE BEEN DEAD, IT STILL PULSATED FROM THE MAGGOTS AND INSECTS THAT TUNNELED THROUGH THE RE-MAINS OF THE CORPSE. After the flies sortied, Havok poked around for a couple more minutes before stepping out of the ferns.

"I saw the flies." Stone smirked. "So there's somethin' dead in there."

"I just found the owner of the head we found back on Ituba Island."

"Any idea who he was?" Havok asked.

"Just guessing really, but he was thin and didn't get out much. I'm guessin' an office or lab worker by the looks of his clothing: a white collared shirt, pleated dress slacks, and dress shoes, all with Russian manufacturer labels. In addition to missing his head, he's missing his feet and hands. Somebody didn't want him identified."

"But they left him in clothing marking him as a possible Russian?" Stone pondered aloud.

"Like you said earlier, they may not be too bright," Havok answered. "But we can't cache our gear here. They may come back."

After inspecting the body and the surrounding bushes for more information, the two men left the gravesite and found a bamboo grove a hundred yards away. Once Havok buried the emergency pack inside the thicket of green stalks, the pair of explorers continued their trek southward. Through the dark, humid tropical forest, they walked and sweated until they reached the interior end of the large bay. By now, their olive-drab clothing was black and heavy with sweat. Damp leaves clung to their attire, and Havok's skin itched ferociously from the razor-sharp bamboo fibers. Here, they sat at the edge of the forest, next to the small stream that escaped the foliage and meandered its way across the beach to the bay. Havok looked out at the clean white sand in front of him and the clear, bright sky. His eyes smarted from the light reflecting off the sand.

Stone kept his eyes on the direction they had just come from, while Havok pulled binoculars from the case on his belt and peered through them at the beach from which the US Navy had rescued Wheatley's father. The white crescent of the sand shined against a dark green forest behind it. The beach was devoid of footprints, trash, or any other sign of human activity. He panned the glasses over the bay.

"See anything?" Stone asked.

"Just some birds," Havok answered, pausing to inspect the uncharted island in the middle of the bay and the tropical growth that grew all the way to the water's edge. He noticed there were no trees on the island; instead, short brush and grass covered the entire island. He noticed something else as well.

"And it looks like the island's changed shape a bit."

"How so?" Stone asked, still looking behind them.

"I don't know," Havok said. "A bit wider, longer, or taller. Maybe it looks different because I'm looking at it from a different angle."

The two men fell silent. Stone kept looking at the jungle behind them; Havok, at the island in the middle of the bay. That's when Havok saw it: a wisp of black smoke rising from the peaked center of the island. Now he knew why the island looked different.

Satisfied, he continued on and used the binoculars to focus on the northern shore. He saw a narrow strip of rocky beach and remnants of an old concrete pier. Other than the three small beaches, a confused wall of forest bordered the bay.

"Doesn't look like anybody is following us," Stone said.

"All quiet on the Eastern Front as well," Havok said dryly.

"Do you think anybody else is on this rock?"

"Somebody took the time to kill and decapitate that body back there. I'll bet his killers are the same assholes who put the holes in my airplane."

"Our airplane."

"Our airplane," Havok corrected himself. "And they're hiding under that island in the middle of the bay."

Stone turned to face the same direction as Havok. "I still don't know why anybody would go through so much trouble for some World War II silver that may not even be here. Plus, is that island in the same spot where Wheatley's father said the Americans dumped the silver?"

"There's obviously something going on here," Havok replied. "But first, I want to see if there's a way to get onto that beach over there so we can at least try to get what we came for."

The hike continued in silence as they followed the edge of the forest that surrounded the bay, and walked under the cover of the tropical canopy. Finally, they came to a spot where they could survey the beach, and the possible location of the silver pesos. There, they heard a noise. Looking past the island in the middle of the bay, at the rocky beach on the other side of the bay a half mile away, they saw a black rubber boat carrying two men depart the rocky beach. The outboard engine whined in the distance as the boat headed for the island.

"Well, we don't have anything to do until sunset, do we?" Stone said.

The two men turned back in the direction they had come from, walking cautiously until they reached the small stream they had sat next to less than an hour ago. They turned and followed the edge of the forest and beach toward the rocky beach. It was not long before they could hear voices and smell the smoke of campfires.

Havok and Stone squatted behind the roots of a banyan tree and peered through a group of ferns to observe their new discovery. Two rows of old single-story cinder-block buildings ran from east to west. The windows were paneless and the doorways were doorless. Worn rain ponchos and thin blankets now hung in their place. At one end of the two rows of buildings was a large two-story building with a wide porch and concrete steps, and at the other end, another large single-story building. Havok also spotted the corner of another building poking out of the jungle to the north of the camp. There was a middle-aged white man wearing a laboratory coat over civilian clothing, with glasses perched on his forehead, standing at the corner, reading something on a clipboard.

They watched as men, wearing the pants of military battle-dress uniforms and blue-and-white-striped jerseys, carried out duties in pairs or in trios: tending a fire, carrying pails of water to and fro, cleaning weapons, or conversing while smoking cigarettes. They all had closely cropped hair or shaven heads and were well muscled. The three men closest to Havok and Stone, about fifty feet away, were passing the time by having a push-up contest.

"We drew the shitty end of the stick this time," whispered Havok.

"What makes you say that?"

"Those jerseys they're wearing are typically worn by Russian special-forces units."

"Well, even without the uniforms, those buggers look mean enough to scare the ugly straight off Maxine Waters with one shot," quipped Stone.

Havok looked back at the two-story building at the west end of the camp. Two men, one looking to be in his fifties and the other in his late twenties, exited the building. They were fully dressed in pressed BDUs and walked with erect postures as they stopped and talked to the soldiers they passed.

They must be officers, Havok thought.

Finally, the two men stopped to talk to the three soldiers recovering from their push-up contest. Sweating heavily, the three men held themselves straight and nodded cheerfully as the older of the two officers seemed to joke with them. The respect was evident.

While not fluent in Russian, Havok knew enough to take caution. He grimaced as he thought back to what Stone had asked just a short time ago: What would Russian Special Forces soldiers be doing on this island?

Havok also thought they were perhaps a bit too close to the camp. He nudged Stone in his side, and they both stood slightly and backed away from the tree.

The sun had long ago passed its zenith and was well on its way toward the western horizon when the hikers arrived back at their boat. After removing their day packs and web gear, Havok and Stone stripped down to their pants under the boat's netting and washed the best they could using a five-gallon bucket of fresh water Manny had filled for them. Now, sitting on chairs on the fantail and wearing dry clothing, they ran combs through their still-wet hair, drank iced-down beer, and discussed their dilemma along with possible options.

"Well, there's quite a bit going on here, but I suggest we check and see if the silver is still there," posed Havok. "If it's not, that's fine, as the search will give us time to let the Russians go to sleep. Once it's late, we can revisit the camp for a better recon; then I'm thinking about a swim out to that island."

"Don't forget," answered Stone. "You mentioned something about a missing university research vessel."

"You're right," Havok said. "I'm sure the ship is playing a factor in all of this."

Manny finished his beer. "What about calling Kilgore?"

"It wouldn't work," Havok replied. "With all that has happened, I'm sure somebody's monitoring Kilgore's comms, which can be traced back to us, and it would tell them we're on this island. Also, if Kilgore was able to sneak that GPS locator device aboard that Chinese frigate and it's still working or not found out yet, they just might be tracking the wrong target electronically, which should still give us time to figure out our next few steps."

They spent the rest of the late afternoon assembling and testing their gear for the night dive and going over the dive plan. They worked until it was dark. Once Havok and Stone made sure their equipment was packed and ready, they sat to eat the simple meal Manny had prepared for them, and they finished the bucket of beers. This would be the last of the cold beer, as they could not afford to run the boat's generator. For dessert, they had stubby bananas that Manny had picked up earlier that day.

By seven p.m. Havok and Stone had pulled their dive packs across the monkey line to the embankment. Each dive pack contained a scuba tank, a regulator, a buoyancy compensator, lead weights, fins, a mask, and a wrist compass. Havok's pack contained a simple wand-type metal detector, and Stone carried a one-hundred-meter-reeled measuring tape. Along with their dive gear, they both wore web gear and carried their weapons. After helping each other with the dive packs, they began their night march, leaving Manny to hide in his observation post.

Havok and Stone plodded southward. Their bodies bent forward to ease their backbreaking loads. They shifted their weapons to the cloth-covered crooks of their elbows and wiped their palms on their sleeves. Havok pulled a saturated handkerchief from one of his pockets to wipe his eyes. It proved useless under the torrent of sweat.

Following familiar ground, they passed the two bays; the smaller one first. As they approached the interior end of the larger, or southernmost, bay, they gave themselves a wider berth to avoid any chance encounter with any Russians from the camp.

After an hour, they approached the edge of the jungle lining the beach from where Wheatley's father had been rescued years ago.

Gratefully, the men dropped their loads and sat down for a brief rest, greedily drinking from their canteens. After five minutes of recovery, Havok stood without saying a word and started getting ready by stashing his weapon and web gear under a nearby bush. After that, he took off his hiking boots and socks and laid them on top of the same bush. Stone followed his lead.

Still wearing their sweat-soaked fatigues, their practiced hands assembled the scuba gear and they helped each other shoulder the equipment. Holding the head strap of his mask and the heel straps of his fins in one hand and the metal detector in the other, Havok, with Stone behind him, followed the curve of the tree line until it met the water.

Havok looked at the night sky. "No moon, but plenty of stars."

"Even still," replied Stone, "it'll still be black as hell at the bottom of this bay."

Havok was not thinking about the black inner space of the bay that would soon consume them; instead, he remembered Wheatley's words. Wheatley had said his father saw the submarine dumping silver two hundred yards straight out from this beach. He took a reading with his wrist compass and noted the heading.

As Havok and Stone entered the still surf, the cold water shocked their warm, sweaty skin. Now in water up to their shoulders, they slipped their fins onto their feet and pulled their masks down over their faces. As the water closed over his head, Havok was surrounded by a black nothingness. He looked down at his wrist and saw the luminous dial of his compass. Once he verified his compass heading again, he used his thumb to turn on the metal detector he held in his other hand. Immediately, he heard a series of clicks. After the self-test was complete, the clicks settled into a slow, monotonous rhythm. Once satisfied, Havok touched Stone's shoulder, and the two men kicked out to begin their search. As Havok kicked forward, hovering just above the sandy bottom of the bay, he let a little air into his buoyancy compensator. Once satisfied with his equipment, Havok crooked his left arm in front of him and followed the orb of his compass dial deeper into the bay. Thankfully, the water was clear and the starlight from the night sky increased visibility. As he kicked, the marred landscape of the bay's bottom glided past him as if he were in a lunar spacecraft skimming along the surface of the dark side of the moon. Miniature craters and scars exploded into view.

Havok counted his ninety-fifth kick and came to a halt by placing the blunt end of the metal detector into the soft mud in front of him. He estimated they had traveled about two hundred yards. He turned to his right. Stone's outline was two feet away, and he saw Stone reach out to him, handing him the brass snap clip on the end of the reeled measuring tape. Stone settled on the bottom, while Havok swam away until the tape became taut. As discussed, he was at the two-meter mark. While Stone sat anchor, Havok swam in an ever-expanding circle at two-meter increments. He kicked methodically while holding on to the end of the tape and listening to the slow clicks of the metal detector. As the minutes ticked by, so did their chances of finding the silver.

Suddenly, at twenty meters out from Stone, the dull series of clicks from the metal detector exploded in his ears, but just as suddenly as it had begun, the din went away. Still, Havok had no doubt he'd passed over something.

Havok stuck the end of the metal detector into the mud to stop his forward movement and to push himself back a few feet. He waved the end of the instrument in front of him until the monotone clicks once again joined in a nerve-racking blast. He laid the detector next to the hot spot and withdrew his knife from the sheath strapped to his inner calf. Still holding the brass clip, he methodically prodded the thick blade into the soft muck until he felt the metal scrape against something. He stuck the knife's blade into the muddy bottom a few inches from the spot and looped the end of the measuring tape around the handle of the knife. Scooping the mud away from the spot where his knife had scraped against something, he dug down, about six inches, until he felt a flat object about the size of a half-dollar. Havok extracted the piece and brought it up against his mask. Though encrusted with a black coating, he knew it was a coin.

He put his find in one pocket of his BC before reaching into the other pocket. He pulled out a piece of Styrofoam the size of a deck of cards, which was tied to a yellow plastic tent peg with ten inches of kite string. He replaced the knife stuck in the mud with the tent stake and tugged on the tape four times, signaling Stone to swim to him. Stone obeyed and reeled in the measuring tape as he swam to Havok. The two men searched the area.

After a few minutes, Havok reached out to a rectangular hole in the mud, and his waterlogged fingers felt wood. The hole turned out to be a crate, which looked like it was about to fall apart. He could see the remnants of nails that were now only lines of round stains in the corners of the box. The nails that held the crate together had long since rusted away. He reached into the box and felt the water passing through his fingers as he searched. He found nothing. Just as Stone was doing a few feet away, Havok searched the area around the crate with his metal detector, but it maintained its monotonous tempo. All Havok saw were other rectangular holes in the mud along with loose scraps of wood. Someone had already been here, and that someone had removed the crates.

The exhaust bubbles escaping the regulator in his mouth revealed disappointment. He thought about the Russians, but dismissed them as the salvagers of the silver. Instead, another suspect came to mind, one that had to do with the missing research vessel and its crew and students. He looked back at the empty box, and his lips formed into a pleasing smile around the mouthpiece of his regulator. Havok kicked himself away from the scarred mud, locating Stone, who was about three feet away searching a rectangular hole himself. Havok tapped Stone on the shoulder. Stone turned his head toward Havok, and Havok saw exhaust bubbles escape Stone's mouthpiece. He also saw Stone hold something up in his hand. It was a dive knife.

Havok had his suspicions about what was going on. He guessed that the crew and students from the research vessel had stumbled on the silver by accident. He also guessed that the Russians were on this island for something very different, but what could it be? Whatever it was, the arrival of the research vessel probably interfered with what the Russians were doing.

Even though the silver had been salvaged and Havok shivered from the immersion in a dark sea, he enjoyed the thrill of the hunt. It was not money, but an adventure with just one more twist. Instead of reaching a climax by finding the money, then taking an avalanche slide down to a disappointed end, the loss of the money became an extension of foreplay that would balance him on the verge of a mind-numbing climax. Havok knew their next step would be dangerous, but what an extension of the foreplay it would be. Havok also knew that Stone wouldn't be so aroused.

The two signaled each other. The swim back to the beach was not that difficult for Havok, as he had his mind on something else. When able to stand, the men removed their fins and plodded from the water, beginning their journey around the edge of the beach and the jungle.

"Find anything?" Stone asked once they were back under the cover of the foliage.

"One coin, an empty box, and a big-time need to find out what's going on around here," Havok said. "Let's look at that knife."

Stone reached down and pulled it from the cargo pocket on his pants, blade first, and handed it to Havok.

Havok accepted the dive knife and hefted it in his hand before bringing the knife closer to his eyes. Under the growing light of a rising quarter moon, he could see etching on the blade.

15

"'PROP OF HSU,'" HAVOK READ.

"Great. So now we know that the missing research vessel was here," Stone replied as he grabbed his socks and boots from the top of the bush. "What's next?"

"Let's cache our gear by the stream we passed over earlier, then go visit our Russian friends again."

Stone let out an exasperated sigh and flicked his sand-saturated sock at Havok's face. "I don't get paid enough for this shit."

Havok jerked his head to the side to avoid the loose-flying sand, and smirked.

Minutes later, Havok and Stone crept up to the camp's western perimeter, wary of the weak moonlight. The camp was dark and quiet except for occasional muted coughs escaping from behind the rain ponchos covering the door and windows of the barrack-like buildings. Luckily, there were no campfires and everybody seemed to be asleep. However, the faint glow of a light leaked from behind the blanket covering the door leading into the first story of the two-story building at the end of the barracks.

Without a sound, Havok followed the camp's perimeter, with Stone following, to a window at the rear of the two-story building. The blanket was thin enough to allow them to see through it reasonably well. A group of men sat around a table. At the center of the table were two bottles of liquor, some glasses, and a camp lantern. Havok saw the two officers from earlier in the day. He also recognized Kang, but there were two other men he didn't recognize. Except for Kang, they wore BDUs. Both Havok and Stone listened to their slow conversation, as the group spoke English.

"I don't know about you," Anisimova said to the group as he lolled in his chair, swirling the clear, fiery liquor in his glass tumbler, "but I'm a bit tired of drinking coal miner's piss and sweating my balls off." He turned slightly to the man next to him.

This man was cleaning his pistol with a rag. That was, until he heard the comment about the vodka. He slowly put the pistol in its holster and shifted uncomfortably in his camp chair. "Sorry, sir," Petroske replied. He knew he could say nothing else. He had fulfilled the vodka order request that Anisimova had sent him while Petroske was waiting in Singapore for his flight to this island. *It's not my fault that Anisimova drank it all.*

Anisimova sipped his liquor and grimaced at Petroske for another second before turning to the sound of approaching footsteps. Heels scraped against loose gravel outside on the concrete porch.

Havok saw a thinly built, forty-year-old man push aside the blanket draped in the doorway and step into the glow of the lantern. The man, dressed in plain civilian clothing, was the same man Havok had seen standing by the corner of the building off by itself. The man looked nervously at Anisimova.

"Sir, the last of the recovered sarin has been sealed into new containers."

"Are they ready for transport to the salvage ship, Andropov?" Anisimova demanded.

"Y-yes, sir," Andropov stammered. "The canisters are staged in the laboratory here on the island, but the captain of the Stalinetz said it will be at least one more day before the storage room will be complete."

Anisimova grumbled, "I don't know why it takes so long to seal off one room."

"We need to make sure the room is leak-proof on the Stalinetz," answered Colonel Yeshenko, who sipped his drink while sitting with his back to the window Havok was peeking into. "How many Americans are still alive?" he asked, looking straight at Andropov.

Andropov responded succinctly, "Except for the professor at the seaplane camp, they're all dead. The last of them died in the lab about an hour ago. One of them dropped the last canister that needed to be repackaged."

"Will it impede our progress?" Kang said, speaking for the first time. He held a snifter of brandy in his hands.

"No. It will not," Andropov responded, turning to Kang, who sat opposite Yeshenko. "I had Ohmsky and some of the men bury them with the others. Then I gave Ohmsky and his men instructions on how to clean the lab. The sarin is all packaged and staged in the lab, waiting for the ship to be ready."

Anisimova sighed after a sip from his glass and looked at Kang. "That damned ship. Couldn't you have found a better salvage ship for this mission? Why did we have to be saddled with that tub sitting out on the bay?"

Kang returned a haughty look to Anisimova. "The international maritime salvage industry is but a small community, and the sudden disappearance of a modern salvage vessel would have been noticed. Also, even my own government watches me and my fleet. Nobody is going to miss a seventy-year-old ex-Soviet salvage ship. Besides, my country has designs on this island in the near future, and we need to recover both the gold and the sarin before that happens, so we cannot be too particular at this point."

Kang and Anisimova looked at each other. Their faces were determined.

"What about our pilot friend?" Yeshenko asked as he ran his index finger around the rim of his glass. "Do we have any information on him?"

"I received a dossier on him and his friend Stone from Shanghai this evening," Kang replied, taking his attention away from Anisimova. "It seems that the two men in question may prove to be some serious competition for your men, Colonel Yeshenko."

"Not simple barkeeps, that's for sure," Yeshenko mused. "I'm still trying to understand how they were able to sneak that GPS locator back aboard your country's frigate."

Havok turned to Stone and grinned. Stone grinned back.

"Well, they may have tricked us the first few days," Kang answered, ignoring Yeshenko's snarky comment, "but when the frigate started to head southeast toward New Guinea, I knew we were not dealing with simple barkeeps. Also, the fact that they killed their cell phones so my government couldn't track them affirms my thesis. I was able to google quite a bit about their façade," Kang replied with confidence, "but my contacts in Shanghai were able to tap into the American Department of Defense. These simple facts may be self-explanatory, but I ask you to read between the lines. That will tell you more, much more. Havok and Stone are US Navy veterans and graduates from the US Navy's diving school."

"SEALs?" Petroske asked.

"No, Major Petroske," said Kang. "They were salvage divers. They graduated at the top of their class, a fact that means they are true competitors who can demonstrate underwater mastery. Other than being exceptional divers, they were members of their elite Special Boat service, which means they are very capable at getting behind enemy lines. I radioed the Kona Wave, or the Shanghai Mariner, two hours ago. They report they are now searching the Tizard Banks, but have seen no sign of them."

"Could they already be on this island?" Petroske asked.

"There is a good chance of that," Varonov replied, speaking for the first time. "I'll call the men on patrol and warn them."

"The two men," continued Kang, "have operated their dive- and flight-charter business for over three years now. They own a vintage American plane, and, as we have found out, Havok pilots it very well. They also attended the US Army parachute school as part of their training in the Special Boat service. Again, we should not trifle with these men. The captain of the Shanghai Marnier informed me that he left two men at a town called Taytay while he took the ship to search right down the coast. Our two men reportedly ran into Havok and Stone, and Havok killed one of them in simple hand-to-hand combat. The surviving man called the ship for a pickup."

Both Yeshenko and Varonov straightened in their chairs. They looked at each other before Yeshenko put his glass on the table and rubbed his temples. The sudden information that had rolled off Kang's lips so easily struck Yeshenko hard. He had known all of his men for many years, and he loved them as only a commander could. They were brave soldiers and true patriots. After a deep breath, Yeshenko grabbed his glass and tossed the liquor down his throat. Exhaling loudly, he said, "This is now personal."

"Gentlemen," Kang continued, "there is no way that these two men are simple barkeeps. I know people, and I know these men are trained and experienced operatives for the American government."

Kang briefly stopped talking to look at Andropov, who still stood next to the table, then stared across the table at Anisimova and changed the subject. "Andropov told me earlier this afternoon that the amount of sarin recovered and saved is about half of the original cargo. Once everything has been tabulated, I might ask a larger percentage of the bullion to offset my losses."

Anisimova also looked at Andropov and could see beads of sweat form on his forehead. Anisimova returned Kang's stare. "You are a businessman and should be used to taking chances with your profits. We will stick to our original deal. You get to keep all the recovered sarin, and we get to keep all the recovered gold. Besides, according to what you said at the beginning of this operation, the quality of the sarin we're recovering is unsurpassed, even by today's standards, especially now that it is a concentrated form. ISIS, or North Korea, or whoever you sell it to will be willing to pay much more for the product now that we have less than what you tabulated. Even further, replicating the product would be a dangerous and costly effort that would not go unnoticed."

"I am not one to take any losses," Kang replied sternly. He sat straighter in his chair and looked directly into Anisimova's eyes. "Besides, no part of this operation could have been carried out without my financial backing. However, staying with our present situation, I have ordered my friends in Shanghai to monitor all cellular and other forms of communication between our two friends and Scott Kilgore back in Subic. Kilgore's an operative for the US government who appears to have taken an interest in me over the last few days. My employees told me that he has been inquiring into my recent travels and banking transactions. Shanghai is also tracking communication with other known associates back in the States, including that special archaeology outfit in Pensacola. The minute Havok or Stone makes a call or sends an email, we will know about it. Also, my crewmen are monitoring every radio frequency, so if the two men use their boat radio, we will know about it too."

"Does that mean the American government knows of our operation?" asked Yeshenko.

"At least those two men do," Anisimova replied.

"Maybe we shouldn't have tried to shoot him down," Yeshenko suggested.

"That is beside the point, and too late to offer now," Anisimova stated, his eyes leveled at everybody around the table. "Yes, he is aware of our operation. I am sure of that. It is my gift to know people. Havok and Stone are not to be ignored, watched, or dallied with. They are on their way here or already here. We must be ready to capture or kill them. Varonov, keep the patrols going," he commanded before turning to Kang. "The radar on the Stalinetz is malfunctioning again, so since you have now joined us, we need to rely on your electronics and radar if the Americans are still trying to make it here, Kang. If they are already on this island, then we can try to catch them if they try to flee."

"Somehow," Kang reflected, bringing his snifter to his lips, "I doubt Havok has a habit of fleeing."

Ignoring Kang's remark, Anisimova continued, "We cannot afford anybody coming or going." Directing his threatening gaze around the table, he stopped at Andropov and leaned forward in his chair. "Remember Dr. Dubrinsky?"

Poor Dubrinsky, thought Andropov. His mind reeled as his body had convulsed at the ghastly sight of his colleague's dismembered corpse. He also remembered the glee on Kang's bodyguard's face as Chiba wiped blood off the blade of his knife while he stood over the corpse.

"Do not be disapproving," said Anisimova. "We did not kill him. It was Dubrinsky's conscience over the death of that first student that killed him." Anisimova spread his threatening gaze around the table. "Now that they are all dead, it is no longer a concern for any of us."

Anisimova leaned back in his chair and tossed down the last of the harsh spirits in his glass, signaling to the others that the meeting was at an end. Everybody stood and finished their drinks. Andropov was the first out the door, and the others turned to file out behind him. Yeshenko was the last to go through, but Anisimova halted him. "Yeshenko, have the salvage ship captain join me for breakfast. I wish to review our current recovery plans."

Yeshenko nodded as he pushed aside the blanket hanging in the doorway.

Anisimova remained in his chair and refilled his glass from the bottle on the table. Before sitting back in his chair, he turned the lamp out and sipped the liquor in total darkness.

Havok and Stone backed their stiffening bodies away from the camp and crept to the edge of the beach but remained in the tree line. They surveyed the pebble-strewn beach and the Zodiac boat with its bow pushed up onto the beach. Under the light of the moon, Havok could see two men wearing dark coveralls and smoking cigarettes under the boat's canopy. The red glow of their cigarettes showed their Asian faces. Havok could also hear the idling of an outboard engine.

Must be waiting for somebody, Havok thought. Kang?

Just then, Havok heard somebody walking through the trees behind them. He turned to see a flashlight beam guide Kang from the trees onto the beach. Kang approached the boat, and the men in the boat flicked their cigarettes over the side. One man went to the bow and helped Kang step into the boat, while the other man stood behind the helm. Once Kang took a seat in front of the helm, the helmsman backed the boat off the beach into deeper water. Havok watched as the boat turned and headed toward the island in the middle of the bay. The silvery wake of the boat scarred the black sea.

"Did you hear the way they went on about us?" Stone whispered. "According to him, we've got Y chromosomes the size of kielbasa sausages. They got us pegged as some sort of super spies."

"Yeah, we're James Bond, Alan Quatermain, and Rambo all rolled into one," replied Havok. "But enough about us. We need to verify what's under that island out there."

"I'm guessin' one Russian-crewed salvage ship and one Chinese-registered multimillion-dollar yacht tied up next to each other and both anchored over a Japanese submarine filled with gold."

"I'm guessing you're right," Havok said, "along with the fact that Kang arrived sometime just recently, which is why that island looks different from when I flew over it. Why don't you get a better picture of this camp, including that building off by its lonesome? I'll bet that's the shore laboratory where they repackaged the sarin and are now storing it. I'm going out to see what's under that island. We'll rendezvous near the stream."

"Make sure no one is on deck, blowing a fag," cautioned Stone.

"Sure, Mom," replied Havok distantly.

Stone could see that Havok's attention was on the island out in the center of the bay. "What'll we do after that?"

"Then, we go look for a seaplane, rescue the professor that they mentioned, and get the hell off this island."

"Do you know where to look?"

"I think so," said Havok. "Anything else?"

"Yeah, who's Quatermain?"

"Forget it. Let's move."

Stone turned toward the camp behind them, and Havok crept the opposite way, along the edge of the beach. After having listened to the conversation between the Russians and Kang, he took extra care with his steps. He treaded past two Zodiacs loosely covered with some palm fronds. Next to the inflatable boats was a row of fuel drums on a three-foot-high wooden rack. The entire area reeked of fuel and motor oil.

Havok waded into the lapping surf and looked out across the dark bay toward an even darker rock.

He laid his rifle in the knee-deep water and pulled a deflated UDT life vest from his trousers' right cargo pocket. After donning the vest and strapping it in place around his upper torso, he blew into the oral inflation tube several times. Ready for his swim, Havok slung his rifle over his head, letting the weapon rest against his back with the barrel pointing down. For a second time that night, Havok let the black sea swallow him. Only his head and the stock of his rifle remained above the surface.

Although he was wearing boots and no fins, Havok glided toward the dark island three hundred yards ahead, and soon, the summit of the island towered above him. He reached out and touched the side of the island. His waterlogged fingers felt cloth. With his face only inches from the side of the island, he discovered it was camouflage netting with leaf-like material added to give it a solid appearance. He felt underwater and found a weighted boom that held the net down. Havok pushed himself under the boom, and remembering Stone's warning about late-night smokers, rose slowly on the other side. For a long minute, he looked and listened, and when he was sure he was alone, he reached out and touched the side of a ship, which rose away from him into a veil of darkness. Little of the moon's light penetrated the camouflage netting. He slid aft, along the barnacle-encrusted hull, trying to find a ladder or rope, anything to help him get on deck. Near the stern, he came across a rope ladder, with wooden rungs, dangling from the deck. He tugged at it before hauling himself from the water. Seawater cascaded off his body. The sound of the running water alarmed him, so he hung on to the rungs, allowing the water to fall off his body and clothing, before continuing. His arms strained as he pulled his body, heavy with wet clothing and a rifle, up the ladder. His hands were numb from the long immersion, and he had a difficult time grabbing the narrow wooden rungs of the rope ladder. Finally, when his head was level with the waist-high bulwark, he waited and looked to see if anybody was on deck. He heard no voices and saw no ends of lit cigarettes, but he did see slivers of light escaping from behind the curtains and blinds covering the windows on the vessel on the other side of the salvage ship.

Kang's yacht.

Havok slid over the curved bulwark and squatted on the deck. He pulled his rifle over his shoulders. Seeing nothing, he grabbed the inflation tube of his vest and started to let out air as quietly as possible.

Once the vest was deflated, he stepped carefully as he inspected the area. He saw that he was standing on the open deck of some sort of salvage vessel. The tiny slivers of light leaking from behind the curtains and blinds on Kang's yacht helped his night vision. Havok walked forward along the port side until he came to an angled ladder that led up to the next level. He made a step closer to the ladder, but stopped as his booted foot kicked a piece of loose metal on deck. Havok froze. The metallic clang rang loud in the still night air. He waited for blinding lights followed by gunshots. When no slugs ripped through his body, he knelt to inspect the metal objects. He felt pieces of round stock, each about the size of his thumb.

Metal left over from welding, Havok thought.

Carefully, he stepped over the scraps, up the ladder, and stopped when his head was level with the next deck of the salvage ship. His eyes roamed the deck in front of him while he pressed the stock of his rifle against his shoulder. The barrel of his weapon sniffed for unseen targets in front of him. To his left, out of the corner of his eyes, he could see an occasional dim light escape from the closed curtains of Kang's yacht. He wondered if Xian was aboard.

All seemed clear, so he took the last few steps of the ladder and moved forward while keeping an eye on Kang's yacht. Hunched over, he moved cautiously until he rounded the forward corner of the superstructure. There it was: a mounted gun on the small deck space just forward and under the bridge of the ship. Havok's assessment about the weapon that had been used to try to shoot him down was correct. There, on the deck, where perhaps a crane had once been, was a swivel-mounted twin-barreled 20 mm cannon with an ammo can, holding perhaps a hundred belted rounds of ammunition, hanging from the breech of each barrel. Havok's assessment about the gunners' failing to lead his airplane when they tried to shoot him down appeared to also be correct. This was an auxiliary salvage ship, not a combat vessel; therefore, the gun was an addition and the crew had probably not received appropriate training in how to use it against flying aircraft.

He stepped past the mount and rounded the front of the superstructure, walking aft along the starboard side until he came to a ladder that led up to the pilothouse level. He climbed until his head was deck level. He could hear the hum of a generator escape from the smokestack to his left. In front of the smokestack, he could see the pilothouse. Taking a chance, he stepped up the last of the steps and crept low alongside the smokestack, stopping just behind the open door of the pilothouse. The muted light from a radar monitor revealed two men. One of them stood in front of the console, slapped the side of the radar monitor, and cursed in Russian. Another man sat at a table near the chart table and sipped from the ceramic mug in his hand. After two more hard slaps from the standing man, the screen brightened and the man turned to his companion. The man with the mug lowered it from his lips and offered it to his companion.

Havok observed the men for a few more minutes, until he decided he had a good idea of the situation. The Russians had a salvage ship anchored above a wreck, and some of the equipment on board the salvage ship was not quite up to standards. In addition, Kang had just joined the Russians, and his yacht was anchored next to the Russian ship. Lastly, the university research vessel had been reconfigured and would more than likely arrive at this island in a couple of days. Ashore, the sarin was ready for shipment, and the last surviving person from the university research ship needed rescue.

He kept low and alert on his way back to the fantail, where he placed his rifle back over his shoulder, reinflated his vest, and slipped over the starboard side into cold water to commence his swim toward the shore to meet Stone by the stream.

16

<hr>

TERUMBU ISLAND, LATE JULY

THE SWIM BACK TO THE BEACH WAS ARDUOUS; HOWEVER, HAVOK PUSHED ASIDE THE EXHAUSTION, AND THOUGHT. His brain, acting like an old tape recorder, played back everything that had occurred in the last few hours, while his body mechanically pulled him to an unseen shore.

Before he knew it, his hands scraped against a rock, and he could hear the slow cadence of water as it lapped against smooth sand, then silently crackled in its retreat. He searched the beach to see if an enemy patrol was waiting for him. All he saw was unruffled sand that glistened like newly fallen snow under the light of the now-uncovered moon. He lowered his feet and pulled the rifle slung across his back over his head. He held the M14 in front of him and waded toward the stream that cut through the expanse of clean, undisturbed sand. The moonlight seemed as bright as the sun's rays, beaming down, exposing him.

Havok remained hunched as he walked upstream and into the jungle. He was about to stand up when he heard a noise that was foreign to the jungle. It was a cough, soft and slight, but still a cough. Quickly but smoothly, he lay facedown in the bed of the flowing stream, with his rifle next to him. With running water splashing against his face, he waited. A few seconds went by before he started to hear mushy footsteps in the jungle mud somewhere off to his left. Hoping he would be mistaken for a rock in the center of the stream, he remained where he was, with his hand under his chest to hide the luminescent dial of his watch. The sound of footsteps turned into a line of camouflaged limbs that filed past him two yards away. The patrol seemed to take forever to pass. Although it seemed like a whole army, he counted only six pairs of legs.

Havok waited a full two minutes after the last man passed, and when he was sure there were no stragglers, he relaxed and moved his hand out from under his chest. The glowing hands of his watch showed it was two fifty a.m. He thought of trailing the patrol in case they ran into Stone, but then thought better of it. He knew Stone, and the smartest thing for him to do was to rest and wait for his friend.

Havok left the stream and crawled up to a group of ferns that crowded the bank. He sat there and shivered, listening to the quiet forest around him. Just after three a.m., a splashing din obliterated the tranquil silence. He craned his head above the broad leaves and looked upstream. A figure was pushing itself to its feet in the shallow stream. Havok sprang from cover and leapt straight at the shadow, landing atop the body and roughly clamping his hand over the man's mouth. He whispered harshly, "Will you shut up, you hemorrhoid! You're waking up the neighborhood."

Stone's body went limp, and Havok removed his hand from his mouth.

"A patrol came by a few minutes ago," Havok whispered into his friend's ear, "and they might head back this way."

"I know," retorted Stone quietly. "I followed them. Now get off me. The water's cold."

Havok helped his friend up, and together they moved several yards farther inland to talk and share a canteen of water.

"Did you get the layout of the camp?" Havok asked.

"Sure did," Stone answered, "including the lab. It was big enough to be a storage building and stout enough to be a typhoon shelter. I'm sure it was both. There's a stack of sealed metal boxes in the middle of the room, with their lids screwed on. There's also quite a few empty containers stacked on a workbench. They're like metal Nalgene water bottles. I'll bet the boxes are full of those things." He paused to take a gulp of the warm canteen water, then asked, "What the hell is sarin, anyhow?"

"The only thing I know," Havok said quietly while still looking around them, "is that it's a man-made nerve agent first manufactured during World War II by both the Japanese and the Germans, and it's deadly. A drop the size of a pinhead can kill anybody standing within feet of it."

"What's next?" Stone asked solemnly.

"Next," Havok answered, "we go find ourselves a seaplane and a professor, and make plans for stealing both the sarin and the professor."

The men stood, gathered their dive gear, and started to make their way back to their boat. By the time the tired pair reached the southern shore of the smaller bay, located halfway between the larger bay and the cove hiding their boat, a gray dawn had replaced the cover of night. They stopped where the jungle gave way to the confused mass of mangrove roots bordering the bay. Havok sniffed the air. A slight easterly breeze brought with it just a hint of campfire smoke. Havok knew they were dangerously exhausted, and with daylight approaching, walking around the island became even more risky. But, as tired as he was, Havok could not sleep without knowing all the variables. The men at the camp last night had said the sarin was almost ready for shipment, and he knew the Russians and Kang could only spend so much time on this island before being found out.

Twenty minutes later, the two men lay prone on the damp jungle floor, observing a different camp from the one they had watched just hours ago. This camp was much smaller than the other one had been and not as shipshape. Empty bottles, opened tin cans, food wrappers, and other trash littered the bare ground, and all but one of the four army tents had wet laundry hanging from the angled anchoring ropes. One man dressed in flight coveralls, a bit paunchy, stood over a dying fire, poking it with a stick. Havok quickly concluded that the personnel here were not like the professionals at the other camp, and to confirm his assumption, other men began to exit the sagging tents dressed in wrinkled green flight coveralls. These men were aviators, not soldiers.

Across from the tents was a large two-engine seaplane painted a mottled yellow-brown. Camouflage netting was draped over the huge airplane and hung down from the wings. The paint job and the netting effectively disguised it from any great distance. Havok recognized the seaplane as a variant of the Russian-made Beriev multipurpose amphibious plane complete with a high-wing and T-tail–engine configuration mounted on a monohull fuselage. The starboard wing of the airplane extended over the ground and into the jungle. Under the wing, Havok could see what looked like a portable workbench with drawers and a large vise mounted to its flat surface. A few feet away, near a thicket of bamboo, an olive-drab rain poncho covered something.

The sun broke free of the horizon's hold and turned a gray dawn into a brilliant blue sunlit sky, signaling the remainder of the camp's residents to leave their tents. As men left the tents, they converged on the man at the fire, who got the fire going again and was preparing a large pot of tea. Most of the aviators were trim, but not as physically fit as the Russians at the other camp. They talked quietly, smoked cigarettes, and joked occasionally while watching the man prepare their tea.

After a few minutes, the paunchy fellow turned his head toward the heap under the wing and said something to his companions. They responded with an outburst of laughter. He stepped jauntily toward the covered pile with a smirk on his face, while his comrades catcalled behind him. As the paunchy man bent down to remove the poncho, a figure underneath it sprang up and launched a punch that landed squarely in the man's crotch. The man howled and doubled over in pain, grabbing at his genitals. The figure on the ground slapped the man's cheek with an open right hand. The sharp crack of the slap echoed into the jungle, and the luckless man hobbled back to a group of howling spectators.

The figure maintained a defensive stance for a minute longer, then sat down on the raincoat. Havok saw that it was a woman. Her hair, though only shoulder length, was matted and uncombed, and she wore only a pair of gym shorts and a tank top. She drew her legs up against her chest and swiveled around on her butt, turning away from her crowd of tormentors and facing the nearby jungle.

"She must be Professor Bonne-Bouche," Havok whispered to Stone without looking at him.

"I've never met a professor with balls like that before," Stone said.

"You've never met a professor period."

Stone ignored the remark, and they turned their attention back to the camp. Havok felt sorry for the woman. Please hold on for just one more day, he begged her silently.

A nudge in the rib cage grabbed his attention away from the woman.

"Time for an Irish goodbye," Stone said. "We'll come back for her tonight."

Not ready to leave yet, Havok turned to his friend. "Hold on, I'm going down to say hi."

Before Stone could protest, Havok slipped the heavy dive gear off his back and disappeared into the surrounding trees.

As Havok circled around the eastern end of the camp, he kept his eyes on the woman. He noticed that under the dirt was the face of a beautiful woman. Though sitting on her haunches, she looked like she would stand just over five feet tall. Other than the gym shorts and tank top, both of which were black with grime, she wore only a pair of leg irons clamped around her dirt-covered ankles. The strain of captivity and being forced to sleep on the ground like a mongrel dog had etched deep lines into her tired face. Still, he could not help but look into her face and gaze at the native beauty that the filth failed to disguise. He admired her beauty and her defiance, both of which probably bugged the hell out of her captors.

But Havok also knew it couldn't last forever. He thought about recent events and assumed that she had been held captive for about two weeks now. Lost hopes would consume her bravery, eventually forcing her to give in to her tormentors and to death. Separating her from her companions, ill feeding her, and forcing her to sleep on the damp ground were all tools used by experts to break their victims' spirits.

***

Pilar Bonne-Bouche sat shivering on the hard ground. Even though it was not cold, the little food she had received reduced the ability for her body to warm itself. Her petite body had long ago burned up what fat reserves it had to begin with. Drained of energy, she found it difficult to hold her head up or even concentrate, and that little show she had just put on for her captors had almost killed her. Sitting on the foul poncho with her tired arms wrapped around her dirty, folded legs, she dared not show them her weakness or her misery. Inside, though, she knew the truth. She was weak, scared, lonely, and had no way of knowing if any of her students were alive or dead.

Desperately she longed for the touch of a friendly soul and to be held in the strong arms of a kind human. Barely able to hold back tears of self-pity, she thought of her childhood and her murdered father, a kind and innocent scientist who had been killed in a landslide caused by the greed of a ruthless mining company owner. The owner she had sought was found on this very island. She remembered the years of following her father around the Pacific, living life out of a backpack, and finally taking his position at the university after his murder. Sadly, she thought now, she would give it all up—the books, her work, the revenge for her father's murder—just for the garment of humanity to envelope her and take her from this evil place.

As she grew ever more despondent, a slight movement just within her peripheral vision seized her attention. She turned her head. Her eyes widened, and the grit under her heavy eyelids scoured her eyeballs painfully. A face emerged from the foliage four feet from her. The face was streaked with dirt and sweat, and an enormous mustache held tiny bits of grass. His eyes were a welcome sight, though. They were bloodshot and raw, but those large browns twinkled and offered the comfort and peace she most desperately needed.

Silently, the apparition spoke to her. She watched the firm lips form the words "Don't worry. Help is here."

Just as quickly as the face had appeared, it melted back into the jungle, leaving Pilar wondering if she had just looked death in the face. She stared blankly for a moment and then realized that the face was not one of death but of life. She lay on her side, wrapped herself in the pungent poncho, and slipped into a deep sleep, a weak smile on her weary face.

****

It was miserably humid by the time Havok and Stone reached the Outfit, and they sweated profusely under the load and the dense canopy that trapped the heat and humidity. Both were thirsty and tired, and their physical condition ordered them to go straight to their boat, but they ignored that order. Instead, they skirted the edge of the small cove, stopping and listening every few feet, until they reached the bush in which Manny was hiding.

"Manny," Havok whispered loudly.

The old Filipino slowly stood and simply stated, "We had company."

Havok and Stone dropped their loads where they stood. Havok said, "Really?"

"Yes," Manny said, turning back to the bush. "Boss, I was sitting down there inside the plant, and a face looked down at me."

The broad-leaved ferns were a little over four feet tall. Havok stepped inside the circle of plants and saw flattened vegetation where Manny had been sitting. Meanwhile, Stone pointed his weapon in front of him and began to search the nearby jungle.

"It was quiet all night. Didn't even hear any animals. I was not sure what time because I was tired and fell asleep, but something woke me up. Maybe a sound. I do not know. I opened my eyes and looked up. His face was staring down at me."

"What'd he look like?" Havok asked.

"He was old with many wrinkles," Manny explained. "His hair was long and gray, and he had a skinny beard, a begote. He looked Asian."

"Did he say anything?" Havok asked.

"No," Manny responded, shaking his head. "He just give me the evil eye, the bad eye."

Havok stood and joined Manny out in front of the bush. He inspected the ground under their feet, looking for several moments before giving up. The area was carpeted with a bright green plant Havok knew as sleeping grass, which was a kind of Venus flytrap. The blades would close when they sensed pressure, like that of a landing insect or foot-steps, then reopen after a few minutes. Many of the blades remained closed because of the three men walking around.

"Don't worry," Havok said. "He's not gonna hurt us. Get us something to eat, then get some sleep. I'll take the first watch."

"Do you know who he is?" asked Stone, still panning the muzzle of his weapon in front of him.

Havok replied, "I think I'm too tired to worry about some old Japanese guy."

"What do you mean, 'some old Japanese guy'?" Manny asked.

"Just a hunch, really," Havok said with a tired sigh.

"He's not part of the Extreme Team over at Cobra Headquarters?" Stone asked.

"If he was," Havok said, "he would have jumped Manny or waited to ambush us."

"I'll buy that," Stone said, accepting his friend's explanation about their visitor, "but how did you figure him for a son of Nippon?"

Havok repeated Manny's description, including the evil eye, which matched the description that Wheatley had given him about his father's Japanese prison guard back in the war and the officer's war wounds he had suffered to his face.

Stone accepted Havok's theory. "From what you say, the man has to be at least a hundred years old. How's it he gets around so easily?"

"I don't know. Maybe the island lifestyle agrees with him. It could also be the water," Havok surmised.

Stone ticked his head to the side slightly. "So what's our next step?"

"Manny's making us something to eat, so get our dive gear stowed. Let's chow down and you two get some sleep. I'll wake you around noon."

"You know something?" Stone said dolefully as he turned to board their boat. "With you around, it's always the same thing: geologists in distress, Russian musclemen chopping off heads, and Japanese hermits. I say, boy, you had better get a life."

Havok chuckled and turned for the group of ferns, leaving his friend to tend to the dive gear. He sat down on the hard, wet ground and immediately regretted it, as his body started to stiffen. His legs were sore from the miles walked and swam, and his shoulders ached from the massive load they had carried. Although racked with pain, exhaustion, hunger, and thirst, he struggled to remain alert enough to stand guard.

Havok waited for Manny to bring him something to eat, and he didn't have to wait long.

Manny hurriedly pulled himself up the line from the boat with a yellow net bag dangling from his belt. He appeared to be excited.

"Look what I found." Manny plopped the bag on the ground in front of Havok. Without waiting for an answer, he squatted and pulled the drawstring apart.

Havok looked into the net bag while pulling the coin he had found on the dive last night from his shirt pocket. He estimated it contained about a hundred blackened silver pesos. He bent to select one of them and compared it to the one he'd pulled from his shirt pocket.

"I found this too," Manny said, handing a folded piece of paper to Havok.

The white sheet of paper looked like it had come from the notepad on their chart table. Havok unfolded the paper and read the few English words.

"What does it say?" asked Manny.

"'Take the money. Leave my home. The other white men will kill you.'"

"That's it!" Stone said angrily.

Havok looked up from the note to see Stone joining them.

Stone looked into the bag. "Listen, that thieving filcher took a dive bag, a can of coffee grounds, a notebook, a carton of cigarettes, and two bottles of scotch, and that"—he kicked the dive bag scornfully—"is a pretty paltry sum for the smokes and the booze. There isn't a store within a hundred miles of here. What are we going to drink when the beer runs out?"

Havok had long ago stopped wondering about Stone's inconsistencies, and answered, "Don't worry about the liquor or smokes. By this time tomorrow, we'll be on our way out of here, and with an extra mouth to feed."

Stone stood with his hands on his hips, seething over the theft. "Has that plan of yours come together yet?"

"Yeah." Havok paused. "But in the meantime, I'll keep guard and you guys get all the food and sleep you can. Again, I'll wake you around noon, Stone."

Obediently, Manny picked up the bag, and both he and Stone turned to make their way back to the boat for food and sleep. In a few minutes, Manny returned with a Tupperware container filled with two scoops of cold rice, canned sardines in mustard sauce, and a warm Coke. Havok accepted the bland food and selected a spot about forty yards away from Manny's guard post. He sat down and shoveled the food into his mouth with a plastic fork while keeping a sharp lookout.

The minutes ticked by painfully slowly. The food had filled his shriveled stomach and, combined with the mounting heat, aggravated the agonizingly slow passage of time. Every second seemed to last a minute. Finally, the hands on his watch struck noon, signaling the end of his watch. He stood and his thighs screamed in protest, barely allowing him to walk stiffly back to the boat. His fatigues seemed to have formed their own exoskeleton, as the dried, salt-encrusted material crackled when he moved.

It had been a quiet watch, and Havok hoped it would remain that way so he could get some sleep. He reached the embankment, slung his weapon over his head, jumped for the monkey line, and pulled himself to his floating home. Stepping into the pilothouse, he placed his pistol, rifle, and web gear on the chart table before going down the narrow ladder into the dark forward cabin. Stone was sleeping on the port bunk with his submachine gun in the crook of his bent arm. He still wore the filthy fatigues from the night before. Manny was in the starboard bunk.

"Stone, it's time," Havok said, roughly shaking his shoulder.

Stone's eyes snapped open, and he tightened his grip on his weapon, but once he recognized Havok, he closed them. After a couple of seconds, he swung his feet off the mattress and slowly sat up, grimacing. He let the weapon rest in his lap while he placed his face into cupped hands massaging his eyeballs. "Anything happening?"

"No, all quiet."

"Good," Stone said with his face in his hands, muffling his voice. "Do you have a plan?"

Havok quickly answered, "Whatever we do will tell our friends we're here. And don't forget there's another boatload of Russians with more hostages out there. Sooner or later, if we don't do anything, they are going to figure out where we ain't. So our first move has to be smart. It's got to give us the upper hand. And it's got to happen tonight."

Stone nodded his tired head and stood. "Here, have a piece of bunk."

Havok sat on the soggy mattress. "Give me about four hours of sack time, and then have Manny relieve you so we can get things moving."

The exhausted men switched places, and as Havok's head sank toward oblivion, he asked himself one question: Where did the Japanese man get those pesos?

17

TERUMBU ISLAND, LATE JULY

HAVOK FELT A HAND YANKING HIM FROM THE DEPTHS OF AN ABYSSAL SLUMBER. When he reached the surface of consciousness, he tried to open his eyes but found they were glued shut. While he had slept, his tear ducts had secreted fluid to flush his eyes of dirt and dried salt, leaving a thick, sticky mucus, He forced his eyes open with his fingers. Finally able to see, he focused on Manny, who was standing over him with a mug.

"Here," Manny said quietly. "It's cold, but it's still coffee. I'm going to relieve Pete. It's late afternoon."

Havok accepted the mug before Manny stepped up the short ladder and out of the forward cabin, leaving him alone. Havok pushed himself upright and sat in a stupor. It took a few minutes, along with a cup of instant coffee, to clear his fuzzy brain. As he recovered, he raised his wrist so he could look at his watch, and smelled his armpit and his clothing.

After draining the cup, he unbuttoned his clothing and slid them off as he stood, letting them drop to the deck. Kicking the clothes out of the way, he squatted. Tugging at the mother-of-pearl knobs on the drawer under the bunk, he pulled out the drawer and grabbed a set of clean clothes and a pair of clean socks. After changing, Havok put on his boots and stepped up into the pilothouse. The little late-afternoon sunlight the jungle canopy and the netting allowed in blinded him. After a minute of letting his eyes adjust to the light, he grabbed his weapons and web gear off the chart table. With everything he needed, he approached the monkey line, but stood aside as Stone slid onto the deck.

"Go ahead and get three or four empty dive or duffel bags ready," Havok ordered. "Whatever you think will be necessary to carry the individual sarin bottles. And grab a couple of entrenching tools."

"All right," Stone answered. "But where are you going?"

"Once we snatch the sarin," Havok replied, "we're gonna have to move fast. I'm gonna see if I can find a spot to hide the sarin, as carrying it with us ain't an option. You know, in case we get caught. Also, I don't feel comfortable with dropping them off at sea, as they might not sink."

"They've invented things called lead weights," Stone responded.

"They've also developed things called leaks and currents," Havok said. "If I can find a spot good enough to hide the sarin long enough for us to get the professor, and away from here long enough to call Scott, then we're good. Once Kang and the Russians know what we've done, they'll take what they have and split as quick as they can."

Stone sighed. "Go ahead, but don't take too long."

Havok answered with a silent nod and stepped past Stone, grabbing for the monkey line. He pulled himself ashore and, once on land, walked to the stream that emptied into the cove. As he stepped into the ankle-deep water, he pointed the muzzle of his M14 in front of him.

For the next three hundred yards, he followed the two-foot-wide stream through lush undergrowth. Alongside the stream, the forest grew thickly. Combined with the thick canopy overhead, this growth cut visibility to no more than three feet into the jungle. Havok came to a small clearing cut in half by the stream. A small amount of sunlight entered through the thinning canopy above. On either side of the moving water, he saw an inviting green carpet of grass covering the open ground. Opposite him was a four-foot-high limestone outcropping over which the water had been spilling for millennia.

Havok walked up to the small pool of water and inspected the area for any possible hiding spot. He looked down at the grass on the sides of the stream and froze. Four feet away was a small patch of sleeping grass, with the leaves closed. He knelt to inspect the leaves. They were empty of trapped prey. Somebody had walked through only minutes before. Havok stood and quickly stepped into the forest to wait and think. He could go back to the boat, or he could wait here for the person or persons to return. After all, it wouldn't be good to run into anybody. Deciding on the latter, Havok selected a couple of broad banana leaves to sit on and waited.

He didn't have to wait long before a man entered the clearing.

The aged Asian man walked quickly and had a concerned look on his face. He wore a short-sleeved button-up shirt that looked like it might have been popular during the early sixties, and although it was old and threadbare, the shirt still looked clean and well taken care of. His white gym shorts were about thirty-five years younger and had the words "HSU Athletic Dept." embossed on the left thigh. He wore a broad-brimmed straw hat.

The old man came from the direction of the boat, but instead of walking up the stream like Havok had done, he emerged from the jungle and stepped across the small clearing and across the stream before disappearing into the jungle on the other side. Intrigued, Havok decided to follow him.

The man's walking had been sure and swift, indicating that he knew the island well. Havok followed well behind him, being careful not to be spotted by the old man or to make any noise. After Havok had been trailing the man for about twenty minutes, the terrain started to slope upward. The angle of the terrain made it difficult to keep an eye on the old man, and within minutes, he lost sight of his quarry. Taking a chance, Havok stood on a boulder to catch a glimpse of the old man, who pushed his way through a solid barrier of hedges that walled off the entrance to the ravine.

As Havok stepped off the rock and put his weight onto a mat of rotting vegetation, the ground gave way. Havok's chest struck a rocky edge, and he let go of his rifle as his arms shot out in front of him. His fingers hooked a dangling tree root that poked through the cracks in the rocks, and the sudden halt wrenched his shoulder. Hanging by three fingers and with his head below the opening in the ground, he waited for the stormy waves of agony surging through his arm and chest to subside, while subconsciously ticking off the seconds it took the M14 to hit bottom. He had counted to five when he heard the echoing crack of his rifle striking a rock somewhere beneath him. Five seconds times thirty-two feet a second meant there was nothing between his hand and his death except 160 feet of air.

"Oh fuck me!" Havok blurted.

After the wrenching pain had ebbed, he grabbed the root with his free arm before carefully pulling himself up and over the edge. He rolled away from the hole and, still lying on the ground, looked back at what had almost taken his life. The opening he had fallen into was about three feet wide with a rocky edge or lip on two sides. He looked under the matting of vegetation and saw that it covered some sort of fissure in the ground. He could only imagine how long this crack ran. As he looked into the black depths, an idea came to mind.

Havok filed that idea away as another idea entered his mind. He stood and headed toward the solid wall of hedges that the old man had entered, massaging his throbbing arm as he did so. But as Havok approached the wall of hedges, the old man came back out. Havok rolled behind a moss-covered rock just in time to avoid detection. The old man walked back down the center of the wide ravine until he was about halfway down the slope. Then he turned in the direction of the Russian main camp.

After Havok saw the man disappear into the jungle, he stepped through the wall of hedges to the other side. What lay before him put the rest of the island to shame. The ever-present canopy covered a clearing about an acre in size. Outside the barrier was the wild jungle. Inside this barrier was a fabricated heaven.

In the center stood a peaked hut that was carefully constructed of materials culled from the island's forests and beaches. Spreading out from the hut was a beautiful green lawn of patiently manicured grass. Opposite Havok, on the other side of the hut, was a well-maintained garden. Throughout the clearing were numerous plants, fruit trees, and flowers. There were also numerous rock formations, which looked like they were used to funnel rainwater to a rock-lined pond teeming with freshwater shrimp. All was blessed by the sweet kiss of sunlight that filtered through the thinning canopy above.

Havok approached the structure and ducked through an open doorway into the cool interior of the hut. He wasted no time, going straight to the back wall where a full bookshelf stood next to a table. On top of the table was a simple candle and holder, an open pack of Marlboros, a bottle of scotch, and a notebook and pen, all of which had been pilfered from the Outfit.

It looks like he was able to put quite a dent in the bottle's contents in the last few hours, Havok mused.

The bookshelf contained a mixture of notebooks, sketchpads, rough reams of paper, and even a worn copy of the April 1965 edition of Playboy. Havok remembered Wheatley's description of his father's captor and the story behind his father's captivity.

The Japanese man must have come back for the silver, thought Havok. But why is he still here, on this island?

Havok studied the bookshelf and looked at the notebook on the table. He figured the best place to start was the present, so he flipped open the notebook on the table and saw today's date at the top of the page. It was written in Japanese, and there was a brief entry under it. Able to read Japanese to some degree, he was able to see that the old man was quite concerned about the presence of everybody else on the island. He looked up at the items on the bookshelf.

He thought it best to start from the beginning, so he selected a worn, old-looking notepad on the far left of the top shelf. The first yellowed page was dated June 26, 1954. Havok scanned the pages of this notepad and read about the man's experiences just after the end of WWII. Once Havok finished with that notepad, he followed up with subsequent pads and books on the shelf, going forward in time chronologically.

A changing person seemed to roll off these pages as time went by. In the first volume, he saw a man who was full of anger and hate, a man who had come here to retrieve the silver so that he could buy his way into the Japanese mafia, the yakuza. His idea was to make enough money from the yakuza to fund Japanese anti-American groups and overthrow the American occupation of Japan. Then Havok read of the reason for the old man having been stranded on the island and an account of his following years. Now, the old man's only concern was how to rid his island home of vile pests. This was a man who wanted only to be left alone with his thoughts and his garden. The only thing Havok could figure out was that over the years isolation had calmed a savage beast. He pulled the last notebook from the lower-right corner of the bookshelf and saw that the pages and entries were dated within the last few months.

Finally, Havok took a moment to look at his watch. He hadn't realized how long he had been there: over thirty minutes now. Havok placed the pad back on the shelf and turned toward the open door. He stopped and thought about leaving a note behind, asking for a meeting, but thought better of it. If the old man found out his self-made heaven had been violated, any sort of fledgling trust between the two might be destroyed. Instead, he looked around to make sure everything was in the same place it had been before he entered the hut.

The sun was setting as Havok retraced his route to the Outfit. He had just crossed the stream with the little pond and waterfall when he heard a noise. Standing behind a tree, he waited, and after a minute, he saw Stone, with his MP5, walking toward him. Havok stepped out from behind the tree. "Is there any reason why you can't stop making any noise?"

Stone immediately pointed his weapon toward Havok, but then pointed the barrel to the ground. "Where ya been? Hooking up with that Chinese version of Sharon Stone?" he asked, ignoring Havok's sarcasm.

"No such luck. Instead, I fell into a hundred-foot-plus-deep hole in the ground and found out about our Asian visitor."

"Oh, is that all?" Stone grinned. "And to think I was worried." He nodded behind him. "Come on. Manny's got dinner waiting for us, and you can fill us in on your plan while we eat."

Havok followed him back to the Outfit. It had turned dark by the time they arrived back at the boat. The two men climbed aboard and met Manny in the pilothouse.

The men ate cold rice and canned corned-beef hash in the darkness of the salon behind the pilothouse as Havok told his companions about their visitor.

"His name is Hirosaki," Havok said between bites. "At the end of World War II, he was stationed in Indochina, where he stood trial for war crimes. The British sentenced him to prison for nine years. Apparently, they couldn't prove murder for the beheading of Wheatley's mates or any other POWs. They got him on cruelty charges instead. In 1954 Hirosaki was repatriated back to Japan. It turns out the American who knew about the silver tried to bribe Hirosaki during the war. That's why Hirosaki tried to have everybody associated with him killed, including Wheatley's father. Anyway, Hirosaki kept the news of the pesos to himself throughout the entire war and while he was in prison. The year he got out of prison back in Japan, he was able to round up some sort of boat and crew, and came here to recover the treasure, planning to use it to join up with some other disgruntled soldiers back in Japan. He also needed the money to buy his way into the yakuza, which started out as a simple black-market organization but morphed into something bigger. There was a lot of underground resurgent movement back then. Its purpose was to get rid of the MacArthur government and reestablish the old military regime. They arrived here on June 26, 1954, and anchored out. On the third day, he and his crew discovered the silver. The diver that found the loot surfaced, waving her arms and yelling to get everybody's attention."

"Her?" asked Stone.

"Back then, scuba was still in its infancy, so they used female pearl divers. Anyway, Hirosaki was alone on the beach, sketching flowers, when he heard the diver yell. He was looking at the swimmer, just like everybody else was, which was why no one spotted the pirate junket sneaking into the bay behind them until it was too late. According to Hirosaki's diary, it took only several minutes for the pirates to board the Japanese ship and capture the entire crew. Hirosaki said he watched from shore while all the males were murdered and their bodies tossed overboard. The pirates spent all night ravaging the females, the liquor, and the foodstuffs. By morning, they finished off the female divers and the booze; then they took the ship, leaving Hirosaki alone on the island."

"That's pretty ironic," Stone said.

"How's that?"

"If the pirates had waited a few more hours for the divers to recover the coins, they would've been a whole lot richer."

"What's even more ironic," added Havok, "is Hirosaki. He came here full of hate and revenge, but got stranded with only a sketchpad, a pencil, and the shirt on his back. Forced to seek out a living, he forgot about prejudice. For him, a simple mango, the medicinal benefits of the aloe plant, or the basic palm frond meant more than a rifle or status. Now, his hard work means he has no wants, no worries, and no problems, which may be why he's pretty spry for someone who must be at least a hundred years old. You know, that peace-of-mind sort of thing."

Havok took another forkful of hash before continuing. "Out here, a human is no better off that a mouse or lizard. They all have to struggle equally to survive and not be eaten."

"Now that we know all about Hirosaki," Stone asked, "what about the goon squad?"

"Over the years, the island did have visitors, but only that—visitors. But about three months ago, a seaplane began flying over the island once a week for several weeks. Then, a little less than a month ago, the seaplane landed to leave behind a dozen soldiers to set up camp—that old Philippine naval barracks they're at now. About a week after the seaplane dropped off the soldiers, a Russian ship with more sailors and soldiers came in and dropped anchor. The soldiers came ashore and disguised the ship to make it look like an island, and the seaplane made its home where it's now anchored, along the southern shore of the small bay between us and the larger bay. Hirosaki's pretty upset about the airplane because they run the engines now and then and it scares the hell out of his flowers. They're not blooming like they used to. Also, the sailors on the ship anchored out in the middle of the bay and began diving operations. This made him happy. Figured if they got what they came for, they would leave."

"But he wasn't that lucky," Stone said after swallowing a bite of rice.

"That's right. Two of their divers died after they had recovered only a few canisters. Hirosaki saw the Russians bury them ashore. That put a screeching halt to everything."

"Until the Kona Wave arrived, right, boss?" offered Manny.

"The Kona Wave showed up and anchored over the silver cache. Hirosaki watched the students diving, swimming, and taking soil and rock samples before they inadvertently found the silver themselves. The students recovered the pesos, and that night, the Russians who were hiding ashore snuck out and captured them. The Russians took the pesos, painted and renamed the Kona Wave, and then made the students dive for the sarin canisters."

The three men fell silent, lost in thought. Finally, Havok looked up at his two friends. "I have a plan, if you want to listen to it."

Stone and Manny acknowledged with nods.

"We'll sneak into that lab building at the Russian camp and stuff as many sarin containers as we can into dive and duffel bags, then beat feet to that crack in the ground I fell through." Havok looked at Stone. "Did you bring climbing gear like I suggested?"

"Sure did," Stone answered.

"Good." Havok scooped the last forkful of rice and hash off the paper plate. "Once we hide the sarin in that underground whatever-it-is, we'll snatch up the professor on our way back to here and get as far away from this island as we can. By daybreak, we should be in a good enough position to call Scott."

***

By ten p.m. the three men stood at the edge of the crevice that had almost taken Havok's life. They peered into the hidden depths using a red-lensed flashlight held by Stone, but saw nothing but blackness.

Havok stuffed his pistol into his waist and pulled a short length of rope and an aluminum carabiner from his pants' cargo pocket. In the dark, his practiced hands looped the eight-foot piece of rope around his waist and crotch and through the carabiner, fashioning a climbing harness.

"Here," Havok said. "Pass me the flashlight."

Stone kept it pointing into the hole while giving it to Havok.

Havok accepted the light and clipped it to his climbing harness upside down.

"You sure you don't want me to go with you?" Stone asked, still looking into the black hole.

"No. I'm only going down there for a quick look-see and to get my rifle back," Havok said, reassuring his friend. "I'll be fine."

Havok stepped away from Stone and picked up a coil of rope. He secured one end around the trunk of a nearby tree. He held the remainder in his hand and walked back to the hole, dropping the coil into it. Where the rope rested against the crevice's edge, Manny taped a slit length of garden hose over the rope as an anti-chafing device. Havok picked up the rope and snapped it into the carabiner, and, with one hand holding the rope above his waist and the other holding the rope under his butt, he turned around and backed up to the black hole. He placed his weight on the line, used his hands as brakes, and loosened his grip. Gravity pulled him deep into the alien bowels of the earth.

Slowly, Havok entered the darkness, his back scraping against rock outcroppings behind him. The humidity and exertion caused him to sweat, and the sweat worked into the scrapes in his skin. He had no idea what hideous denizens eeked out a survival in the depths, but the stinging pain kept him from worrying what was or was not beneath him. Beyond the hellish glow provided by the dangling light, he could see nothing. Suddenly, the rocky wall in front of him disappeared and he found himself swinging freely in what seemed to be a large dome-shaped cavern. He heard the echoing drip of water. Havok looked down at the slithering mass beneath him on the floor.

18

. . . .

TERUMBU ISLAND, LATE JULY

TWO HOURS LATER, THREE SWEATING FORMS CROUCHED IN THE STILL JUNGLE TEN YARDS AWAY FROM THE REAR WALL OF THE MAKESHIFT LABORATORY. After making sure they were alone, Havok leaned over and whispered to his companions, "Ready to work off your Wheaties?"

"Oh, yeah," Stone answered, "and that lovely twelve-hour siesta aboard the air-conditioned yacht did so much for my complexion."

Havok had learned to ignore Stone. He knew Stone was as tough as two-month-old Arizona roadkill. Stone was just not happy unless he had something to complain about.

The men stood and stepped to the laboratory, carrying empty dive bags. Reaching the rear door, Stone pushed against its wooden double panel. The door opened just as Stone had said it would.

The three men filed into the building and closed the door behind them. Stone pulled a small LED flashlight with a red lens from his pocket, pushed against the small rubber switch at the end of its handle, and jammed it between his teeth. Under the weak dull-red glow they could see gray metal boxes stacked in a large square on the concrete floor in the center of the room and a workbench against the wall with empty containers on it.

Havok leaned his recovered rifle against the wall behind him. As a testimony to American arms manufacturers, the rifle was still operational, although the wooden stock was a bit gouged. He pulled a Phillips screwdriver from his waistline and stepped over to the boxes. They were one foot wide by one foot tall and three feet long. Four screws secured the lids, one at each corner. He used the screwdriver to remove one screw at a time from a box on the top layer of the stack. After pulling out the last screw, he carefully tugged at one end of the lipped cover, breaking its wax seal. He pulled back on the cover, and inside, two rows of ten green canisters stood upright, held tightly in place by foam packing. Havok selected one canister, hefting it in his hand. It weighed about eight pounds. He placed it back into the crate and, grabbing the crate's end handles, placed the crate on the floor.

Now Stone and Manny started on their own boxes. The three men took care loading the canisters into the empty dive bags layer by layer. Within thirty minutes they had four bags fully loaded with death-laden containers. Leaving the bags alone for a minute, they replaced the covers of the boxes and restacked them as they had been. Before they screwed the lid on the last box, Stone pulled out a dive glove, a coil spring a little bigger than a finger, and a screw and washer.

"What're ya doing with that?" Havok asked.

"You'll see," Stone replied as he went to the workbench and grabbed an empty container. Returning to the box, he placed the container inside, standing it up. Next, he unscrewed the lid and poured half a canteen of water into it. After screwing the lid back on, he stood the spring on the lid of the container, dropped the washer and screw into the spring, and, with his screwdriver, threaded the screw through the lid. Once the spring was securely in place, Stone fitted the dive glove over the spring with the spring holding up the middle finger of the glove.

"Great," Havok said as he watched Stone lay the cover over the glove and spring, folding it over. "Do ya always have to find a way to piss people off?"

Stone replied with a devilish grin on his face, "Well, they need to butch up then, don't they?"

Havok shook his head as he turned to a full dive bag. "Come on."

Manny and Stone followed Havok's lead and shouldered one bag each, along with their weapons, while Stone and Manny grabbed the straps of the fourth bag to carry between them. Although Manny weighed just over one hundred pounds, he had no problem carrying the same amount of weight as Havok and Stone. Havok pushed his screwdriver into his waistline, grabbed his M14, and followed his friends out of the building. Closing the door behind him, Havok took the lead, starting out on the route that led to the building.

They had only walked about twenty yards when, without warning, Havok slammed into another person. Havok smelled tobacco.

The man blurted a single word in Russian as Havok's weight, and the weight he carried, bowled him forward. Without even thinking about it, Havok used the surprise and excess weight to his advantage. He dropped his rifle, pulled the screwdriver from his waist, and pushed the man off his feet. As the pair went down, Havok jammed the crossed tip into the man's chest. When the two bodies collided with the ground, Havok's weight drove the shank between his victim's ribs. He could hear the great expulsion of air leaving the man's windpipe as warm blood gushed over Havok's hand, making him lose his grip on the plastic handle. Only a gurgling sound and the spastic quiver of the man's legs accompanied his death.

Havok rolled off the Russian while pulling the screwdriver out of the man's chest. Now lying on his back on top of the full dive bag, Havok flipped the tool over, pointing it into the black air and searching for any other threat. All he could see were faint traces of moonlight that squirmed through cracks in the canopy, but a figure loomed over him, blocking the moonlight.

"You all right?" Stone asked with uncharacteristic concern.

"I'm fine," Havok answered, "but I think I put a hurtin' on Ski here. Help me up."

Stone reached down and grabbed Havok by a bag strap, pulling him to his feet as Manny joined them. Manny looked at the body and then lifted his shotgun, pointing it around into the jungle as he looked for other late-night walkers.

"Come on," Stone whispered. "Can't hang out all night long."

"Manny, grab my rifle and pack it for me," Havok ordered. "Stone, help me get him on my shoulders."

After Stone folded the Russian over Havok's left shoulder, the three men and a corpse continued their journey, leaving behind only a few bloodstains on the matted vegetation.

Unknown to the three men, another man had died thirty feet away. The man clutched an empty vodka bottle. Unlike his comrade, he had died with a smile. This smile was several inches long, and it went from ear to ear below his chin.

The hike to the cavern was taxing. The added weight stressed the men's already-spent muscles. It was past midnight by the time they reached the crack in the ground, and Havok knew they were running out of time. After placing their heavy loads on the ground, Stone retrieved their rappelling gear from under a pile of leaves, and they went to work. Havok strapped on his climbing assembly, an entrenching tool, and a light, and lowered himself into the opening. The red glow from his light cast an evil glare beneath him. Havok guiltily expected a little red man with green eyes, horns, and a broad, fangy smile to materialize and congratulate him on his murderous deed.

The walls of the crevice disappeared, and Havok found himself hanging just under the dome-shaped roof of the cavern. He looked down at the pile of dried vegetation and animal bones, and the insects that had made the floor directly under the crevice their home. He kicked his legs and started to swing. When the arc of his swing was right, he released his grip on the rope, landing squarely on the large boulder next to the pulsating mass of vegetation, bones, and insects. After yanking the rope away from the gathering swarm of tiny, clacking, and hungry creatures, Havok tightened his grip on the rope and gave it four tugs. The rope disappeared into the blackness above him.

Remaining on the boulder, he unsnapped his flashlight from his climbing harness and panned the narrow light around the cavern. Long, craggy stalactites pointed down from the curved roof. Many of them dripped water, which created a field of stalagmites covering the flat cavern floor. The air was damp. Stepping off the boulder, he passed the pile of desiccated vegetation and made his way to a recess in the sloping ceiling. The recess was located where the cavern walls met a floor of hard-packed sand strewn with various-sized rocks and stalagmites. Once inside the miniature sub-cavern, Havok placed the flashlight on a rock, pulled the entrenching tool from his belt, and began digging. The dull scraping sound bounced off the roof of the cavern, keeping him company.

Within three minutes, the reddish-black lump of a dive bag was lowered into the cavern with Stone harnessed to the same line just above the bag. Together, both the bag and Stone dropped to the floor. While Havok kept digging the hole, Stone unclipped himself and the bag from the line and tugged it four times. Manny, on the surface, pulled the rope out of the cavern. He lowered the remaining bags one at a time, while Stone unclipped the loads and shouldered them, carrying them one at a time to where Havok was digging his hole. Havok heard the sound of a rope rubbing against its chafing gear above him as Manny started to lower the dead Russian into the cavern. To Havok, looking up from his hole and wiping sweat from his eyes, the dangling corpse looked just like hell's archangel descending into the cavern. He remembered a quote he'd heard once: "The devil whispered in my ear, 'You're not strong enough to withstand the storm.' To which I whispered back in the devil's ear, 'I am the storm.'"

Why did I think of that passage now? he wondered, wiping his brow one more time before returning to his work.

Once the hole was deep enough, Stone helped him line the bottom of the oval-shaped grave with the canisters. When the last container was in place, Havok and Stone placed the body on top of them. Stone helped cover the sarin and the body with sand, using his feet and hands, while Havok shoveled it in with his entrenching tool. The air was thick and humid, causing the men to stream sweat, which soaked the dry sand as it covered the dead and deadly contents. When the grave was covered, the men stood to inspect their work.

"Kind of fitting, isn't it?" said Stone.

"How's that?"

"What he came for, he's stuck with forever."

Havok nodded and gathered his gear. Stone did the same, and they did their best to wipe out any evidence of their work by smoothing the sand and redistributing vegetation.

By two thirty a.m. Havok and Stone were back on the surface after having climbed back up the rope using tired arms and foot-cinching ropes. Manny stashed the climbing gear. The two men drank water from their canteens, and then all three of them shouldered their weapons and web gear. When all was ready, Havok turned in the direction of the seaplane. His friends followed.

With the excess weight buried behind them, Havok and his companions set out at a mile-eating gait and quickly covered the distance. Soon they were squatting at the edge of the seaplane camp, watching from behind dense foliage. They had no problem finding the location again in the early-morning darkness; all they had to do was follow the smell of campfire smoke, which hung in the tropical air. As the three men crawled toward the camp, glowing embers from a dying fire cast a flickering hue on the center of the encampment. Snores came from inside the sagging tents, along with an occasional cough. There appeared to be nobody on watch.

Havok whispered to his mates, "Hang on. I'm going to get a guest for tonight's dinner."

Stone responded woefully, "I hope she doesn't like beer."

****

Pilar's body ached at every joint and muscle because the last ounce of her body fat had been consumed long ago to produce body heat. Now, with no padding left, the moist, cold ground became unbearable to her. When morning came, she knew she would no longer be able to resist any of the bastards. She wouldn't even be able to hold an arm up by then. Hungry, sore, and wallowing in self-pity, she failed to notice the black-green ghost stealing away from the fast hold of the jungle. The ghost snatched her up so fast she became dizzy, but she could still feel the embrace of strong arms.

A dirty and sweaty face, inches from hers, whispered the words she had longed to hear: "Don't worry. You're safe."

Havok held Pilar tightly against him as he dashed back in the direction of the Outfit. Manny and Stone followed. She could feel his biceps press against her back, but she did not mind the discomfort, as everything was fine now. She had no idea who he was or what was going on, but the warming embrace of another human set her mind at ease. No longer would she feel discomfort or pain. Finally, the jostling movement stopped, and she felt herself being placed on the ground. Another man's voice came from somewhere in the darkness.

"I send him out for pizza, and look what he comes back with."

Pilar removed her face from the first man's chest and saw two other forms. The man who still held her with one arm spoke up: "Here you go, Pilar."

The man shoved something into her mouth, and she tasted the most wonderful thing: peanut butter.

He squeezed a lump of the oily goo into her mouth from an MRE packet and then pulled it away. It only took a few seconds for her mouth to salivate enough to moisten the peanut butter so she could swallow it whole. She then felt the lip of a canteen against her lips. She swallowed five gulps before the man pulled the canteen away.

"That's enough for now," the benevolent voice said. "I don't normally treat a girl this way on our first date, but you can have more water later."

"Mister," croaked Pilar, "right now, between you and the peanut butter, this is the best date I've ever had." It hurt her to speak, but it was the most welcome pain.

"All right," Stone said. "I know you two are having a real hoot, but I think it's time to split. When our friends wake up and find out they've lost the family jewels, there are going to be a lot of pissed-off Slavs running around here."

Havok looked at Pilar's dirty face. "Excuse my friend here. His eloquence is lacking somewhat these days."

"To me, he's a perfect gentleman," she said.

Havok reached into the cargo pocket of his trousers and pulled out a bundle. "Here, put this on."

Pilar accepted the bundle, which was a sweatshirt, and as she gratefully slipped the extra-large clothing over her shivering body, the sudden warmth, along with the peanut butter and water, was too much for her. She collapsed into a deep sleep.

****

They reached the Outfit by four a.m., and Havok woke Pilar and instructed her how to cross the rope onto the boat. When the four were aboard the boat, Havok took Pilar into the salon behind the pilothouse and told her to lie down on the sofa. Stone stepped into the pilothouse to start the engines, while Manny went into the forward cabin for a blanket. Now that they had buried the sarin and rescued the professor, they could escape this island, and once safely on their way, they could radio for help and give a description of the disguised university research vessel.

"Shit!"

Havok, who was looking at Pilar's wide eyes as she was trying to take in what had happened in the last half hour, asked, "What's the problem?"

"We had a visitor again," Stone said dejectedly.

"Let me guess," Havok responded. "He took the last of your smokes?"

"Negative. He ganked our radio."

The words hit Havok hard as he realized their situation had suddenly changed, and for the worse.

As if to confirm his dread, Stone continued, "Not only that but the engines won't turn over."

Manny stepped up from the forward cabin with a folded blanket in his arms. He saw the empty mount on the console in front of the helm where the marine radio used to be.

"Manny!" Havok ordered, looking at Pilar, who was slow to understand the sudden change in plans. "Get a pot of coffee going, fry up something quick for breakfast, and get a bag ready to go with all the ammunition and canned goods we have. Looks like we may have to jump ship. Stone, let's look at those engines."

Havok walked past Pilar and opened the hatchway to the engine room. He knew what to expect. Then he stepped down the short ladder with Stone right behind him. Havok's expectations were confirmed: the valve covers, rocker arms, fuel injectors, and jumper lines of the two twelve-cylinder aircraft engines had been beaten off and lay strewn about the deck in pieces. They looked over at one of the start batteries and saw the handle of a claw hammer sticking out of the side. Battery acid still dripped from the wide crack in its side.

"You know he didn't stop here," Havok said.

"Yep, I bet he threw our laptop and your cell phone into the South China Sea as well," Stone replied. "I told you to always carry your cell phone with you, but thank God for me. I've got my cell phone." Stone reached for his back pocket.

"Go ahead, replace the battery and call Scott," Havok said, still looking at the broken engines. "Shit's gonna hit the fan when they realize that Pilar, along with one of their soldiers, is missing, and it won't take long for them to figure out who's behind it all." He looked at his watch. "It's four thirty, and I think we have about two hours at most to get some hot chow into us and to come up with Plan C."

Havok turned, went up the ladder leading out of the engine room, and looked at Pilar on the sofa. Halfway asleep, she looked so vulnerable. He could hear Manny rummaging through the pantry in the forward compartment, and he could smell the coffee brewing. While the other three people on the boat were busy doing something, Havok was thinking about their next move. Stone disrupted his thoughts.

"Damn it!" Stone grumbled as he stepped up from the engine room. "I just got an out-of-office reply. One helluva time to go on a vacation or a company retreat!"

Havok thought for a second before responding. Both he and Stone had known Kilgore for many years, and they knew how he operated. "I doubt he's on either one. We just need to go to ground and find an Alamo for the time being."

By five a.m. Manny had filled his backpack with ammunition and canned goods. The open backpack sat on the stern deck next to the gas cans and Havok's and Stone's filled backpacks. The three men and Pilar sat in the salon drinking hot coffee and eating heated canned corned beef off paper plates. The sun, still below the horizon, was just starting to illuminate the eastern sky.

"Why did Hirosaki do what he did?" Stone wondered just loud enough for Havok to hear. "I thought the last thing he wanted was us hanging around. Why would he smash the engines and steal our comms? Why would he force us to stay here?"

"It could be a case of island fever or castaway crazies," Havok replied as quietly as Stone had spoken. "Remember, he may be over a hundred years old, but he was still a Japanese soldier, and raised with the samurai concept. Two men enter, one man leaves. It's either the Russians or us. He has locked us into mortal combat with the intention of letting the winners take the spoils and leave his island paradise, and pretty damned quick."

"Or it might be a simple case of him being bored and wanting to have somebody to mess with," Stone said.

Manny downed the last of his coffee and stood. "Boss, anything else?"

"Go look to see if we can squeeze any more ammo into our backpacks," Havok ordered.

Manny went into the forward cabin to see what else might be of some use.

***

"I don't know who you two are," Pilar said after a gulp of coffee, "but thanks for rescuing me."

"No problem," Stone grumbled as he lit the cigarette that dangled from the corner of his mouth. "But the word rescue might be the wrong word choice right now."

"Never mind him, Pilar," Havok said, giving Stone a stern look. "We've got you safe and sound."

"How did you know my name?" Pilar asked. She held the almost-empty coffee mug close to her lips with both of her hands. "Were you sent here to rescue me?"

"Actually, no," Havok answered. "It seems like all of us here are victims of circumstance. I just happened to hear about you thirdhand. As for the rescue, we came here for something else but just stumbled into this mess."

Although Pilar did not need to ask—she had accepted the inevitable long ago—she did anyway, hoping her question might bring back her students: "What about my students? My friends? Did you find them?"

"Sorry. They're all dead," Havok said bluntly. He knew of no other way to tell her.

Pilar sat there, feeling a guilt take her body over. She had argued to stay with her students, but the Russians wouldn't listen. Instead, she'd found herself separated from them and bound up like a forgotten dog in the backyard. She then thought about the ship's crew. "What about the ship and its crew?"

Havok gulped his coffee before answering, "We overheard Kang and the Russians talking. They repainted the ship, gave it a new name, and put their own crew in charge. They've spent the last week or so looking for us." He paused and looked deep into Pilar's eyes. "How many crewmen were there?"

"Seven, including the captain. The university maintains a small crew because the students carry out most of the watches and menial tasks to give them shipboard experience." Pilar noticed the battle dress the men were wearing. "Are you Marines or something?" Pilar put the mug to her lips and tilted the remnants of syrupy coffee into her mouth.

"Sorry. It's just like we said," Stone said, exhaling cigarette smoke through his nostrils. "We're innocent bystanders who came out here for silver, but unfortunately, you and your group happened on it first. Now, here we are too."

"No problem." She held out the mug for more coffee. A white film stuck to her lips. "You're welcome to all of it. The Russians took it after they captured us."

"I know," Havok said as he refilled her mug.

She looked quizzically at the two men. "You two know a lot about me."

Havok realized his rudeness and apologized. "I'm Joe Havok, and this lump here is Pete Stone, my partner."

"Partner in what?" she asked.

"Just about anything, but mostly a bar slash dive shop up in Subic," Havok answered. "I met a knowledgeable Australian at our dive shop who let me in on a long-lost secret about the silver. After that, I flew on down to this island for a look-see and some asshole put holes in our airplane. I managed to get back to Subic to collect Pete and Manny, and we all came back."

"That was you in the plane?" Pilar asked, remembering the panic he had caused.

"Affirmative. I was just lucky that they were bad shots."

"It wasn't from bad shooting. The big gun on the ship jammed on them right after they started shooting. When they finally fixed it, you had flown off. I heard all about it from listening to the Russian at the seaplane camp. When they failed to shoot you down, the pilots received a message to clean and check their machine gun. There's one mounted at the front of the seaplane. It's like the one on the ship."

While Pilar spoke, she appraised Havok. His clothing, damp from the trapped humidity, fit snugly over a muscular torso. His arms bulged out of the rolled-up sleeves of his shirt, the knotty biceps stretching the cloth. His skin was tanned but not overly so: he was done just right. The two things that attracted her most were his eyes and his enormous mustache. The large brown orbs exuded confidence. A hint of crow's feet at the corners suggested a jovial nature. The thick reddish-brown mustache clashed with the soft, caring eyes. It made a bold statement, revealing a roguish side. The mustache reminded Pilar of Wyatt Earp. He was attractive, and she could tell he was his own man.

Havok became aware of her gaze, but Stone mercifully broke it. "Hey, Pilar, I'll show you mine if you show us yours."

"Sure," Pilar said, straight-faced as she sipped her coffee while turning to Stone.

"First," Stone said, removing the cigarette from his mouth and knocking off the ash, "we have a headless corpse not two miles from this spot, but his head managed to walk to an island north of here. There's an armed Russian ship anchored over a World War II Japanese submarine with a gazillion smackers in gold and a ton of germ warfare stuff. Then, we have two camps chock-full of Russian sailors, commandos, murderers, and scientists, all of whom I think had a little bit too much lead in their drinking water. Following them around is a Chinese mining industrialist packing his own private harem. All these crazy cats are as thick as thieves, but they can't seem to stand each other's company. To top it off, this island comes complete with its own hermit."

"Well, that's about what I've got, except the hermit," answered Pilar. "Who's he?"

"Long story short: it seems this island comes with its very own Ben Gunn," Havok said.

"Ben Gunn?" Stone asked with his head tilted. "I thought his name was Hirosaki?"

"Haven't you ever read Treasure Island?" Havok asked.

"Did it come with wiring instructions or a centerfold?" Stone asked. "If not, then no, I haven't read it."

Exasperated, Havok quickly explained, "Gunn was a pirate that Long John Silver marooned on an island after burying some treasure. Gunn came to haunt Long John Silver later on, and it seems that Hirosaki has haunted us by wrecking our escape plans."

Havok turned to Pilar. "Now, show us yours."

Pilar spoke: "We came on a university-sponsored research project, but for me it was personal. We were conducting an environmental impact study while I was following Kang, trying to get evidence on his destructive mining operations. Unfortunately, we followed him here and stumbled across his other criminal activities. Before our capture, the Russians used their own divers until two of them died. After our capture, they started using my students. The Russians separated me from my students on the first day. I heard about their torturous work only by listening to the Russians. And that corpse you mentioned used to be one of their scientists."

"Dr. Dubrinsky?" Stone offered.

"Yes, Dr. Dubrinsky. The Russians had two biochemists. Andropov is the other chemist. He is a patriot and an actual member of the group.

He staunchly believes in their cause. Dr. Dubrinsky was an outsider. He was only in it for the money. I guess he got cold feet, though, after some of my students died. He must have suffered a bout of conscience. He protested, but the leader of that murderous lot wouldn't listen. Dubrinsky threw in the towel and escaped by boat one night. It took the Russians a couple of days to track him down, but they finally got him. He was dismembered, and his headless and handless corpse was brought back as a warning for others who might've had similar thoughts."

"And to make it hard to identify the body in case it was discovered," Havok added.

"That's right. That might've led authorities back to their organization." Pilar grew silent for a moment before continuing at almost a whisper. "It's my fault. I lied to everybody to get this project underway. It was my own selfish vengeance that brought them here."

Havok and Stone recognized her avalanche into remorse, and Stone was the first to speak up in an attempt to keep her attention elsewhere. "How did a Japanese sub end up here with all that gold and sarin? And how did the Russians find it?"

"I can't tell you how the Russians found it," Havok interjected, "but I think can tell you how it ended up here. One of the biggest mistakes the Japanese made in World War II was the misuse of their submarine force. Instead of attacking merchant fleets, as the Germans did, the Japanese used their submarines to attack only warships and to resupply their beleaguered island garrisons once the Allies started their island-hopping campaign across the Pacific. I figure the sunken sub is an I-400 class, one of the largest class of submarine ever made. I'll bet the submarine was loaded with pillaged gold from all over Southeast Asia and then ordered to make it to Japan or Indochina to continue the war effort. The Japanese also had special units trying to manufacture all kinds of secret weapons, including chemical weapons, in places like northern China and Manchuria. Ergo, the Japanese probably had another secret facility somewhere in Southeast Asia where they made all kinds of weapons, including sarin. They tried to ship it north, but lost in the end.

"Now we have Russians salvaging what they need to create a new nation, with Kang here as some sort of investor or backer in the whole scheme. Before we rescued you, we snatched their sarin and hid it in an underground cave near here. The only way to it is through a crevice in the ground."

Stone looked at Pilar. "What's your connection with Kang?"

"He's a millionaire who owns a fleet of ships and enough equipment to mine on every continent," Pilar responded. "He owns the bottom half of the Philippines. Apparently, one of his mines caved in there recently, on the island of Mindanao, killing a dozen miners. A lot of his miners around the world have died because of his skirting safety regulations."

Havok turned to Pilar and asked, "Why are you following him?"

Pilar's lips suddenly compressed, and she looked away from Havok into the distance. "He killed my father," she said with a vengeful, distant stare in her eye before continuing in a low, cold voice, "About four years ago, my father and I were working with the University of Nevada to conduct a study on the impact of open mining on public lands. Kang had an operation out in the desert, and one day, my father went out to speak with him. He had flown in with his senior staff to inspect his mine that day. It was an open-pit mine, and while my father, Kang, and his staff, along with several miners, were down in the pit, under-digging caused a landslide. It buried everybody. Only Kang escaped alive. Since then, I've vowed to follow in my father's footsteps. I've spent the last few years collecting evidence of the damage Kang has caused. I was able to collect enough information to shut Kang down in the States at least."

"It's amazing how shit like that always floats to the surface," Stone remarked, crushing out his cigarette butt in the ashtray on the table. "Well, at least he's no longer operating in the States."

"It doesn't matter. There's a whole quorum of other companies waiting to take his place, most of them foreign, but all have the same impact. These companies lease public land from the government," Pilar explained, "just like the ranchers do, except these companies dig deep holes in the ground and process the soil while using poisonous chemicals to extract the silver, platinum, or gold."

"Then," Stone said, "they ship all that precious metal to a foreign bank, and Uncle Sam gets stuck with a few measly bones in rental fees and quite an expensive mess to clean up."

"Yes," Pilar said, turning her attention back to Stone. "In the end, all that's left is a huge pit in the ground, piles of toxic soil, a poisoned groundwater system, and bought-off politicians who look the other way. Remember when Hillary Clinton, while secretary of state, was accused of taking bribes to let Russians mine American uranium? Crap just like that."

Changing the subject, Stone asked, "So what's your take on Anisimova?"

"He's a hideous animal," Pilar responded with a different form of hate in her eyes. "He told me a lot about their organization. Men like that need to brag. It makes them feel good about themselves. You could compare him to any other despot. Like Hitler and Stalin. He kept bragging about being some sort of top dog in a Russian separatist movement. In the States, I guess you would compare the movement to the KKK or some other white supremacist group. He does say things like 'All Afro Americans ought to be fenced inside Florida.' He has caused a lot of trouble worldwide because of his mouth."

"If he's such a pain," Stone responded, "I'd have thought the Russian government would have dropped him like a hooker with leprosy."

"The Russians can't afford to dump him. Or at least Putin can't for right now," Pilar responded. "Putin is, in reality, a dictator, and has arrested numerous opponents, but Anisimova may be a little too hot to touch right now. He has too much support from certain segments of the Russian populace, and perhaps the only thing the Russian parliament and Putin could do is ask him to tone it down."

Everybody fell silent for a moment and took the time to look out the cove's entrance. The sun had peeked above the horizon, and they could see Manny closing his backpack. Havok looked at his watch. It was almost six a.m. He sighed. "I'll bet the Russians are waking up by now and are probably realizing two people are missing. Or at least that you're missing. Pilar, grab another roll and follow us. Stone, let's shoulder our gear and weapons, and find ourselves an Alamo."

"Do you really have to call it that?" Stone asked.

But before Havok could respond, the sudden volley of machine-gun fire erupted, followed by two exploding fiery balls spewing burning gasoline all over the stern deck and all over Manny. Instinctively, the men dove for the deck, but Pilar remained seated with a bread roll in her hand, stupefied by the sudden violence invading her new, peaceful world.

Havok yelled at her, "You'd better get your butt on the floor with me, and do it now!"

As Pilar dove for the safety of the hardwood deck, she heard the anguished screams of a man being burned alive. The horrifying scream lasted but a few seconds. The roar of an instantaneous inferno replaced it. All three could feel the heat as the burning gasoline on the stern deck set the camouflage netting alight. The fire spread rapidly, and after only a few seconds, the roaring of the flames was joined by the sudden hissing of compressed air. The scuba tanks, secured along the starboard side, were splattered with flaming gasoline, which increased the internal heat and pressure. The increasing pressure forced the rupture discs in the valves to burst, relieving the excess air pressure inside the scuba tanks, preventing them from exploding.

19

. . . .

TERUMBU ISLAND, LATE JULY

Dawn arrived over the Russian camp, and with it came the commands of NCOs mustering their squads for roll call. Reluctantly, Anisimova rose with the dull light and the age-old military custom of morning parade.

With the sarin removed from the submarine, the Russian's recovery of the gold inside the submarine had become unimpeded, and the amount of gold ingots breaking the surface was beyond anyone's imagination. The sight of the bullion was intoxicating for everybody, and Anisimova looked forward to wresting the last ingot from the submarine and leaving this island.

He stood up from his army cot and stumbled toward his washstand. He splashed water from a steel pitcher into the waist-high basin just as his orderly pushed aside the blanket draped over the doorway and entered the room, carrying a breakfast tray: a mug of boiled tea, a jar of jam, a saucer with pats of butter, and a tin of biscuits.

"Here's your breakfast, sir," the young private said. "I also have messages from the seaplane camp and the communications room."

"What is it, man?" Anisimova said after spitting rinse water out of his mouth. He stood and ran his wet fingers though his hair.

"The seaplane camp reports that the professor ran away, and the Kona Wave—I'm sorry, the Shanghai Mariner, reports that its crew has searched every square meter north and east of here. No sign of the Americans."

Before Anisimova could respond, Yeshenko roughly pushed aside the blanket, almost pulling it from the nails above the doorway. He remained in the doorway while he spoke. "Go ahead and tell the ship to return. I've found our Americans."

Anisimova scowled questionably as water dripped from his chin. "What do you mean you have found Havok? Have you seen him?"

"No, but the missing sarin and two missing men prove that he has arrived!"

"'Missing'? The sarin is missing?" Anisimova blurted as he felt a warm liquid feeling deep within his bowels.

"Yes," Yeshenko replied. "Get dressed and I will show you."

The veteran soldier did an about-face and stepped from the door, letting the blanket fall back into place.

Minutes later, Anisimova, Yeshenko, Petroske, and Ohmsky, along with a few curious soldiers, stood outside the rear double doors of the laboratory. They saw Andropov standing next to the stack of boxes. He held the lid of one box in his hand; the lids of other boxes were on the concrete floor, propped against the stack.

Everybody could see the erect and gloved middle finger that Stone had rigged to pop out of the box.

Yeshenko, after a minute of surveying the room, turned to the jungle surrounding the building. His piercing gray eyes scrutinized the ground around the building. Finally, he spotted a trail of disturbed vegetation. He followed the trail around the corner of the building, with the others following. Yeshenko walked until he came to a patch of bare ground. He squatted and examined boot prints in the wet earth.

"These prints are deep, indicating heavy loads," Yeshenko observed. He spat out orders without looking up from the boot print. "Ohmsky, go to communications. Contact the patrol. Tell them to listen for boat engine noises. Now that Havok has the sarin and more than likely the professor, his team will try to escape with both, if they have not done so already."

"Yes, sir," Ohmsky replied.

Before Ohmsky left, Anisimova sputtered out his own orders: "Yeshenko, get everybody out searching, including those useless airmen. If they can't guard one female, then they can get off their backsides and earn their food."

For once, Yeshenko had to agree with Anisimova. He turned his gaze from the boot print to Ohmsky. "Everybody!"

"Yes, sir," the sergeant repeated, and with a hurried salute, he turned toward the camp. The soldiers that had shadowed the group followed Ohmsky back to the center of camp.

Yeshenko continued his search of the area, with Anisimova and Petroske doing the same. After a few minutes, Yeshenko spotted something that made his heart wrench with pain: a cluster of black flies. He squatted and waved the buzzing insects away. What the flies left behind was a huge glob of dried blood that glued a clump of leaves together. He stared at the morbid remains of a missing soldier. After a minute of silence, he heard more buzzing off to his right. Enraged, Yeshenko stood, clenched his fists, and followed his ears to the buzzing. Several yards away, he found another cluster of flies gorging themselves on a meal of thick, dried carnage. He also noted a different type and size of footprint.

Yeshenko stepped to the others, who waited for his assessment.

"What's wrong?" Anisimova asked.

"I found what happened to my missing men," Yeshenko said through compressed lips. "Those two men have been with me for years. Their killers will pay."

Petroske spotted the blood as well and knew what it meant, but he could not understand why Yeshenko was so upset. The love that Yeshenko had for his men was useless. After all, these men were soldiers and volunteers. No one should shed a tear for them.

"The men were killed separately," Yeshenko said. "And their bodies were carried in different directions. I believe the stories the men have been saying about being watched are true. There is somebody else on this island besides us and our friends from Subic."

***

While Yeshenko was contemplating the events that had occurred over the last few hours and the implications of this new information, his junior officer, Lieutenant Varonov, was leading a patrol to the north of the island. Though he was Yeshenko's aide-de-camp, Varonov was bored with camp life and administrative duties, so he'd put himself on the patrol rotation to break up the routine. He never faltered in his duties to Yeshenko, though.

Varonov, having just received a phone call about the missing sarin and professor, looked to his right and left, and saw armed Russians waiting to follow his lead. He regarded, through the tangled jungle, the slight tinge of bluish gray highlighting the eastern horizon and the blue sea under it. As he stepped slowly forward, he turned his head to the foliage to his left and immediately brought his AK-47 up over his head while squatting. His quick movement signaled the five men to do the same. He lowered his weapon and pointed its muzzle directly in front of him. In the growing light, Varonov and his men could discern camouflage netting and the vague structure that the netting covered.

Hot coffee, Varonov thought. As he sniffed the smell of boiling coffee in the early-morning air, he could also hear low voices coming out from under the netting. He thought back, remembering the last time a patrol had been ordered to scout this area. That was three days ago, just when Kang arrived on the island along with his up-to-date radar on his yacht. These Americans ae sneaky bastards, Varonov thought as he contemplated his next move. He recalled Kang's words from their meeting the other night. "These Americans are well-trained and experienced operatives, and not to be trifled with."

Varonov, wondering why the Americans had not yet departed the island, looked down at his AK-47. All of his men were similarly armed. They squatted with their weapons at the ready, waiting for his orders. The message he had received from base camp was that the sarin canisters were missing, along with the professor, which more than likely meant both were aboard the boat. A plan formulated in his mind.

Varonov held out two fingers at the two men closest to the inland end of the cove. Using his V-shaped fingers, he pointed those two fingers to his own eyes, then to them, indicating for them to make their way to the other side of the cove and guard that side of the boat. He mouthed the words five minutes, then twisted slightly and looked back at the other three men. He held out his rifle, directing them to cover this side of the boat. Once Varonov was confident his men understood their silent orders, he nodded to them. The patrol moved out as ordered.

Under Varonov's watchful eyes, the patrol slipped noiselessly into the trees surrounding the Outfit only yards away. He gave the two men who were making their way around the other side of the boat and cove five minutes to get in position. Then he pointed his index finger at the men with him and then at the end of the netting facing the opening of the cove, indicating for them to shoot at the stern of the vessel. He assumed that the sarin was on the boat, perhaps in the forward compartments, and shooting at the boat was a dangerous move for them all, but he had to disable it somehow.

Voronov rose slowly and shouldered his assault rifle. Taking aim at the rear of the netting, he let loose a short burst. The men with him followed suit, firing a short burst each, and everybody could hear the slugs thud into the dense tropical-hardwood hull planking.

A brilliant explosion flashed in their faces and surprised them. Burning bits of both the boat and the net arched from the explosion into the tree branches above the cove before drifting down to land on the remaining section of netting and the water. Within thirty seconds, the entire aft section of the boat was aflame. As the Russians watched the blaze consume the boat, they heard an inhuman scream escape the howling inferno and billowing smoke. They could also see a dancing shadow through the netting. Mercifully, the scream lasted only a few seconds.

Soon after the scream died away, a wreath of blinding, acrid smoke enveloped the Russians. The net was made of nylon, and as it melted, an oily cloud of black smoke filled the small cove. With no wind passing through the enclosure, the blinding fog had nowhere to go. It cut visibility to less than a foot.

Suddenly a deafening barrage of gunfire exploded from the boat, along with the high-pitched hissing of air. Voronov threw himself to the ground just as he heard an AK-47 return fire. A sapling two feet away from him shattered as bullets slapped into its narrow trunk. Smoke-induced tears streamed down his blackened cheeks, and the smoke burned the lining of his throat. Other assault rifles joined the firefight, and the entire cove was nothing more than a stirred-up beehive with bullets flying all over the place.

However, just as suddenly as the gunfire from the boat had erupted, it stopped, but his men kept firing. At first, he thought the Americans were firing, but it didn't take more than a few seconds to realize that it was not ammunition being fired, but ammunition exploding in the inferno.

Fearing friendly casualties, Varonov yelled out into the blinding smoke, "Cease fire! Cease fire!"

The Russian weapons became silent, but the flames that were actively consuming the Outfit filled the silence, along with the hissing of compressed air from the scuba tanks. For long minutes, six throats coughed painfully. Twelve eyes cried and strained to look through the results of their work. However, all Varonov and his men saw was a grayish void.

While they searched the thick smoke, Varonov heard the ringtone of his cell phone. He answered the call.

***

An hour later, Varonov stood at attention in front of Yeshenko. He avoided looking into Yeshenko's eyes.

Standing at the edge of the cove, away from the rest of the men, Yeshenko reprimanded Varonov. "All you had to do was wait! Could you not have waited? You are not a simple conscript. I thought you knew better."

"Sorry, sir," Varonov said sincerely. "I just wanted to find a way to disable the boat and prevent their escape. I did not plan on the fire."

He had been with Yeshenko for years and had never let his commander down before. They were like father and son, and the fact that

Varonov had disappointed the colonel was more painful than any amount of punishment he could receive.

Yeshenko did not respond to the apology. Instead, he looked over at the edge of the cove. Now that the smoke had cleared, he could see nothing but the burned-out hulk of the American's boat. Charred wooden frames, the tops of two engines, and other boat paraphernalia, including the scuba tanks, poked above the soot-covered water. Yeshenko knew it had just been a simple mistake, but Varonov's actions may have ruined their only chance to retrieve the sarin and capture the men who took it. Yeshenko had to do something to maintain discipline. The Americans had arrived at the island without being found out, two of his men were dead, and both the professor and the sarin were missing, all due to a lack of discipline and alertness.

"Lieutenant Varonov," Yeshenko said after a sigh. "Get men to search the boat for bodies and containers of sarin. I want to make sure both the sarin and the Americans are accounted for, even if the sarin canisters exploded under the fire."

Varonov stood straighter. "Very well, sir."

Varonov turned to two soldiers who stood near him. He gave them both a nod, and each man handed his weapon to another nearby soldier before starting to unbutton his blouse.

Yeshenko returned his attention to the boat in the cove. The once-pristine cove was now a burnt and ravaged hell. The air smelled of thick, acrid smoke. Tree leaves had been turned brown, and the cool, clear water of the cove was black with floating oil and soot. Yeshenko watched as two of his men, stripped to their trousers, took turns diving amid the wreckage. One man remained on the surface to catch his breath and clear his eyes and nostrils of fuel and oil, while the other man pulled himself through the wreck, feeling for bodies and sarin canisters. Although what was left of the main deck was only two feet underwater, visibility was next to nonexistent. Long minutes ticked by before they found what they were looking for.

Yeshenko saw one diver stop, his chin just above the filthy surface of the water, as he grabbed at something unseen under the surface. To the horror of most everybody watching from the embankment, a black torso with ragged strips of pale red flesh hanging from its bones suddenly bobbed up. The diver who had dislodged the corpse reeled back as the ruptured skull and long, grinning teeth shocked him.

Yeshenko had spent a career fighting in wars from Syria to Venezuela and had witnessed his share of bodies in burned-out vehicles and houses. The diver who backed away from the grinning corpse evidently hadn't seen death like Yeshenko had. He joined the other diver, who was clinging on to a tree root that poked out of the rocks at the edge of the cove.

Standing at the cove's edge, Yeshenko looked at the blackened corpse as it bobbed gently in the water, black flies smothering the burnt flesh. After a few seconds, he turned his attention to the two men. "Could you recognize it? Was it the professor?"

The diver coughed and spat out black phlegm before answering. "It was very hard to recognize sir, but it was about the same size. I think so."

Yeshenko wasn't ready to gamble on an assumption. "Varonov," he said, still looking at the body, "have the men search the surrounding forest and the beaches."

"Yes, sir," Varonov replied, having anticipated his superior's order. "The men have already started."

20

....

TERUMBU ISLAND, LATE JULY

WHILE THE RUSSIANS EXPANDED THEIR SEARCH FROM THE COVE, THE OUTFIT'S THREE SINGED AND EXHAUSTED SURVIVORS PULLED THEMSELVES FROM THE ROLLING SURF THAT WAS ASSAULTING THE ISLAND'S EASTERN SHORE. They sluggishly stumbled across the narrow, rocky beach to the dark foliage ahead. Once undercover, their spent bodies collapsed. Their eyes smarted terribly from sweat, salt water, and the brilliance of the bright morning sun, and their lungs coughed forcibly, trying to rid themselves of toxic smoke.

After several minutes, Stone spoke: "Manny didn't have to go like that."

"Did he have any family?" Pilar asked sorrowfully. Although she had only known her rescuers for a few hours, she correctly surmised that they were tough men, hard-core by nature. But she also saw something else. She looked past Havok's stoic facade and into his eyes, which were rimmed with red. He seemed to be on the verge of crying. Although his tears could have been caused by the smoke and salt water, she sensed it was something else.

"Yes," he said softly. "He had a family and he was a good man."

Havok fought against the rising guilt that tried to rip him apart. If he hadn't asked Manny to come along, Manny would be alive, happily playing with his grandchildren.

"They have finally done it!" fumed Stone, his voice thick with vengeance. "These Rambo dropouts have pissed me off for the last time. Manny did not deserve to die like that!"

"I know, Stone, I know," Havok said absently. His mind was turning its gears, trying to plan their next move. He knew it was cruel to dismiss his friend's death so soon, but the survivors could not afford the distraction of grieving over Manny's death; they had to get busy if they were to keep on living themselves. "Come on. With any luck, the Russians will spend the morning looking for our bodies in the Outfit. Meanwhile, we need to retrieve our cache pack and get cleaned up." He looked at the scratches on his arms. "It won't take long for a minor cut to get infected, or for them to smell us if they get close enough."

Wearily, Stone and Pilar rose to follow Havok into the island's interior. As they walked, Havok consoled himself: At least Manny is with the Outfit: he always did love that boat.

The team took a circular route into the island's interior before turning south. Finally, they walked up to the bamboo grove where they had stashed the rucksack. The smell of the nearby headless and handless corpse hung in the still tropical air. Stone and Pilar kept watch while Havok stepped into the thicket of rigid stalks. He brushed aside the covering vegetation, lifted the pack off the ground by a shoulder strap, and backed out. Once he was free, Havok opened the top of the pack and pulled out a bundle wrapped in black plastic and green duct tape, and handed it to Stone before shouldering the bag. Stone tugged at the plastic and tape, uncovering a well-oiled black MP5 submachine gun and two thirty-round magazines.

Havok, Pilar, and Stone walked back in the same direction they had just come from. As they walked, Havok's mind went back to their provincial escape. He had known that the law of averages would catch up with them and had not been surprised by the attack. The guilt he felt was not in allowing themselves to be attacked, but in the death of Manny. The only reason he had wanted Manny to come along was to nursemaid them and the boat. Now Manny was dead, horribly burned alive while trapped in the confines of a dark, lonely compartment. Havok vowed with a heavy conscience that he would assume Manny's paternal responsibilities; he now had a family.

During the attack, while Havok, Stone, and Pilar had lain on the deck, they had heard Manny's dreadful screams but could do nothing for him. The aft half of the boat had quickly become a holocaust of flames from the ten gallons of gasoline stowed on the deck, along with the compressed air escaping the ruptured blowout discs of the scuba tanks. Like a bellows for a blacksmith's forge, the air fed the flames. Thankfully, the screams only lasted a few seconds, but once they stopped, Havok's thoughts turned to Stone's and Pilar's survival. The smoke from the fire had become a thick, stagnant cloud, and while they lay there choking, Havok realized they had a thin sliver of hope. Once the smoke was thick enough, Havok stood to grab three towels hanging from a chair next to them. He leaned over the side of the boat to soak the towels, then wrapped one towel around his head and dove for his friends just as a burst of machine-gun fire broke out to starboard. The bullets thudded into the bulwark where Havok had been standing only seconds before. Immediately, more weapons joined in. He noted the inaccurate fire and knew the opposition was firing blindly.

"Here, put these on," Havok ordered his friends, throwing each a wet towel.

"Those pinheads are gonna hurt somebody if they ain't careful," Stone retorted as he wrapped a towel around his head and face.

As if someone had overheard Stone, a voice, yelling in Russian, rang out from the south embankment and the shooting stopped.

"You always have something to whine about, don't you?" Havok chided over the thunderous crackle of the building flames.

They waited for the smoke to build even thicker to provide cover, and Havok hoped that he and his two companions could hold out until then. Invisible flames screamed at them through the dense smoke even though the hissing from the scuba tanks was starting to lessen. Though the wet towels protected their heads, sparks and floating embers landed on their clothing. As their clothing caught fire, they beat the flames out with their hands.

Eventually the smoke became thick enough. "Let's go," Havok said.

Havok had slipped through the dive gate at the side of the boat and into the soothing coolness of the water. With his eyes at water level, he had barely been able to see the entrance to the cove under the dark-gray veil. Stone and Pilar had joined him, and all three had swum out of the cove.

Now, Havok turned his thoughts away from their miraculous escape and back to their current predicament. He looked at Pilar as they walked. A thick coat of black soot covered her face, and her hair was tangled and singed.

Pilar became aware of his gaze.

"What's wrong?" she asked.

"I was just wondering how much more interesting our first date was going to become," Havok mused, hoping a little joke would help the situation.

"I hope it's like that old beer commercial," Pilar responded in kind. "'It just doesn't get any better than this.'"

"You know something? I like you," Havok said with uncharacteristic truthfulness. "Most women would have become hysterical by now."

"Boy, you really know how to compliment a girl," Pilar said. Without wanting to admit it, she knew the only reason she was not a hysterical nutcase was Havok. With him around, she felt as if nothing would happen to her. "Hey, big boy, how about that shower you promised?"

"I thought you would never ask," Havok responded.

The afternoon sun was still burning away over the island when the bloodied castaways found a small, rocky, and uneven clear patch in the forest. The sun shone, and Havok spied a shallow pool of water much like a large birdbath among the tumble of exposed rocks. The captured rainwater was clear and inviting.

"Stone, you go ahead and take first guard," Havok ordered, slipping the pack off his back.

Stone did not answer, as he already had his eyes on the jungle around them. He just nodded, pulled up the muzzle of his assault weapon, and moved off to find a spot where he could observe the most likely avenue of approach.

"Pilar," Havok said as he opened the top flap of the pack, "strip down to your underwear. I'll get us some soap and lotion." He pulled out a roll of clothing: bundled-up jeans and a T-shirt. "I carry a little bit of everything, including a change of clothing. Since I only have one set, you get to be the lucky girl." He also pulled out a pair of men's underwear and couple of washcloths, and placed them on the edge of the rocky basin filled with water. "But I get the underwear. Be right back."

Pilar had learned by now not to question anything Havok said or did, even if it meant stripping for him. So she did as ordered before walking up to the shallow pool of water. She squatted down and reached into the pool with cupped and blackened hands. After the fire's blistering heat, the salt water, and the exhausting trek through the humid jungle, plus the fact that she had not bathed in many days, the fresh, cool water hit her skin like a refreshing arctic blast. She massaged the water into her face, enjoying the sensation. She stood to run her wet fingers through her snarled hair, and as she did, she watched Havok poke around the jungle floor. He was like a boar rooting for food. After a few minutes, he stepped up next Pilar and laid several pieces of a dirty red root and a broken stem of a cactus-like plant on a rock at the edge of the water.

"What's all that?" she asked, turning her attention to Havok, who was pulling off his ragged shirt. He submerged it in the pool of water, wrung it out, and spread it over a nearby rock.

"We may be out here a while," he explained. "So we better get used to using nature's storehouse."

He placed two pieces of the red root on one of the washcloths, which he then folded. He dipped the washcloth in the clear water and then began to wring the wet towel in his hands. As he crushed the roots inside the washcloth against each other, the washcloth started to form a mass of soapy bubbles. He held it up for Pilar. "Here you go."

"I'm impressed," she said as she accepted it.

"Mind if I join you?" Havok asked. He dropped his pants and rinsed them in the pool before spreading them on the same rock with his shirt. He squatted next to the rock-filled water basin and washed his face before running his wet fingers through his hair. "There's not much water, and we need to save some for Stone, so just wet and wash your face, armpits, and open sores or scratches. And don't forget your crotch."

He didn't wait for a reply, but used his hands to splash water on the cuts on his forearms while leaning over the rocky basin.

Pilar did likewise before using the soapy towel to scrub her arms and legs, and the cuts she could see. As she did, she watched Havok. His tanned skin stretched across his muscular back. Every movement was a delight to watch, as muscles rippled under the thin epidermis. Without shame, she found herself longing for a chance to run her fingers down the center of his back. She realized that she had not been this aroused in years. All the man had to do was turn and look at her and she would melt like butter, but she also knew this was not the time. It took effort for her not to lie down and open herself to him.

"Here," Pilar said, handing the washcloth to Havok. "Your turn."

He took the washcloth and proceeded to scrub his wet skin. "Go ahead and take your panties and bra off and rinse them in the water. Also, rinse off your skin and cuts. Check yourself all over. Keeping clean out here is going to be vitally important, and leaches can find the damnedest places to hide."

Without a second thought, Pilar stood to unsnap her bra from behind. After letting it drop into the pool of water, she pushed her panties off her hips and tossed them into the pool with the bra. Squatting back down, naked, she did as ordered and splashed water on her arms, legs, pits, and finally her crotch. It felt so good, but then she remembered prior visitations from Kang's whore: Xian and her penetrations.

By now, Havok was doing the same, and Pilar saw his manhood through his wet underwear. She looked down at herself. Her nipples were erect. Havok rinsed away the last of the soiled soapy patches, leaving nothing behind but smooth, tanned skin. Water ran down his chest and stomach muscles as if the water droplets were steel marbles in a pinball machine. Pilar wondered if this man knew how sexy he was. He produced a scene no soap company or its world-famous supermodel could ever reproduce. Pilar hoped that she would be able to enjoy sex again.

Havok stepped from the rocky water basin, reached into the ruck-sack, pulled out a white towel, and quickly dried off before passing the towel to Pilar. While she dried herself, Havok picked up the piece of cactus-like stem from the rocky edge of the basin. A green sap oozed from the severed stump. Havok started dabbing the goo on his many cuts and scrapes.

"What's that?" Pilar asked.

"Aloe vera," Havok said as he looked for more cuts to cover. "Nature's wonder medicine. Here, let me put some on you."

Naked and heady with his attention, all she could manage to croak out was "OK."

With a damp towel hanging about her head, she stood naked and let a man she had only known for a few brief hours touch her body inti-mately. He inspected her as if she were a horse for sale. She was so light-headed that she did not feel the cool, soothing sap as he covered her cuts and bruises.

"Looks like you'll live," Havok said. "Hope you didn't mind me checking you for ticks."

"Purely my pleasure," she said, trying to act as though this was a daily event.

"Come on, let's get dressed," he said, tossing the aloe vera aside. "We wouldn't want Stone to see you naked."

They quickly dressed while looking at each other without saying any-thing. After a minute, Pilar was dressed, but both the T-shirt and jeans were too big and too long. She cuffed the pant legs up almost to her knees and rolled up the sleeves on the T-shirt.

"You know," Havok said while buttoning his shirt, "all you need is a broad-brimmed straw hat perched on the back of your head and you'd look just like Rebecca from Sunnybrook Farm."

Before Pilar could reply, she saw Stone step out of the jungle. He was not carrying his weapon.

"Do not move!" roared a heavily accented voice. "You are surrounded!"

Pilar turned her attention away from Stone and toward the other figures as they emerged from the jungle around them. All were dressed in camouflage military BDUs.

"Hello, Professor," Anisimova said as he stepped out from behind Stone. He was carrying Stone's assault weapon and wore a smug grin.

Havok looked at Anisimova and the large man next to him, who wore sergeant stripes on his BDUs. The men seemed to be opposites. The man self-identified as Anisimova was trim, well groomed, and dressed in pressed camouflage BDUs, while the man next to him had been, at one time, well muscled but was now going to fat.

"Good day, Mr. Havok. I am glad we finally have a chance to meet," Anisimova said, turning his attention from Pilar to Havok. He held out his hand. "I am Deputy Commissar Nicholai Anisimova."

"Howdy," Havok answered, grasping the hand in front of him.

The handshake was more than a courteous gesture. It was a personal test of strength. First, Anisimova's eyes had searched for a weakness; now his hands searched for a chink in the other man's armor. After a tense minute, the handshake was unlocked and Anisimova asked directly, "Now, Havok, without any further waste of time, will you and your comrades please tell me where you have hidden the sarin?"

Havok put on the most honest face he could muster. "What sarin?"

Anisimova had expected that answer. "All right. No matter. In time you will tell us, and you can be sure of that. In the meantime, I hope you do not mind if I let Sergeant Ohmsky take you to our camp. I shall see to the professor's comfort myself."

***

By early evening Havok and Stone stood on the porch outside the building that Anisimova occupied. Their hands were bound behind them with rope. They faced several people with whom they were quite familiar by now. Both of the Americans showed signs of a recent interrogation at the hands of Ohmsky: cut lips and blackened eyes.

"Sergeant Ohmsky tells me that you two claim complete ignorance of the disappearance of our sarin," Anisimova stated as he reclined comfortably in a field chair, casually sipping a glass of vodka.

Havok studied the man closely with one eye almost swollen shut. Anisimova was a fit and proper-looking man. *He looks like he could be at home in a Monte Carlo casino or riding a polo pony,* Havok surmised. *Perhaps too proper to be out here, but perhaps not.*

"That's a fact," Havok said. "Haven't a clue."

"And I suppose you know nothing of two missing spetsnaz as well?" Anisimova asked. "Two missing men?"

"Nope, do not have the slightest." Havok had hidden his surprise well when Ohmsky had asked him the same question earlier.

"Well, I am afraid that only leaves us two choices."

Stone turned to face Ohmsky with a sneer. "I guess beating us is no longer an option," he interjected. "You've tried that, and, by the way, tell your man Ohmsky here that the WWE is still looking for flabby, washed-up athletes to fake wrestle for a bunch of bored and easily entertained Americans."

Ohmsky responded to the comment by cuffing the back of Stone's head.

"You are right, Mr. Stone," Anisimova said, smiling. "But before we explore those options, I am assuming you're the one who placed that glove with the spring in one of the boxes that once held our sarin."

Stone grinned and winked at Anisimova.

That reaction took Anisimova aback, but just for a second. "Beating you is no longer an option. I knew it was a useless endeavor anyway. I guess I simply allowed Sergeant Ohmsky a bit of sport." Anisimova looked back into his glass of liquor. "One option could be shooting one of you to encourage the other to speak up."

"You don't have much of an imagination, do you?" Stone retorted.

Anisimova ignored the flippant remark.

"Of course, there is the other option." Anisimova tilted his head toward a sitting man who appeared to be about thirty years old. He was well tanned and wore a striped jersey and swim trunks.

"This is Renko, our diving officer and captain of our salvage ship. He tells me that the recovery of the gold is occurring at an expeditious rate; however, the submarine's depth is forcing his men to observe the decompression tables, thus slowing down the recovery efforts. We are close to recovering the last of the gold, but your help will still be useful. To put it bluntly, if you do not care to tell us where the sarin is, then I am sure Renko would not care to observe the decompression tables with you two after we have recovered the last of the gold." Anisimova paused and looked intently at his two captives. "I am told decompression sickness can be quite painful and can cause paralysis, if not a slow death, but I am sure you two are very well aware of that."

Anisimova now turned his head to face Renko.

The dive salvage officer, who had been studying the two Americans quietly, pulled his glass of vodka from his lips and looked at his wrist-watch. "It's late in the day, and my men should be finishing up the diving operations and will spend tonight putting away the gold. I can use them at first light tomorrow, though."

"I totally agree," Anisimova said, "and in the interim, I am sure we can find some accommodations in the center of camp where we can keep an eye on them."

"What about Pilar?" Havok asked.

The edges of Anisimova's lips curled into a disturbing grin. "I have had the opportunity to witness Xian's talents, as I know you are aware. Kang told me about your little tryst with Xian earlier on a far-different island," Anisimova responded. "Pilar was not too receptive to Xian's advances, but that doesn't matter to Xian. Perhaps the professor did not feel you had the need to know."

Havok had spent a night with Xian and could just picture what she had forced on Pilar.

"Before I turn you two over to Renko," Anisimova said while swirling the liquor in his glass, "I am curious about one thing. How did you find out about our operation? Do any of your compatriots know of this place?"

"Mister," Havok answered, "I don't know what kind of shit you've been smoking, but you're way off. Stone and I just came out here for some silver coins. We own a dive shop up in Subic, and some old drunk told us about the silver."

"Sorry, we don't believe you," Anisimova said. "We have access to your records and know of your military service and personal history. We even know who your fellow operatives are. Kilgore for example."

Stone gasped in mock surprise. "What? He's a spy?"

Anisimova ignored Stone. "If you two are only simple barkeeps, then why did you not stay away after we shot at your airplane?"

"I thought it was just some Chinese patrol boat trying to scare off the competition," Havok replied, a look of irony on his face. "Countries have been fighting over these islands for years. I figured they wouldn't notice a couple of ex-swabbies stopping by for a few days of recreational scuba diving. Tourists do it all the time."

"You two are not tourists!" Anisimova stated, pointing his glass at Havok. "As you Americans say, your story is wearing thin. So again, why are you on this island? Although we have your silver coins, I believe that the peso story is simply a cover, a front for something more purposeful. No one goes through that much effort for a cache of silver coins."

"You got us," Stone interjected, shrugging his shoulders. "We have an addiction, and it's called getting ourselves into situations just to get out of them, and we do not need any government helping us to do that."

Anisimova fell silent and gave Stone a tired look. "I am curious, Mr. Stone. Do you have any other surprises waiting for us other than a glove with an erect middle finger?"

Stone returned an "I told you so" look and followed it with a dire statement: "We are the simple barkeeps that Satan tried to warn you about."

Anisimova shook his head uncomprehendingly and then turned his attention back to Havok. "You are here to destroy our movement."

Havok responded with a truth that he hoped would strike Anisimova hard. "If you had minded your own business and kept your shit together, everything would be just fine. We would have our silver. You would have your gold and sarin. And the professor would still be leading her little troop of geology scouts around, trying to save the world."

"Ohmsky, take them out of here!" ordered Anisimova, cutting off any further discussion.

***

The night passed long and hard for the two prisoners. They were tied to an iron stake at the foot of the steps that led up to Anisimova's quarters. It was not the fact that they slept on the cold, damp ground with only the clothes they wore when captured that bothered them. The lack of food did not bother them either, and the beatings they received from Ohmsky were taken in stride. They were hard men, used to discomfort, and even Stone accepted his new surroundings without his customary complaining. The fact that both of them faced an almost guaranteed death had not rested for long in their minds either. It was the thought of Pilar's suffering that bothered them. These two things occupied their minds: how to escape their predicament and how to rescue Pilar.

21

TERUMBU ISLAND, LATE JULY

At five in the morning, the island came to life as the Russians emerged from their barracks and started on familiar duties, which included restarting campfires and smoking cigarettes. The Russian avoided looking at the two Americans still tied to the stake. In the waning darkness, Havok and Stone saw Ohmsky sitting in a canvas chair several feet away. He watched them while smoking a cigarette.

"Good morning," Stone said to Havok through swollen lips.

"How are you feeling?" Havok asked. "Sweet Pea didn't hurt you none, did he?"

"He wouldn't last two rounds with Ronda Rousey."

Suddenly, Ohmsky sat straight in his chair, then leaned forward. He looked at Stone and pointed with the cigarette pinched between his fingers. "You know Ronda Rousey?"

Stone looked at Havok before turning to Ohmsky. "Yeah, you want her autograph?"

Ohmsky studied Stone for a minute before leaning back in his chair and puffing on his smoke. "You do not know Ronda Rousey," he said with a smile. "She is classic American athlete and great actor. What would she want with asshole like you? She has class."

"Suit yourself," Stone replied, shrugging his shoulders and turning his attention back to the camp. Apparently, Russians think a bit too much of The Expendables 3.

Both men were hungry and tired, but they were more worried about the professor. They turned to look at Pilar, who had been roughly dumped on the ground near them around midnight. She wore a set of leg irons along with the same clothes she had been captured in. Swollen black-and-blue eyes marred her sleeping face, but they knew Xian had left marks elsewhere. Throughout the evening hours, Havok and Stone had listened to her assertions of ignorance that escaped from the two-story building before them. Her screams had come between the sharp cracks of a whip. Havok and Stone also knew that Xian had had an audience who watched silently and with enjoyment.

Despite the suffering over the last weeks, Pilar had found the resolve to reveal nothing. Havok had tugged madly at his bindings as he listened to the agony. Sometime halfway through the torture, he had been ready to break free, but something had held him back. The fact that Pilar still possessed the strength to resist gave him the courage to hold out. It would have been stupid to have made a move at that time. Havok remembered his SERE school training: survival, evasion, resistance, and escape. There will always be an opportunity. The trick is to never John Wayne it and to wait for the right time.

Now, in the growing light, two other Russians joined Ohmsky. The trio exchanged words in Russian. Ohmsky stood, flicked his cigarette butt away, and stretched his massive bulk. Then the three men stepped up to their captives and untied their bindings. Havok and Stone felt the pain as the blood rushed back into their hands. The Russians pulled the pair to their feet and led them through the camp, past the row of fuel drums, to the edge of the narrow, rocky beach where the inflatable boats were stowed. One Zodiac, with a Russian sailor sitting on the portside gunwale near the coughing outboard engine, was surrounded by a noxious mist of oily blue exhaust. He waited several feet from shore with a lit cigarette hanging from his mouth, watching Havok and Stone wade into the water and climb into the boat. Once aboard, the man grabbed the tiller arm of the engine, twisted the throttle, and steered them toward the Stalinetz.

The Zodiac covered the distance quickly, and within a few minutes, its bow bumped against the boom holding down the netting that covered the salvage ship and Kang's yacht. The sailor yelled something in Russian while waving his arm back and forth. Ash fell from the man's cigarette. Havok and Stone understood his message, and they reached out to push aside a flap in the netting. The operator juiced the engine for a second and steered the boat past the opening and up against the swimmer's ladder that Havok had used two nights ago. Havok reached up and grabbed a rung, holding the boat against the hull of the ship so Stone could disembark.

Havok followed Stone and, while doing so, noticed the ship sat quite a bit deeper in the water. There must be a lot of gold down in those bilges, he thought.

As the two Americans slid over the bulwark, they found themselves stranded on the open fantail among a ship of strangers. Havok and Stone stood, with their bare feet feeling the rough wooden deck, watching the immense amount of work going on as they plotted any possible means of escape. None of the busy sailors or divers paid their newest guests the slightest attention. It was as if the Americans did not exist. Havok saw an open hatch in front of him, flush with the deck. He stepped up to the hatch and looked inside. He saw a gear-storage room with a brand-new, shiny steel deck and four walls covered from top to bottom with lumpy canvas bags. The bags looked like sandbags lining the walls of an army bunker in Iraq. Havok presumed these bags contained the silver pesos that the students from the Kona Wave had recovered.

This must be where they plan to store the sarin, he thought.

Across the deck from them, four divers, who wore torn and faded wetsuits and scratched scuba tanks on their backs, climbed over the side of the salvage ship. Another man, wearing work clothes, sat in the enclosed bucket seat of a twelve-foot electric crane. The operator used hand controls and foot pedals to use the crane to lift a rusty thirty-five-gallon oil drum with holes punched in its side and hoist it over the side, after the divers. Havok also saw a bundle of electrical wires snaking over the bulwark.

He turned his attention away from the divers and the crane operator to size up the ship. The fantail took up about one-third of the ship's deck, and forward of the fantail was the superstructure. On either side of the superstructure, an angled ladder led up to the second level, and between the ladders, next to a doorway, was an alcove. A steel welding table and acetylene and oxygen tanks stood under the starboard ladder. Scrap metal littered the deck at the ladder's base. Havok remembered kicking some of that round stock the other night. Under the portside ladder a rounded stainless-steel tank lay horizontal on four steel legs. Havok recognized it as a recompression chamber, and it looked big enough to house two men at a time.

Renko interrupted Havok's surveying. Like his men, Renko wore practical work clothing. He also held a tin plate with two flat biscuits smeared with chunks of cold butter and jam. Two mugs of steaming tea also rested on the plates. He offered Havok and Stone their breakfast before telling them to sit down on the double bitt behind them. Havok and Stone accepted the food, wolfing it down shamelessly while listening to Renko. The Russian salvage master looked at them with hard eyes.

"Gentlemen," Renko said, "I am not a soldier or a politician. I am a diver, and that is what I expect from you two. You will dive with my teams, but they will rotate. You will not. You will surface for the mid-day meal and when the sun sets. When your tanks run empty, I will send down new ones to you below."

"Sounds like a lot of work for a couple of crackers," Stone interjected through the chewed biscuit in his mouth.

"Right," Renko acknowledged. "If my men tell me that you worked hard, you'll be given the same rations as they. If there is any hint of non-compliance, you'll not have the luxury of a dry biscuit. Understand?"

The captives nodded their heads while sucking the last of the sweetened tea from the chipped mugs. Now they had a chance. Instead of starvation rations, they would receive full meals that would keep up their strength and assist in their escape. Havok thought back to his

SERE training again. Never John Wayne it. Take your enemy for whatever you can.

Renko continued his instructions: "After you surface tonight, you will be fed and then locked in the recompression chamber. It saves me the trouble of assigning a guard. If, by the end of our recovery of the gold, you have not informed us of the location of the sarin, I will not feed you or let you use the chamber. You will be useless to me, and you will be given back to Anisimova. Clear?"

Renko received two ambiguous stares.

"Good. Now, about the dive itself . . ." Renko briefed his new divers on the submarine's layout and the recovery process. At the end of the brief, Renko signaled to a group of sailors. The sailors brought over masks, work boots, weight belts, and tanks with regulators. They brought no wetsuits. Renko turned to leave but stopped to give the Americans a final warning: "I am in communication with the camp. If my men below lose sight of you for more than five minutes, I will radio the main camp, which will not bode well for the professor. I am told that the Chinese woman has taken quite a liking to her."

"Hey," Stone said. "Not to make light of our situation, but what do we do when natures calls?"

Stone saw that Renko had to stop and think for a moment before answering. After he figured out Stone's American slang, he answered the two men: "Somehow, I think you two have quite a bit of practice at thinking through uncomfortable situations." He turned away from the Americans as his men handed over the dive gear.

Havok and Stone accepted the gear and started to suit up.

"Great," Havok said while checking his regulator. "We're facing life and death here, and all you're worried about is how to take a dump." He saw that Stone went silent to think about something. "What are you thinking about?"

Stone, checking his own regulator, answered, "I'm just trying to remember the deepest depth I've ever had to force a war hammer." He turned to Havok. "I'm thinking with the male half of my brain. You, dipshit, seem to be thinking with the other half. You need to get your male half back in the game."

Havok shook his head and turned back to his dive equipment.

Once they were ready, the Americans climbed over the bulwark to join the divers already below. With the aid of thick anchor ropes that disappeared into the depths of the bay, Havok and Stone simply descended into the depths. As they did, the rising bubbles from the divers below greeted them. At fifty feet, Havok and Stone were welcomed by the ghostly outline of a submarine's tilted conning tower that materialized out of the greenish-gray beneath them. The rising sun was still not bright enough to light the underwater world, so they couldn't see the entire wreck. At seventy feet, they floated just aft of the conning tower and saw a severely damaged hull.

Havok's guess about the type of submarine had been correct. It was an I-400-class cruiser submarine with an elongated seaplane hangar. The hanger took up most of the available deck space fore and aft of the conning tower and bridge. As Havok and Stone pulled themselves forward past the conning tower, they saw a launch ramp that took up most of the forward deck that the hangar did not occupy. From Havok's knowledge, the hangar could accommodate three seaplanes with folded wings. The submarine lay canted to port. Dozens of jagged holes, with shards of rusting metal, peeled outward like flower petals. The holes must be the result of explosive cannon rounds that tore into the metal skin, Havok thought.

Havok and Stone continued to pull themselves forward and rounded the forward end of the seaplane hangar. In front of and below them was an open round hatchway just forward of the hangar and to the side of the launch ramp. The bundle of electrical wires snaked into the hatchway, while a weak light leaked out, illuminating a Russian diver hovering above the hatchway. He wore a full-face mask equipped with a telephone cable that connected him to the dive supervisor on the salvage ship. Suspended next to the diver was the punctured oil drum hanging by a wire rope.

Havok swam up to the hatchway and peered inside the short vertical tunnel. A vague glow illuminated the submarine's interior. An occasional air bubble escaped from inside the submarine, while the echoing clinking of metal indicated that divers moved about inside it. The Russian diver signaled Havok and Stone to enter.

Just as Havok was about to tuck his head into the round opening, he noticed the sun's rays penetrating the depths and brightening the water around them. He looked over and saw the ghostly outline of a single-masted sailing vessel resting in the mud some yards away. Though the outline of the vessel was fuzzy, it appeared to be in quite good condition. He could see no damage. It was as if someone had simply pulled out the bilge plug and let it sink. A jab in his side from the waiting Russian diver made Havok stop looking at the sailing vessel and turn his attention back to the hatch.

A diver's head appeared in the circular coaming at the bottom of the hatchway. The Russian diver inside the submarine crooked his gloved finger, directing the Americans to enter. Havok dove into the hatchway headfirst. Stone followed. It was a tight fit with the scuba tanks on their backs, but after banging their way down, they found themselves in the submarine's crew quarters. The Russian divers, who had entered first, had disappeared into the spaces aft or forward of the crew's quarters. Havok could hear them clunking about, but the diver who had signaled them waited. When both of the Americans had entered the quarters, the diver held up a fist, signaling them to stay there.

Just then, Havok saw a movement above him and he looked up. The drum was being lowered into the submarine, banging against the metal of the hatchway entrance as it did. He watched until it hit the angled deck. The wire rope it hung from remained taut. The Russian diver disappeared through an open watertight doorway into a compartment aft of the crew quarters.

One electric light mounted to a pipe along one wall provided a weak and ghostly illumination. The rest of the electric wires went through the hatches forward and aft to power other lights. A maze of pipes, valves, gages, lockers, and a wide variety of equipment surrounded Havok and Stone. The two men could also see a shimmering carpet two feet above them. It looked like a floating pool of mercury. The air bubbles that had escaped from the dive regulators over the last few weeks had collected into trapped air pockets. Exhaust bubbles from Havok's and Stone's regulators disturbed the air pocket.

Since the submarine lay at an angle, all the gear that was loose when the submarine had sunk lay piled up in the valley formed by the deck and the bulkhead of the compartment. The jumbled mass included a ragged bunk mattress, mess gear, clothing, and human remains. The knobby ends of long bones, splintered ribs, and pieces of broken skulls poked out of the gray mess. The bones were the remnants of poor sailors who had died a slow and horrible death while trapped inside a sinking iron coffin. Nevertheless, the Russians appeared to have had no concern for the dead Japanese sailors. It was evident that the Russians simply trampled on the bones as they carried out their task to recover the gold from inside the submarine.

I hope we don't end up like that, Havok thought. He shivered slightly and waited for the work to begin as the water, although relatively warm, started to sap his body heat.

The Russian diver who had greeted them before reappeared, coming in from the space aft of them. He walked as if he were a pantomime. He held a yellow brick close to his chest. Havok met the diver at the watertight door and relieved him of his precious load, stepping on the bones of dead Japanese sailors as he did. He turned around in time to see Stone accepting a gold ingot from a Russian diver who had appeared in the forward watertight doorway. The work began as Havok and Stone dumped their paving-brick-sized ingots into the hanging drum.

After about fifteen minutes of work, the drum was full. After signaling the Russian diver who remained outside the submarine, Havok grabbed the bottom of the drum and helped guide it as it was lifted out of the compartment. While waiting for its return, Havok and Stone continued to retrieve the gold ingots from the other divers and pile them on the mattress in the center of the room.

Eventually, the drum was lowered back into the submarine, and they filled it with the gold ingots piled on the mattress. Even though kept busy loading the gold, Havok and Stone both kept an eye on their air gauges, and when one of the divers came to the watertight doorway with another ingot, Havok showed his air gauge to the Russian. Havok also pounded his chest with a fist. The diver nodded in understanding, handed Havok his ingot, and held his fist vertical, indicating for Havok and Stone to stay and wait. The diver walked past Havok and pulled himself up through the hatch. Havok dumped the gold into the drum and waited.

Two divers exited the forward torpedo room, handed Stone their gold, and then pulled themselves up through the hatch. The drum followed them with Havok guiding it out the hatch. Just as the basket disappeared, two scuba tanks and regulators were lowered into the compartment on a rope. Havok and Stone swapped out the tanks and regulators. In less than a minute, the two empty tanks were pulled up through the hatch. The men waited for a new team of divers, a pile of gold ingots at their feet.

Hunger and cold plagued them. The tank straps and lead weights that chafed their skin and dug into their hips caused the morning to slip by painfully slowly. When they had switched out tanks a third time, their tongues felt as if they had quadrupled in size. The compressed air and rubber hoses dried their mouths, while the salt water sucked away what remained of their vital body heat. Their shins and kneecaps were bruised from knocking against metal.

With every passing minute, the pair was becoming weaker, and finally, with their fifth set of tanks, came uncontrollable shivers. If they did not get warm soon, they would surely die as their core temperatures reached dangerous lows. Somewhere, though, they found the strength to continue. Bruised legs carried spent bodies, and weakened arms carried heavy ingots. No longer did Havok care about watching their bottom time. His numbed mind and pain-racked body mechanically went back and forth.

Finally, to Havok's and Stone's immense relief, a Russian diver approached Havok, handed over an ingot, and gave him a thumbs-up. Havok dumped his load in the basket and waited for Stone, who was near the aft hatch, waiting for an ingot. The Russian diver who had signaled to Havok guided the basket through the hatch and followed it out. When Stone joined Havok, they also exited the submarine. Outside the wreck, warmth-giving light filtered down. In the center of the shimmering carpet above, Havok saw the two black hulls of the salvage ship and Kang's yacht.

Slowly, Havok and Stone rose toward life and warmth, resisting the urge to blast straight up, to free themselves from the grip of the cold depths. Their survival instincts remained intact, demanding that they ascend as slowly as their air supply would allow. Havok imagined the dissolved nitrogen in his bloodstream coming out of solution and turning into bubbles that would boil his blood, causing excruciating pain and death. When the men reached fifteen feet, they joined the Russian divers at their decompression safety stop. Another scuba tank and regulator hung by a rope. Half the size of a standard scuba tank, it served as an emergency bailout bottle. Havok and Stone hung on to the rope holding the bailout bottle and regulator and sucked the last of the air out of the tanks on their backs. Stone spat out his mouthpiece and grabbed at the regulator from the bailout bottle. He took two deep breaths before passing it over to Havok, who had just spat out his mouthpiece.

The sunlight and warmth that pierced the watery barrier was not enough to stop their uncontrollable shivering, but it was a start. Also, the thought of warmth, food, and fresh water combined to give the two men a new determination. They looked at each other through their masks, sending a message. The two Americans made up their minds: they would not be beaten.

When their three minutes were up, the Russian team leader kicked and started to rise. The other Russian divers followed. Havok and Stone, though, remained where they were. The bailout bottle would give them about another fifteen minutes of decompression time, and the two men needed to take advantage of every second of decompression time they could.

The team leader stopped to look down at them when he reached the surface, while the rest of the divers pulled themselves up the ladder hanging off the Russian ship. He knew what they were doing, and even though he was not supposed to give them any breaks, he felt sorry for them. The Americans had worked hard all morning, so what did a few extra minutes of decompression time matter? He floated at the surface, watching them for another several minutes, until he saw Havok spit out the regulator mouthpiece and look at him. Havok rose toward the surface, exhaling bubbles out of his mouth on the way up. Stone followed him, exhaling as well. When their heads broke the surface, the team leader climbed up the ladder, leaving Havok and Stone to fend for themselves.

After hanging on to the rope ladder a few minutes, Havok and then Stone struggled up the rungs and over the bulwark, where they collapsed on the deck. Even though a thick net covered the ship, the little sunlight that leaked through the netting warmed them. They lay on their sides, prostrate and shivering, soaking up the weak sunlight. After about five minutes, they felt strong enough to sit up to unbuckle their scuba gear. While their shaking hands struggled with the wet straps and metal clips, a crewman placed a tray on the deck next to them before returning to his shipmates inside the ship.

When Havok and Stone were finally free of their burdensome gear, they pounced on the tray, which held a plastic gallon jug of water and two mess tins, each heaped with boiled potatoes, cabbage, a chunk of fish, and a thick slice of brown bread smeared with butter. Though the two men's tongues tasted like rubber and their gums were raw, the bland food might as well have been the best French gourmet fare. After attacking the food and licking the empty plates clean, they drained the jug of its sweet, fresh water and lapsed into a deep sleep, brought on by full stomachs, warm air, and the exhausting toil below.

For an unknown number of minutes, Havok and Stone recuperated. They were lost in the depths of unconsciousness when a diver shattered their welcome respite by kicking their ankles. Grudgingly, Havok and Stone labored to their feet, donned a new set of scuba tanks, and climbed over the bulwark, joining a team of divers already in the water. As a whole, the dive team descended back into the depths to continue emptying the submarine of its precious bullion. The supply of gold seemed inexhaustible.

Back inside the submarine, the divers struggled to fill the metal drum. Above, Russians on the deck of the salvage ship sweated to empty the drum every time it surfaced and stow the ingots wherever space was still available below deck. The men not involved in the recovery process were busy recharging scuba tanks and maintaining the air compressors. In one form or another, everybody supported the massive effort.

Eventually, as the sun disappeared behind the island and darkness started to set in, the final team of divers surfaced to climb up the swinging rope ladder. Again, the Russians left Havok and Stone to use a refilled bailout bottle and fend for themselves. At the safety stop, Havok looked down and saw a very weak light far below him. It was light leaking out of the hatch on the submarine. The Russians hadn't turned the light out. Havok kept looking at the dim illumination until the bailout bottle surrendered the last of its air. Havok and Stone hauled their spent bodies up the ladder before falling over the bulwark. Eventually and excruciatingly, the Americans were able to wrestle free of their equipment. They crawled to their waiting meals. That was when Anisimova made his unwelcome appearance.

"Hello," Anisimova said, gloating over his captives. The weak red glare of the deck lights bounced off Anisimova's tanned cheeks and carefully manicured and pointed beard. He looked like Satan himself. Behind him, crewmen prepared equipment for the next day. "How are you this evening?"

"Just ducky," Stone garbled through a mouthful of potato. He held the plate up against his lips and sat cross-legged. He did not bother to look up.

Havok was a bit more civil. He leaned against the bulkhead of the superstructure, eating fish with his fingers and looking at Anisimova impassively. "We're fine."

"Do you find your work a trifle too difficult?" Anisimova asked.

Havok lied, "Not really. It's kind of a busman's holiday."

Anisimova slightly bobbed his head sideways in acknowledgment. "Since our last discussion, have you thought about revealing the location of the sarin?" he asked.

"Told you, shipmate," Havok replied. "We haven't a clue about your sarin."

"All right, then," Anisimova said.

Havok noticed a hint of anticipation in Anisimova's voice.

"If you wish to be so difficult about this matter, I am sure Renko will not be so lavish with your meals tomorrow, or any other niceties his men have allowed you today. I am told we might have one more day of recovery left, and I will make it a point to make sure it passes quite slowly and painfully for you two. Good night, gentlemen." Anisimova left the men alone to finish their meal.

Stone watched Anisimova walk away and turn the corner to the superstructure. "Thanks for pissin' off Doctor Evil. Work's going to be even harder without grub."

"Don't sweat it," Havok said. "Renko is not going to lose two good divers just because Anisimova requests it. But"—Havok paused to swallow his last bite of fish—"we'll probably run out of gold to find by this time tomorrow, and even Renko won't give a shit about us at that point. We've got to figure out a plan before then."

After they finished their food, Havok and Stone stood to look for Renko, but before they could take one step, the door at the rear of the superstructure opened and Renko stepped through the door, closing it quickly behind him.

"Are you two ready for the chamber?" Renko asked.

"You're going to have to work on your English," quipped Stone. "That didn't sound too good."

"I was just helping my men stow the ingots in the bilges," Renko said, ignoring Stone's remark.

"Yes, we are," Havok answered. Though extremely tired, he was able to roughly calculate the amount of time they were at depth and the time they were allowed to decompress underwater during their safety stops against their surface intervals, and he figured that the decompression chamber might not be needed. However, every little bit would help.

"You two did well today," Renko commented, turning to face the recompression chamber. "Follow me."

"I don't suppose that means you'll let us go?" Stone asked as he fell in behind Havok and Renko.

Renko answered with a slight, companionate smile. He led them to the open entrance into the recompression chamber.

Havok squeezed his frame through the round hatch and into the small steel chamber. Stone followed him, and between the two of them, it was a tight fit. They each sat on a narrow bench facing each other with their backs bent to match the curvature of the chamber.

"I always did hate the economy package," Stone said. His voiced echoed out the open hatch. "I wonder if it's too late to ask for an upgrade."

Renko sighed and looked away from them. He shut the hatch. Havok watched Renko through the tiny glass porthole as the man moved over to a mass of valves against the steel bulkhead and manipulated the various handwheels. The air inside the chamber turned thick and warm. Beads of condensate started running down the curved steel shell. Soon, the internal pressure gauge needle was pointing to one hundred feet. Havok could see Renko double-check the valve alignment before stepping out of sight. Inside the round steel shell, the occupants, still wearing their saltwater-soaked clothing, made themselves as comfortable as possible by stretching out on the narrow benches.

In the confines, Stone spoke with his eyes closed, his voice echoing off the steel inches from his face: "What do you think?"

"About what?" Havok asked, staring at the steel inches above his head.

"About us, the professor, and the god-damned San Diego Chargers," Stone blurted with genuine irritation.

"I think the professor is in dire need of our help, and I don't think the Chargers will have a chance in hell of making it to the Super Bowl this year."

"OK then, was that so hard?" Stone snapped. Then suddenly changing his tone, "Why doesn't Anisimova just cap us and call it a day?"

"Sorry, but for somebody like Doctor Evil, it would never be that humane. He gets his fix by pulling the wings off his victims before he squishes them between his fingers."

"I had to ask."

Havok and Stone went silent, stretched out the best they could on the short, narrow benches, and fell into a deep sleep.

Early the next morning, a man rapped his knuckles on the glass of the small porthole in the chamber's hatch. Havok and Stone woke with such agony it was hard for either of them to remember if he had ever been that sore before. Their joints and muscles ached. Their skin itched from wearing salt-encrusted clothing. Their mouths tasted like camels had shit in them while they slept. Havok tried to yawn but found his jaw locked. He yearned to stretch and anxiously watched as the diver at the porthole unlocked the round steel hatch and opened it.

Havok looked at the depth gauge mounted just above the hatch; they were at sea level. He also remembered the drop in temperature while half asleep. A chamber operator must have slowly bled off the pressure and brought them back to the surface figuratively while they slept.

Havok and Stone crawled out of the chamber. They could barely straighten their bodies. Instead, they hobbled out to the fantail, where each received a mug of hot sweetened tea and a buttered roll with liver spread and salty cheese. Once they wolfed down their breakfast, the backbreaking torture began all over again.

Throughout the morning and the early afternoon, after their lunch, Havok and Stone toiled and felt pain incurred from the previous day's work. They cursed the gold; however, as the day passed, both men had to wait longer and longer for Russian divers to emerge from the doorways fore and aft of the crew's compartment.

They must be running out of gold, Havok thought.

About two in the afternoon it was time to switch out the Russian dive teams, and the departing divers signaled Havok and Stone to follow them. Not really knowing what was going on, they followed the ascending divers until they reached fifty feet. One Russian turned and signaled for the two Americans to hold on to the bundle of electric cables and to wait. The Russian dive team surfaced while a replacement team dove past Havok and Stone. After a minute, Havok realized what was going on. They were indeed running out of gold, and instead of making them wait inside the submarine, the Russian divers were allowing the Americans to decompress, albeit slightly, at a lesser depth and to enjoy the little sunlight that did penetrate to fifty feet. Havok again looked down at the weak light that escaped the hatchway and thought about the Russian divers. I hope we don't have to kill any of these men.

By sunset, with the submarine now empty of gold, the American divers, almost crippled by now despite the subtleties given by the Russian divers presumably without Renko's knowledge, crawled from the black water and lay sprawled and shivering on the deck.

Havok's shaking hands were finally able to unclip the shoulder straps of the scuba tank on his back. Rolling away from the tank, he struggled to sit up, and as he did, Anisimova loomed out of the darkness.

"Hello. How are we doing this evening?" Anisimova greeted them cheerfully. "I hope today's efforts were agreeable."

"Can't complain," Havok replied, noticing Anisimova's expression, which told him the man's cheer was maniacal. Havok looked past Anisimova to where five commandos, including Ohmsky, stood. "I take it this is not the type of visit that we have all come to love."

"Correct, Mr. Havok," Anisimova said with a nod. "It seems the professor has received reports of your working conditions. She has grown quite concerned about your welfare and has finally been persuaded to reveal the location of our sarin in return for your better treatment."

"Where did she say it was?" Havok asked, hoping she had misled them.

"In an underground cavern about three kilometers from your boat," Anisimova responded, looking down his nose at Havok. "We discovered the entrance when one of Yeshenko's men fell into it. We are setting up equipment to recover his body and the sarin."

"Glad you have concern for your men," Havok said, disguising his disappointment.

"Renko says you have worked hard, and due largely to your efforts, the recovery is complete." Anisimova folded his hands behind his back and stood a bit straighter. His excitement was apparent to both Havok and Stone. "We have the gold and now the sarin, which means your services are no longer required."

"Thanks, pal," Stone said. "I always knew you would work us into an early grave."

Havok ignored Stone's comment. Instead, he was able to push himself up into a sitting position while looking at Anisimova in the growing darkness, trying to guess Anisimova's next move. He did not have to wait long.

"Ohmsky," Anisimova turned to the Russian sergeant. "Tie their hands, and get weight belts with enough lead to ensure they will stay put. I will meet you back here in a couple of minutes. I need to see Renko."

It was almost black now on the stern deck of the salvage ship, but Havok could still see Ohmsky's face when he received Anisimova's order. Ohmsky sighed and looked at the deck. His shoulders dropped as well.

By the time Anisimova returned, Havok and Stone had weight belts wrapped around their ankles and their hands were tied behind their backs.

"You men have been like maggots picking at my flesh," Anisimova stated, a hint of satisfaction in his voice. "I am glad to see that our relationship will soon be ended."

"Are you done?" Havok asked with no emotion.

Anisimova balked at Havok's lack of contriteness. The passiveness in Havok's voice and face irked him. He wanted to gloat in his victory, to toy with them as a cat would toy with a dying mouse. He wanted the men in front of him to grovel at his feet, begging for their lives. Instead, Havok and Stone stared him down, though they were within seconds of their own deaths. They had removed his pleasure.

"I am discarding you just like the trash you are," Anisimova snarled. Like flicking an unseen insect from his coat sleeve, he waved his right hand, and Ohmsky reached out and pushed the two men over the side.

22

TERUMBU ISLAND, LATE JULY

A SILHOUETTE OF COMMANDOS LINED THE CREVICE AS TWO OF THEIR NUMBER LEANED AGAINST RAPPELLING ROPES, BALANCING THEMSELVES ON THE EDGE OF THE OPENING. One of the two, a corporal, spoke into the small mouthpiece of the radio headset strapped to his uncovered head. He was testing the equipment. Once Yeshenko heard the corporal's voice on his headset, he ordered the men below. Silently, the two men lowered themselves from the protective watch of their comrades.

The soldiers slid down the ropes and into the fissure. Flashlights dangled from their cartridge belts and lit their way as they descended. After a few moments, they found themselves swinging in the spacious underground cavern, where their lights illuminated the body of their fallen comrade. The men stared at the ghoulish site, watching the body move. The corporal lowered himself farther, halting six feet above the cadaver. He saw the clothing move from the hundreds of insects that feasted on their unexpected meal. The light hanging from the corporal's belt passed over the man's face, revealing a grinning mask of death. In less than two hours, insects had consumed his eyes and lips.

The other soldier, hanging several feet above the corporal, shuddered at the sight of their friend. "Poor Sergei. Is there any chance he survived the fall?"

The corporal looked up from the corpse at the private above him. "Nyet. He's dead. Let's get him out of here before those damned bugs eat him down to the bone."

The men lowered themselves to the floor, landing on either side of their comrade. The private bent over the corpse to weave his climbing rope through the shoulder straps of the man's web gear. The corporal made his report to Yeshenko, who stood 160 feet above him.

"Colonel, we're on the cave floor and we found Sergei. He's dead."

When the soldiers had finished securing the rope, the corporal added, "He's ready to be lifted out."

"Stand clear," Yeshenko ordered.

The men in the cavern stepped back as the men on the surface took up the slack in the rope, and as if the corpse had come back to life, it jumped to its feet. The insects that were not quick enough to latch on to a piece of flesh cascaded off the puppetlike body. The dead man soared upward through the hole in the rounded ceiling as if he were Lucifer himself.

After watching their friend rise out of the cavern, the men began their search for the sarin. First, they used their flashlights to scan the dry, sandy carpet of the cavern floor, looking for the tiniest clue, the smallest disturbance. When the beams of lights failed to find any sort of track, they moved out from where they stood. For many minutes, busy light beams danced about the floor and walls of the cavern and stabbed into every crevice. Finally, the corporal's light found something out of the ordinary.

"There," he said, pointing with the beam of his light.

The private turned and saw the corporal looking into a small cul-de-sac. He joined the corporal and saw the same thing. The sand inside the cul-de-sac was different from the sand outside of it.

"Sir," the corporal said, speaking into the mouthpiece. "We have found an area that looks like it has been recently disturbed. We are going to start digging."

"Very well," Yeshenko's distant voice replied.

The corporal and his charge placed their lights in crevices and angled them so that they lit the floor before unclipping their entrenching tools from their belts and beginning to scoop away the sand. They dug with a mission. Soon, their sweat mixed with the sand and the sweat of previous men, and their efforts paid off when the blades of their shovels struck something firm. The corporal set aside his tool to scrape away the loose sand and expose a patch of camouflage clothing. They had found one of their missing men.

The diggers worked fast to uncover the body, and as they pulled his body out, the two men uncovered another missing soldier. The second dead soldier was faceup and laughing at them with a great, bloody smile that went from ear to ear under his chin.

The corporal said aloud, "Did the Americans really have to cut his throat?"

The private sighed. "Well, it's done. Let's get him out of there."

The two men grabbed the top dead man by the feet and the shoulder straps of his web gear, pulling him from the shallow grave. They turned back and pulled the second man from the bottom of the grave, expecting to see the bottom lined with canisters of sarin. However, there was no sarin.

The corporal reported their findings: "Sir, we have both missing men but no sarin." His voice echoed throughout the domed cavern as he spoke into the mouthpiece.

"Keep digging," Yeshenko ordered over the headset. "It has to be there!"

"Yes, sir," the corporal replied.

Back on the surface, Yeshenko took his eyes away from the black hole and looked to his right. Varonov stood next to him. "Call the base camp. Have them get the Americans out here. If they won't tell us where the sarin is, we'll hang them upside down over this hole until they do. Tell that Asian pig to ask the professor again too. Tell him to tell Xian not to be so nice this time."

Varonov turned to call the camp on his cell phone, leaving Yeshenko to stare back into the crevice. For thirty minutes, the men below dug farther into the grave. When they hit solid rock, they started to dig around the edges of the grave.

Thirty minutes later, Yeshenko paced back and forth along the rim. Soon his earpiece crackled with the dreaded news that he had expected to hear.

"Sir," the corporal reported, "we have dug down a meter. There is nothing down here except two dead spetsnaz."

Still, Yeshenko was not willing to give up. "Spread out and keep looking. Either the Americans are lying or they moved it."

Yeshenko waited for the Americans while trying to figure what had happened to the nerve gas. Finally, Varonov approached Yeshenko with a confused look on his face. "Colonel, it looks as if Deputy Anisimova went aboard the Stalinetz and executed the Americans an hour ago. They're dead, sir."

Yeshenko could not believe what he had heard. That impatient fool had killed the men before they had recovered the sarin. Killing the prisoners before the goods were within their hands went against all common sense and practicality. On second thought, though, Anisimova's move did not surprise Yeshenko. Anisimova was a bully, and men like him were afraid of men like Havok and Stone. Anisimova might have impressed politicians with his intelligence and earned the respect of the public with his boldness, but professional soldiers who had to survive on their wits and honor despised the man. The only reasons Anisimova was in charge of this operation were his knowledge of the wreck and his ability to incur favor with the real leaders of their movement, who were all back in Russia.

After a few moments, Yeshenko's anger subsided. Still looking into the crevice, Yeshenko gave his orders: "Varonov, get four more men in there and have them look another hour. I'll return to camp with the rest of the men. In the meantime, I need to have words with Anisimova."

Yeshenko returned to camp while six flashlight beams danced energetically over the cavern's floor and craggy walls, searching for any clue. Hellish lights and dilated pupils inspected every nook and cranny. Nothing escaped the soldiers' attention—nothing except a partial footprint almost completely covered by a four-foot-tall chunk of limestone that was wedged into a narrow vertical crack that split the cavern's back wall.

***

Back at the base camp, inside the second-story room above Anisimova's, a heap lay on the floor. Standing above the prostate figure was Xian, her face flushed with the erotic excitement from the beating she had just finished giving Pilar.

Xian decided to take a break and accepted a glass of wine from Chiba, Kang's bodyguard. After filling her glass, Chiba placed the half-full wine bottle on a table next to the doorway. There were several bottles of liquor and wine on the table along with glasses. Chiba had watched the beating, and his pleasure showed. His thickset frame was capped with a head that was attached to his shoulders without the presence of a neck. Kang, sitting on a camp chair, held a glass of whiskey and smiled.

"I am sorry, Miss Bonne-Bouche," Kang stated, "but if you refuse to give us the real location of the sarin, we shall have to continue with this foreplay. As much as I detest my present associates, I did make a substantial investment in their endeavors, and I will not let you destroy this opportunity."

"You aren't beating me for just the sarin," Pilar grunted through swollen lips.

"You are correct," Kang replied with a smile. "You have been a thorn in my foot for many years. Due to your efforts, my companies cannot legally enter the US to participate in projects that other companies are conducting this very minute. Now you are following me around the South China Sea to cause me more trouble. Yes, I am enjoying this. Again, please tell us where Havok hid the sarin."

"I told you what Havok told me," Pilar stated as she struggled to sit up. "What about Havok and Stone? Are they still on the Russian ship? Are they OK?"

"They are still alive," Kang replied. He was unaware of Havok's and Stone's execution. "But from what I hear, they have been worked near to death. That is, they were worked near to death until you told us where the sarin was. Now, since it is not where you said it would be, I fear their tortuous work may begin again. Unfortunately"—Kang paused to sip his whiskey—"no matter what the Russians do to those two, I do not think Havok and Stone are the type who will break. No, they will be the cause of their own demise unless you are that cause. You had better be totally honest with us."

"I have been truthful with you." Pilar was sitting upright now. "If the Russians haven't found the sarin, it is because somebody moved it or they're digging in the wrong spot. I know Havok told me the truth. He had no reason to lie."

"For your sake, Miss Bonne-Bouche, let's hope he did tell you the truth," Kang warned.

23

TERUMBU ISLAND, LATE JULY

UNDER THE VEIL OF MOONLIGHT, TWO HEADS QUIETLY BOBBED TO THE SURFACE OF THE COAL-BLACK SEA JUST OUTSIDE AND AFT OF THE FALSE ISLAND. Havok and Stone remained motionless as they sucked in great amounts of air through open mouths as quietly as they could. After a few minutes, they glided under the camouflage netting to the starboard side of the Russian ship. While they hung off the rope ladder, recouping their strength, they listened for voices but heard none.

"Did you really have to drop me on my head?" Stone whispered.

"I just saved your life, and you still have room to complain?" Havok replied. "By the way, your head landed on a mattress."

"Fine. Thanks for saving my life, but did you really have to drop me on my head?"

Havok didn't reply. Instead, he stared at the rope ladder, thinking of a plan, and of their narrow escape.

Their survival had been close.

Their bound bodies had sped downward in the water, but Havok did not fight or struggle against his bindings, knowing it would be a waste of energy. Instead, he waited to hit the bottom. As he counted off the seconds, he could see nothing but the weak light escaping the open forward hatch of the submarine far below him. It seemed like hours, but Havok had subconsciously counted off ten seconds when his plunging race came to a sudden halt. The men's bare feet struck the edge of the submarine's deck, but the stop was brief. Their feet slid over the curved hull, the weights pulling them downward. A second later, their feet plunged into mud.

Havok could feel the muck around his ankles, which also covered the buckle of the weight belt. He could also feel the corroded steel of the sub's hull against his back. By then, his lungs were climbing into his throat, trying to escape to the surface without him. At the same time, dozens of thoughts raced through his brain. Havok knew his brain would start shutting down from lack of oxygen, but something brushed against him. Was it Stone going through his death throes? He didn't know, but it saved his life. As he was pushed sideways, his hands scraped across the jagged edge of torn metal. He ran his bindings up and down against the jagged metal, and he felt the steel slice into his flesh. He didn't care, as they had been down for over a minute and were running out of air. Finally, the rope snapped and his hands flew apart. He bent over and thrust his hands into the mud, fishing with his slashed fingers until they felt the large metal buckle. He struggled feverishly to release it. By now, Havok was seeing racing bright lights. Death was near.

He didn't know if it was him or the Virgin Mary, but something forced open the buckle, and he felt his feet pull themselves from the mud. He desperately needed to reach the surface and life, but he could not face leaving his friend behind. He knew Stone was off to his left, so he leaned over and reached out with his arm, waving it back and forth. He found Stone, who himself was thrashing furiously, struggling against his bindings and the lead weights. Havok didn't waste time with the rope, but pushed his hands into the thick mire at Stone's feet. He found the buckle, snapped it open, turned around, and stuck his arm between Stone's arm and chest, in square-dance fashion. Havok used his free hand to pull both of them up, along the hull of the submarine. Once they were on the deck, he saw the light coming from the open hatch. Forcibly, Havok pushed Stone toward the hatch and threw him through it headfirst. Havok followed Stone, and seconds later, both of them were sucking in the air trapped in the pocket inside the submarine.

Neither man said anything for the longest time as they came to grips with their miraculous survival. They simply breathed in as much as they could, with their eyes closed. Their laborious breathing echoed against their eardrums in the tiny air pocket.

After a while, Havok asked, "You ready?"

***

Now, somewhat recovered, Havok said, "Time to spike a gun?"

"I hope I get to see Anisimova's face when he realizes we ain't dead," Stone whispered back. "He tried to drown us, but all he did was throw us into the briar patch."

"Now you can recall your literature?" Havok responded as he pulled on the rope ladder. "Come on."

Havok slid over the bulwark with Stone right behind him, and when both of them were lying flat on the deck, they crawled forward, feeling their way cautiously. Stone passed Havok and was the first to reach the ladder that led to the upper deck, while Havok paused to collect a few pieces of round steel stock that lay scattered about the deck: leftovers from the welding table. He scooped them up and stood, ready to follow Stone up the ladder, when suddenly a brilliant white light blinded him. Havok froze where he stood and looked through the open watertight door directly into the ship's interior. The massive body of one of the divers filled the frame only four feet in front of him.

Although the diver's body faced Havok, his head was turned, looking back at his unseen shipmates. A fury of Russian curses pummeled the unthinking man, and just as quickly as the door opened, it was snapped shut, burying Havok again under a blanket of darkness. Havok realized how lucky he was, and he knew the longer they remained on board the more of their luck would evaporate. With his night vision ruined, he stuck his hands out in front of him, searching for the handrails of the ladder. He found them and followed them up to where Stone was waiting for him. Hunched over, Stone led Havok forward until they reached the single-barreled cannon. Without speaking, each man knew what to do.

Stone's hands caressed the cannon barrel until he found what he was looking for. With both hands on the charging bolt, his tired arms slowly pulled it back, exposing the breech. "Go ahead, make their day," he said through clenched teeth.

Havok removed the belted ammunition and inserted three pieces of the stock, one at a time, into the breech, pushing them as far as they would go into the tapered barrel, making sure they were snug. He placed the ammunition back into the breech as well. "All right, let it go."

Stone eased the bolt forward, completing the gun-spiking operation, and within minutes, the men were in the water, swimming toward shore. Reaching the beach at the apex of the bay thirty minutes later, Havok and Stone dragged their bodies from the grip of the cold sea and collapsed onto the smooth sand, warming themselves with the dull rays of the weak moon.

"You know something?" Stone said as he recovered from the half-mile swim. "I would really hate to be the first guy that fires that thing up."

"It's not gonna be pretty," Havok answered, staring at the moon, lost in thought.

"I sure could go for a hot beef steak right about now," Stone said.

"If we're lucky, all we're gonna get tonight is a cold can of beans, and that's going to have to wait."

"Ain't you the Galloping Gourmet."

"I never claimed to be Graham Kerr."

"Who's that?"

"Forget it; let's get moving."

Grudgingly, the men stood and walked toward the main camp. Though they remained cautious, Havok gambled there would not be any patrols out that night. The Russians thought they were dead, the gold was safely stowed, and, as far as Havok and Stone knew, the Russians had recovered the sarin from the cavern. They arrived at the camp's perimeter and skirted around it until they were behind the two-story building where Anisimova occupied the lower floor and where Xian had been torturing Pilar on the second floor. They could see dim lights leaking through the rain ponchos that covered the windows on both levels, as well as familiar voices coming from the first story.

"What do you mean you killed them?" Kang said. His anger was apparent.

"That is correct," Anisimova said defensively.

"Then you're a fool for doing so," Yeshenko blasted. "At least until we recovered the sarin. All we found were my two missing men, and I lost a third just finding them. Kang, did you ask the professor if she knew where else it could be?"

"Yes, she clings to the same story," Kang said. "She's upstairs with my bodyguard. Somehow, I believe her. She says you are looking in the wrong spot or somebody else moved it."

"No matter," Yeshenko said, shaking his head. "We will begin our search again in the morning. It is too late to do anything now."

He turned to leave the room, but Kang stopped him.

"Before you leave, can I offer you a piece of advice?"

"Yes, Kang," Yeshenko said wearily. His voice revealed the strain of the last few days.

"In recent weeks, you have tried to kidnap Havok and his friend, to shoot him down, and to burn them alive. Now, your comrade here has drowned them. They seem quite tenacious, so I suggest your divers verify that the execution was carried out successfully."

Yeshenko, committing his first mistake since being on the island, agreed. "That is sound advice, and I will have them do so by first light." He nodded his head while looking at Anisimova with disdain and then at his watch. "It is late. I am going to bed. Just make sure your bodyguard leaves the professor in walking condition. I will collect her at sunrise."

Havok and Stone heard the sounds of people leaving the building. They looked around the corner and saw Yeshenko walking toward the center of camp. They also saw Kang round the corner, where he climbed the rusting steel steps up to the second floor. After listening to a brief exchange in Chinese, they watched Kang and Chiba walk down the steps and toward the beach. After a minute, they also saw Anisimova leave the building and walk to the two-story building at the other end of camp.

Havok knew they had only minutes to work. They quickly covered the few yards to the steps leading up to the second floor and took them three at a time. At the top landing, they entered the room. They saw Pilar lying on her right side with her hands tied behind her back. She appeared to be sleeping. Havok knelt down and placed one hand on her shoulder and the other over her mouth, touching her gently. At first, she jerked away, but she looked up and recognized Havok's face in the darkness. As he untied her and helped her to her feet, he heard booted footsteps landing heavily on the metal steps.

Stone searched for some sort of weapon while Havok shoved Pilar into a dark corner. Stone kept looking at the bottles on the table next to the door, and it looked to Havok as if Stone couldn't make up his mind which bottle to grab.

"Pssst!" Havok hissed, holding his hands up in despair.

Stone looked at him and held his hands up as well. "What?" he mouthed.

Stone saw the don't-fuck-with-me look in Havok's wide eyes.

Exasperated, Stone dropped his hands and grabbed the bottle of chardonnay. He held it over his head and firmed his body up against the doorframe. They heard approaching footsteps, and then the man's thick skull entered the room. The thought of what would happen to them if they did not put this behemoth down for good gave Stone's weak arms renewed strength. The coiled springs of his arms snapped loose, thudding the bottle across the crown of the man's skull, shattering the bottle.

The force of the blow brought a muted grunt from the victim. His body bowled forward as Stone jumped on his back and rode him to the ground. As they landed, Stone grabbed Chiba's ears and viscously smashed his face into the concrete slab three times. Pilar listened to the sounds of bone and cartilage breaking. With Stone still on top of the dead man, he went through the pockets of his clothing, relieving Chiba of a 9 mm, two extra magazines, and a stiletto knife. Havok looked around for anything useful and came up only with a canteen of water, which he passed over to Pilar. He turned to help Stone drag Chiba's body into a dark corner. Havok grabbed Pilar and led all three of them out of the room, down the stairs, and into the darkness of the jungle.

Halfway to the seaplane base, the escapees stopped for rest and water. They took turns emptying the two-quart canteen before speaking. "You know something?" Havok said, speaking to Pilar for the first time in days. "Rescuing you is becoming a full-time job."

Pilar swallowed the last gulp of the water and then passed the empty canteen back to Havok. "I'm glad to see that I'm keeping you gainfully employed, but how are we getting off this island?"

Havok answered, "We're going to start with getting ourselves an airplane."

"We're going to fly out?" Pilar asked, and a smile came to her face at the prospect of leaving this island of death and misery.

"After we take care of a few items first," Havok said. After pausing for a moment, he had to ask, "Pilar, what's going on with the sarin?"

"I'm not sure. I told the Russians just what you told me. They found the cavern and the grave with two dead Russians buried in it, but no sarin. Did somebody move it after you buried it?"

Havok thought for a moment before responding, "Well, I only killed the one Russian, so I think we owe Ben Gunn a nice piece of cheese."

"There you go with Ben Gunn again," Stone said. "What do you mean by that?"

"I'll tell you later, but you're right: it's time to get ourselves an airplane."

***

Four loud and drunken men sat around the folding army table. They all wore their flight coveralls, and two of them wore shoulder holsters that held semiautomatic pistols at their sides. On the table, three almost-empty vodka bottles, two rolls of toilet paper, a jar of pale green liquid, and a plate of pickles surrounded the battery-operated lantern in the center of the table. Two other men sat by a dying campfire, sharing a bottle, a magazine of some sort, and quiet conversation as one of them held it up to view the centerfold in its entirety.

"They seem to be celebrating," Stone surmised.

"They are," Pilar answered. "They're leaving tomorrow morning and taking some excess gear and some of the soldiers back early."

"Back to Mother Russia?"

"Indirectly. One of them is bragging about what he is going to do when he gets to Da Nang. It sounds like some sort of pit stop."

"Well then, are we going to take that Popsicle stand or what?" Stone said impatiently.

"Just hold on to your saddle sores, Pete. I'm waiting for an opening."

Two minutes later, the opening came.

One of the armed men stood, said something, and grabbed a roll of toilet paper.

Havok watched the man stumble toward them. "Pete, you and Pilar get as close as you can to the table, and keep your eyes on the guy taking a dump. When he comes back out, you two jump the other armed man at the table." He looked at Pilar. "Know how to use a pistol?"

"Yes."

"Good." Havok handed her the bodyguard's pistol, and before he left he warned, "Don't think twice about shooting any one of those guys if you have to. They're so drunk they're liable to do anything."

The three of them remained squatting in the bushes, letting the Russian pass. Pilar and Stone then edged closer to the camp, while Havok looped around and approached the squatting figure from behind. The smell of the area told him to watch his step. The man jerked and wobbled as he squatted, creating a mess on his right foot and the leg of the flight suit. Havok sighted the holster and casually stepped up behind the man. He snatched the revolver from the holster and jammed it against the man's neck; then he grabbed the man's collar with the other hand and pulled the Russian to his feet.

The pilot did not know what was happening, but he knew enough to stand peacefully.

Havok pushed the barrel of the revolver harder against the man's neck and held him at arm's length. Although drunk, the man got the message and walked back toward the table. The pilot stumbled into the open, and the violence erupted so fast it seemed to be over before it had started.

As soon as Havok and his captive entered the clearing, Stone and Pilar leapt from the jungle, jumping at the table with the other men. Pilar jammed the barrel of her pistol against the other pilot's cheek, while Stone yanked the sidearm out of its holster and pointed it at the other men at the table. The larger of the two men by the campfire threw down the magazine he was holding and jumped to his feet. Stone quickly aimed at him and pulled the trigger twice in quick succession. Two slugs tore into the man's chest, knocking him back onto the bright red coals of the campfire. He was dead before landing. The sitting pilot took advantage of the distraction. He grabbed at the barrel, yanking the pistol free from Pilar's hands. Havok saw the flurry of movement in the flickering shadows, and in a split second, he removed the pistol from his captive's neck and leveled it at the rising figure between Stone and Pilar. He fired twice into the man's face and then rammed the barrel back into the neck of his now slightly deaf captive.

Pilar jerked her head away as bone and gore slapped against the side of her face. The slaughter also splattered all over the table with a piece of toothed jaw knocking over the lamp. Abrupt silence reigned supreme throughout the camp; only the crackling of the fire could be heard as flames consumed the legs of the corpse.

"We did not mean to kill your chums," Havok said, speaking in English. "They were stupid. If you behave, you all will live through this night, I promise."

The Russians answered him with uncertain looks.

Havok pointed his pistol at the man next to the fire and flicked the barrel. The man grabbed his dead friend by one arm and dragged him from the fire. Havok returned the barrel to the neck of the man he was holding. "My friend and I are going to get something, and the professor will stand guard. If you make an attempt to escape or harm her, all of you will die, understand?"

The men looked at their dead comrades and then nodded their heads vigorously in agreement.

"Pete, find some rope."

Stone disappeared into the shadows and soon returned with a coil of nylon rope. He grouped the Russians together by the campfire while

Havok approached Pilar. She was wiping blood from her face with toilet paper. He bent over and pulled the pistol from the dead pilot's grip and handed it back to her. "Hang on to it this time. Pete and I are going back to the Outfit for some possibles." Through the dancing light of the campfire, he could see the fear and apprehension in her eyes. He grabbed her arms firmly. "Don't worry, we'll be right back. If any of them move, shoot them all."

"What about the others? Maybe they heard the gunfire at the main camp."

"I doubt it. It's too far, and besides, it's a chance we have to take." Havok could see the worry in her face. "Tell you what, go hide over there in the jungle and watch the Russians from there. If anybody shows up, come to us, all right?"

Pilar nodded her head.

"Good." He gave her a reassuring wink while flicking a piece of skull from her shoulder. "I'm going aboard the seaplane for a couple of minutes first." He left her to watch the Russians, while Stone made sure they could not loosen their bindings.

Havok quickly ran through the cavernous interior of the aircraft. He found a light switch on the curved wall and turned on the dim overhead lights. He looked around the inside of the airplane, spotting the nose gun with two large aluminum boxes of ammunition in a small compartment under the seats of the cockpit, along with a toolbox and a sampling connection for the fuel systems. Satisfied, he left the plane and found Stone, who was dunking a pickle into the jar of pickle juice to wash off brain matter.

"How quick can you make a couple of bombs out of scuba tanks?"

"Quicker than a politician jumping in front of TV camera," Stone said before chomping on the pickle.

***

After the run through the humid jungle, the salt water felt shockingly cold against Havok's skin as he slid into the watery grave of his boat, and longtime friend. Stone stood guard at the edge of the cove. Through the darkness, Stone watched Havok's shadow wade through the exposed wreckage, gathering needed materials.

With knowing hands, Havok searched through the remains of his once-proud boat, finding first a waterproof flashlight. He used it to help find other needed items: a coil of rope, four scuba tanks still in their racks, and four weight belts, each with several three-pound weights. He had everything they would need; the seaplane would provide the rest.

By two a.m. Havok and Stone had made it back to the seaplane with their load tied to their backs. They cautiously approached the camp. The fire was now a pile of glowing embers, and the dim light silhouetted four men as they sat up against each other, snoring loudly.

"Pilar," Havok whispered loudly as he stepped to the table. There was no answer, so he eased the load off his back and pulled his pistol from his waistline. "Pilar?"

A figure burst from the jungle to his right. Poised and ready to fire, he waited until the dying fire exposed the running figure. Pilar's smooth brown face came in from the light and plowed into Havok's chest. "I've been so frightened. Please say you'll never leave me again."

"Promise," he said honestly. "Have any visitors?"

She shook her head vigorously against Havok's chest with her arms wrapped around his waist. When she had settled down, she noticed the scuba tanks. "What are these for?"

Stone, who had already dropped his load near the workbench, was eating another pickle. He answered Pilar, "Welcome to Bomb Making one oh one."

"You're going to help Stone while I learn how to fly a Russian seaplane."

Havok checked the Russians to make sure their bindings were still secure. Then he entered the huge airplane, making his way to the cockpit. They needed to accomplish quite a bit within the short time they had until sunrise: Stone had to manufacture four bombs and then learn how to operate the 23 mm cannon, while Havok had to learn how to fly the Russian multi-engine seaplane. Although he had logged almost fifteen hundred hours of airtime, most of that was in single-engine aircraft. The sight of the numerous gauges was almost overwhelming. Havok shrugged his shoulders and repeated to himself, An airplane is an airplane is an airplane. He looked in the seat pockets for the usual check-off lists found in any airplane. Havok found the lists and started to review the images in the instructions.

Meanwhile, Stone and Pilar got themselves busy making bombs. The first thing Stone did was to lay one empty scuba tank on the workbench and place the first-stage valve in the vise bolted to the bench. Next, he opened the drawers under the work surface of the bench until he found a strap wrench. Placing the webbing around the base of the scuba tank, Stone pushed on the strap's lever until the tank started to turn. Satisfied, Stone continued turning the tank until it popped free from the valve. He removed both items and placed them on the ground before grabbing a second tank to repeat the process.

"While I'm doing this, Pilar," Stone said, "find me some containers to hold fuel."

Without saying a word, Pilar obeyed by walking over to the camp table and grabbing the jar of pickle juice. After tossing out the liquid, she searched the ground for more empty food jars or cans. By the time she returned, Stone had managed to remove all four valves from the tanks.

"Pilar, since you're a diver, go ahead and strap a weight belt with weights to the shoulder of each of these tanks. I'm going to do the stuff to finish making our bombs."

"You know what you're doing," Pilar replied.

Stone reached out to grab the jars from her hand and gave her a wink as he turned.

Entering the airplane, he left the jars on a bench seat inside before going forward and dropping into the small bow compartment where the weapon was mounted. He poked through two large ammunition boxes, each one containing about one hundred rounds of a deadly mixture of tracer—high-explosive incendiary armor-piercing rounds.

"A hell of a pig in a poke," Stone mused.

He pulled apart the linked ammunition and selected four high-explosive rounds; then he linked the belt back together. Clutching the rounds in his hand, he left the airplane and saw that Pilar had already strapped the lead weights on the scuba tanks.

"Looks good."

"Thanks," she said, looking at the rounds in Stone's hand. "What kind of material are you going to use to fill the tanks to make them explode?"

"I'm planning on filling each tank with about a gallon of gas from the airplanes. Then I'll thread the rounds into the necks of the scuba tanks. Why?"

"I can see your reasoning for using the big bullets as fuses. Dropping them from any height should set them off, but why the gas? Why not use the propellant from more of those rounds? I'm no bomb expert, but I can think of several advantages of using the explosive propellant in granular form from the bullets instead of gas. First, a couple of handfuls of the propellant powder or dust, which I assume is self-oxidizing, would have more of an explosive air-to-surface ratio. Second, having a gallon of gas sloshing around inside the tanks doesn't provide the same surface-to-air ratio. Lastly, I believe the flashpoint for gas is quite high, much more so than loose powder, and it has to be in vapor form. After all, that's what you're trying to do, right? Maximize the explosive potential of your bombs?"

Pilar paused long enough to see Stone give her a quizzical look. "However, I know you would have thought of it eventually."

Stone paused for a minute while looking at the rounds on the workbench. After a nod of his head, he looked at Pilar. "Hey, it's been a long day, and I'm a bit beat. That is sound advice."

Pilar smiled at him. "Just trying to do my part."

"Well," Stone continued, "it's nice to see that not all of you academics are politically biased dullards. There's hope for the American education system after all."

"Good," she said. "I'll take that as a compliment. Now go ahead and get me more rounds. I'd say maybe a dozen or so. I'll finish making the bombs, and you can spend the time to get familiar with the gun in the bow of that airplane."

Stone straightened up a bit and answered with a salute before turning to the airplane. He searched the bow of the airplane and found two extra ammunition boxes. After giving Pilar twelve rounds, he returned to the gun mount. He sat in the hard bucket seat behind the weapon. It was a Russian 23 mm antiaircraft gun. He grasped the weapon by its bicycle-like handlebars and moved it around. The weapon was positioned on a short mount with the barrels inserted through a hole in the Plexiglas, which allowed some movement. Stone could see that the weapon was not an original part of the plane, but inserted sometime later, haphazardly, but it was functional. He pulled back the charging handles twice to make sure the weapon was operable, ejecting two rounds as he did.

"Do you think they'll work?" Pilar asked with one eyebrow raised as Stone pulled up beside her. He saw the four tanks with explosive rounds threaded into the neck openings upside down and the weight belts strapped to their shoulders. The empty casings and projectiles lay separately on the workbench. A pipe wrench lay next to the vise.

"Lady." Stone drew back slightly. "I see that you may have missed your calling in life. Now help me get them on board."

Havok was in the cockpit, struggling his way through the flight instructions. He decided to give his tired eyes a break and turned around, looking aft, into the cabin. He saw Stone and Pilar working to load the bombs through the fuselage door and noticed that Pilar was smiling. The sparkle in her eyes reinforced a new determination to survive. With Pilar's smile firmly imprinted on his mind, he went back to his studying, but he realized the instructions were useless, so he tossed them aside and started to study the controls and gauges. He also realized that he had begun to notice many little things about Pilar, insignificant mannerisms to which, in other women, he would not have given a second thought.

***

As a steel-gray light softened the black eastern sky, the surviving Russian pilot woke up. His legs were damp from the early-morning dew, and his head thundered from vodka. As he sat recovering from his stupor, he looked up at his airplane and spotted three people standing on the port wing, dropping the camouflage netting. Sorrowfully, he realized it was not a bad dream or the vodka.

24

TERUMBU ISLAND, LATE JULY

ANISIMOVA WOKE TO THE SOUND OF YESHENKO STOMPING INTO HIS ROOM, HIS COMBAT BOOTS STRIKING THE CONCRETE FLOOR HARD AS HE ENTERED.

"God damn you, Anisimova!" Yeshenko shouted. "Renko sent his divers down, and the two Americans are not there. Also, I looked in on the professor upstairs, and all I saw was one dead obese Chinese bodyguard."

Anisimova, still fogged by sleep, didn't comprehend the seriousness in Yeshenko's voice. *I guess the professor was stronger than she looked,* he thought.

Just at that moment, both of them heard the distant sound of the seaplane engines firing up. Now Anisimova woke to realization, but he dared not show his panic. "They must be warming up the engines," he said as he stood up from his bunk in his underwear.

"Are you sure?" Yeshenko asked with a sneer as he turned to the door. He'd heard the desperation in Anisimova's statement. As Yeshenko stepped toward the door, the sound of the engines deepened. He turned around and glared at Anisimova bitterly. "You fool! Listen to that! They are taking off. Havok is alive."

Yeshenko left the doorway to organize the troops, but Anisimova remained in the room, trying to come to grips with the sound of his future dissolving. After a large shot of vodka, the stunned man quickly clothed himself and stepped out from his room. He joined Yeshenko, Varonov, and Ohmsky, who waited for the rest of the Russian soldiers to collect their weapons and gear. Yeshenko saw Anisimova approach with his face ashen and downcast. Gone was the look of a man who thought he was superior to others. Now he wore the face of a man who was looking for a way out.

Anisimova saw Yeshenko staring at him, and he tried to return to his old self. "Colonel Yeshenko, I want a full report as soon as possible. If we do not find the sarin and if the Americans escape, we will not be too welcome back home."

"And we can blame you for that, you fool!" Yeshenko exclaimed, spitting out the words as if they were venom.

"Do not worry about blame; we can live with that," Anisimova said. "It's Putin's cleaners that we have to worry about. After a mess like this, he'll select the best of his janitorial staff."

"Unlike you, I do not fear death," Yeshenko stated. "It is called being a man."

***

Meanwhile, aboard the salvage ship, Renko sat in the brown vinyl-covered bridge chair on the port bridge wing. Drinking a mug of tea, he wondered what had happened to the Americans. Did sharks eat them already, or did a current wash the bodies away? While pondering, he watched the disguised Kona Wave pull into the bay and anchor over the same spot the silver had been recovered from earlier. Through the holes in the camouflage net, Renko's eyes followed the research ship's mooring until he saw the seaplane fly away from the island.

They must be testing the engines, he thought.

***

In the air, Havok struggled to smooth out the flight of the lumbering bird. The takeoff had been relatively easy, but once in the air, the plane pitched and yawed, mostly from Havok overcorrecting the unfamiliar plane. He extended his upwind leg for that reason, to give him time to get familiar with the huge bird and its controls. He flew away from the island until the aircraft flew straight and level. It responded to his hands exactly. He had conquered the huge, weighty warbird, and now it was his, like a freshly broken mustang, spirited but willing to do his bidding.

Havok gently banked the airplane to starboard, easily maintaining his altitude of five hundred feet, coming around half circle. He made small adjustments to the trim and throttle controls until the small green dot ahead was an unwavering target in the center of his windshield. Soon the sparkling center of the island was expanding into view. They were committed now. Havok pushed the small button on the yoke with his left thumb and spoke into the boom mike positioned in front of his mouth. "Whenever you're ready, Stone, but just give our diver friends a bit of breathing room first."

"No problem, and I hope I see nothing but assholes and elbows escaping that ship," Stone replied into the mike in front of his mouth. Sitting in the chair just behind the gun, he, too, felt obligated to give the Russian divers at least one brief warning.

Havok sat in the left seat feeling ecstatic. He had mastered the seaplane, he had the upper hand, and Pilar was sitting by his side in the copilot seat. He looked over and gave her a reassuring wink. She wore ragged and stained clothing, and her short hair was a confused tangle of dirt and filth. He liked what he saw.

Pilar was tense and scared. Even though Havok had spiked the gun, she worried about the outcome. She just wanted to leave this horrid island, but when she looked over at the pilot and he winked, her spirits suddenly rocketed upward. His reassuring glance, coupled with his natural self-confidence, transpired to give her a new sense of confidence in their chances of survival.

As the seconds ticked by, the island became a perfect picture ahead of them, a bright green throw rug on a sparkling blue carpet suddenly set ablaze by the morning sun as it burst from the eastern horizon behind them.

Stone was the first to see it. "Looks like we have a sprouting fleet down there. See that?"

Havok and Pilar craned their necks to look out over the instrument panel and could see a ship. "That looks like the Kona Wave!" Pilar exclaimed.

"Great. Another target to shoot at," Havok said jokingly, but deep down he was concerned. Not wanting to frighten Pilar, he asked, as if he were asking for another lump of sugar in his coffee, "Did they arm it?"

"When they took the ship over, they brought on board the small guns they all carry and one big machine gun, just like the kind Rambo carried in his movies."

Havok pictured an M60 machine gun. Whether it was an M60 or not, a belt-fed squad automatic weapon, and a good gunner, could easily reach the large aircraft with those .30-caliber rounds. "That'll do it. Do me a favor, Pilar: go aft for some sort of body armor—you know, a flak jacket. There's one near the red toolbox."

Pilar bent forward and turned out of the cushioned bucket seat. When she stepped past Havok, he said, "Also, go ahead and sit on that toolbox. I'd hate to see you take a bullet in the butt, at least before I get another chance to see it."

"Sound pretty sure of yourself, don't you?"

"Shouldn't I be?"

They stared at each other for a few seconds before Pilar broke the eye contact. "We'll see." She said it as if it was a promise.

Below, in the gun deck, Stone gripped the long trigger handle of the cannon, and it roared and bucked in his hand. The false island was about a mile out in front when the airplane shook violently for about three seconds. Both pilot and gunner saw the fabricated maelstrom erupt behind the stern of the island.

Havok kept aiming the airplane's nose at the ship while hoping to see men swimming from the ship. So far, he saw none. After one minute, the aircraft shook violently again as Stone squeezed the long trigger and the cannon roared. Both men watched the first of the tracer rounds arch lazily out in front of the plane and tear up the water behind the false island again. However, that second warning was short-lived, as the remaining rounds from the burst disappeared into the dark green shroud. Finding his mark, Stone did not let go of the trigger but continued to send two almost solid lines of glowing orange miniature missiles soaring into their target. Stone gradually depressed the flaming barrels as the plane flew closer to the target.

Come on, people, Havok pleaded. We're trying to give you a chance.

The plane blasted across the bay's narrow mouth, and Havok could hear the metallic clicking of small-caliber rounds slapping into the skin of the plane: ground fire from Russian AK-47s. Almost masking the slap of the small-arms fire was the rhythmic thumping of the plane's 23 mm gun, and along with the thumping came the acrid odor of cordite.

Before Havok knew it, the firing ceased as Stone could depress the barrel no farther. They flew over the now-smoking ships, and Havok continued straight ahead, flying across the island toward its western wall. Luckily, the only rounds that had struck the airplane were AK-47 7.62-caliber rounds. Havok mentally thanked God that their gun-spiking operation had worked.

"Pete, need time to reload?"

"Doing it right now," Stone replied, "but next time I think I'll sit on something a little thicker."

"You hit?" Havok asked as he checked the gauges on the panel in front of him.

"Don't sweat me; just fly this thing. Go and turn. My trigger finger is getting itchy."

Havok commenced his turn, and Pilar, taking advantage of the lull, poked her head into the cabin with the flak jacket dwarfing her. Havok looked at her without saying anything and then looked ahead into the windshield. He straightened out his turn, and they both saw a column of black oily smoke roll from the fake island. They could also see Kang's yacht speeding away from the devastation, its gleaming hull standing out against the coal-black fog.

"Hey, our friend is leaving," said Stone over the intercom. "We gonna ruin his day too?"

"Let him go. We're after the Stalinetz." Without looking at her, Havok read Pilar's mind. "Don't worry, we'll get him later."

"Scout's honor?"

"Scout's honor."

At three-quarters of a mile out, Stone began his murderous hammering again, sending two arcs of explosive rounds toward the ship's forecastle. But as the plane flew closer, they started taking small-arms fire again. Before, it had been sporadic, but now it reached a full-fledged barrage as the lead hailstones started punching through the aircraft's skin from the sides and bottom. The duel was fierce now, a two-barreled cannon against a storm of AK-47 and machine-gun fire. In less than two minutes, the plane closed the gap between the duelers, and Stone ran out of ship to shoot at. They had passed through the pall and over the stricken ship when the side window suddenly exploded.

Only Havok's lightning-quick reactions saved his eyesight. When the window blew out, he turned his face away, and shards of glass sliced into the back of his head and neck. He faced forward and saw Kang's yacht ahead as it escaped out the tight mouth of the bay with a few miniature whale spouts trailing behind in his wake. Stone had managed to spray a few rounds his way before the smoking weapon had seized up from the heat.

"The gun's jammed," Stone reported.

Havok disregarded the sting of his wounds and banked his aircraft to the right. As the shadow of the seaplane crossed over the dissipating wake of the yacht, Havok noticed the stench of something else replacing the strong, acrid smell of gunpowder. He looked down at the dashboard and saw blue smoke creeping out from under it. The gauges no longer worked. The ground fire must have reached the electrical circuitry and caused a short. Soon, great volumes of smoke started rolling out from under the console.

Havok yelled into the intercom, "We're on fire up here, and I won't be able to fly this crate much longer! I'm circling around to the right. Is that gun still out?"

"Damn thing bit it," Stone replied. "They didn't oil it like they should have."

"Well, get your eggs ready to drop. We'll put two on the ship and two on the camp. I don't want to try to land with those things rolling around back there."

Havok did not expect an answer. He looked ahead as he continued his turn. The choking fumes of the smoldering electrical fire brought tears to Pilar's eyes. However, the shattered window at Havok's side allowed in rushing air that blew away the blue smoke. "Sit in the copilot's seat and strap yourself in. Then open up that vent on the side there," Havok ordered, pointing to a small handle and a series of slots in the cockpit wall.

Still wearing the flak jacket, Pilar did as ordered and sat down. She opened the vent, which blew away enough smoke to allow her to see out the window. Havok was still banking the aircraft when she saw the Kona Wave swing into view. On deck, she could see several men running around before the research ship disappeared beneath her, and she could see that Havok had turned the seaplane toward that billowing column of smoke.

Havok aimed the plane past the smoke at the invisible ship behind it. Just before they entered the smoke, he felt a thump come up from behind them. "You OK back there?"

"You ever try to open a door at a hundred miles an hour?" Stone yelled. "Damned thing ripped right off its hinges. Do ya think the owners will get pissed?"

Havok didn't respond. At that time, the world went black, and a split second later, the plane burst through the other side of the black cloud. A blast of gunfire tore into the nose of the airplane, knocking Havok's right foot off the rudder pedal. He looked down and saw blood gushing from his boot and draining out the small bullet hole in the floorboard. He yelled back into the cabin, "Did you drop our eggs?"

"Sure did, and there were some awfully pretty cherry blossoms back there," Stone replied, "but I didn't see anybody swimming from the ship."

Havok sighed, knowing he had just killed men who'd saved their lives. "Well, stop patting yourself on the back, and drop the last two on the camp."

255

25

TERUMBU ISLAND, LATE JULY

Aboard the burning ship, Renko lay bleeding on the bridge, listening to the anguished death cries around him. Hungry flames surrounded the bridge as if they were prowling wolves waiting for a chance to leap through the shattered windows and pounce on torn survivors.

Only moments ago, this ship had been alive with the heartbeat of machinery throbbing below and men walking her deck. Now, the machinery and many of his men were dead, torn apart or burned alive from the furious assault. None had suspected that the approaching aircraft was about to slash their lives and their cause to ribbons. At least not until the water astern of the Stalinetz had boiled from the lead hailstorm. Then, realizing they were about to be attacked, men dove for cover inside the ship or behind whatever they could find for shelter. However, the second burst came, and the explosive rounds tore through thin steel and the wooden deck and into soft human flesh. The rounds also struck the pressurized welding tanks on deck. The oxygen and acetylene bottles exploded, sending shards of razor-sharp steel soaring across the deck like miniature scythes. In the engine room, armor-piercing rounds penetrated the wooden deck above and gouged out huge chunks from the main engines, generators, and men.

Renko heard the cannon fire from the bridge wing and went to the small deck behind the bridge. When he reached it, a sledgehammer struck him in the ankle, knocking him to the deck. He looked down at where his foot used to be. In its place, a ragged stump pumped out a stream of bright red blood. Suddenly, the plane's gun ceased its murderous hammering, replaced by the thunderous roar of the aircraft engines that screamed past only meters above him. After the plane passed over, silence replaced the din. Renko could now hear the screaming of men and smell oily smoke. He knew now the ship was aflame. He picked himself up and hopped on one leg back to the bridge to organize a defense and the fire parties. He knew he had only minutes before the plane would start another strafing run.

The surviving members of the bridge team managed to establish communications on the ship's phone circuits and tried to get some sort of order. In front of the bridge, the gun crew manned the gun, and other men worked at clearing away a section of netting for them. Renko picked up his binoculars and looked through the hole in the net while a seaman applied a tourniquet to his stump. He could see the aircraft, two miles ahead, turn back toward his ship, and he knew this was his only chance. He could also hear the harried screams of seamen as they fought the raging fires that worked to consume the ship.

Renko, ignoring the pain of the traumatic amputation, told the gunner, via a telephone talker, to fire when he was ready. He did not want to destroy their aircraft, but his own ship and the lives of his men were at stake. The airplane approached, and Renko watched the silent duel develop. From behind, he could hear flames building in their crescendo, reaching a pitch that drowned out the screams of the fire parties and wounded. The gun crew ignored the carnage aft and trained their weapon, the long barrels searching out their target in the bright blue sky.

At three-quarters of a mile out, Renko heard the metallic slap of rounds slamming into the forecastle. Though only a mere fraction of a second long, the pause to return fire seemed to last an eternity. Renko did not need the binoculars now. He dropped the glasses, letting them hang from his neck by the strap, and gripped the helm tightly, his knuck-les turning bloodless. He looked up at the plane then and at the man holding the horizontal trigger bar of the gun. The gunner leaned for-ward with his right eye pressed against the hard rubber sight piece. His hand squeezed the firing trigger, and the cannon bucked and roared as the weapon exploded.

The bolt group assembly blew sideways from the breech, knock-ing the assistant gunner away from the weapon. He was dead before his body hit the deck. In shocked disbelief, Renko watched the smoke swirl around the mount and blood from the dead man run to the nearby scup-pers. He took his eyes off his men just in time to see exploding bullets race from the forecastle to his bridge, like fiery footprints left behind by some invisible racing demon. The demon reached the bridge, and the glass and steel of the bridge exploded around Renko, shredding him and his bridge team to pieces. Long after the roar of the aircraft left him and the screams of dying men faded away, Renko lay still, mourning—not his own death but the death of his ship. He died before the airplane returned to drop two bombs.

Ashore, it was chaos. When the fight first developed and it became apparent that Havok did not intend to fly off, a crowd gathered on the beach, expecting quite a show. They were confident of the outcome. Everybody carried their AK-47s, and two men were busy setting up a PKM machine gun on a workbench on the beach, eagerly sighting them on the faraway plane and waiting for it to come within range. A long belt of ammunition hung from the breech, and cans of more ammuni-tion were positioned on the workbench next to drums of gasoline. The crowd saw black cotton balls of smoke roll away from the aircraft, stain-ing the blue sky.

Soon the duel erupted as a fury of lead spat out from the beach at the plane. The storm of fire lasted for over a full minute, until the aircraft was out of their range. The soldiers lowered their smoking weapons and looked at the Stalinetz. Smoke billowed from it.

"Varonov, get men out there to help the sailors," Yeshenko ordered.

"Yes, sir," Varonov replied as he turned to collect men.

Petroske, standing nearby, observed as events unfolded. The pistol that Anisimova had given him hung uselessly from his clutched hand, his trigger finger teasing the trigger.

Anisimova stood behind the crowd and watched the events unfold as well. He knew the gold was lost, at least for now. The sarin was definitely gone, and his chances of leading a new country had just gone up in smoke. The men who really led their movement were hard-liners, idealists who were not very forgiving, and they would not tolerate anything but success. Anisimova realized this, but he did not care. Those stupid men back in Russia had only an insane dream; they could have their fantasy country. It was also doubtful that Putin would allow a group of usurpers to take half of Russia for their own country. Anisimova was not an idealist; he was a man out for himself. He would have to start fresh again, and he knew where. If he was lucky, transportation, in one form or another, would be available to him for his escape, and he would be the only man to survive this fiasco. He could come back for the gold.

Yeshenko was thinking of something much different from Petroske and Anisimova. He was thinking about the pilot in that airplane while watching it circle over the western half of the island. With an appreciation that only a person like Yeshenko could understand, he smiled. He admired the man. Many times, they had tried killing or capturing Havok, and every time, he had come out on top. Yeshenko would be honored to know him as a friend and comrade.

He put aside his thoughts of admiration when the aircraft turned for another firing run. Varonov and his men, in two Zodiacs, reached the ship but held off because of the smoke and men jumping ship. Men who were not wounded saw the futility of fighting the raging flames and abandoned their hoses, escaping through gaping holes in the netting and swimming to the Zodiacs. Yeshenko and the men on the beach waited for the opportunity to send up another unforgiving blast of small-arms fire. When it came, it mixed with the death blows the airplane was hammering out as Russian gunfire challenged the sturdy frame of the seaplane. For a brief ninety seconds, a hail of lead smacked into the unwavering hull, and as the aircraft sped out of range, the men saw a thin veil of smoke trailing behind it. The uniformed men cheered and slapped each other on the back at the result of their marksmanship, and they applauded even louder when they saw the plane try a run on Kang's retreating yacht. Its gleaming white hull escaped toward the bay's narrow mouth with miniature whale spouts chasing after it. The men on the beach were soldiers who believed in something thicker than power and wealth. They detested the Chinese deserter.

The bay was a mess. The rising column of black smoke blotted out the sun, and the water was covered with soot, debris, and leaking oil from the burning ship. The heat from the flames reached out at the men on the beach, while the men in the Zodiacs picked survivors from the water.

Yeshenko watched the smoking aircraft circle around to the other side of the bay. For a moment, he thought they were going to attack the research ship, destroying their last form of transportation. He watched as the airplane turned to make a third pass over the salvage ship, and saw his soldiers aboard the Zodiacs staying away from the burning ship and collecting men who swam from the wreckage. The airplane completed its turn and committed itself to a third run. However, this time he did not hear the seaplane's cannon fire, nor did he see any puffs of smoke from the cannon. Instead, the plane disappeared into the pall of oily black smoke that towered above the salvage ship. Immediately, he saw two huge fireballs displace the shroud of smoke, followed by the seaplane blasting out of the smoke, straight at the men on the beach. The thunderous clamor of the turboprops drowned out the clamor of the screaming flames that consumed the ship. With lightning-like reflexes, the men pointed their gun barrels into the air and blasted away at the plane less than two hundred meters in front of them.

In a second, the plane was atop them and then beyond. Most saw the gray tanks drop from the side of the plane. Those lucky men turned and threw themselves behind any sort of available cover. The remaining men were so engrossed in the huge target that filled their vision that they did not see the falling tanks and were yanked off their feet like puppets being controlled by unseen strings. The exploding cylinders sent chunks of lead and aluminum shrapnel to all points of the compass, igniting the gasoline-filled drums lined up on the long workbench, splattering the men who operated the PKM machine gun with flaming gasoline. The two men howled in agony and stumbled in the soft sand, away from the exploding drums. Yeshenko shot them with his pistol, knowing it was the right thing to do. They collapsed, and flames started to consume their bodies.

The airplane was gone now, forgotten in the wake of death and destruction it left behind.

26

．．

TERUMBU ISLAND, LATE JULY

HAVOK STRUGGLED TO BREATHE THROUGH THE CHOKING SMOKE THAT SEARED HIS THROAT. Only the bullet holes and two vents allowed in enough cool, clean air to survive on.

"Stone!" Havok yelled through spasms of painful coughing. "Strap in. This thing ain't taking us anywhere but down."

Stone poked his head up into the cockpit between Havok and Pilar. "Make sure you set this thing down near a beach. I don't feel like trying to outswim a boat full of armed commandos."

"I'll try," Havok said as Stone's head popped out of view.

Havok circled low over the island and, this time, aimed the aircraft at the small gleaming white beach at the other end of the bay. He gently rolled out of his turn at one hundred feet. Ahead he saw the two ships: one, a flaming grave settling in the water; the other, clean and alive, anchored along the southern shore.

He was taking a chance flying past the research ship with its machine gun, but he needed a straight, long path to land the large airplane. He pulled back on the throttle and lowered his flaps in increments, slowly bleeding off air speed and altitude, until he was fifty feet above the water and at 120 knots, stalling speed. He passed between the two ships and chanced a peek at the research ship to his left. He saw several men on deck. Instead of blasting away at a choice target less than a hundred yards away, they were running around the main deck madly, like a confused colony of ants. He looked right and caught a passing glimpse of the minesweeper, with the netting burned away, low in the water and smoldering.

He looked ahead and adjusted his aim point, just ahead of the white beach. At twenty feet, Havok pulled back the throttle and flared the plane. The hull dipped into the sooty black water. It bounced roughly back into the air, but he maintained backpressure on the yoke and the plane settled back into the water. He released his grip on the yoke and steered with only his feet. Looking over at Pilar, he said, "Get aft and be ready to jump. Grab anything useful and tell Stone to do the same. After I beach this thing, I'll join you back there. Now go!"

Needing no further encouragement, Pilar unbuckled the seat belt and hurriedly left her seat. Havok steered the plane until he felt the nudge as the hull dug into soft sand. He threw off the headset and killed the ignition, then joined Stone and Pilar, who were standing by the large side door. The only thing they carried were the four pistols they'd collected the night before, spare pistol ammunition, a small first-aid kit, and a one-gallon water jug.

Havok stepped between his companions, out the door, and into the calm surf. He sank up to his neck, and the salt water bit into his wounds. He disregarded the pain and held his hands up to grab a pistol and the water jug from Stone and then waded ashore with his friends following.

Havok turned and saw men aboard the research ship lowering a Zodiac from a davit. He looked over at the minesweeper and saw that only the top of the ship's electronic mast remained above water. The smoke was no longer billowing and rolling away; instead, it was now a stagnant black fog bank. Unseen to Havok, along the northern shore, buried behind the fog bank and the tangled mangrove swamp, was a party of Russian commandos bent on revenge.

With throbbing wounds, the injured party stumbled across the sand and reached the jungle, gratefully accepting its protection. Havok looked back at the wet and bloody footprints they left behind in the white sand.

Beyond their tracks, he saw a Zodiac with four men on board peel away from the Kona Wave. He grabbed Pilar's hand and started running. They buried themselves in the island's overgrown interior. After five minutes of exertion, they dropped to the ground and started on the jug of water, emptying the plastic jug in one round.

"Now what?" Pilar asked, dragging the back of her hand across her mouth.

Havok looked at her dirty, tear-streaked face and wondered if he would ever see her cleaned up. He didn't have a clue what was next, but he couldn't admit that to her. She had been rather hardy in her efforts to survive this island so far, and the last thing he needed was to reverse that stoutness. "We need to put another mile or so between us and them, and fix ourselves up."

For two miles, Havok and Stone led Pilar through the jungle, walking in silence toward the western rim. Secretly, Havok hoped that these men would just cut their losses and leave on the research ship. He knew the Kona Wave still had hostages for a crew, but he wasn't worried about them. He was, instead, more worried about Pilar. While they walked, sweat and exertion irritated torn flesh, and the exertion exhausted their thirsty bodies.

Soon Havok spotted a large banyan tree surrounded by a forest of broad-leaved ferns. They went inside and rested in relative peace while they took turns dressing their wounds.

"We can't stay here long," Havok said. "There could be Russians three meters from here, and we wouldn't be able to see them. We need to be someplace where we can see them coming." He noticed a small cut above Pilar's left eye. "But first we need to fix ourselves up. Here, let me take a look at that cut, Pilar." He opened the first-aid kit and tended to her bruised cut.

"I bet you were one hell of a Boy Scout," Pilar said, looking at his strong face.

"I got my share of merit badges," he said as he finished wrapping gauze around her head to hold the bandage in place. He avoided Pilar's admiring gaze by looking at Stone. "Let's take a look at your scratch."

Unabashed Stone, leaning on his back and feet, lifted his butt off the jungle floor and pulled his trousers down. Once the trousers were down by his knees, he rolled over the exposed tree root. Havok went to work immediately. The wound itself was superficial; the bullet had dug a long, deep trench in the pale flesh of his right buttock, leaving behind a gouged and swollen muscle.

"What do you think?" Stone asked, his face an inch above the dirt.

"How many fingers do I have up?" Havok said, holding up two fingers.

"Two. Why?"

"Good. No brain damage." Havok wiped the wound with an antiseptic pad. "It looks more painful than anything."

"Not my butt," Stone said. "I mean the fix we're in. Our backs are against the wall."

"Yeah, but so are theirs." Havok stretched a butterfly bandage across Stone's wound.

"How's that?" said Stone.

"Simple," said Havok. "They haven't got their nerve gas, and now they just lost their precious gold, their ship, and probably a good portion of divers, sailors, airmen, and soldiers. We forced them to shoot up their own airplane, and with half of its crew dead, it's not likely they'll repair it soon. Next, the friendly neighborhood loan shark seems to have picked up stakes, and I'll bet he's ready to call in his markers."

"They still have the Kona Wave," Stone said, "and can leave on that ship if they want to."

"They could," Havok said as he sat back and looked at his work. "But they still have its real crew to deal with. In addition, Anisimova is going to have to pull something from his hat besides a hot, steaming turd before he goes back to Mother Siberia. His superiors won't be too happy if he leaves here empty-handed. Go ahead and pull your pants up. Good as the day you were born," Havok lied. Even though he had cleansed the wound and applied butterfly stitches, without proper care, a nasty scar was the least of Stone's worries. Out here, infection could kill him. "Leave it to you to get shot in the butt."

"You're right," Stone agreed as he rolled over. "I wouldn't want to face his bosses now." He stood, grunting in pain. "Your turn."

Havok leaned back against a root and wrenched the boot off his right foot. The wet leather and sand scraped against the heel, sending shivers up his spine, but his face remained steady. He held up his foot for Pilar, who peeled off his sodden sock. Under the sock was a foot wrinkled from prolonged saltwater immersion. She felt a lump.

"It's still in there," she said.

"I know; take it out," Havok demanded calmly.

"You asked for it," she said as she reached for a pair of tweezers in the first-aid kit. "You know it's going to hurt."

"Know what you're doing?"

"First time for everything," Pilar said honestly, and she began to dig for the spent bullet. Though lodged just under the calloused skin, it took almost a full minute for her to dig the pointy copper-jacketed slug free. She held it up for Havok. Except for a few beads of sweat on his forehead, his expression had remained a casual, disinterested gaze.

"Didn't that hurt?" she asked.

"No," Havok lied. "After penetrating the fuselage and then going through the sole of my boot, it must have been pretty much spent."

"I guess so," she said.

She laid down the bullet and started on the glass splinters in his neck. It took another fifteen minutes to clean and dress the wounds. After all had been cared for, the group inspected their weapons and stood. Havok turned and looked into Pilar's eyes. The black Asian orbs sparkled curiously.

"What's wrong?" he asked.

"Oh, nothing," Pilar answered, a hint of mirth in her voice. "It's just that all we need now is a drum and a fife and we would look just like those guys in that painting—you know, The Spirit of '76."

"There's something else we have in common with those guys," Stone said.

"What's that?" she asked.

"They're all dead."

27

··

TERUMBU ISLAND, LATE JULY

THE BLOODIED TROOP OF COMMANDOS RACED THROUGH THE JUNGLE ALONG THE NORTHERN SHORE OF THE BAY. Through the tangled web of the trees, they caught occasional glimpses of the beached seaplane and a black Zodiac with four men racing away from the Kona Wave, its blunt bow pushing a creamy white wave in front of it.

"Good," Yeshenko said under his breath as he ran ahead of his men. With him and his men coming in from two directions, capturing the Americans should be easy. Still, he would have liked to use every available body, but he knew he could not. Yeshenko was forced to leave behind the company medic and two men to assist the wounded. He also left behind Dr. Andropov, who would have been useless out here anyway. The surviving airmen managed to stumble into the camp once the air assault was over. He ordered them to follow and to see what they could do with the seaplane. Anisimova and Petroske volunteered to stay with the airmen.

Yeshenko led the commandos who, just a short time ago, had watched their ungodly cause go up in flames and then sink beneath the still waters of the bay. The Russian soldiers ran toward the men who had caused it all, and their mouths watered for the taste of vengeance.

Yeshenko stared ahead into the jungle as his sweat-drenched body ran, hoping for a final battle. As far as he was concerned, in a few hours there would be two groups of people on this island: the victors and the dead. He did not know which would be which, but it would be decided today. As the Russians cleared the jungle and ran out to the open beach, they saw the Zodiac, which sat next to the still-smoking seaplane, with numerous sets of footprints pointing into the jungle.

"Radioman!" Yeshenko roared.

A soldier with a field radio strapped to his back ran to Yeshenko. He, like all the others, breathed heavily, gasping for breath. "Yes, sir."

"Do we have the men from the Kona Wave on the radio yet?"

"Negative, sir."

"Keep trying!" he ordered, and then turned his attention to Varonov. "Get on that airplane and put out the fire. Everybody else, catch your breath and drink water, as you're going to need it."

Most of the soldiers had canteens on their belts. They pulled them out and sucked down the water as if it would be their last drink of the precious fluid, and shared with those who didn't have any. Varonov pulled out his canteen and a handkerchief. He dowsed the handkerchief and wrapped it around his face before running into the surf. Columns of blue-gray smoke still climbed from the shattered windows of the cockpit. He waded through the surf to the open side door, hoisted his body up, and threw himself inside.

Yeshenko watched his aide disappear into the smoke, while emptying his own canteen in seemingly one gulp. He placed it back in its pouch and wiped his forehead with his right forearm. He looked back at the airplane and saw a red fire extinguisher fly out the open door with his aide following it.

Varonov waded back through the surf, while the airmen and the surviving pilot burst from the jungle and collapsed in the sand. Anisimova and Petroske came after the airmen. Yeshenko could see Anisimova was close to panic, his eyes wide and darting as if he were a rat inside a maze trying to find the exit.

"The fire is out; only the wires are smoldering. The airmen can take care of the rest," yelled Varonov as he stepped out of the surf.

"Fine." Yeshenko turned and looked at the airmen lying in the sand. "Get off your asses and do something with that plane. Varonov, have the men form a skirmish line, each man five meters apart. You guard the end of the northern flank, and I will take the other end. Now move!"

Varonov organized the men while Yeshenko approached Anisimova. "Well, it has not turned out like we planned, has it?"

Anisimova looked around, avoiding Yeshenko's accusing eyes. "No, it has not. What do you think we ought to do?"

"Now you ask for help," Yeshenko said sharply, despising the man in front of him. "You stay and salvage what you can from this expedition. I will take my men and go after the Americans. Have the pilot listen on the radio; we will plan from there. Do not make a move until you hear from me, understand?"

Anisimova nodded.

"Move out!" Yeshenko yelled to his men.

The men obeyed his command and moved forward into a dark jungle that would become somebody's grave forever. While the men moved, Yeshenko thought about Varonov and what had brought them here. They had served together for many years and had a relationship that only true soldiers could understand. They served while watching the collapse and ethnic poisoning of their country, along with the squandering of its wealth, gobbled up by foreigners. They had tried to stave off the dismantling of their beloved nation by fighting a civil war and savage battles at home. Yeshenko had devoted his life to Russia, sacrificing things other men his age found a necessity, such as family, friends, and a place to call home. For Yeshenko, the military was his home and Varonov was his family.

***

Havok, Stone, and Pilar marched steadily inland toward the steep volcanic rim while trying their best to ignore painful wounds. Surrounded by the jungle, Havok felt naked and exposed. He could not shake the desperate feeling as if he were an injured animal trying to find a hole in which to die. Soon the ground gradually began to slope up and the trees thinned out, giving way to brush, until they were out of the jungle, looking up at the island's rocky western barrier. About fifty yards up the slope Havok saw a jumbled mass of boulders. "Wait here. I'm going up to check those rocks."

Stone and Pilar did not say a word; instead, they plopped their weary bodies where they stood. Havok turned from his friends and bounded up the slope, over rocks bleached almost white, and through the sparse vegetation that managed to survive the fierce sun. He climbed over the large boulders and then disappeared. A minute later, he reappeared and walked back down the slope with Pilar watching him. Wearing a seven-day growth of beard, and torn leather-and-canvas boots and rags for clothing, he was the most handsome man she had ever met.

Havok reached out his hand for Pilar to grab. "Come on."

He led them to a small open area among the volcanic rocks. The floor, a few square yards in size, was level. After they kicked a few rocks out of the way, it was smooth enough to allow them to lie down in some comfort. Above the hideout was a brief rock overhang that offered shelter from the broiling sun. Best of all, their small redoubt offered an excellent view of the terrain in front of them. Nobody could approach without being seen.

Pilar and Stone lay on their backs with their eyes closed, while Havok lay on his stomach, peering through gaps in the boulders that ringed them. To his right he laid out one-quarter of their arsenal: a .38-caliber revolver and twenty extra bullets. So far, all was quiet, but Havok fought hard to stay awake for the next two hours while his raw eyes searched the jungle beneath him. He desperately needed sleep, but he knew that his friends needed it just as much as he did. To keep himself conscious, his fuzzy mind tried to think of all possible sources of rescue and escape. No idea was too far-fetched or too grand, including heading back to the bay at night and recapturing the Kona Wave.

Suddenly, as his tired mind pondered their chances, his gritty eyes spotted movement below. He turned his head to the left and strained to see what had caught his attention. At first he saw nothing, but after a few seconds, a striped ghost materialized from behind a tree. The commando held the butt of his rifle close against his shoulder with its barrel tasting the air in front of him like a snake's tongue, quickly darting about, searching for prey he knew was near. The Russian advanced slowly. Off to his right, another striped ghost materialized, then a third to his left. Havok watched the line of commandos advance slowly through the thinning jungle. The first man was slightly ahead of the other two and closest to their redoubt.

Without taking his eyes off the man, Havok reached out and carefully picked up the revolver. His left leg stretched out behind him, nudging Stone. Havok heard the soft rustle as Stone rolled over into a prone position and crawled up next to him. Stone knew better than to say anything. He peered through gaps in the boulders at the soldiers below and then reached back and grabbed the second revolver and the semiautomatic pistol.

Havok twisted his body to the right and looked through another gap in the boulders. His heart sank as he spotted another group of men. This group did not form a skirmish line like the others; instead, the four men held themselves together in a small knot. They wore the same uniforms as the skirmishers, but also wore broad-brimmed jungle hats that disguised their features from any distance. One of them was armed with a PKM that had about three feet of belted ammunition dangling from the breech, and they all wore two belts of ammunition across their chests in Mexican-bandito fashion. The group did not move, but only squatted behind the trees and watched the other Russians move forward.

Havok turned his attention back to the skirmishers. The first commando was halfway up the slope, only thirty yards away. He stood there inspecting the rocky precipice from afar as Havok stared out through the small gap at him. It felt as if the soldier was looking straight at him.

Havok considered waking Pilar but then thought better of it. Havok turned back and watched the soldier. The man was still standing there, not moving but searching the area ahead of him. After several seconds, it appeared the man was satisfied that the scatter of boulders was empty; he turned around, ready to join his comrades at the base of the slope. As he started down the slope, the tense silence was shattered by Pilar as she moved ever so slightly, waking from her slumber and kicking a rock. The soldier turned to face the disturbance, ending his own life. Havok jammed the pistol barrel between the boulders and fired twice. The rounds thudded into the chest of the unlucky man, knocking him backward down the slope. Even before his body slammed into the ground, Havok heard the sharp crack of Stone's automatic, followed by a barrage of gunfire from the soldiers below.

The rocky overhang seemed to explode into a million pieces as the commandos blasted away at the slope, forcing Havok and Stone away from the gaps in the boulders to cover their faces with their arms, protecting themselves from the flying rock splinters. The deafening volley continued until all the Russians found cover.

Havok chanced a peek out into the jungle below. He spotted only an occasional glimpse of a shadow stealing forward, like a pack of rats descending upon a piece of cheese, scurrying in the darkness, stopping every few feet to sniff the air. Havok knew it would not be long before they were within grenade-throwing distance. One grenade in here and they would all be hamburger.

"Stone, we can't let them get close."

"Well," Stone responded, "at least to sunset. By then we should be able to sneak out."

"Are you sure?" Pilar asked.

Havok turned and looked into her face. "No problem. We wouldn't let anything happen to you." He looked deep into her eyes, sending a message of reassurance and confidence. Then he looked over at Stone.

"Stone, keep an eye on your flank. They may try to circle around you."

Stone answered with the single crack of his automatic, stopping a soldier as he slithered up the slope on his stomach. Havok turned his attention back to his own flank. He saw the four other Russians climb up the slope. They were too far away for pistol accuracy. Time was running out. All that those four men had to do was to get up behind them, and it would all be over.

Havok could do nothing about them for now, so he turned back to the men in front of him, and the sporadic duel continued. As he watched the shadows in front of him, he thought about the men off to his right. They behaved differently from the skirmishers, and there was something familiar about one of them. A soldier burst out from behind a small shrub about twenty yards in front of Havok, aiming for a desk-sized piece of lava. Havok drew a bead on him with his pistol as he squeezed the trigger. The hammer fell on an empty chamber, and the soldier fell safely behind the boulder. Havok cursed and reached for his last five bullets. He quickly reloaded and then searched for his target. The man was gone, and so was Havok's patience.

The afternoon sun burned away at the slope, and its heat reflected back up, broiling the trapped victims inside the redoubt. Between Stone and Havok, they accounted for several Russians, killed or wounded, but there were still about a dozen men out there, including the men who were getting above and behind them. Havok wondered when they were going to do something; the waiting was murder.

The soldiers took advantage of the available vegetation and craggy terrain and moved within thirty yards of the redoubt. Havok knew they had only minutes to live. Without seeing who threw it, Havok spotted a black object arch through the air, toward them. He yelled a warning and threw himself backward, landing on Pilar as the grenade landed on the boulder that covered him, exploding two feet above their heads. The blast was deafening, and Havok felt shrapnel tear into his back and legs. A thundering volley of gunfire followed.

"This is it!" Stone yelled. He rose to his knees with a pistol in each hand and fired at the rush of soldiers charging the last few yards. Havok had rolled off Pilar and started to get to his knees when he heard the sound of machine-gun fire erupt above and behind him. He waited for the rounds to tear into his back. When the burst ended and he felt no pain, he could not understand what was going on. The men in front of him had stopped their charge and fell back, running back into the jungle with spouts of dust chasing close on their heels.

Havok didn't quite understand what was happening, but he did not question fate. He got to his knees and fired the last of his bullets at the retreating Russians. The rhythmic mechanical clap of the machine gun was replaced by a familiar voice.

"Hi, pal."

Havok turned to look at the boyish face of Scott Kilgore as he ran past the redoubt, his bright beach-boy smile shining from beneath the shadow of his mustard-yellow Russian-army floppy hat. Kilgore didn't wait for a reply but continued his downhill gallop, firing his weapon from the hip with the belted cartridges dangling from the weapon and swinging madly. Following him were three men that Havoc didn't recognize. One was a rather roguish-looking man, another was a large and sweaty Polynesian, and the last was a toothpick of a man with a beet-red face and pointy beard. They held AK-47s close to their shoulders, firing three-round bursts at the disappearing targets.

"Captain Morgan!" Pilar yelled joyously.

"Who's that?" Stone asked.

"The captain of the Kona Wave: we have the ship back!"

"Well then, are we gonna just stand here, or are we gonna get into this fight?" Stone roared. He leapt over the boulder that had provided him cover only moments before, and disappeared over the edge of the redoubt.

"You stay here, Pilar," Havok ordered. "We'll be right back."

Havok kissed her roughly on the forehead before joining Stone and the sporadic bursts of machine-gun fire below. She looked over the boulder and saw her two saviors picking up weapons from the corpses that littered the slope and then following Captain Morgan into the jungle.

Havoc and Stone ran as fast as their bleeding legs could carry them, each carrying two AK-47s. They caught up with Kilgore and the others who were taking cover behind trees, firing at invisible Russians who were now at the edge of the jungle and backed up against the slope. The Russian force had been swung back just like an opening door, and now that door had hit the wall. They dared not leave the cover of the jungle, but took refuge behind a large banyan tree with huge roots that broke the ground and spider-webbed out from the thick trunk. The victory that was almost within their grasp had been cruelly wrenched from their hands at the last literal moment. Now it was the Russians who fought for their own survival, pressed hard by Kilgore and the other Americans.

Gradually, the intense firefight slackened as the commandos died at the base of the banyan tree, one by one, desperately fighting for survival. One man, the young officer, jumped up from the crooked tree roots and leveled his weapon at Havok, who lay prone on the ground only ten meters away. He screamed and charged toward Havok, pulling the trigger on his AK-47 and not letting go until a blast of withering fire from three different machine guns tore into his chest and face, throwing him backward.

Havok wondered what had possessed the man to make a suicidal stand like that. Maybe he had been angered by the deaths of his comrades, or perhaps he had just refused to die like some dumb beast in a slaughterhouse. Whatever the reason, his useless death seemed to trigger a defiant last stand by the surviving Russians.

An intense barrage erupted from the tree as four Russians stepped out and blasted away at the Americans. Only Ohmsky did not fire at the Americans; instead, he ran forward and grabbed the dead officer by his collar, dragging him back behind the tree. As he dragged the dead man over a tree root, the four standing Russians all died simultaneously as bullets ripped into them. Ohmsky joined them in death as his skull detonated, spraying the tree trunk with blood and gore. His body pitched forward, landing heavily on the ground, and shook with several jerky spasms before going limp.

An eerie silence took hold of the battlefield. Havok looked over the carnage, suspicious of the sudden silence. Several bodies lay strewn around the base of the tree with a layer of blue-gray smoke lingering three feet off the ground, covering them. The entire area reeked of cordite. A voice rang out from behind the tree, destroying the silence: "Havok, are you out there?"

"I'm here, Yeshenko."

"I knew you would survive this," Yeshenko replied. "You fought well."

"You gave me no choice," Havok said, defending himself.

"Perhaps in another time, in another place we could have been friends, even comrades."

"It still can be that way. I hold nothing against you, Yeshenko. You're a professional soldier, and nobody can hold that against you. I'm sorry about the men we've killed. Come out and give yourself up, and your men too."

"I'm sorry, I cannot do that nor can my men. They are all dead. Now I must do something that you have refused to do."

For a second, Havok pondered the cryptic sentence, but the sharp crack of a pistol shot answered his question. The Americans looked at each other questionably and then cautiously approached the tree.

Havok noticed the torn bark and the clear sap that bled from the tree and ran down the trunk, mixing with the blood of the dead Russians, seeping into the ground. He held his weapon out in front of him with his finger on the trigger as he came around to the other side of the tree, but when he saw the scene in front of him, he lowered his weapon, knowing that the time for killing had ended. Before him were Yeshenko and Varonov, who lay curled in Yeshenko's lap, dead from either the chest wounds or the massive head injury. The entire left side of his skull above the ear was ripped back, with large pieces of bone hanging from the cranium, attached only by flaps of skin. Blood mixed with the clear liquid that dripped from the exposed gray matter.

Yeshenko sat with his back against the tree trunk, his left arm pinned under the young officer's head. The other hand held a smoking pistol, and Havok could see the results of its work. He had a neat little hole in his left temple, surprisingly free of any blood. Havok stared at the tender scene until Kilgore walked up next to him.

"Come on," Kilgore said, slapping Havok on the back. "It's over with."

Stone joined the two. "Thanks, Scott. Just when we got them where we wanted them, you gotta show up and hog the show."

Kilgore was about to respond when they all heard the distant rumble of aircraft engines starting up. He pulled a black Motorola radio from his back pocket and spoke into it. "This is Kilgore. What's happening?"

A distant voice crackled from the handset, thick with a pronounced Hawaiian accent. "Looks like da whole batch are flying da coup."

"OK, Cheng. Sit tight. We're on our way back with the professor and two lowlifes in tow." Kilgore slid the radio back into his back pocket and then asked a question that Havok and Stone were longing to hear: "You mugs want a beer?"

***

Anisimova, along with Petroske and Andropov, looked out a window in the rear of the thundering seaplane. He stared at the smoking gravesite of his compatriots and the destroyed remnants of power and wealth until the green dot disappeared somewhere over the horizon. Once out of sight, he turned around in his seat and looked past the other survivors of the bloody island and through the cockpit window up front, into a new future. There was no way he could go back to Russia now, not even Siberia or Europe. By this time tomorrow, he would be a wanted man, hunted by the biggest governments in the world. He had to lie low, consolidate his position, and begin a new campaign. He knew exactly where to go. Of course, the pilot, Andropov, and the others, all except Petroske, could not be allowed to live once they got there. Anisimova knew that he still maintained some influence over Petroske. He could drop Petroske off somewhere and watch him from afar, and if ever needed, he could contact him and use him as an inside man. Petroske was always good at worming his way into a select crowd. He was also a good dupe.

28

TERUMBU ISLAND, LATE JULY

THE SUN POISED LOW OVER THE WESTERN HORIZON, CASTING A LONG SHADOW ON THE COBALT WATER ASTERN THE ANCHORED **KONA WAVE.** The ship's crowded lounge resembled an inner-city emergency room; however, no hospital ward could offer the same serene ambiance. Stained wood paneling and soft lights eased tired eyes; cushioned furniture, a thick carpet, bandages of all shapes and sizes, and clean, dry clothing relieved bruised flesh; and ice-cold beer brought relief to parched throats.

Havok sat at the end of a reddish-brown vinyl-covered sofa with a green bottle of Carlsberg in his bandaged hand. He shivered from the air-conditioned air that blew across his freshly washed hair. After a long sip of beer, he spoke to Kilgore who sat on the floor beside Captain Morgan: "So, how did you end up on the Kona Wave?"

"I was intrigued by the information I retrieved for you. There were so many loose ends, I had to figure out a way to tie them together: Kang, the missing Kona Wave, the changing Google images of this island, and the suspicious movements of key Russians figures, to mention a few. After hours of solo detective work, I decided to ask for help. The problem was my bosses sent the info I gave them up the chain of command, all the way to the White House, which refused to send in any military aid.

They said no joy with the current political situation in the South China Sea and all. The president would not allow for any official aid. So I laid a plan of my own, which included BB over here. What's that saying? 'It's easier to ask for forgiveness than to beg for permission.'"

Havok turned to look at the roguish man sitting in a chair and drinking a bottle of San Miguel. About as lean as Stone but a bit more muscular, BB sported a tawny complexion accentuated by a thick black flowing mustache. He looked like the pirate captain in the rum commercials.

The mustachioed man looked back at Havok. "I'm Bon Brule Lafitte, and I was in Key West conducting some field research for SPAN when I got a coded text from Scott, who asked me to join him. I hopped on the next plane to help out an old friend."

"Were you in the Teams as well?" Stone asked from his seat on the carpeted floor. His back rested against the panel-covered steel bulkhead. He, too, held a beer in his hand.

"Nope, I wasn't a SEAL," BB answered. "I'm just your average everyday ex–airborne Ranger who does contract work for SPAN, but when I heard I was rescuing you two, I couldn't say no. You have quite a reputation back at SPAN, at least with one person."

"Any relation to your namesake, Jean Lafitte?" Stone asked.

"It depends on which family drunkard you're talking to," BB responded.

Changing the subject from the discussion about BB's relation to the historic pirate, Havok turned to face Kilgore. "So how did you recapture the Kona Wave?"

"I work with a trading firm that does favors for me that I return in kind. The firm owns a few coastal freighters that do legal shipping along with a bit of smuggling around the South China Sea, and they were able to get us to within twenty miles of here without raising suspicion. They put us over the side in a Zodiac small enough not to raise any concerns with radar signatures. We hit the water early last night and arrived before dawn, which is when we saw the Kona Wave. We beached the boat, covered it with palm fronds, and swam over and climbed aboard as she was anchoring and freed Captain Morgan and his crew." Kilgore slapped Morgan on the back as they sat together on the floor.

Morgan responded with a smile and sipped his fourth whiskey. The flush from the alcohol further accentuated his reddish complexion.

"Fortunately," Kilgore continued, "the Russians on the ship were so busy trying to put holes in you that we were able to seize the moment. We walked up behind the distracted Russians and overpowered the whole kit and caboodle."

"Just like that?" asked Stone as he reached into the cooler next to him for another beer.

"Just like that," echoed Kilgore after a sip. "Unfortunately, we had to kill a couple of them, and one of Morgan's men received a broken arm. On a more positive note, though"—Kilgore's eyes twinkled as he spoke the words—"you guys seem to have inherited quite a sizable treasure. What are you going to do with it?"

All heads turned to Havok, including Pilar's. She sat at Havok's feet wearing a clean pair of gym shorts and an extra-large T-shirt. The soft sunlight coming through the porthole reflected off the smooth, tanned skin of her face. Her black eyes waited for an answer. Havok looked at Stone, who maintained an expressionless face, giving no hint of his thoughts.

"I want to do the right thing here," Havok said as he turned to look at Kilgore. "I think Stone and I are happy with just keeping the silver."

Kilgore scoffed. "What do you mean, 'the right thing'? So far this month, you've slept with a married woman and killed at least ten Russians, and now you're trespassing on an island perceived to be owned by a communist nation, and it isn't even the end of the month yet."

"I'm just being practical," Havok answered, remembering June Johnson, and her husband, for the first time in days. "That gold was pillaged during World War II and found on a Japanese submarine just off the coast of an island claimed by several nations. Once the news of our little adventure leaks out, every swinging dick, including the parents of those dead students, will claim the treasure, and I don't want to be part of that circus. Stone and I came here for the silver, which will be much easier to claim and keep anyway. That said, when I dive for the silver, let me know if anybody wants me to grab them a gold ingot or two. Also, it would take us weeks to dig through that burned-out wreck to recover that much gold, and it isn't wise to hang around that long. Let somebody else go through the trouble for the gold. Besides, like Kang said, the Chinese government has a growing interest in this island, and no matter if they want it for an airbase, a communications-jamming facility, or a roadside rice wagon, we don't need to be here when they show up."

"So we leave the gold to them or let Anisimova come back and get it?" Morgan asked.

"No," Havok replied. "Once we're away from this island, we can start notifying people. I'm sure the US Navy can scrounge up a submarine and a complement of divers. It wouldn't take much for a sub to come in and sit on the bay floor while the divers covertly recover the gold."

"As always, you seem to have a plan, so what do we do right now?" Kilgore asked.

"First," Havok said, looking around at the inhabitants of the room and easing his beer bottle to his lips, "we need to finish these drinks. Then we anchor the Kona Wave over the gold."

Havok pointed the neck of his bottle at Kilgore and spoke directly to him: "After that, you and BB and the rest of the crew go ashore, bury all the dead you can find, and recover any weapons and ordnance you come across. Also, mark the mass grave of the students so their bodies can be recovered when the time comes. I'll dive to collect the silver. The Russians were courteous enough to bag the coins and stack them neatly in a space meant to store the sarin safely, so the recovery should take only a few hours. I'm going to need Stone to man the J-davit on the stern to bring up the bags, and I'll need Pilar and Cap'n Morgan to stow them below."

Havok looked at the brass chronometer on the wall before speaking again. "We still have about an hour before sunset, so let's get moving. I figure, if it all goes right, we can be done by midnight."

"Shouldn't we also look for the sarin?" Kilgore interjected. "That's one thing that doesn't need to fall into the hands of some pint-sized country with a half-wit leader."

Every Garden of Eden must have its serpent, Havok thought, before saying, "Don't worry about the sarin. It's in good hands."

"You sure?" Kilgore asked as his brow furrowed.

"I'm sure," Havok stated confidently. "Ben Gunn has it under control."

"I don't understand the reference," Kilgore said.

Havok winced. "Don't you guys ever read? Ben Gunn was a pirate in Treasure Island. He was marooned on an island but found buried treasure and relocated it before Long John Silver could get it. Ben Gunn kept it out of the pirate's hands until the good guys showed up. Our island comes with its own version of Ben Gunn, a Japanese hermit who, I believe, has it all under control. The best thing is to let him keep it. The Russians did do a good job repackaging the sarin, and the US government can monitor this island even if the Chinese take it over. I'd say let's give it about five years, until time catches up with our Ben Gunn, and then I think we can put the X on the treasure map for the US government. Remember that X marks the spot."

Kilgore nodded his head in agreement. "And when the times comes, I'm sure you and Stone may ask the government to turn a blind eye now and then. Right?"

Both Havok and Stone shrugged their shoulders.

Kilgore sighed before continuing, "If all goes well tonight, we should be out of here in the morning and on our way back to Manila for fuel before heading to Guam, aka American territory. Then we can notify the authorities that at least the Kona Wave is still afloat."

Morgan chimed in: "We are in quite a pickle with a lot to explain, so I'm not sure about sending out a radio message just yet. Besides, there are at least two people, government employees that, who aren't even supposed to be here."

"I agree," Havok said. "We can't explain everything over a simple radio message. Let's just get away from here in the morning, and then we can figure out how to let the world know what happened to the ship and those students. There's also one more thing: In the book, Ben Gunn hid quite a bit of treasure, and all he wanted in return was a nice piece of cheese. Kilgore, round up some liquor and smokes for our friend before you leave the ship."

He turned to Captain Morgan and looked down at Morgan's tumbler. The cheery smile quickly disappeared from Morgan's face.

Stone spoke quickly: "Hey, I'm sure if we dig through both of the Russian camps, we can come up with plenty of smokes and liquor."

Still looking at Morgan's tumbler, Havok said, "There's a difference between processed cheese and finely aged extra-sharp Wisconsin cheddar, but go ahead. Keep some Marlboros and a bottle of liquor each."

"Excuse me for briefly being Scottish, but I agree with Stone," Morgan stated. "There's plenty of liquor ashore, so I don't see why I have to give up mine."

Havok didn't answer. Instead, he turned his head slightly to the side while still looking at Morgan.

Captain Morgan let go a sigh of resignation. "I'll give up the Canadian Club, but I'm keeping the Jameson, dammit!"

"Fine," Havok answered, then turned his attention back to Kilgore. "Also, in the future, I suggest we have a SEAL team sneak in monthly deposits of scotch, Marlboros, and porn mags. Anyway, are we ready?"

By five p.m. Kilgore and his team had already reached the shore of the bay in two Zodiac boats, and the Kona Wave's propellers were happily disturbing the still waters. After weighing anchor, Morgan, with Fetu at the helm, glided the ship across the bay and watched from the bridge as Havok, with the help of one of Morgan's crew members, released the large pelican hook that held the anchor chain in place. Once the anchor was deployed, its chain raced through the hawse pipe. When the chain clanked to a stop, Morgan pulled back on the engine controls, guiding the ship aft-first over the wrecks of the salvage ship, Japanese submarine, and sailing yacht. After Morgan felt that he had backed the ship enough, he spoke into his handheld walkie-talkie. "All right, guys, head aft and deploy the stern anchor."

Leaving the crewman on the bow, it took Havok and Stone a couple of minutes to reach the stern, where they repeated the same process of releasing the pelican hook and letting the anchor chair race through a closed chock block. Once again, the chain clanked to a halt.

"The anchor's deployed," Havok said into his walkie-talkie.

Morgan, still on the bridge, waved for the crewman on the bow to start bringing in some chain slack via the electric windlass. At the same time, Morgan pushed the engine controls forward to idle the ship over the wrecks. Once he was satisfied that the ship was over the wrecks, he signaled for the crewman on the bow to stop the windlass and lock the chain in place. Once the crewman did as ordered, Captain Morgan spoke into his walkie-talkie, ordering Havok and Stone to do the same. Now, with just enough slack in both the bow and stern anchors, the ship was securely anchored over the wrecks. Morgan stepped out onto the bridge wing and looked down into the water. He could see air bubbles and rainbows of fuel, along with bits of body parts, erupting on the surface of the water as they escaped from the wreck of the salvage ship below, spreading pollution to the shore two hundred yards away.

Minutes later, Havok donned a worn wetsuit and scuba gear. Once dressed out, he climbed over the stern's handrail and splashed through the black film that blanketed the surface of the bay. He rolled over and started to kick his way downward, fighting against the rising current of oil and air bubbles. Though the sun had yet to disappear over the western horizon, the weak rays could not penetrate the murky water, so he used a dive light to try to see his way through the attacking air bubbles and stream of fuel. Brushing aside the occasional foot or other body part, Havok saw the Stalinetz's ghostly superstructure materialize out of the gloom. At sixty feet, he reached the charred ruins of the main deck. The ship landed nicely between the submarine and the single-masted sailing yacht, and was at an even keel.

As Havok trained the beam of his light onto the deck of the Russian salvage ship, several members of the ship's crew greeted him from under the thick oaken beams. Until yesterday, these crew members had been human beings. Now they were gaunt caricatures floating in the water with faces burned away and with blackened stumps that used to be hands and fingers. The blackened stumps pointed accusingly at him while long, exposed teeth chided him, blaming him for their predicament.

Turning away from his accusers, Havok inspected the deck of the salvage ship with his dive light and saw that the fire had consumed practically everything above the waterline, exposing the engine room, steering room, and the steel-lined gear locker. With so much having been consumed and exposed, the silver would be easy to recover.

He kicked over to the hatch of the fireproof room and saw where some of the cannon rounds Stone had fired earlier had punched through the steel. He pulled on its twisted metal. After several tugs, the hatch, along with its hinges, gave way. He laid the square sheet steel to one side and shined the light into the room. Most of the lumpy canvas bags lining the four walls remained intact, though a few had been ripped open by the cannon rounds. Silver pesos lay spilled on the deck of the room. Havok looked up and saw a steel-mesh basket being lowered by a rope. He kicked up several feet to grab the bottom of the basket. Turning back over, he kicked downward and dropped into the silver-lined room while pulling the basket with him through the hatchway.

He worked hard, placing heavy bags of silver coins into the basket, which could hold five bags. Once the basket was full, he gave the rope five determined tugs, signaling Stone to lift it out of the gear locker. After an hour of labor, he watched the basket leave the room for the tenth time and poked his head above the coaming of the hatch. A replacement scuba tank dangled in the dark water. He changed out his tank, tugged on the line holding the empty one, and waited for the empty basket to return.

By seven p.m. the sun had set and Stone turned on a deck light. Havok was still working below, but Pilar was just returning from helping Captain Morgan stow the recovered bags of silver coins in the bilge space under the engine-room deck plates. Her clothes were stained with sweat. She carried two plastic bottles of water..

"Cold water?" she asked.

At her words, Stone looked up from his work. His face was streaked with sweat and grease. "Thanks. Here, take a seat."

They both sat on the double bitts next to the J-davit to wait for the tugs on the rope. She held her bottle with both hands, lost in thought. Stone gulped his water, waiting for Pilar to speak first.

"Tell me about Havok," she said. "Has he always been the way he is?"

"What do you mean?" Stone asked, pulling the bottle away from his lips.

"It seems like he has tunnel vision and doesn't like anybody getting in that little circle of his, does he?"

"Yeah, you're right," Stone said, fingering the neck of the water bottle. "He's like a Roman sphincter."

"Roman sphincter?" Pilar asked.

"You know, a group of soldiers who march in formation with spears and shields. They roll over everything in front of them and push the roadkill to the side."

"You mean a phalanx, and they are Greek, not Roman."

"I know what they are. I was just trying to be funny." Stone paused to look at the bottle. "I'm here to tell you, no one has ever broken through Havok's shields and spears."

"I love him," she abruptly admitted. "Do you think he loves me?" Her eyes searched Stone's face, looking for the answer she wanted to hear.

Stone's shoulders dropped slightly as he tried to think of a proper response, but he didn't want to tell her the truth. He didn't have the heart to tell her that she was just one more woman who had queued up waiting for her turn at him. *Now it's my turn to be the douchebag*, he thought as he answered, "Unfortunately, he does."

He regretted saying those words as they left his mouth.

Before she could ask him what he meant, Captain Morgan came up behind her. "I see that Havok's tugging on the line," he pointed out.

Stone and Pilar turned to look at the line as they stood. Stone, still holding his bottle of water, pushed the green button on the winch motor. The rope attached to the winch started to retract. Pilar and Morgan waited for the basket full of silver coins to reach the deck.

The time slipped by, and the work paid off as the silver bags were hauled from the salvage ship. The room was almost empty by now, and Havok guessed that there were only two or three more loads left. The bags were stacked in one corner, and as he moved to grab a bag of coins, he saw something underneath it. It looked like a Russian version of an old-fashioned Craftsman toolbox, the type that would be sitting on any garage workbench back in the States. Havok continued to place bags of coins in the waiting basket, wondering why the toolbox was there. A half hour later, all that remained in the room was Havok and that toolbox. Under the light from his flashlight, curiosity took over, and he started to open the drawers of the toolbox. He was mildy surprised. The drawers were full of precious stones and pearls. The precious stones, separated by type, included sapphires, rubies, garnets, and diamonds, most of which appeared to have been worked and placed into settings as jewelry but removed from their settings at some point.

Well, it looks like Uncle Sam gets a bit in its treasury, Havok thought as he looked at the wealth. He was about to close one of the drawers full of loose diamonds, but stopped as he spotted a gold ring with a huge diamond set into it. At least one ring had escaped the smelting pot. Some lucky woman must have one hell of a rich husband, Havok told himself as he also thought about one particular woman in his life. He sighed through his regulator, and the escaping bubbles told him no. He ignored the message from the bubbles and grabbed the ring, slipping it into the neck of his wetsuit.

At last the basket, and Havok, surfaced next to the hull of the Kona Wave. The whine of two outboard engines approached from somewhere off in the darkness. Kilgore, BB, and their teams were returning, which signaled that the salvage efforts, both ashore and under them, were complete.

While waiting for Havok to spend an hour in the recompression chamber, the group showered and changed clothes. By one a.m. everybody, including Havok, who took a brief minute to shower and change into a dry pair of swim trunks, was eating sandwiches and sliced fruit and drinking a few more beers.

"Get everything wrapped up ashore?" Havok asked Kilgore between bites of a ham sandwich.

"Yep," Kilgore said. "We placed three bottles of whiskey and two cartons of cigarettes out in open view at the camp before we started cleaning up, and when we came back, the cheese was gone. We also marked the graves of the students, buried the Russians in a separate spot, and came back with a small arsenal of automatic and semiautomatic rifles and RPGs."

Kilgore was tired, and it showed. Exhaustion showed on all of their faces.

Havok popped the last bite of his sandwich into his mouth before standing. "I think it's time. Captain Morgan, I suggest you put a man on watch. The rest of us should get a few hours of sleep. I suggest we get underway soon after dawn. And, BB, glad you were able to join us."

BB raised his beer bottle in salute.

Havok turned to look straight into Kilgore's eyes. "Thanks."

"No sweat, Joe," Kilgore said quietly.

Havok crossed the room and stopped at the cooler next to Stone to grab two beers. Straightening, he turned to Stone. "See you in the morning, Pete."

Everyone watched him walk to the door, including Pilar.

He spoke as he reached out for the knob: "I'm gonna have a couple of barley pops, then get some shut-eye. Good night."

Havok left the lounge and walked down the passageway to his room. Everybody else, except Pilar, followed suit and filed out of the room, saying good night to Pilar on the way out, leaving her to her thoughts.

Pilar, sitting on the floor, looked at the brown bottle in her hands, but in her mind, her eyes still followed Havok as he walked out of the room. She sat there, picking at the bottle label with her thumbnails, wondering about the man who had just left without saying good night to her. As she continued to pick at the label, a thought occurred to her: He said good night to everyone else. Does that mean he doesn't want to end our night? He did grab two beers, so does he expect me to come crawling to his room? At that thought, she stood and stomped from the empty room, down the passageway, past Havok's stateroom and to her own, vowing to never knock at his door.

Inside Havok's room, the man casually reclined on the lower bunk of the two-tiered bunk. Two thick pillows propped him up in a half-sitting position, while his tired eyes stared ahead at the clean white paint on the aft bulkhead. He was troubled, not by the gold or the death of many men, but by the vision of his own future, a threatened future. His mind was a million miles away, and he did not hear the soft knocking at the door at first. Finally, the weak tapping penetrated his subconscious and pounded directly on his gray matter.

"Come in," he said without turning to look at the door.

It opened slowly. Pilar squeezed her head into the gap. "Are you decent?" she said a bit meekly, ashamed that she had indeed given in and knocked at his door.

Havok answered by grabbing the second beer from the nightstand next to the bunk, along with a bottle opener. He popped the cap off and held it out to her.

Bastard, she thought as she stepped into the room. She closed the door behind her before reaching for the bottle. "Thanks."

Although she was only assuming Havok's failure to say good night to her was so that she would follow him to his stateroom, she wore nothing under her T-shirt. She hoped her rigid excitement was not showing. She stepped to the bed and took the wet bottle from his hand.

Bastard acts as if women come crawling to him all the time, she thought. She felt blood rush to her head but did not know why. Was it the exhaustion from the last few weeks and the sudden rescue? Or was it because of the man in front of her?

She joined him on the bunk, sitting cross-legged at the other end, facing him. They did not speak, but just looked at each other and sipped their beer.

That's when Havok noticed her lack of underwear. Why did she have to come in without panties? he thought. For some reason, an image of June Johnson popped into his brain, which was immediately replaced by an image of Apple. A pang of guilt replaced her image quickly, though. He tried to hide his guilt by looking disinterested.

Finally Pilar broke the silence. "You look bored. What? You don't want me here?"

"I am. I do," he lied.

"How can you be bored after what just happened in the last few days?"

"It's a personal quirk," Havok answered. "Call it post-adventure stress syndrome or something."

"So that's it," Pilar said, thinking she was getting a step closer to understanding the man in front of her. "It's just a game to you."

"Isn't that what makes life worth living?" Havok said, relieved that she did not see through his deception.

She looked deep into his large brown eyes. "Who are you, really?"

He paused, reflecting on her question and back on a life that seemed long distant. "I'm just a small-time businessman living in a small town."

"Wrong," she countered. "There isn't anything small about you."

Unable to contain herself any longer, Pilar leaned over to place her beer bottle on the tiled deck before trying to rise to her knees. The bunk above them prevented her from straightening. Bent over, she clumsily attempted to cross her arms in front of her and pull her T-shirt over her head. After an embarrassing minute, she was successful, and she dropped the T-shirt next to the beer bottle. She leaned forward on all fours and crawled between Havok's legs, reaching into his shorts. She was right: there was nothing small about him.

With nervous anticipation, she leaned forward to tease his nipple with her tongue. Havok responded by rolling her onto her back, taking over. For years, she had isolated herself in her work, only occasionally experimenting with men, who, for the most part, were inept. She had no idea it could ever be like this, nor could she believe this rough-cut soldier of fortune with scarred, calloused hands could be so lovingly sensual. He made it seem so effortless. After several mind-numbing orgasms, she collapsed into a well-deserved coma-like sleep. They both slept like the dead until someone began beating on the door. The racket yanked them from their oblivion, and that was when they heard Kilgore's voice though the door.

"Joe, we have an issue."

29

TERUMBU ISLAND, LATE JULY

Everyone aboard the Kona Wave stood on the ship's fantail. With heavy hearts, they looked across the disappearing darkness of the early morning toward the center of the bay's mouth. A newly arrived vessel blocked their departure. They could see the square splinter shields that protected the crews of two swivel-mounted machine guns facing them from the main deck. One gun was near the bow, just forward of the superstructure, and the second was closer to the stern, just aft of the superstructure. Sailors, wearing light-blue or gray battle-dress naval uniforms stood next to the weapons. The rising dawn also revealed a large bow gun on what looked like an eighty-foot patrol boat. While everybody looked at the boat, Havok did so as well but noticed something that gave him alarm.

"Now what?" Pilar asked, her tone heavy.

Havok noticed the heaviness in her voice. He also thought about the odds they had suddenly been presented with. They did not appear good.

"I'll let them make the first move," he responded as he turned to Kilgore and BB, who stood on either side of him. "In the meantime, though, we need to ready what automatic weapons we have: the small arms and RPGs too. Get them stashed where you two think best.

Height will be our friend. And do it without being noticed by our friends over there."

"I agree," Kilgore nodded. "I don't think they're here to ask if we need a jump."

From there, Havok's group of survivors dispersed and made ready for battle and their escape. Cheng, the ship's chief engineer, checked to make sure the main engines were ready, while Stone, Fetu, Kilgore, and Lafitte readied the weapons and transported them discretely to the bridge and the bow. Havok, along with Captain Morgan, examined the vessel anchored in the mouth of the bay. They watched as the foreign crew lowered a whaleboat from its davit on the main deck. Once in the water and loaded with several men, the boat left the shadow of the patrol boat, joined the early-morning sun on the water, and sputtered its way toward the Kona Wave. The monotonous mechanical knocking echoed across the still water and early-morning air.

Havok turned his attention from the boat and looked at Captain Morgan with a determined face. "Come on; let's tell them we've got Triple A coming for us."

Minutes later, Havok, Stone, Pilar, Kilgore, BB Lafitte, and Morgan stood on the starboard quarterdeck watching as the whaleboat's crew, all of whom were Asian and, with the exception of the coxswain, holding AK-47s in their hands, made their landing at the foot of the Kona Wave's accommodation ladder. While holding an AK-47 in one hand, one sailor jumped onto the landing with the whaleboat's bowline in his other hand. He bent over and quickly wrapped the rope around a cleat. The coxswain pulled the throttle in reverse idle, holding the boat against the platform. Another man, also holding an AK-47, jumped onto the platform, stepped up the angled ladder, and looked at the people staring down at him. Havok inspected the sailor and took full warning.

The man on the platform, like his mates in the boat, wore sun-faded blue camouflage BDUs, but what alarmed Havok was that they bore no sign of rank or nationality; instead, there were dark spots on the cloth where patches had once been sewn. Havok looked over at the patrol boat at what had alarmed him earlier. On the bow, he could see fresh spots of gray paint covering the ship's identifying numbers. He also saw that the patrol boat did not have any flags hoisted from the halyards of its mast. The cover-up work meant only one thing: these men played pirate when convenient, and navy when necessary. They might serve their country faithfully at other times, but today they were serving themselves.

When the unmarked seaman reached the quarterdeck, Havok stepped from the crowd to face him directly. "Can I help you with something? Captain . . . ?"

The man ignored Morgan and looked over the Kona Wave.

Havok continued to look at their visitor.

The man had a narrow face with pointy features and a scraggly mustache. After a moment the man spoke. His squeaky, high-pitched voice matched his rodent-like appearance. "Is this the Kona Wave?"

"Why is that any of your concern?" Havok countered.

"Do you know that you have been reported missing and lost at sea?" the man asked.

The hairs on Havok's neck snapped to attention, but before he could say anything, Captain Morgan spoke, sealing their fate.

"I suppose we probably have been. See, we had some mechanical misfortune over the last couple of weeks, but we're leaving for Manila to report in."

"So you haven't made contact with the outside world?" the sailor said as his squinty eyes became even narrower, with a growing smile.

"No, we . . . ," Morgan started, then hesitated before finishing, "haven't."

"It seems strange that you have remained out of contact with the outside world," the man countered. "Perhaps you are, or were, up to something that you do not want others to know about. Where are your students?"

Pilar jumped in, trying to hide her panic: "They're all asleep but will be up soon."

"Ah, you must be Professor Pilar Bonne-Bouche," the man stated. "Have your students discovered anything of value?"

"No," Pilar said. "They're only students, not prospectors."

"Prospectors?" the man repeated. "Who said anything about gold or silver? Isn't that what prospectors do?"

The smug look on the man's rat-like face, and his comment, told Havok that he didn't believe Pilar's statement. Instead, Havok was sure they were just about to receive their ultimatum, which the man had probably repeated a hundred times.

"Let us waste no more time," the man said. "This island belongs to my country, and you people are trespassing. Before I can let you leave, you must pay a fine."

Kilgore spoke up, but his voice was terse: "You're right. We have something that might be a bit problematic. The students discovered a small cache of Philippine silver pesos left over from World War II. We'd be happy to hand them over if you let us go."

The man turned to Kilgore and surveyed him for a few seconds before speaking. "That was rather quick. And I think you are not the type to give in so quickly. We will take your silver, but it will not be enough."

"You bloody bastard!" Morgan exploded. "You are not acting on behalf of your country. Otherwise, you'd be wearing insignias and displaying your hull ID proudly. You're just using your country as an excuse to rob us."

Ignoring Morgan, the man finished vocalizing his ultimatum while pointing the barrel of his AK-47 at Havok. "I will have a boarding party come back in thirty minutes. You will turn over all cash, tobacco, liquor, jewelry, weapons, and portable electronics that you have on this ship—along with the pesos you mentioned." The man's voice became ominously threatening. "If I am not satisfied, my men will search this vessel. They will also search every woman on board, if you know what I mean." He leered at Pilar's crotch before turning his attention back to the group. "Any questions?"

He received hateful stares instead of a verbal response. The man gave one final warning before stepping down the accommodation ladder: "Do not disappointment me."

A minute later, the stunned people aboard the Kona Wave watched the whaleboat plow through the water back to the vessel anchored in the bay's mouth.

"You know, we could pile up everything he mentioned here on the quarterdeck," Stone said, "but that wouldn't stop him."

"You're right," Havok said. "He just came over for a recon, and his demands of booty were just to make things a bit easier for them. I'd say that in about thirty minutes they'll return with at least two boats and more men in each boat."

"He can kiss my arse," Morgan fumed, his normally red face taking on an even darker scarlet hue. "That pinched-faced rodent ain't getting a bloody stick of gum off this ship."

Havok, lost in thought, absently reminded Morgan of their position. "I think those two heavy-caliber machine guns on the stern and that gun on their bow may say otherwise. We have quite a mixed bag of RPGS, squad automatic weapons, and small arms, but nothing that can match that gun."

"What kind of gun is that, Joe?" Pilar asked.

"It's at least a twenty-five millimeter. Probably a forty millimeter," Havok replied, rubbing his chin. "And after a few well-placed shots, it could sink us where we sit. But they don't want to sink us, at least not just yet."

Pilar was becoming frantic. They had just escaped one death, now they were facing another, and the men around her were acting as if a southern sheriff named Bubba were ripping them off.

Morgan looked over at Pilar's wide eyes. "Pilar, I'm sorry," he said with a heavy heart. "They're not going to let us go no matter what we do or give them. They know that the world thinks we're already dead, and our good friend is going to take advantage of that fact."

"We could radio out now," she said. The desperation in her voice was apparent to everybody.

"They got us trapped, Pilar, so it wouldn't do any good at this point," Morgan said.

Havok responded, "Remember that we weren't supposed to be here. In the meantime, however, our friends here expect to have a boatload of goods and a slightly used research vessel that can either be converted or cut up for valuable scrap and be on their merry way before anybody shows up."

"I'm sorry," Morgan apologized. "I just wasn't thinking."

"Don't sweat it, Cap," Stone said. "None of us were. We've been so busy the last few days, no one has had time to think. We'll come up with something, won't we, Joe?"

Havok did not answer right away. He just kept staring at the patrol boat that blocked their escape. It was a single-decked ship about eighty feet long, with streaks of rust staining the gray hull. Finally, he answered, and expectant ears heard his instructions. "Pete, get me a set of scuba gear. Captain, get me a small grappling hook with about thirty feet of knotted line."

"It's now time for the cold face," Morgan answered without question as he turned to collect the gear.

"Scott and BB, go ahead and take an RPG launcher and two rockets, a loaded pistol, and an extra magazine, and wrap them all in plastic."

Kilgore did not question the order either. He knew Havok had a plan and that it would be a waste of time to ask him what it was. Instead, Kilgore and BB left the quarterdeck to collect those items.

Pilar looked at Havok with hesitant eyes. "What are you going to do?"

Havok took his eyes away from the pirate vessel and planted them firmly on Pilar. "I'm going to get us out of here."

The Kona Wave needed a good captain and crew to get back to Hawaii, and they needed good machine gunners to escape. His plan offered their only possible chance at survival.

Minutes later, Havok was sliding down a rope that hung over the Kona Wave's side opposite the pirate ship. He wore a faded blue wetsuit with a weight belt around his waist, along with a strip of duct tape wrapped around his chest, which held a hand-sized, plastic-wrapped package against his wetsuit. Over that, he wore a scuba tank strapped to his back. Clipped to one of the shoulder straps was a coil of knotted line and a small grappling hook, all bound together with more duct tape. Clipped to the other shoulder strap was a length of line that dangled away from Havok. The other end was in the water. The line was taut because it was tied to the plastic-wrapped RPG and extra grenades.

Pilar watched him, and halfway down the rope, he looked up at her. Her eyes were red and puffy from a constant stream of tears, and he almost changed his mind about going. That single second scared him more than the prospect of a violent and lonely death. He was used to making his own way on sure footing, but that second of confusion was frightening. He knew what was happening, and he refused to admit it. The only thing he did admit to himself was that this was their only way out.

***

Within thirty minutes, Captain Minh of the Vietnam People's Navy stood on the port quarterdeck of his patrol boat. He watched his boarding team, all armed to the teeth, load themselves into the two whaleboats tied alongside the port accommodation ladder. They didn't bother hiding their greed and lust for the liquor, tobacco, cash, and women, all of which awaited them just across the bay. The loot was a mouth-watering supplement to their meager pay. For these men, piracy had become a worthwhile venture. With five men, aside from the coxswain, already loaded in the first whaleboat, Minh stepped into the second whaleboat, becoming the fifth member of the boarding team in that boat. He looked at his men and assured himself that he and his men were enough to subdue everyone on the research ship, while the twelve men left aboard the patrol boat were enough to man the two machine guns and bow gun. Minh turned to his coxswain and signaled for him to start the boat's engine.

Once started, the coxswain pushed the throttle forward, and the little four-cylinder marine diesel engaged the propeller. The men on the two whaleboats held AK-47s in their hands and held their eyes on the research ship in the middle of the bay. They all failed to notice the few bubbles that rose from the depths below to erupt between the ship and the patrol boat.

Twenty feet beneath the surface of the water, Havok heard the inboard engines come to life and was glad to hear their echoing rumble fade away. Now he would have a smaller number of sailors to deal with. Havok rolled over underwater to look up. The wakes of the two boats scarred the smooth pale-blue barrier above him as they pulled away from the patrol boat. Havok knew he had to work fast, as he had a lot to do and couldn't risk the boarding teams figuring out what he was up to. He passed under the hull of the patrol boat and then angled upward, watching his exhaust bubbles race to the surface and gambling everybody left on the patrol boat was watching the boarding teams and not the surface of the water around them.

Finally his hands touched the hull, and he glided up along the starboard side until he surfaced amidships. He surveyed the length of the patrol boat and was relieved to see nobody leaning over the handrail smoking a cigarette. He won that gamble.

Now, alongside the hull, he kicked off his fins and unbuckled his weight belt, letting it fall away into the depths below. He then unclipped the coil of knotted line and the grappling hook from the shoulder strap of the scuba tank along with the length of rope clipped to the other shoulder strap. Now, holding the items in one hand, he unbuckled the scuba tank and let it fall away too. The two lead weights that he had secured to his tank quickly sank the tank. The wetsuit he wore gave him slight buoyancy, which allowed him to loop the rope that he'd used to tow the RPG and extra grenades around his waist. He then unwrapped the coil of knotted line and grappling hook. He loosened the coil and tossed the hook up over his head. It sailed up over the deck railing, reached its zenith, then dropped, and one of the hooks snagged the deck railing. He grabbed the rope and pulled himself out of the water, up to the deck, eight feet above the waterline. After he climbed over the railing, he lifted the grappling hook free of the railing and dropped it back into the water before he pulled at the lanyard that trailed behind him.

He yanked the bundle from the water, and when the bundle was in his arms, he threw himself against the superstructure behind him. His only protection was the overhanging bridge deck above and a steel ventilation trunk in front of him, which ran straight up and down, providing ventilation to some space below. Behind him, there was nothing, except an unmanned swivel-mounted machine gun, clear to the fantail.

He poked his head around the foot-wide trunk and looked forward along the starboard side. Up on the fo'c'sle, beyond another unmanned swivel-mounted machine gun, was his target, the cannon. It was almost completely surrounded by a skirt of steel, gapped only in the back for the gun crew and ammunition handlers to walk in and out. Inside, two sailors sat in their hard steel seats on either side of the weapon's breech. They lounged at their stations while watching the boarding teams.

Havok removed the package duct-taped to his chest and unwrapped it. It contained his pistol and another magazine. Sticking the extra magazine in the neckline of his wetsuit, he squatted and put the pistol down on the deck. Next, he ripped the plastic from the four-foot-long bundle he had towed, and pulled out the long green rocket launcher with the oblong warhead already in its muzzle. He removed the tape that held the second RPG round to the weapon and laid that on the deck in front of him as well. With no time to waste, he stepped out from behind the trunk, shouldered the loaded RPG, and kneeled. He took aim down the tube's open sights, looking through the gap in the gun tub, and pressed the trigger. The weapon roared on his shoulder.

Just as Havok fired, one of the gunners, sitting in the right chair, shifted in his seat and exposed his leg. Havok watched the trail of lazy smoke fall behind the warhead as it entered the gun mount. The thick round punched through the seaman's leg, amputating it at the knee. The round missed the gun mount itself and smacked into the side of the tub, already splattered with flesh and bone. Just like the sailor's leg, it fell uselessly to the deck.

"Shit!"

It took about one second for the sailor to realize he had just had his leg knocked off and for everybody else to realize something had happened. Cursing the dud, Havok picked up the second, and last, grenade. He slammed the short broomstick-like tube down the weapon's muzzle and shouldered it to fire again, but before he could take aim, a sailor with an AK-47 jumped between him and the mount, filling the open sight. Havok moved behind the vent just in time to avoid a burst of gunfire. The bullets marched in line down the deck to where he was kneeling, throwing up flecks of metal, sparks, and paint chips.

Havok dropped his RPG next to his feet, snatched up his pistol, and, without taking aim, pointed the pistol at the advancing sailor and blindly fired two rounds. The rounds tore into the sailor's chest, and as the dead sailor collapsed, Havok heard a noise behind him. Still kneeling, he spun around and saw another dressed in greasy coveralls and carrying a pipe wrench. Once again, he held the pistol in front of him and fired twice. The bullets ripped into the man's stomach and he doubled over, falling first to his knees and then to his face, dead. An exploding fusillade of gunfire tore down the already-scarred deck from the bow of the patrol boat, with bullets tearing into the dead sailor and striking the ventilation trunk. The sailors were firing blindly from around the corner of the forward superstructure. Havok could hear the rounds punching their way through the vent's metal on the other side. He knew that under the withering fire the metal would be perforated like a cheese grater and no longer provide any protection. He also knew that all they had to do was drop a grenade from somewhere above him. Either way, the only chance he had at survival was to jump overboard and swim for the swampy shore.

Trying to ignore the flying bits of paint and metal erupting from the main deck as bullets chewed at the steel, Havok saw the invitingly green jungle, but he thought of the people who depended upon him. He could not desert them. With a fatalistic resolve, he put his pistol down and grabbed the RPG. Many things went through his mind at that particular moment, and the one picture that stayed was the Kona Wave steaming out of this bay. With that billboard firmly plastered in his mind, he swung out from behind the vent into a hail of bullets.

Havok leveled the weapon on his shoulder, looked down the open sights, and, with bullets passing him, squeezed the trigger. The rocket bucked on his shoulder, but the swoosh of the ignition failed to mask the agonizing impact of bullets as they tore into his right thigh and shoulder, knocking him on his back. The next thing he felt was the force of the explosion as shock waves reverberated through the ship's hull. The small-arms fire ceased. When Havok lifted his head and looked down at his chest, he saw a most wondrous sight. A dense swirl of black smoke encircled the gun mount, and from under the smoke escaped the bright flashes of a building fire.

Shaking from severe pain, he rolled back behind the holed vent. He picked up his pistol, ready to take on all comers. The abrupt silence ended with the echoing blast of a ship's horn. The long, rolling blare of the horn reached his ears and the near shore, a signal that meant his friends had seen the deck gun knocked out of action and were on their way.

The distant blare of the horn disappeared over the canopy of the jungle only to be replaced by the crackle of small-arms fire. The gunfire came from the portside, and the symphony of machine-gun fire joined the choir. Havok knew all the attention was back on the Kona Wave as she attempted her escape. He stood with his right leg throbbing painfully and pulled the extra magazine from the neck of his wetsuit. With his half-empty pistol in one hand, a magazine with fifteen rounds in the other, and two bullet holes in him, Havok hobbled aft down the starboard side. He had almost reached the end of the superstructure when a watertight door flew open, knocking him against an overhead deck support. The door slammed into bruised muscle, and the stabbing waves of agony forced him to release the grip on his extra magazine, dropping it over the side.

In nauseating throes of pain, Havok looked into the dark interior of the ship and saw a surprised sailor standing in the doorway. He lifted his pistol and fired a bullet straight into the man's face. From only inches away, the impact blew off the back of the man's head. In a bizarre, surreal moment, Havok watched as a chunk of bloody skull splattered against the bulkhead behind the dead sailor, where it stuck. As the man's body crumpled, Havok saw something still clasped in his hand. It was an old-fashioned US Army pineapple grenade with its safety pin still in it. He snatched up the grenade and continued hobbling to the end of the superstructure and toward the din of machine-gun fire.

He looked across the deck and saw two men standing at the aft swivel-mounted machine gun on the portside. One man was firing at the Kona Wave, which was still out of Havok's view. The other man helped feed the cartridge belt into the machine gun. Both of them were intent on the Kona Wave and ignored the growing pile of empty shell casings at their feet.

Inching up behind the gun crew, Havok could now look around the corner of the superstructure. The research vessel, which was pointed directly at the patrol boat, was building up speed. Between the patrol boat and the Kona Wave, Havok could see the two whaleboats racing back to the mothership and safety. He could also see an occasional white splash near the boats, which told him that Kilgore, BB, and Stone were pouring accurate fire into the boats. He could hear the distant thumping of the machine guns mixed with reports of AK-47 fire as survivors in the boats tried to fight back. But the fight did not last long as the last of the survivors in the boat were cut down, falling backward onto their dead shipmates. Over their heads, two strings of tracer rounds from the pirate ship struck the high bow of the Kona Wave, creating flashes of intense sparks and angry tufts of black smoke. Kilgore, BB, and Stone continued their deadly fire, but now at the patrol boat itself. From a closing distance, two sets of machine guns dueled with each other in a grudge match. Havok could see that, in the narrowing distance, the pirate gunners were finding their mark. Two arcs of tracer rounds sailed murderously into the bridge of the Kona Wave, while the bullets from the American machine guns were bouncing harmlessly off the splinter shields protecting the gunners crowding behind them.

With their escape too close to lose, Havok squatted and placed his half-empty pistol on the deck. With both of his hands free, he held down the firing handle of the hand grenade with one hand and pulled at the safety pin with his other hand. Throwing the safety pin over his shoulder, he held the grenade while holding down the firing handle and reaching for his pistol. Now, armed with a weapon in each hand, he stepped toward the machine-gun crew in front of him and emptied his pistol into their backs. After firing the last round, he jumped over their bodies while throwing his now-empty pistol over the side and continued toward the second machine gun. They were so intent on the Kona Wave that they failed to see Havok or the hand grenade that he flung at them. Both of the sailors were sliced to ribbons by the grenade's shrapnel as it exploded at waist level.

Silence now commanded the firefight. Among the acrid clouds of spent gunpowder and carnage, Havok stood alone. A torrent of blood and sweat ran down his heaving chest as he looked at the results of his work, then at the approaching bow of the Kona Wave, her steel hull coasting to a gentle stop twenty feet from the pirate ship. Up on the fo'c'sle he saw Kilgore, Stone, BB, and Pilar looking down at him. The look on their faces revealed the shock of the unholy sight. The water around the patrol ship was turning crimson from the blood that ran off the deck of the patrol boat in the bay. Havok tried to raise his right arm and wave to them, but he found he was too weak for even that. He realized he was too dead to stand. To the horror of the people watching from the bow of the Kona Wave, Havok folded, his body striking the deck hard. Now only a company of broken bodies manned the ship.

Seeing their friend collapse, Stone and Kilgore hurled themselves over the bulwark, falling to the water below, and swam to his aid, not knowing if he was alive or dead.

***

The task of collecting the dead bodies that littered the deck of the patrol vessel and filled the two boats was finally complete. After all the cadavers were stowed below and locked inside the patrol boat, Captain Morgan, with the help of Cheng and Fetu, rigged a towing hawser to the bow of the dead ship and raised her anchor. Once ready, Captain Morgan, standing at the helm of the Kona Wave, took the damaged ship and its macabre load into tow, and both ships headed eastward.

Below deck, in the cool confines of Havok's stateroom, a nervous Kilgore extracted the last slug from Havok's body. It was a good thing he was unconscious because, even though Kilgore was a corpsman as well as a SEAL, it had been years since he'd performed combat surgery. His shaking hands held a set of forceps, and as he dug for the last piece of lead in Havok's body, he managed to twist and pull torn muscle. After long minutes and a lot of sweat, Kilgore finally put this medieval operation to a merciful end by sewing up the last bullet hole.

At dusk, and in water over four hundred feet deep, the towline was released and Captain Morgan brought the Kona Wave around full circle, bringing her portside against the starboard side of the patrol vessel. He and Fetu, armed with sledgehammers, boarded the boat and went below to the engine room. They smashed every valve and pipe fitting that led to the sea. When they finished their mission, they jumped back aboard the Kona Wave and minutes later, armed with beers, watched it settle in the sea.

"What do you think their nationality was?" Stone pondered aloud.

"They weren't Filipino," Havok said as the bow settled lower in the water.

"I'm guessing Vietnamese," Kilgore answered, but then sighed. "I'm going to have to report this mess, and my boss is going to hate having a hot, steaming turd in his lap." He turned to face Havok. "Why the hell did you have to run into a drunk Aussie?"

Havok smiled. "If I hadn't run into that drunk Aussie, I think our government would've had an even bigger mess on their hands."

Kilgore didn't answer but turned his attention back to the sinking boat.

With its engine room filling, the boat began an increasingly faster slide stern first, and as the burning red sun dipped below the western horizon, so did the bow of the vessel. Leaving behind only a whirlpool and a few bubbles to mark the grave of twenty-two unknown souls.

The next morning, clear and bright, found the Kona Wave halfway to Manila. Everyone on board was sleeping through a majestic sunrise, all except two men. One at the helm, who watched the floating compass face, and a second man, who sat on a white lifejacket locker on the bow, wrapped in bandages and sipping a mug of coffee.

Havok sat on the locker watching the orange-blue horizon, staring at the rising sun, but not seeing it. Not only was he lost to the world, he was also lost to himself. Though clean strips of cloth tightly bound his torn and bruised flesh, nothing could bind the thoughts running through his mind. All his life, love had been a death threat, something he always kept at arm's length. He thought back on the many years, about women he had known, and his thoughts settled on Apple: simple, little, loving Apple.

While he sat there battling with himself, he felt the light touch of a hand on his good shoulder. He looked up to see Pilar.

"Mind if I join ya?" she asked with a bright smile while holding a cup of coffee.

He didn't bother answering; he just patted a spot on the locker next to him.

She sat, sharing the dawn with Havok. After moments of silence and a few sips of coffee, she spoke. "How you feeling?" she asked, placing her left hand on his thigh.

"Well, other than being turned into a poster child, I feel super," he lied.

"You know, that was a pretty brave and stupid thing you did yesterday."

"Tweren't nothing, ma'am," said Havok as he pretended to tip an invisible hat.

"If you had gotten killed, how could I take you back to Hawaii and show you off?"

Those words hit him like a shotgun blast to the gut. He felt like he was going down for the last time, and he grabbed at the only life ring in sight: desperately he lied. He turned to Pilar and looked into her eyes. "Pilar," he said and then halted, as the words were hard to find.

Pilar sensed his uneasiness. It scared her.

"You know that I make it a habit of burning toast and I always leave the toilet seat up."

With a confused look, she responded, "I don't care."

"I already have somebody else!" He didn't know where those words had come from, but he regretted saying them as soon as they escaped his mouth.

It was Pilar's turn to feel a gut-wrenching blast now as the painful betrayal gripped her. While she knew practically nothing of this man's past and his other lovers, the last few days with him had made it seem as if they were meant to be. Her world just splintered into a million pieces. Numb and mortally wounded, she stared at Havok, who shamefully turned his face downward, avoiding her eyes. "You pig!" she scorned. "The love that I gave you, the time we spent together, I thought you wanted all that!"

"I don't know what I want," Havok groaned honestly.

"You know what you want, and it's only yourself!" she spat angrily, tossing her coffee cup over the handrail. "All you do is trample all over the world like some sort of 1930s comic-strip hero." All the pain that had built up over the years finally let loose, and she struck Havok across the face with a vengeance. Then she left, crying.

Havok continued to stare at the deck. After several minutes, he reminded himself of something June Johnson had said, what seemed like a century ago. I am that douchebag.

30

SUBIC BAY, PHILIPPINES
MID-AUGUST

"How's the calamari?" Havok asked as he stared at his margarita.

"Could use some more seasoning." Stone stopped chewing long enough to answer Havok and sip his margarita, placing the glass back on the table. A salt crystal clung to his upper lip. "You seem to be thinking a lot lately. About Pilar?"

BB, relaxing with his own margarita, quietly watched the two men.

Havok tasted his margarita and shifted cautiously in his seat. Though they'd had time for their wounds to heal, some were still tender. He looked down at his wrists and saw the jagged white scars against his tanned skin. He also felt the cool northerly breeze on his cheek and heard the soft country lyrics of a Kenny Chesney country song hitch a ride on the waft. They were sitting at Kilgore's bar, waiting for him to arrive. "A bit of everything, and she says hi."

"She's fine then?" Stone asked.

"HSU told her to take a semester off and gave her a research project to work on instead," Havok said, removing a grain of salt from his lips and licking it off. "Sort of a recuperation process, I guess."

"She'll be fine. It's us we have to worry about," Stone said. "Junior said the modifications to our new boat are coming along nicely. It's a sorry replacement for the Outfit, but it'll be in the water in two weeks. However, I haven't given up finding something sexier."

"Good," Havok said. "I'm getting bored stiff."

"Well," BB said, "don't forget that you promised to help us on that Caribbean project."

Havok sat a bit straighter in his chair. "No problem there. Have you firmed up things with corporate?"

Before BB could answer, Kilgore bounded up the steps to his bar, holding a yellow envelope in his hand. As he passed the bar, he made a circular motion to Mercedes, who stood at the bar. He walked up to the table, threw down the envelope, pulled out a chair, and sat down.

"Still pissed?" Stone asked.

Kilgore grunted before answering, "It still galls me. When I asked for help to rescue you thugs, the brass told me they couldn't get involved. The White House has their own way of dealing with the Chinese government, and an overt American military intervention in the South China Sea wouldn't be good for business just now. So it was all me. I ended up using precious favors. But once everything came out into the open, the president's press secretary went to the podium claiming that the president had authorized a covert special ops to recover American personnel and property, and a half-billion dollars in treasure, which was kept out of the hands of terrorists."

Mercedes swung by the table, carrying a tray with another round of margaritas. She stood next to Stone, who looked up at her with a twinkle in his eye. After collecting the empty glasses, she nudged Stone's shoulder with her hip as she moved on.

Havok noticed the sentiment between the two of them and thought back. Stone had always treated Mercedes with respect. Havok then thought about Apple. He told himself he needed to make up for years of disrespect.

"But forget about our gutless leaders," Kilgore said dismissively, and grabbed his margarita. He quaffed the drink and then placed the glass back on the table. "Nothing like the first drink of the day." Now, with a cheery smile on his face, he looked at the three men. "I got some bizarre good news and some great good news. Which do want to hear first?"

"I've always been a bizarre-good-news-first man myself," Stone responded.

"Good," Kilgore said. "It seems that when Kang escaped Terumbu he headed straight for Hong Kong. However, his government wasn't too keen on the hornet's nest he stirred up. It interfered with their future plans concerning the South China Sea." He paused pensively. "So they wanted to have a word with him. Kang knew he was in a serious jam, so he left his yacht in Hong Kong, where he and Xian caught a flight to Canada. He was going to hide out on a property he owned outside of Vancouver and run his business from there until things settled down. The problem was that the top bidder for his sarin was Kim Jung Un, and, as we all know, he is bat-shit crazy and paranoid as hell. So he sent a covert grab-and-snatch team to Vancouver, drugged Kang, and flew him back to North Korea. Once there, he was taken to Un's palace and strapped to a medical gurney in a special room."

Havok sipped his margarita. "Let me guess. Un's getting bored by executing his victims the old standard way: death by forty-millimeter antiaircraft cannon at twenty paces."

"Yes," replied Kilgore. "In this case I think he outdid himself. In the special room, he had a starved dog held in a cage, and every morning at eight, for about two weeks, he had doctors medically amputate one of Kang's body parts and feed it to the dog in front of him while he was conscious. They started out with the fingers and then the toes, then moved on to the lower, then upper, limbs. The last parts to go were the genitals and tongue. All that was left was a torso and head."

"Ouch," Stone responded.

"But this is when it gets really weird," Kilgore continued. "Every night at six, he had Kang wheeled into his television room, where he was forced to watch the old Brady Bunch shows with Un. It seems Un gets fixated on certain American TV shows and movies. The worst part, though, is that Un would also dress up like Hillary Clinton—wig, pantsuit, and all—while watching the shows."

Stone coughed slightly and pushed the basket of calamari away.

Kilgore looked at Stone and smirked. "Un got bored, so he ordered his men to toss a living and breathing Kang into the dog's cage and had the meal video recorded."

Stone looked at Havok. "Let's make sure we never take a job in that part of the world."

"No worries," Havok said, and then turned to Kilgore. "And what about Xian?"

"I don't think she has anything to worry about." Kilgore sipped his drink. "She wasn't a key player in that mess, and she is now the proud wife of an aged and wheelchair-bound Canadian oil tycoon."

Havok had nothing against Xian and even wished her luck in some way. He looked back at Kilgore. "So what's the good news?"

"I've been made privy about a deeply buried paramilitary group," Kilgore stated.

"How deep?" Havok asked.

"So deep that anybody who knows about the group has to look up to see down," Kilgore explained. "They call themselves the Pagan Raiders, but are officially called the Special Component Recovery Unit, or SCRU."

"Mercenaries?" Havok suggested.

"Better. They do what the DEA, FBI, NSA, or the CIA can't do legally or get away with. Besides, no self-respecting government employee looking to the future and a job in management wants to risk being asked embarrassing questions about any knowledge of the group at any congressional nomination hearings. Anyway, they are about to visit a drug lord's villa in Vietnam. They plan on extraditing him back to the US."

"Why should that concern us?" Havok said as he sat even straighter in his chair. "We don't have a dog in their fight."

"You should," Kilgore responded with a smirk on his face. "Here's your chance to play Frank Buck and 'bring 'em back alive.'"

"Do you mean the drug lord and a certain house guest who may be hiding out in Vietnam, meaning Anisimova?" Havok asked as he remembered holding a grieving and shaking Catalina in his arms when he told her about her husband's death.

Kilgore looked into the eyes of his friends. "You know him. You could be a big help in capturing him and his sponsor, and bringing them back to the States for trial: a kind of two-for-one sale."

"If we go through the trouble of dragging his ass back to the States," Stone said, "he'd better not end up being let loose on a technicality or getting locked up in Club Fed."

"No chance of that," Kilgore affirmed. "He's being charged with the murder of those students, international drug-trafficking, and kidnapping. If for some reason he doesn't end up in an electric chair, there are some Eastern Europeans who would love to save us the juice." Kilgore looked hard at his two friends. "This little operation is not for the faint-hearted and is not supported by the Vietnamese government. They won't be very receptive to the American agents invading their country. This is voluntary and unofficial. What do you say?" Kilgore looked over at BB. "I know you showed up late for the party, but you're more than welcome to join in."

BB looked at Kilgore and lifted his glass in a salute. "I would, but I've already committed myself to getting our Caribbean thing finalized." He turned to Havok and Stone. "You two have your fling, and I'll see you in Pensacola."

Havok retuned the salute with his own glass and looked at Kilgore. "How do we get inside Vietnam?"

Kilgore pushed the yellow envelope across the table to Havok and looked at him with a beaming smile. "When was the last time you guys jumped?"

31

SUBIC BAY, MID-AUGUST

BACK AT HIS STUDIO HAVOK OPENED THE ENVELOPE AND STARTED TO READ THE THREE-PAGE TYPED BRIEF. Halfway through, he heard the door open. He looked up and saw Apple, wearing the bar's uniform and carrying a six-pack of bottled beer. She didn't say anything but walked over to him, pulled a beer from the six-pack, and handed it to him. He accepted the bottle and watched her as she turned to the refrigerator. After placing the six-pack on a shelf in the fridge, she grabbed a Sprite before closing the door. Then she sat on the bed and used the bottle to smooth a crease in the bedspread. Havok could see her mind was a million miles away.

Without thinking, he reached into his pocket and pulled out the diamond ring he'd salvaged off the Russian ship. Holding the ring out, he blurted, "Apple, will you marry me?"

He saw her eyes close ever so slightly as her hand squeezed the Sprite bottle. Veins stood out on the back of her hand. She didn't answer right away. Instead, she kept staring at the bedspread. She seemed not to notice the diamond ring in his hand. Havok waited, giving her time to answer when she was ready.

It was a strange silence.

Finally, she looked up. "Why do you ask me now? Do you really love me? Or is it because you feel guilty that my father died on one of your adventures?"

Havok saw the reflective look on her face. He sighed. "No, it's not because of your father's death. It's just that now I realize how much you've cared for me and put up with my crap. I want to do right."

"So you think you owe me for my service?"

"I didn't mean it like that," Havok said, regretting those last few words.

"You never said you love me," Apple said, staring at the bookshelves.

He paused. "I don't know what to say, Apple. I do love you. Again, will you marry me?"

After a minute, she responded, "Mercedes said you're going to Vietnam to kidnap somebody."

"Yes, we are," Havok said firmly, "but we'll be back. It'll only be for a few days."

"But then you're going to the Caribbean right after that."

"Yes, we are, but we'll come back after that."

"How long will that trip take?" Apple asked as if she already knew the answer.

"Only a few weeks," he replied weakly.

"What about after that? Where will you go next?"

Havok could not answer that question.

Apple broke the awkward silence with a deep sigh. "Mr. Joseph Havok, no, I will not marry you and you can keep your ring." She returned her gaze to the books. "Our lives together as a husband and wife were not meant to be. Your life is in those books. Or if not in those books, it's in some cave in Mexico or a shitty bar on Mombasa." She turned to look at the screen on the laptop, which sat on the rolltop desk. "Or looking for an ancient underwater city off the coast of Cuba. If we got married, you'd feel obligated to stay here, which would destroy us both. If you took me with you, what would 'M' have to say about it in Pensacola? She's on that side of the world, waiting for you, and I am on this side of the world. She keeps sending you books with notes in them, so what would she have to say about me following you around?"

"I just want you to be happy," Havok stated.

"I'm happy for our time together," Apple said as she turned to face Havok. She had a pleasing smile on her face and a hint of a tear in one corner of her eye. "Nothing can take that away. Just as you will always find another adventure, I will eventually find somebody else to marry and live with. That is our future. In the meantime, you finish reading what Kilgore gave you and then take a shower, because you're taking me to Olongapo for a movie."

Apple stood up from the bed, kissed Havok on the forehead, and left the room, leaving Havok to his three-page brief and his thoughts. He looked at the unopened beer bottle and thought about how fortunate he really was: I've never been so gratefully indebted to anybody like her. I don't deserve her.

32

··

THAILAND, MID-AUGUST

THE BRIEF WAS CLEAR AND DIRECT. Havok, Stone, and Kilgore were to catch a commercial flight to Bangkok; rent a car and drive to Pattaya Beach, a resort area seventy miles southeast of Bangkok; and check into the Royal Garden Hotel and pose as tourists. To the south of Pattaya Beach was the town of Sattahip and a Royal Thai naval base, the training ground and headquarters for their naval special forces. Because of the similarity in topography, and because they were to operate at night in Vietnam, they would train at night, then make their way back to Pattaya each morning and sleep during the day.

The flight to mainland Asia was uneventful, allowing each man to be alone with his thoughts.

After landing in Bangkok, Kilgore checked out their car from the rental center, a mundane white four-door sedan, while Havok and Stone retrieved their luggage. They then drove to Pattaya, passing the many baht buses that shuttled the local population up and down the flat countryside. They checked into their hotel, just off South Pattaya Road, the main drag of the resort town, and visited old haunts. When dusk approached, they piled into their rental and made their way to Sattahip.

The two Thai guards at the gate sweated profusely from the early-evening tropical heat, wet spots staining their uniforms. One of them stepped out of the guard shack and peered through the tinted glass before Kilgore had a chance to lower the window. The guard seemed to be expecting them because, as soon as he saw three white males, he yelled something to the other guard inside the small shack, who then picked up a cell phone.

The first guard signaled them to pull off to the side of the road and wait.

Their wait was short. In a couple of minutes, a giant of a white man, wearing tiger-striped BDUs and jungle boots, stepped out of a nearby two-story wooden structure. Bamboo blinds covered the inside of the building's windows. The man lumbered toward the car with an easy gait despite his immense size. Havok saw no nametag or insignia patches on the uniform.

Kilgore rolled the window down but kept the car's air conditioner going.

The man bent down and peered through the driver's-side window. He looked them over cautiously and then said, "Kilgore?"

"In the flesh," Kilgore answered, flashing a huge smile.

The man's smile matched Kilgore's. "Park next to the building I just came out of." He allowed the car to pass and then followed it as Kilgore drove the short distance and parked it under the light at the corner of the building.

Kilgore, Stone, and Havok left the car, retrieving their luggage from the trunk, and walked up the bare wooden steps to a plain brown door. The uniformed man opened the door and all four of them stepped inside a large room. The room was dim and cavernous with sparse furnishings. A dozen seated men eyed the new arrivals with cautious suspicion. Though not as imposing as the first man, they all appeared to be tough and professional, and all wore the same type of camouflage BDUs, also without badges or distinctions of rank. Most wore civilian ball caps denoting the names of states or sports teams.

"Gentlemen, this is Joe Havok, Scott Kilgore, and Pete Stone."

The seated men warily inspected the new arrivals, sizing them up like wrestlers before a big match. Havok, Kilgore, and Stone did the same. Intense, hardened eyes clashed against one another.

"Let's get started," said the big man, breaking up the silent duel. "I'm Blane Tucker, and I, like everybody else in this room, am a member of SCRU. I believe you know what that stands for. You'll learn everybody's names as we go along." Tucker turned and faced the entire crowd. "The purpose of our mission is to infiltrate a villa located just outside of Da Nang. You are going to bring out two men, Tang and Anisimova. Their photos are included in the briefs I hope everybody had a chance to study. Tang is probably the biggest drug manufacturer, trafficker, and pusher around. His cliental is definitely not exclusive. Then there is Anisimova, who's not only a Russian separatist wanted by his own government, but also Tang's partner in the heroin trade. The type of heroin that these two are turning out is twisting many minds into zombies in both the US and Russia. Both Tang and Anisimova are old friends and have been partners for years. Now, we're going to bring them both back to the States."

One of the men, who sat near the far wall, raised his hand. "Is the Vietnamese government still in the dark about this?"

He appeared to be perhaps the youngest man in the room and wore a Minnesota Vikings ball cap, which was perched jauntily on the back of his head.

"Yes, Bergdahl, they are. Most of Tang's relatives run the government and are paid a decent sum. We couldn't take a chance at informing them," Tucker said as he looked around the room sternly. "I must stress that we cannot leave anybody behind. If, for whatever reason, you're not at the extraction point, you must make it to the alternate extraction point. We are not supposed to be there, and Uncle Sam will not admit to anything."

"So what else is new?" Stone joked, breaking the ice. He received a couple of chuckles, but most of the men still viewed them warily.

"The basics of the operation are as follows," Tucker continued. "We will parachute in, landing at a marked LZ manned by people on our payroll, about four klicks from the villa. Far enough away that the sounds of the helicopters won't alert our targets at the villa and our direction won't telegraph our intended target, just in case we are tracked by radar. We will make our way to the villa, and the helicopters will land at another LZ two klicks from the villa to wait for us. This will be our primary extraction point. We will complete our mission and make our way there. In case our primary LZ is compromised, there is a second extraction point near Ba Na, about ten klicks from the villa. Both extraction points are on the maps that you will be given as part of your issue; they will be marked in code. Make sure you study those maps carefully. Any questions?"

"Why are we bringing civilians?" asked Bergdahl, seeming to question the presence of the three new arrivals. Havok studied his young face. He was handsome, with Nordic features. Well-muscled, he held himself with extreme self-confidence.

"Easy, Bergdahl," Tucker said. "These civilians just had a run-in with Anisimova less than a month ago. They know him, and they have a pretty heavy score to settle."

"This ain't a grudge match," Bergdahl retorted. "This is the real thing, and I don't think we should operate with amateurs just because their pussies got hurt."

Havok looked around the room at the rest of the agents. He saw others nod in agreement. He also saw Tucker staring at Bergdahl.

"Listen here: these two men kept a cargo of sarin gas out of the hands of terrorists along with a half-billion dollars in gold and diamonds. Also, I'm guessing that any one of these amateurs could kick your ass without even working up a sweat," Tucker said, staring the man into silent submission. "If you don't like the way I run my ops, you can always resign and see if the Eighty-Second Airborne will take you back."

The younger man averted his eyes to the floor.

"All right," said Tucker, biting his ire, "let's finish this brief."

The brief lasted another fifty minutes. Afterward, Tucker led his newest recruits to a backroom in the same building. There they drew their field gear: canvas parachute bags stuffed with packed parachutes, web gear, boots, and BDUs. They put on their fatigues and web gear, stashed their remaining gear in assigned lockers, and then joined the rest of the team, who waited on a grass-covered field behind the building. Their training began as the sound of helicopters approached.

Sixteen men, each equipped with parachutes and night-vision devices, parachuted from helicopters crewed by US Army Special Ops pilots, aiming for the faint infrared markers that ringed the drop zone. After the three-thousand-foot jump, the team would spend time on an improvised range, shooting brand-new AK-47s with the aid of their night-vision devices. If there was going to be any shooting going on, then the brass casings left behind couldn't be associated with the Americans. The time on the range would be followed by a six-mile land-navigation course back to a country villa. The team had selected the site because of its similarity in construction and terrain to the target villa in Vietnam. Once at the site, they would practice breaching the walls and accessing the rooms where their targets would be sleeping.

The first night of training proved relatively easy and, with one exception, went by without a hitch. The commando team had just landed and were stuffing their parachutes into their rucksacks when a sharp crack rang out in the darkness.

Havok and Stone were the first to reach a struggling form on the ground. Stone turned on his red-lensed flashlight and saw a man lying on the ground, holding his foot with both hands. It was Bergdahl. Next to him, on the ground, was his AK-47. While Stone held his flashlight, Havok helped remove the soldier's boot to inspect the injury. Havok shook out the remains of his big toe.

Stone squatted next to the gunshot victim and comforted him. "You know something, friend? I feel plumb stupid. I've had it all wrong. I had no way of knowing that the best way to get them to drop their guard was to shoot yourself in the foot."

"Fuck you," the man hissed.

"No, I think you just fucked yourself, pal."

Just then, Tucker walked up behind Stone and peered at his man on the ground. He shook his head before speaking. "I knew I shouldn't have allowed you on my team. Go ahead and see if the Army will take you back. See me in five years once you've grown." Tucker then turned away.

The next three nights were spent fine-tuning their drill. The team had to be at peak efficiency if they were to complete their mission and return. Havok and Stone also knew that, for the team to accept them, they had to prove themselves to the others. They did so by always being the first ones out of the aircraft, the first ones to the target villa, and the ones with the best range scores. By the start of training on the fourth day, they were the most respected members of the team.

***

On the fifth night, the team found themselves at sea. The Macau Lady, a dilapidated coastal freighter, sleepily made its way south along the coast of Vietnam twenty miles away. On the ship's dark and lonely main deck sat three large transport containers with tarps stretched across their tops. Registered as a Malaysian vessel and a veteran of the Asian trade, the old vessel slowed to a stop, and a radio call went out to the ship's owners in Panang. The ship's captain reported that the engines had broken down again, and they would have to spend a few hours on repairs.

Once the owners acknowledged the information, the ship sprang to life. Men who seemed to well up out of the rusty decks climbed all over the containers and rolled the canvas tops back. After removing the tarps, the men pulled pins out of the corners of the containers and gently lowered the fake metal sides, revealing three MH-60 special-operations-capable stealth helicopters that squatted inside. Their crews, the SCRU team, and Kilgore, Havok, and Stone waited patiently in the helicopters while their ears strained to hear that one brief radio transmission.

It came.

The pilots started their engines, and when they were at full power, the large insects lifted themselves off into the midnight darkness. Two minutes later, with only the exception of the ship's running lights, the dented freighter went back to sleep, slowly drifting southward. Its engines were still being fixed.

The jump was flawless. Havok, like everybody else, dove into nothingness. At one thousand feet, he pulled the ripcord and felt the opening shock of the rectangular chute. He looked up to ensure his lines were not tangled. From what he could tell, they were free and clear of each other. He couldn't see the canopy above him; it was the same color as the night sky. He looked down and could see only the same thing that the others saw, a fuzzy black blanket under him with a group of diminutive green lights. Barely visible, the pinpricks of light outlined the drop zone, a rice paddy about two hectares in size.

Agents were in position, ready to mark the LZ with infrared markers and guide them to the villa. The agents were Vietnamese peasants employed by the US government for the last twenty years. Their first mission, twenty years ago, had been to report any evidence of American POWs still in Vietnam. Now they kept an eye on the flourishing drug trade.

Havok's body slammed into the flooded rice paddy without warning, jarring his back painfully. It took precious seconds for him and the rest of the men to extricate themselves from the clinging mud and climb up the narrow dike. This was the time when they were most vulnerable, helpless in the mire; they could be shot down where they stood. After Tucker had a full head count, he led the file of men off the path to the jungle's edge where two Vietnamese men materialized from the foliage, silently greeting them.

One of them stepped past the line of American men to gather their chutes; the other man just turned around and walked back into the jungle. The Americans followed the man to their target, four kilometers ahead.

Thirty minutes later the group approached the villa. In the dark, they could see the old-style French-colonial mansion. Its unique, imperial audaciousness clashed with the simple peasant huts that surrounded the vast grounds of the estate.

The team split into three groups. After hours of practice, they knew exactly what to do and where to go. The first group followed the informant to remove the guards and set up a defensive perimeter. The other two teams waited in the bushes until Tucker, who squatted next to Havok, heard the all-clear signal on the earpiece looped over his ear. He acknowledged the transmission and then whispered to the leader in charge of Havok's team. The man nodded and turned to his team, which included Havok and Stone. Nothing needed to be said. The team leader simply stood silently and walked toward the side of the mansion. His team followed. They had been assigned the job of capturing Anisimova, who took up quarters in a spacious guest cottage behind the mansion.

Under the blank witness of the moon, which had just made its appearance from behind the partially overcast sky, Kilgore, Havok, Stone, and the rest of the team skirted the shadows of the jungle along the edge of the expansive lawn behind the mansion. They found themselves behind a cottage that was raised three feet off the ground and surrounded by a wide porch. Havok looked down as they approached the target and saw the body of a guard who had died minutes ago, staring blindly at the night sky. The six men darted out from the bushes and covered the ten yards of open ground to the porch.

Havok and Kilgore stepped up onto the porch and tested the planking. The wood was as sound as the day it had been nailed into place. Still wearing their night-vision devices, they peered through a side window that they knew from their plans was the target's bedroom window. Inside they could see two fuzzy green outlines lying naked on the bed, sleeping. They had already factored in the second person. Kilgore also spotted a bottle of vodka and a glass on the nightstand.

With everybody else in covering position, Stone stepped up to the porch and the men circled around the front door. Kilgore gently tugged on the door handle only to find it locked. Stone carefully placed his weapon on the deck and pulled a small leather case from his right trouser cargo pocket. He opened it and removed two long, thin metal picklocks and went to work. Within thirty seconds, Stone put his tools in his pocket and turned the handle. Staying low, the men opened the door and stole into the front room and down the hall to bedroom.

Stone approached Anisimova's partner on the left side of the bed. He again placed his weapon on the floor and pulled a black cloth sack and a roll of duct tape from his other pants pocket. Havok did the same thing on his side of the bed while trying not to step into the beam of moonlight that entered through the window and landed on Anisimova's sleeping face. On a silent count of three, they struck.

Havok reached to secure Anisimova, and Kilgore grabbed the vodka bottle by the neck. As soon as Havok touched him, Anisimova's eyes flew open, but before he could react, Havok jumped onto his chest, pinning his arms at his sides. At the same time, Kilgore smashed the heavy glass bottle across Anisimova's face. The sound of the breaking nose echoed in the darkness. Havok used the precious seconds to slap a wide piece of tape across Anisimova's mouth. Next, he slid back and wrapped the roll of tape around the pair of wrists that Kilgore held together for him. Once Anisimova's wrists were secured, Kilgore slipped his own cloth sack over Anisimova's head, pulling the drawstring tight.

When they were finished, Havok looked across the bed and saw a young girl, perhaps sixteen to eighteen years old judging by her naked build, kicking blindly at her kidnappers. The men ignored their captives and scurried around the room, looking for clothes to dress the two people. Havok could hear them struggle on the bed, trying to shake their bindings. He could also hear Anisimova trying to breathe through the heavy cloth, duct tape, and a shattered nose filled with mucous and blood.

"You think he'll choke to death?" Kilgore asked.

"It will take a lot more than a broken nose to kill him," Havok answered.

"I got mine," Stone said cheerfully.

Everybody turned and looked at Stone. They saw that he had wrapped a black shirt around the girl's shoulders.

Carrying their captives over their shoulders like two sacks of rice, the men bolted from the cottage and joined the other two teams at the spot where they had split up only a few minutes ago. Standing on weakened and shaking knees was another person also with a black cloth sack over his head. Tucker completed a hurried head count and then radioed in, "Mission complete." When he received his confirmation, the Americans, with three captives, melted back into the jungle. Havok remained at the end of the column. As he turned to look behind them, he thought, The snatch went off too easy. Too damned easy.

∗∗∗

Unknown to Tucker and the rest of the Americans, Tang had had the opportunity to hit a silent-alarm button next to his bed before the Americans threw the bag over his head. Also, although most of the staff were sound asleep, one man was not. Having girl problems back in Saigon, the man, Tang's driver, was sitting in a secluded section of the grounds, mulling over his predicament. As he sat in the darkness with his cell phone in his hand, contemplating how to solve his problem, he heard footsteps—lots of footsteps.

The scene at the Vietnamese air force base outside Da Nang was one of urgency as the duty officer received the alarm and the phone call from the driver. He, in turn, called on the helicopter crews and soldiers waiting in the barracks and hangars nearby. Though not suspecting any immediate danger, Tang had requested, through government connections, that a Vietnamese military contingency always be on standby, ready to rescue him at a moment's notice. Two French-made Gazelle helicopters, each armed with ten two-inch rockets and two M60 machine guns along with six hundred rounds of 7.62 NATO ball ammunition, lifted off with their crews and a squad of soldiers each.

***

On the ground, after thirty minutes of a forced march, the American commandos reached the primary extraction point and saw the three stealth helicopters waiting for them. Their guides had earned their money and disappeared back into their normal lives.

The team approached the aircraft, and as they stepped up next to the open side doors, Havok dropped Anisimova from his shoulder and removed the sack from his head. The lower half of his face was a bloody mess where snot and thick blood gooped down his throat and matted his chest hair. Anisimova looked at Havok with an intense hatred while he noisily sucked in air through his shattered nose. Havok removed a canteen from his web belt and drank the warm water. "That job as a deputy director fell through, huh? Don't worry about it, though; shit like you always end up on top."

Stone pulled up next to Havok and slid his load from his shoulders. "I guess being a white supremacist is too rough these days. The drug trade is more up his alley. The pay is better, and you still get to ruin people's lives."

"Let's just hope he doesn't ruin anybody else's life except his own from now on," Havok said. "By the way, how's your date?"

Stone turned to his left and removed a jackknife from his pocket. He cut the duct tape around her wrists but didn't remove the cloth sack. Before the guides departed, one of them told her to keep the hood on until she heard the helicopters fly away.

By now, the rest of the American commandos had already loaded themselves in the helicopters, and Havok and his team were doing the same. Suddenly, the reverberating sounds of a helicopter engine approached from somewhere in the darkness.

That doesn't sound good, Havok thought as he turned to push Anisimova forward.

The pilots of the three American helicopters heard the same noise and frantically started their engines. Havok and Anisimova were the last men in the paddy, only five feet from the door, when the entire area was suddenly set ablaze in blinding light.

Havok, shocked, froze in mid-stride. Anisimova reacted immediately and used the change in fortune for his survival. He turned right and fled from the harsh light. Havok stared ahead at the gaping door of the helicopter and at the waiting arms that were close enough to touch, arms that could pull him to freedom and life. He then looked right, at the bounding animal that had caused so much pain and misery for so many people. Havok turned right and disappeared into the darkness, followed by a pair of two-inch rockets as they exploded in the mud between him and the helicopter.

Everyone was startled at the suddenness and ferocity of the attack. What followed happened so fast that nobody could recall the details except for the anguish that each man felt in his own way. The American pilots, knowing they could not be caught on the ground, engaged their blades and increased their engines' rpm. Stone, sitting on the edge of the side door, felt the aircraft lift away from the rice paddy and his friend. All he could see was his own hand reach out for Havok, who stood alone in the thick black water. Stone stood to jump out of the chopper but was held back by the other men in the aircraft when they realized what he was going to do. The helicopter escaped the bright light and left behind a trail of unseen exhaust and sorrowful screams.

The lead Vietnamese pilot, Lt. Vihn, had just received an update over his headset as to where the American helicopters were waiting. The driver had followed the group of commandos and kept the air base updated. Vihn led the other helicopter to the scene, and through his own night-vision goggles, was able to capture the site on the ground. He saw the first two helicopters and fired two rockets. Vihn saw his rockets explode uselessly in the mud. He recovered quickly and radioed in the incident, informing the base of the two men left on the ground. Vihn and the other helicopter followed the unknown helicopters into the darkness. He knew he had the advantage of home territory, as well as probably having more fuel than the invaders, meaning they would have to set down somewhere.

Now alone in the communist country, Havok tried to follow the diminishing sounds of the rotors beating the jungle below. Ahead he could hear the splashing and the horrid rasping as Anisimova tried to run through the knee-deep ooze and breathe through a clogged nose.

For Anisimova, this was his last chance at survival. With hands still bound, he reached up and ripped away the tape on his mouth. He gulped in great amounts of air, which immediately increased his strength. He reached the dike and climbed it. Once on dry ground, he ran down the narrow footpath. Now it was his turn to hear the man behind him struggle in the thick water.

Anisimova turned around when he no longer heard the sound and then saw a shadowy figure climb the precarious rise. Anisimova ran as fast as his wet, naked legs could carry him, knowing he had only seconds. He saw a buffalo-drawn plow in front of him, sitting there like some sort of metal scarecrow in the moonlight. He ran to the blade of the plow and began to rub the thick tape across the rusty metal, sawing away at it. In two seconds, his wrists sprang away from each other, just as Havok's body loomed above him, blocking the moonlight as he slammed into Anisimova.

Now that Anisimova was able to fight back, he did so with a bitter vengeance. Angered beyond reason, full of insane hate, he threw Havok aside like a ragdoll. Havok sailed through the air and landed on his back in the putrid water of the paddy. He tried to get up, but the equipment he wore glued him to the bottom. Before he could free himself, Anisimova was atop him, straddling his waist. Havok felt strong fingers close on his throat, keeping his head underwater. He tried to breathe but gagged on warm water that tasted like shit.

Anisimova grinned and laughed madly. All those years of poverty and want had made him murderously evil. Twice within a single month, vast power and wealth had been cruelly snatched away, and now the man responsible for his avalanche back into poverty was under him, struggling in a shallow sea of waste and filth, dying. Anisimova tightened his grip. He could feel the man under him weaken.

Anisimova was so intent upon choking the life out of Havok that he did not see the fist leave the water and smash into his already-broken nose. The first punch sent shock waves of agony sawing through his skull; the second punch made Anisimova shit himself, forcing him to loosen his grip. With his remaining strength, Havok pushed Anisimova away.

He rolled away from Anisimova, and between deep gasps for air, he saw Anisimova flounder in the water, holding his face in his hands and screaming in agony. The screaming that started out sounding inhuman was made worse by blood, mucus, and animal waste as it ran down his heaving throat, choking him. Havok crawled away from his opponent, hoping to get a few precious seconds between himself and Anisimova. He knew Anisimova had gone beyond the edge; he was now a rabid, diseased animal that would be nearly impossible to stop.

Havok managed to pull himself free of the clinging mud and get to his feet. His trembling right hand reached for the K-bar on his web belt. Desperately, his fingers tried to clear the mud from the snap that held the knife in its sheath, while the enraged animal rose from the mire, his pain subsiding. Havok gave up on the knife, knowing that even if he did get it out of the sheath, the five-inch steel blade would not be enough to stop the madman.

The two spent warriors stood there, stooped over and gasping for breath. Their world consisted of only this fetid square piece of swamp, and only one man could live in it. Foregoing all thoughts of power, wealth, or life, they charged at each other. Their bodies clashed, and their fists pounded away at each other. Havok took several kidney-busting blows to his abdomen, forcing him to vomit. As he was spewing out wastewater and stomach contents, he continued to send blows against Anisimova's shattered nose.

They fought like two junkyard dogs that had never known anything but pain, misery, and hunger. For the longest minutes, the nearby jungle listened to the muted grunts and agonies of these two men until one of them collapsed back into the mud.

The figure swayed above the prostrate body in the paddy and then made his way back to the dike, crawling up the incline until his body lay flat on the narrow footpath, his chest heaving under great strain. After a brief respite, he forced himself to sit up and pulled a canteen from his web belt. Havok used the water to rinse his mouth of the vomit and vile taste, and then threw the empty canteen at Anisimova, who struggled in the paddy, trying to get a foothold. Havok was about to step back into the arena and finish off the gladiator when somebody pulled up next to him.

He looked wearily to his left and saw a man dressed in black fatigues, carrying a pistol. He spoke in English but with a Russian accent. "Do not stand up."

Havok recognized Petroske from Terumbu Island. Under the bright moonlight, he saw more black-dressed shadows lining the crisscross of footpaths. His heart sank.

Petroske turned to the other men and said something in Russian. Two men walked down from the dike and into the rice paddy. They grabbed Anisimova by the armpits and dragged him out of the water and up the dike, depositing him next to Havok.

Everybody remained silent as they stared at Anisimova. He was quickly recovering from the duel and soon realized that his compatriots surrounded him. At first, his eyes betrayed a frightened uncertainty as he surveyed the picket of stark figures, until they fell on Petroske.

"Petroske! Good to see you, my old friend."

Petroske helped his former superior to his feet and then handed him a canteen.

Anisimova rinsed his mouth with the warm water and spit out the fetid bile. He handed the canteen back to Petroske and then stared down at Havok. Now it was finally over. Havok would be dead, and he was safe from extradition to the States. He was tired and had had enough. Anisimova stopped staring at Havok and looked at Petroske. "Shoot him," he ordered in English.

Havok heard those two words and saw Petroske raise his pistol. For some reason, Havok took the time to look at the pistol. He closed his eyes and heard the echoing click of a slide being drawn back. Knowing he was about to die, he gave his life one more chance at survival. He lurched to his feet just as the sharp crack of the pistol exploded behind his left ear. As he fell forward off the dike, he was amazed at how painless death really was; he did not feel the bullet's impact. Instead, he felt the bone-jarring shock as his chest slammed into the decline of the dike, his face just kissing the paddy water.

After about a minute, when the pain in his chest subsided and he could still hear the soft night breeze blowing across the black water, he realized he was still alive. He quickly pushed himself into a crouching position and turned around to peer over the top of the dike.

One of the black figures said something in Russian.

Petroske lowered his pistol and looked at Havok. "This is your lucky day. I was told not to kill you. We were ordered here to take care of Anisimova, which we were about to do until you took him from us. We followed you here to see how this night would develop."

And with that simple statement, Havok saw the soldiers walking off the dikes and melting back into the jungle, disappearing like ghosts. Havok looked to his right and saw Anisimova's body lying sprawled out, facedown. The entire right side of his head was a sliding mass as blood and fluid leaked from his cranium.

Havok did not move; he simply tried to absorb what had happened. Either Anisimova's superiors or the official Russian government, embarrassed at the attention brought to them by Anisimova, had ordered him hunted down and executed the old-fashioned Stalinist way of doing things: a single bullet to the skull.

With a body racked with pain and a mind filled with wonderment at his miraculous survival, Havok stood and climbed back up the dike. He glanced once more at the body and then turned east, toward the alternate extraction point. Pulling his map from his pants pocket, along with a small flashlight, Havok reviewed his route and stepped forward while thinking about all that had happened within the last month. He then thought about Apple. She was right: there was no way he could live life without facing it. With a smile, he started to think about the search for a lost pirate fleet. It was an easy job—perhaps just too easy?

Maybe I'll just have to burn more toast, he thought as he walked away with a spring in his step.

9 781950 906543